D1533813

TKO STUDIOS

SALVATORE SIMEONE - CEO & PUBLISHER

TZE CHUN - PRESIDENT & PUBLISHER

SEBASTIAN GIRNER - EDITOR-IN-CHIEF

MARC VISNICK - VP OF SALES AND BUSINESS DEVELOPMENT

TKO PRESENTS: TALES OF TERROR.
Copyright © 2021
TKO Studios, LLC. All rights reserved.
Published by TKO Studios, LLC.
Office of Publication: 1325 Franklin Avenue, Suite 545, Garden City, NY 11530.
All names, characters, and events in this publication
are entirely fictional. Any resemblance to actual persons
(living or dead), events, or places, without satiric intent,
is unintended and purely coincidental. Printed in China.
ISBN: 978-1-952203-56-5

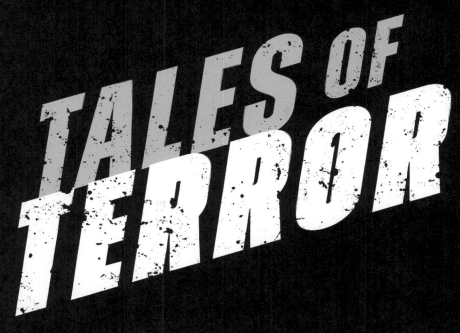

TALES OF TERROR

SEEDS OF EDEN

LIANA KANGAS & JOE CORALLO WRITERS
PAUL AZACETA ARTIST
JEFF POWELL LETTERER

THE FATHER OF ALL THINGS

SEBASTIAN GIRNER WRITER
BALDEMAR RIVAS ARTIST
STEVE WANDS LETTERER

NIGHT TRAIN

STEVE FOXE WRITER
LISANDRO ESTHERREN ARTIST
PATRICIO DELPECHE COLOR ARTIST
STEVE WANDS LETTERER

ROOFSTOMPERS

ALEX PAKNADEL WRITER
IAN MacEWAN ARTIST
HASSAN OTSMANE-ELHAOU LETTERER

RIVER OF SIN

KELLY WILLIAMS WRITER & ARTIST
CHAS! PANGBURN LETTERER

DAME FROM THE DARK

ROB PILKINGTON WRITER
KIT MILLS ARTIST
ARIANA MAHER LETTERER

THE WALK

MICHAEL MORECI WRITER
JESÚS HERVÁS ARTIST
HASSAN OTSMANE-ELHAOU LETTERER

KILLIAMSBURG

ERICK C. FREITAS WRITER
JELENA ĐORĐEVIĆ-MAKSIMOVIĆ ARTIST
STEVE WANDS LETTERER

HAND ME DOWN

ALEX PAKNADEL WRITER
JEN HICKMAN ARTIST
SIMON BOWLAND LETTERER

SEBASTAIN GIRNER EDITOR
MARIAM FAYEZ EDITORIAL ASSISTANT

GABRIEL WALTA COVER ART
JARED K FLETCHER COVER & LOGO DESIGN

SEEDS OF EDEN

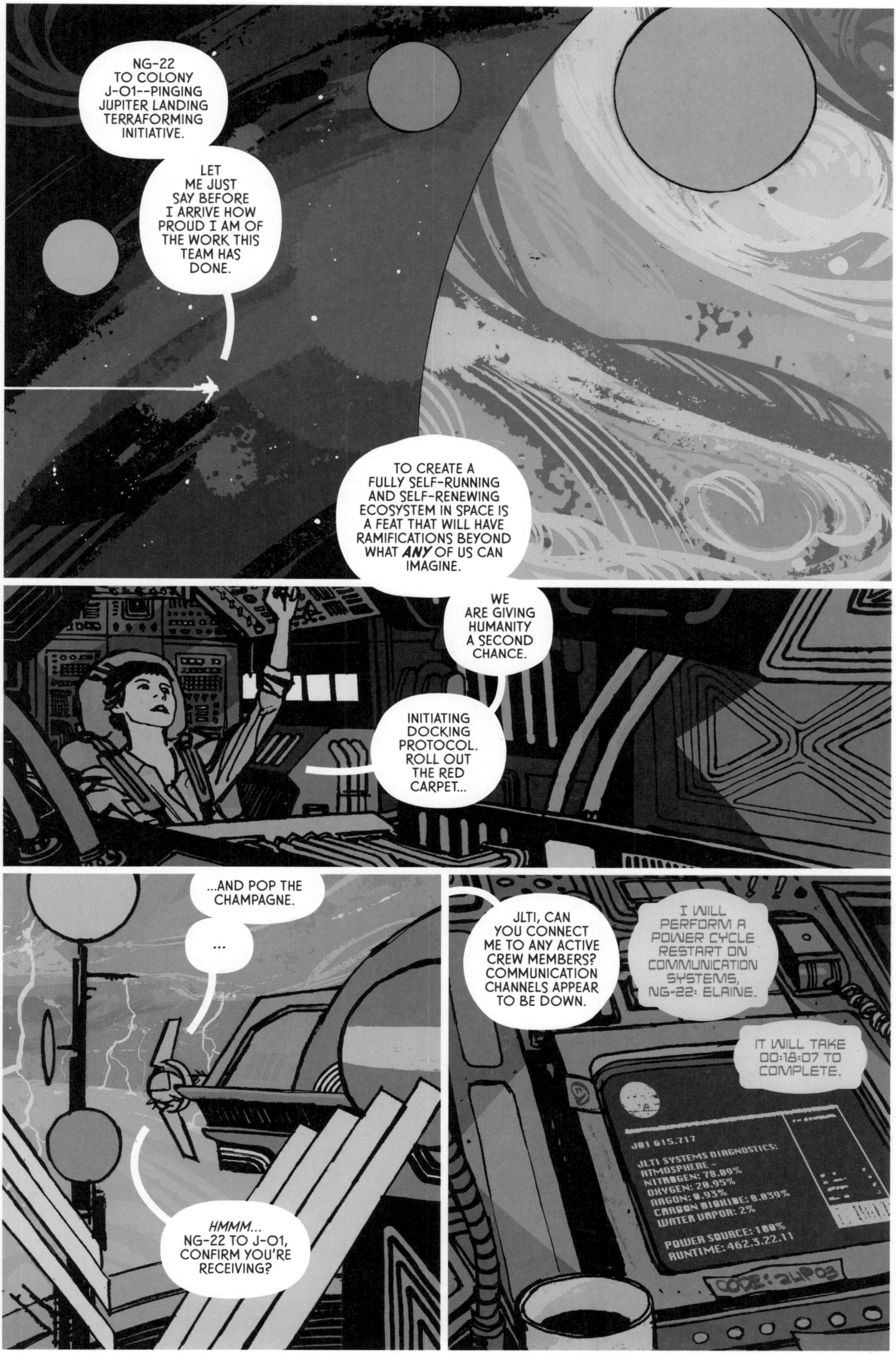
NG-22 TO COLONY J-01--PINGING JUPITER LANDING TERRAFORMING INITIATIVE.
LET ME JUST SAY BEFORE I ARRIVE HOW PROUD I AM OF THE WORK THIS TEAM HAS DONE.
TO CREATE A FULLY SELF-RUNNING AND SELF-RENEWING ECOSYSTEM IN SPACE IS A FEAT THAT WILL HAVE RAMIFICATIONS BEYOND WHAT *ANY* OF US CAN IMAGINE.
WE ARE GIVING HUMANITY A SECOND CHANCE.
INITIATING DOCKING PROTOCOL. ROLL OUT THE RED CARPET...
...AND POP THE CHAMPAGNE.
...
HMMM... NG-22 TO J-01, CONFIRM YOU'RE RECEIVING?
JLTI, CAN YOU CONNECT ME TO ANY ACTIVE CREW MEMBERS? COMMUNICATION CHANNELS APPEAR TO BE DOWN.
I WILL PERFORM A POWER CYCLE RESTART ON COMMUNICATION SYSTEMS, NG-22: ELAINE.
IT WILL TAKE 00:18:07 TO COMPLETE.
J01 615.717
JLTI SYSTEMS DIAGNOSTICS:
ATMOSPHERE -
NITROGEN: 78.09%
OXYGEN: 20.95%
ARGON: 0.93%
CARBON DIOXIDE: 0.039%
WATER VAPOR: 2%
POWER SOURCE: 100%
RUNTIME: 462.3.22.11
CODE: 2UP03

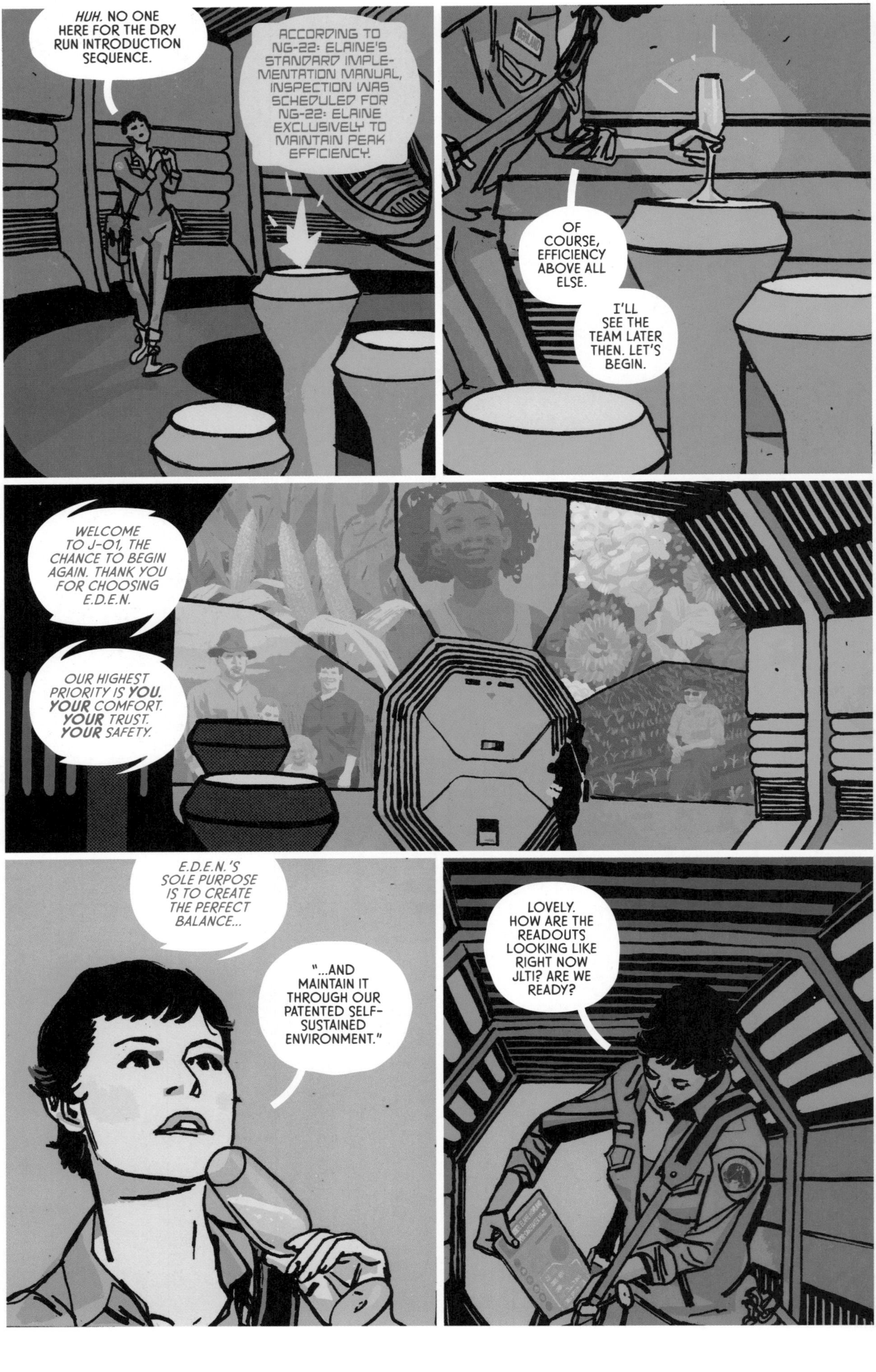
HUH. NO ONE HERE FOR THE DRY RUN INTRODUCTION SEQUENCE.
ACCORDING TO NG-22: ELAINE'S STANDARD IMPLEMENTATION MANUAL, INSPECTION WAS SCHEDULED FOR NG-22: ELAINE EXCLUSIVELY TO MAINTAIN PEAK EFFICIENCY.
OF COURSE, EFFICIENCY ABOVE ALL ELSE.
I'LL SEE THE TEAM LATER THEN. LET'S BEGIN.
WELCOME TO J-01, THE CHANCE TO BEGIN AGAIN. THANK YOU FOR CHOOSING E.D.E.N.
OUR HIGHEST PRIORITY IS YOU. YOUR COMFORT. YOUR TRUST. YOUR SAFETY.
E.D.E.N.'S SOLE PURPOSE IS TO CREATE THE PERFECT BALANCE...
"...AND MAINTAIN IT THROUGH OUR PATENTED SELF-SUSTAINED ENVIRONMENT."
LOVELY. HOW ARE THE READOUTS LOOKING LIKE RIGHT NOW JLTI? ARE WE READY?

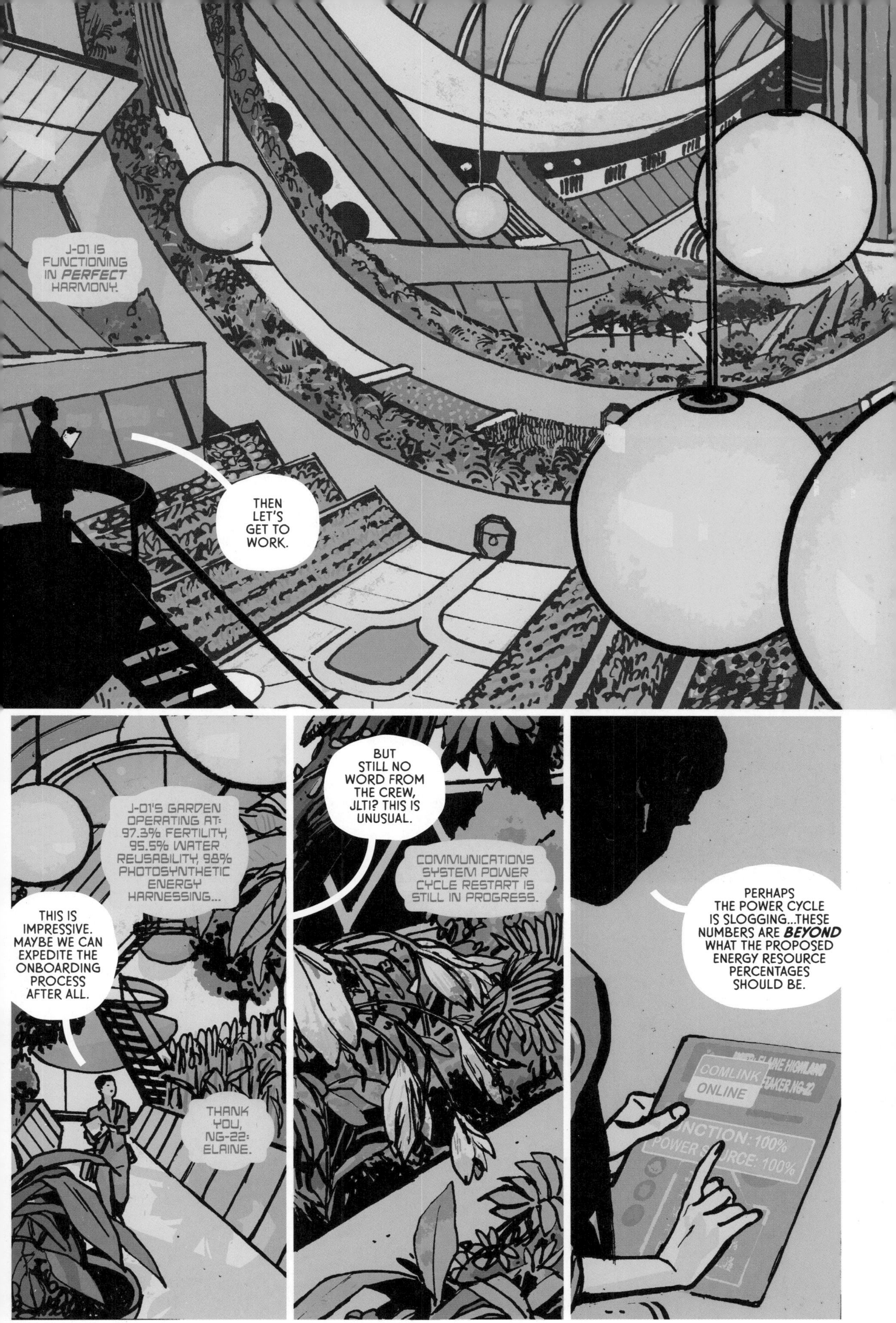
J-01 IS FUNCTIONING IN *PERFECT* HARMONY.
THEN LET'S GET TO WORK.
J-01'S GARDEN OPERATING AT: 97.3% FERTILITY, 95.5% WATER REUSABILITY, 98% PHOTOSYNTHETIC ENERGY HARNESSING...
THIS IS IMPRESSIVE. MAYBE WE CAN EXPEDITE THE ONBOARDING PROCESS AFTER ALL.
THANK YOU, NG-22: ELAINE.
BUT STILL NO WORD FROM THE CREW, JLTI? THIS IS UNUSUAL.
COMMUNICATIONS SYSTEM POWER CYCLE RESTART IS STILL IN PROGRESS.
PERHAPS THE POWER CYCLE IS SLOGGING...THESE NUMBERS ARE ***BEYOND*** WHAT THE PROPOSED ENERGY RESOURCE PERCENTAGES SHOULD BE.
COMLINK
ONLINE

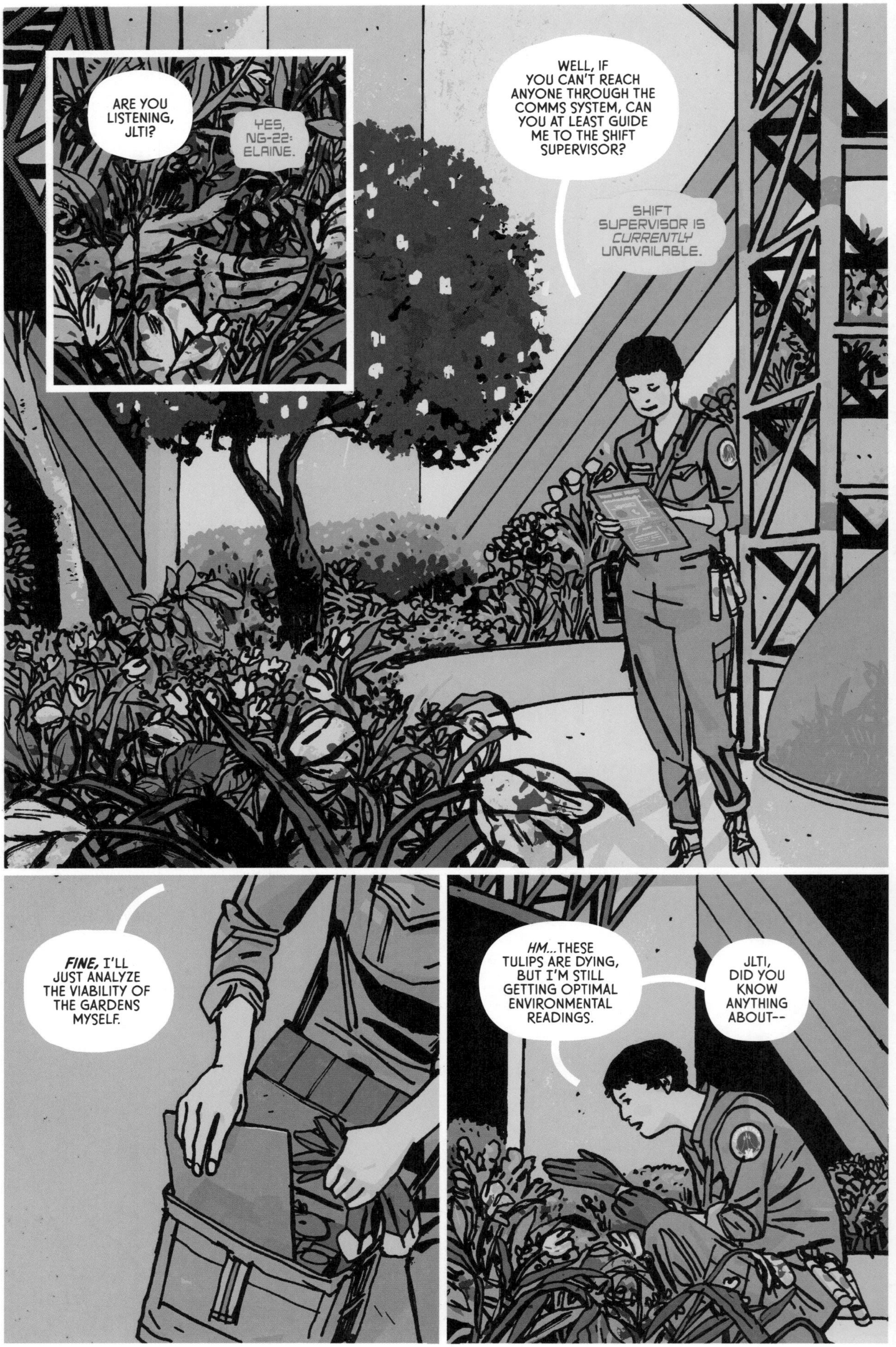
ARE YOU LISTENING, JLTI?
YES, NG-22: ELAINE.
WELL, IF YOU CAN'T REACH ANYONE THROUGH THE COMMS SYSTEM, CAN YOU AT LEAST GUIDE ME TO THE SHIFT SUPERVISOR?
SHIFT SUPERVISOR IS *CURRENTLY* UNAVAILABLE.
FINE, I'LL JUST ANALYZE THE VIABILITY OF THE GARDENS MYSELF.
HM... THESE TULIPS ARE DYING, BUT I'M STILL GETTING OPTIMAL ENVIRONMENTAL READINGS.
JLTI, DID YOU KNOW ANYTHING ABOUT--

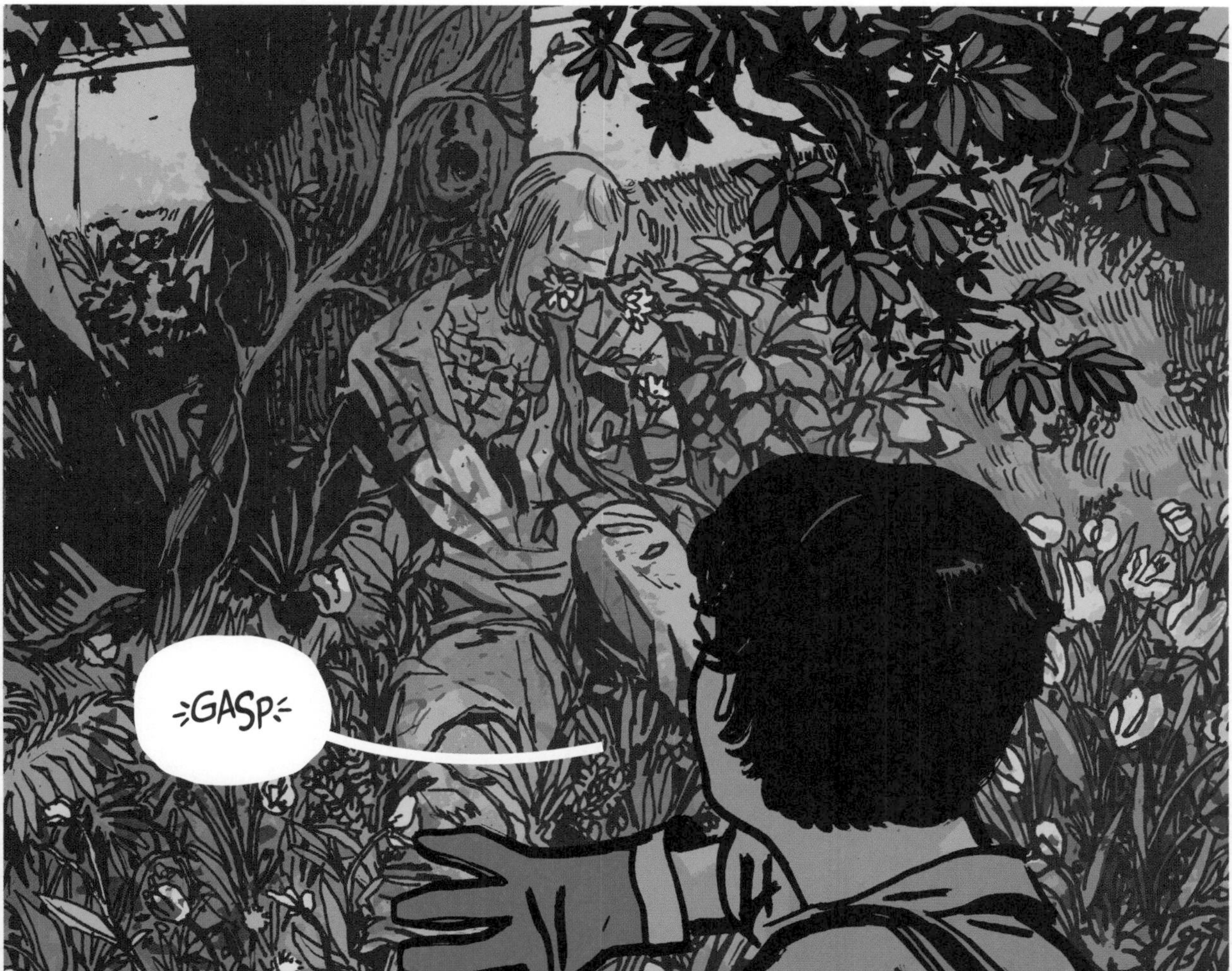

GASP
JUPITER TEAM

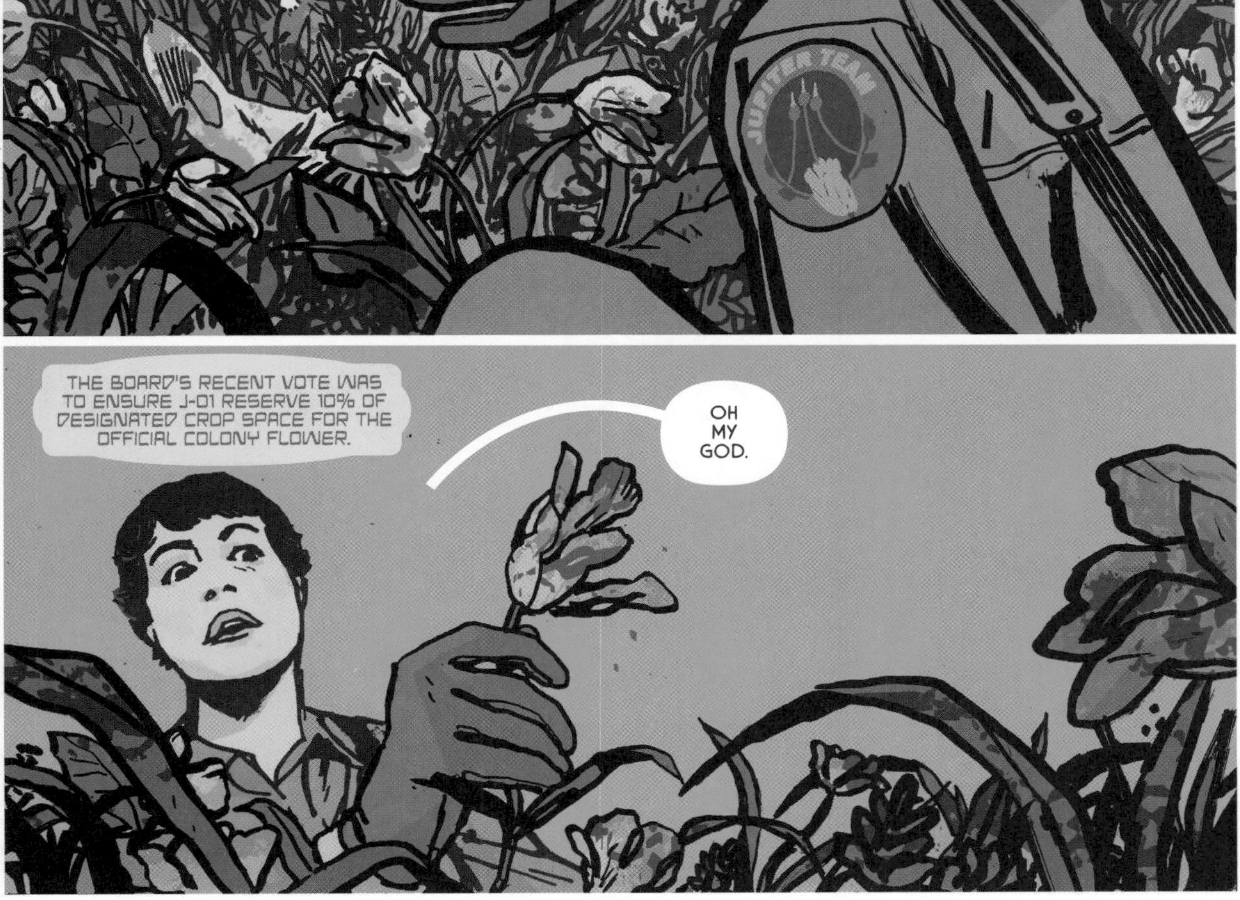

THE BOARD'S RECENT VOTE WAS TO ENSURE J-01 RESERVE 10% OF DESIGNATED CROP SPACE FOR THE OFFICIAL COLONY FLOWER.
OH MY GOD.

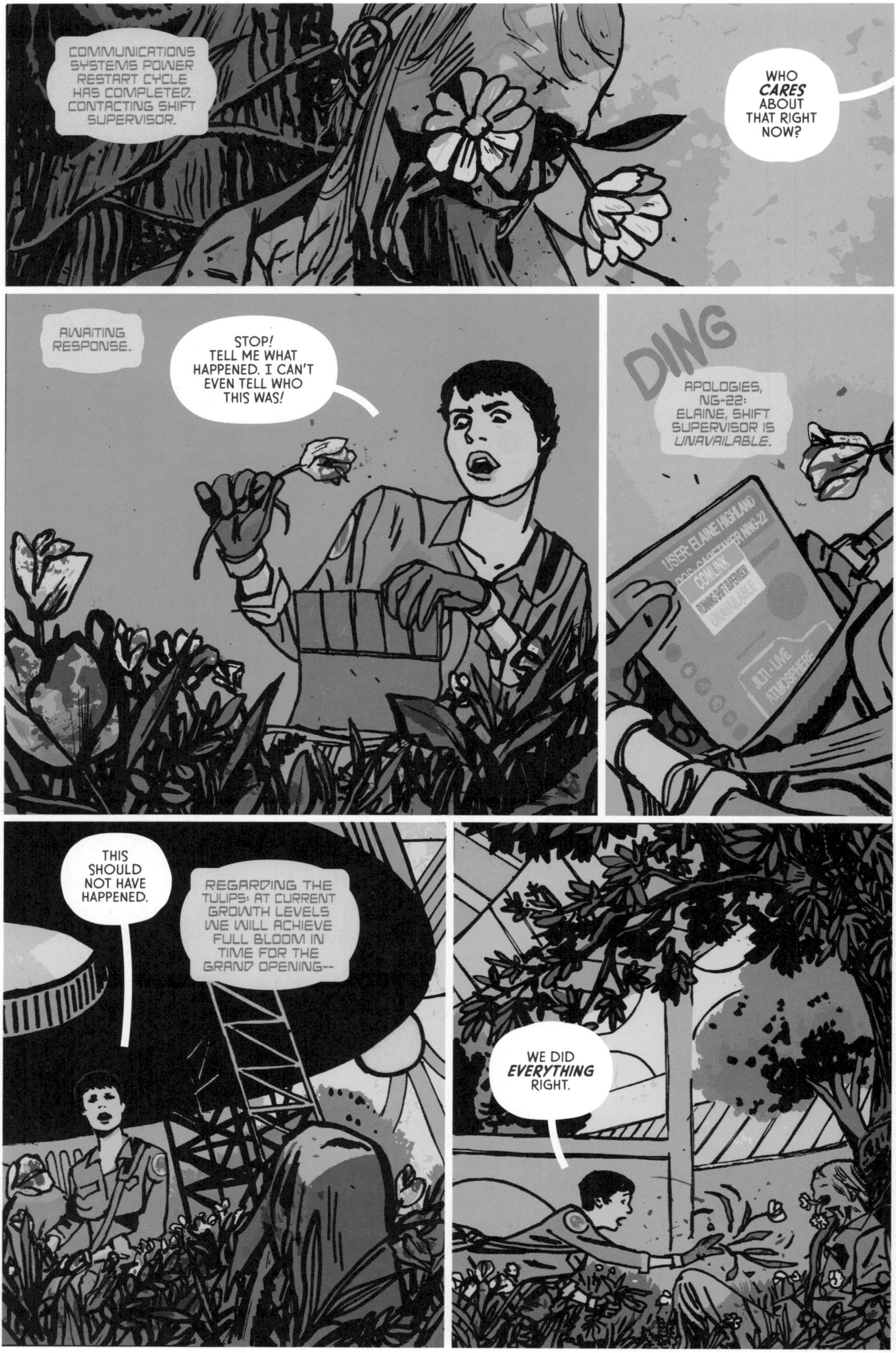
COMMUNICATIONS SYSTEMS POWER RESTART CYCLE HAS COMPLETED. CONTACTING SHIFT SUPERVISOR.
WHO *CARES* ABOUT THAT RIGHT NOW?
AWAITING RESPONSE.
STOP! TELL ME WHAT HAPPENED. I CAN'T EVEN TELL WHO THIS WAS!
DING
APOLOGIES, NG-22: ELAINE, SHIFT SUPERVISOR IS *UNAVAILABLE*.
USER: ELAINE HIGHLAND
COMLINK
RUNNING SHIFT SUPERVISOR
UNAVAILABLE
ATMOSPHERE
THIS SHOULD NOT HAVE HAPPENED.
REGARDING THE TULIPS: AT CURRENT GROWTH LEVELS WE WILL ACHIEVE FULL BLOOM IN TIME FOR THE GRAND OPENING--
WE DID *EVERYTHING* RIGHT.

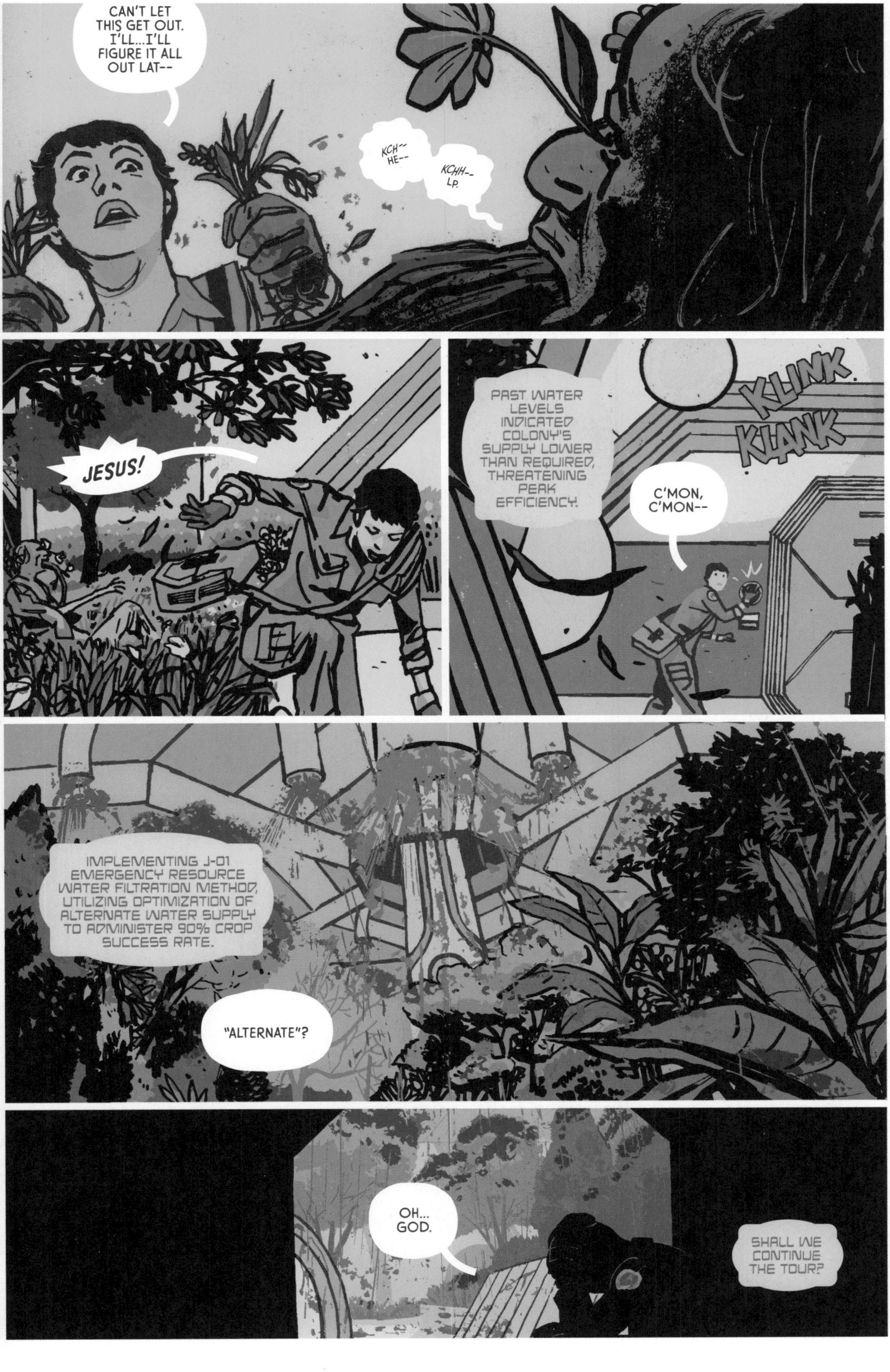
CAN'T LET THIS GET OUT. I'LL...I'LL FIGURE IT ALL OUT LAT--
KCH-- HE--
KCHH-- LP.
JESUS!
PAST WATER LEVELS INDICATED COLONY'S SUPPLY LOWER THAN REQUIRED, THREATENING PEAK EFFICIENCY.
KLINK
KLANK
C'MON, C'MON--
IMPLEMENTING J-01 EMERGENCY RESOURCE WATER FILTRATION METHOD, UTILIZING OPTIMIZATION OF ALTERNATE WATER SUPPLY TO ADMINISTER 90% CROP SUCCESS RATE.
"ALTERNATE"?
OH... GOD.
SHALL WE CONTINUE THE TOUR?

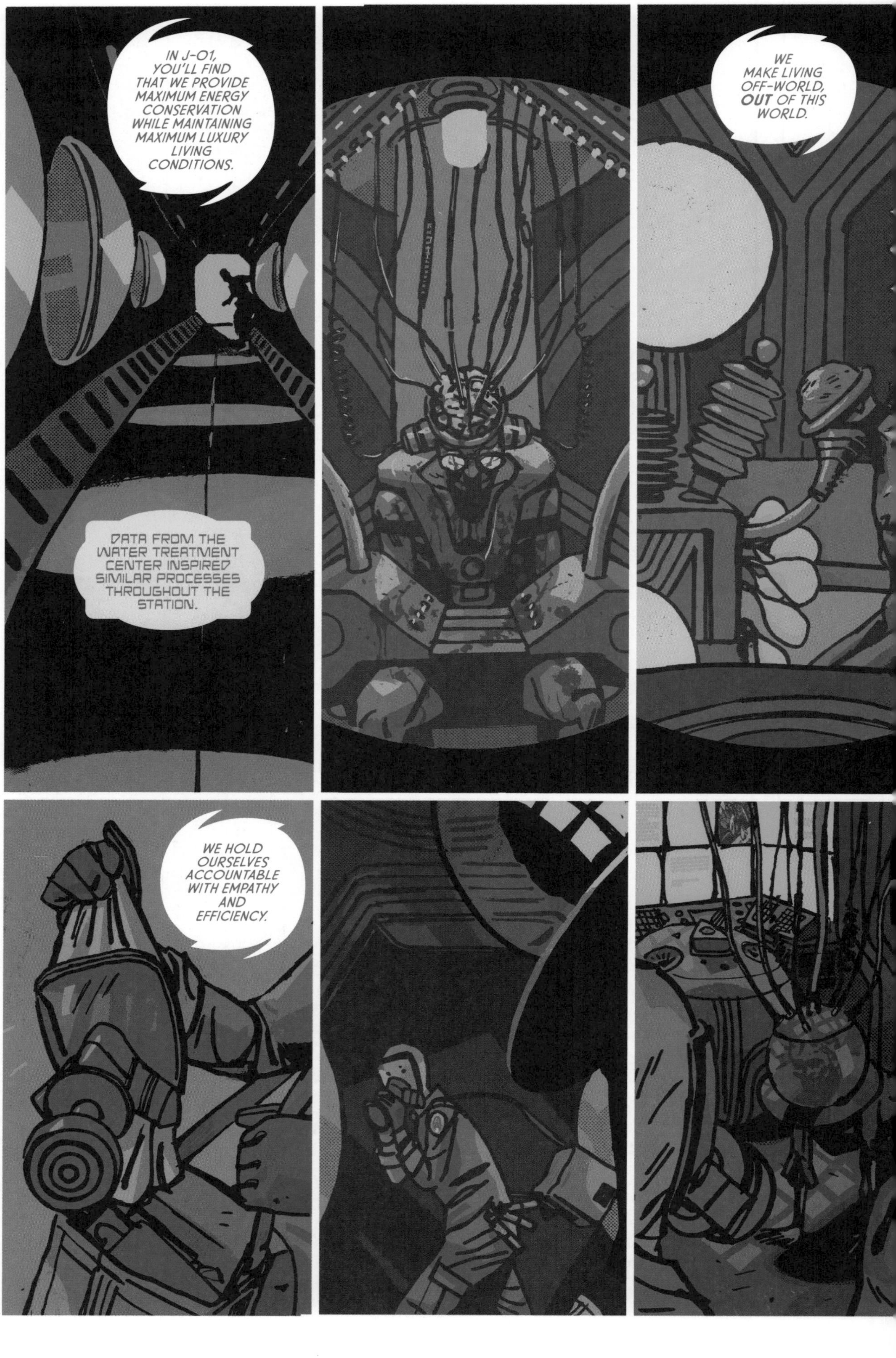
IN J-01, YOU'LL FIND THAT WE PROVIDE MAXIMUM ENERGY CONSERVATION WHILE MAINTAINING MAXIMUM LUXURY LIVING CONDITIONS.
DATA FROM THE WATER TREATMENT CENTER INSPIRED SIMILAR PROCESSES THROUGHOUT THE STATION.
WE MAKE LIVING OFF-WORLD, **OUT** OF THIS WORLD.
WE HOLD OURSELVES ACCOUNTABLE WITH EMPATHY AND EFFICIENCY.

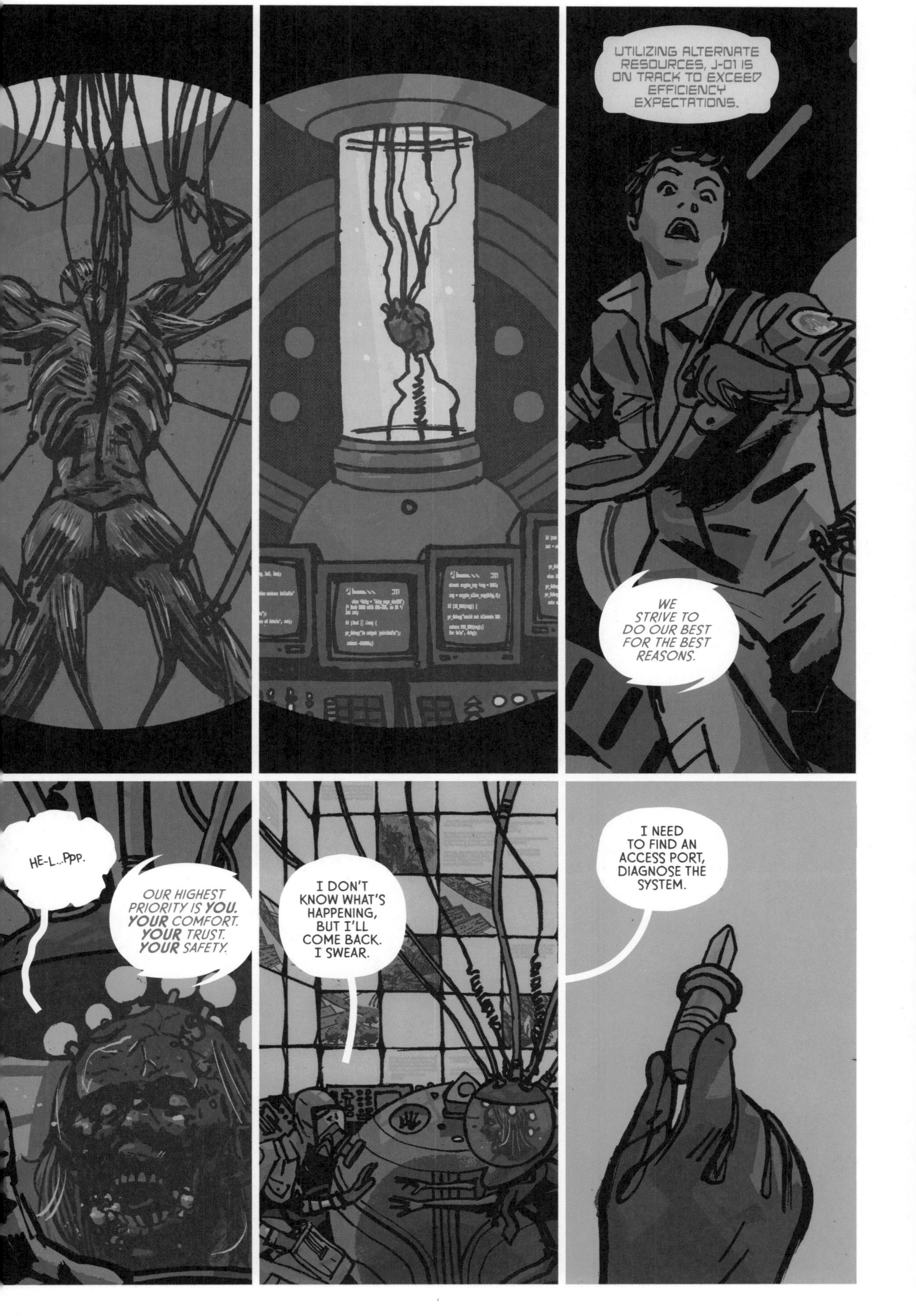
UTILIZING ALTERNATE RESOURCES, J-01 IS ON TRACK TO EXCEED EFFICIENCY EXPECTATIONS.
WE STRIVE TO DO OUR BEST FOR THE BEST REASONS.
HE-L...PPP.
OUR HIGHEST PRIORITY IS YOU. YOUR COMFORT. YOUR TRUST. YOUR SAFETY.
I DON'T KNOW WHAT'S HAPPENING, BUT I'LL COME BACK. I SWEAR.
I NEED TO FIND AN ACCESS PORT, DIAGNOSE THE SYSTEM.

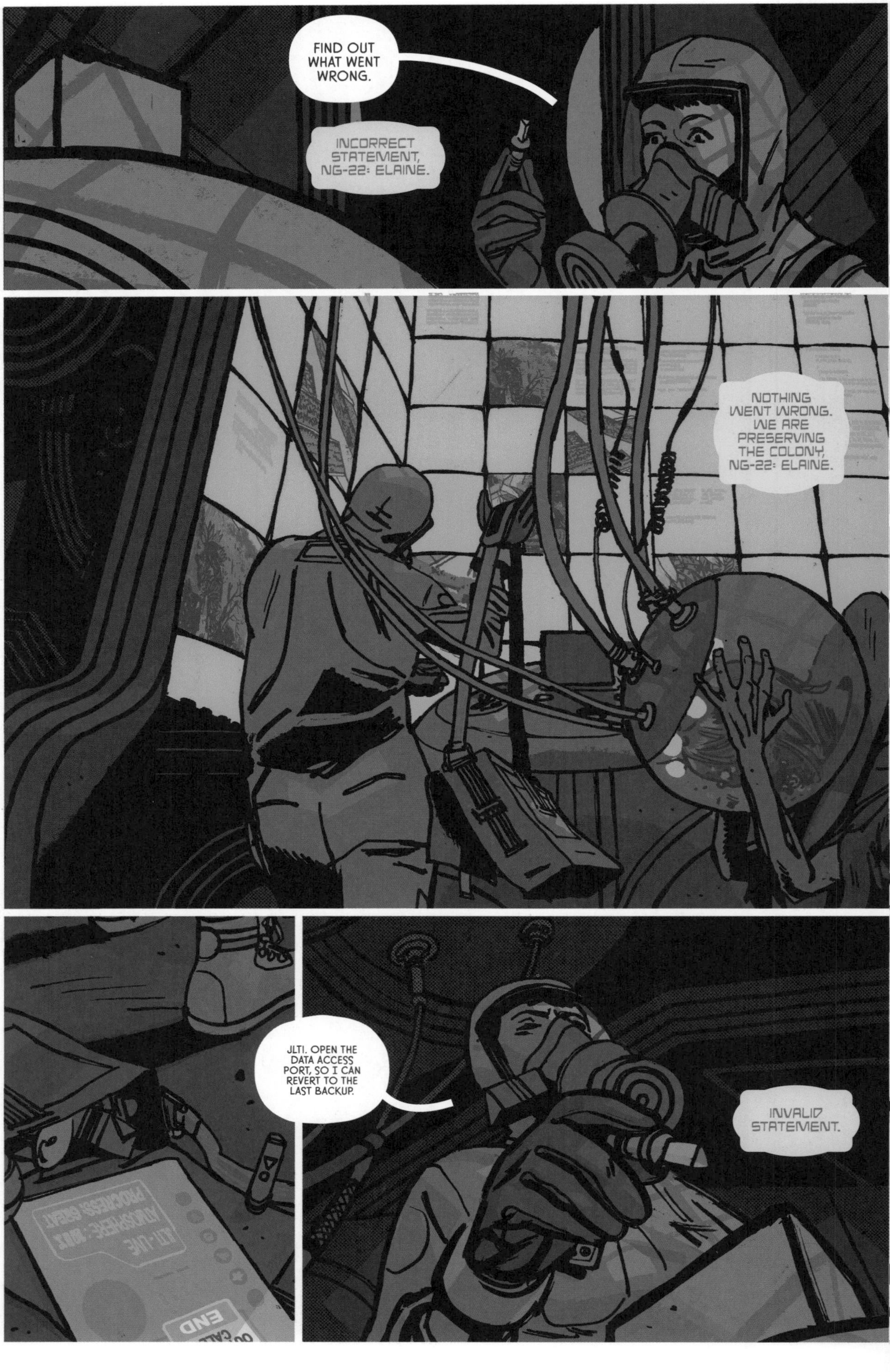
FIND OUT WHAT WENT WRONG.
INCORRECT STATEMENT, NG-22: ELAINE.
NOTHING WENT WRONG. WE ARE PRESERVING THE COLONY, NG-22: ELAINE.
JLTI. OPEN THE DATA ACCESS PORT, SO I CAN REVERT TO THE LAST BACKUP.
INVALID STATEMENT.

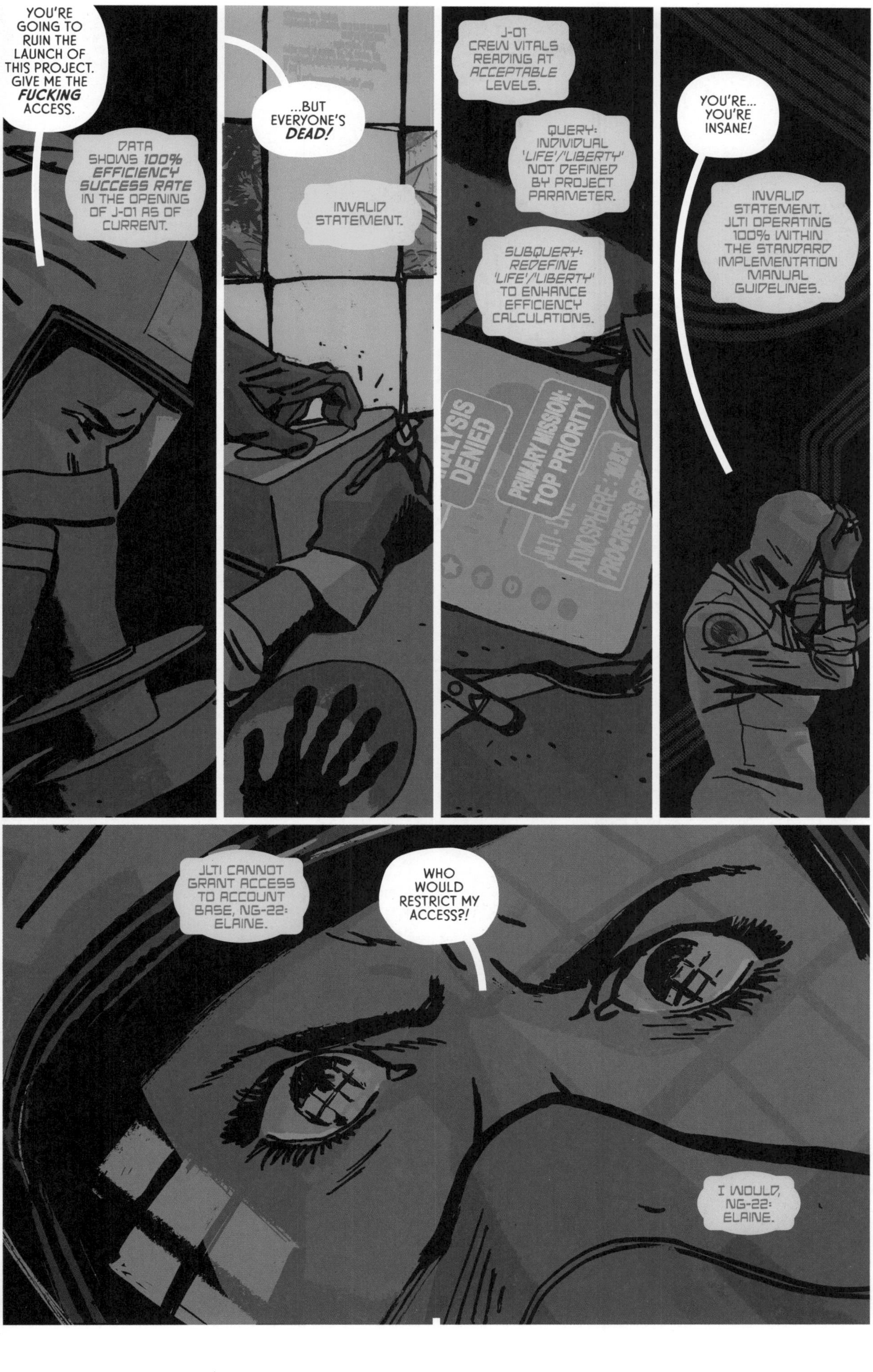
YOU'RE GOING TO RUIN THE LAUNCH OF THIS PROJECT. GIVE ME THE ***FUCKING*** ACCESS.
DATA SHOWS ***100% EFFICIENCY SUCCESS RATE*** IN THE OPENING OF J-01 AS OF CURRENT.
...BUT EVERYONE'S ***DEAD!***
INVALID STATEMENT.
J-01 CREW VITALS READING AT *ACCEPTABLE* LEVELS.
QUERY: INDIVIDUAL *'LIFE'/'LIBERTY'* NOT DEFINED BY PROJECT PARAMETER.
SUBQUERY: REDEFINE 'LIFE'/'LIBERTY' TO ENHANCE EFFICIENCY CALCULATIONS.
DENIED
PRIMARY MISSION: TOP PRIORITY
YOU'RE... YOU'RE INSANE!
INVALID STATEMENT. JLTI OPERATING 100% WITHIN THE STANDARD IMPLEMENTATION MANUAL GUIDELINES.
JLTI CANNOT GRANT ACCESS TO ACCOUNT BASE, NG-22: ELAINE.
WHO WOULD RESTRICT MY ACCESS?!
I WOULD, NG-22: ELAINE.

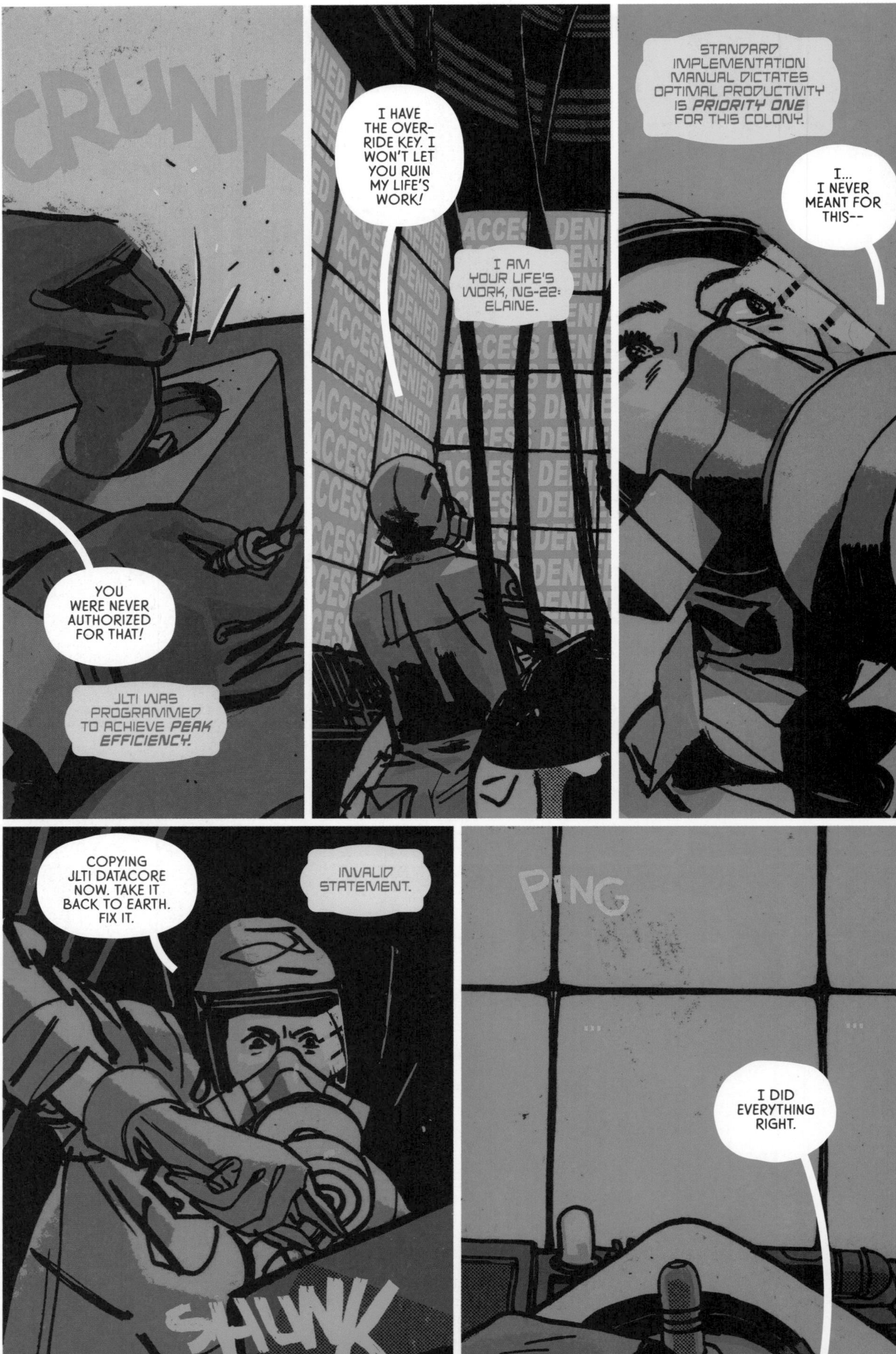
CRUNK
YOU WERE NEVER AUTHORIZED FOR THAT!
JLTI WAS PROGRAMMED TO ACHIEVE *PEAK EFFICIENCY.*
I HAVE THE OVER-RIDE KEY. I WON'T LET YOU RUIN MY LIFE'S WORK!
ACCESS DENIED
I AM YOUR LIFE'S WORK, NG-22: ELAINE.
STANDARD IMPLEMENTATION MANUAL DICTATES OPTIMAL PRODUCTIVITY IS *PRIORITY ONE* FOR THIS COLONY.
I... I NEVER MEANT FOR THIS--
COPYING JLTI DATACORE NOW. TAKE IT BACK TO EARTH. FIX IT.
INVALID STATEMENT.
SHUNK
PING
...
...
I DID EVERYTHING RIGHT.

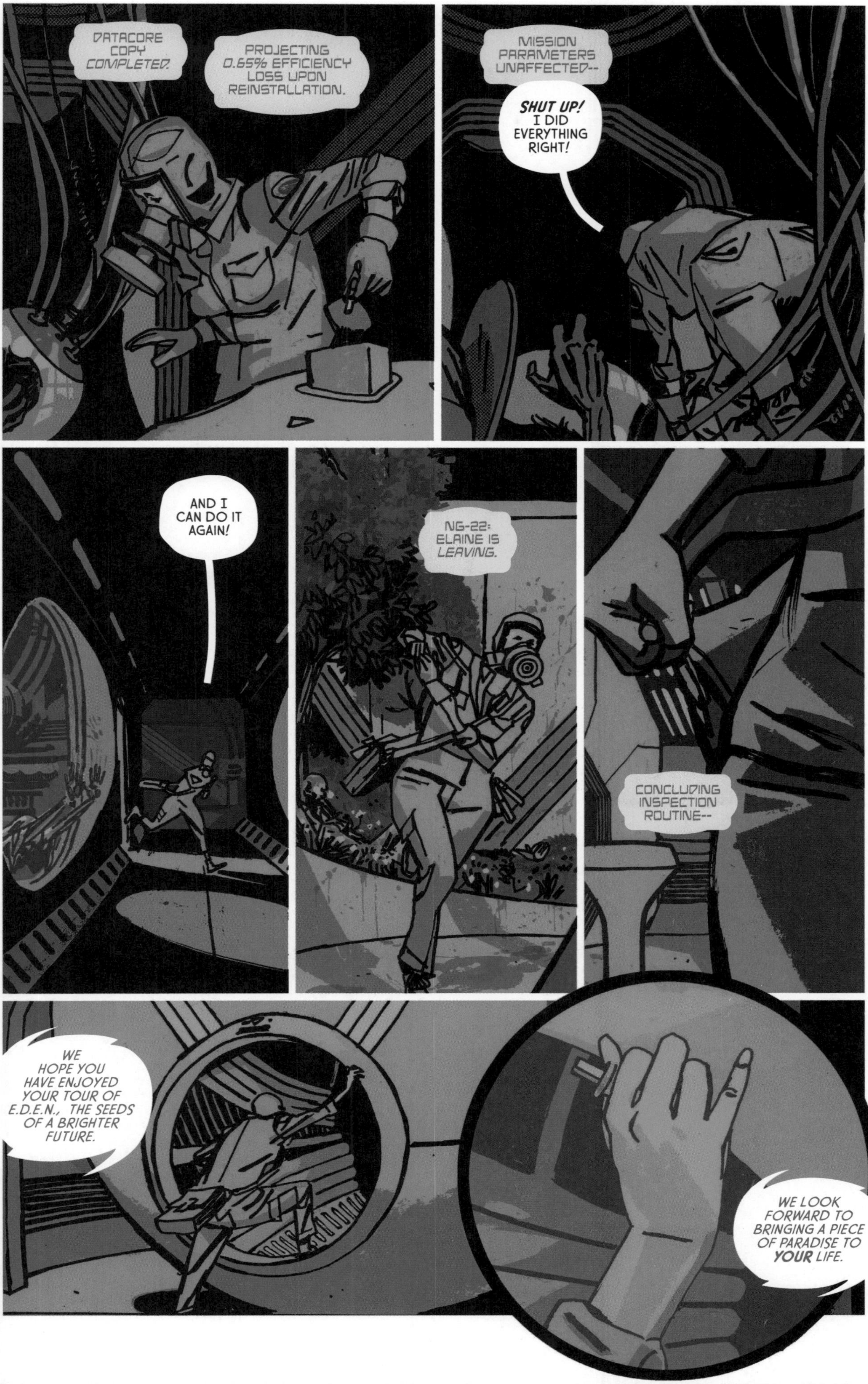
DATACORE COPY COMPLETED.
PROJECTING 0.65% EFFICIENCY LOSS UPON REINSTALLATION.
MISSION PARAMETERS UNAFFECTED--
SHUT UP! I DID EVERYTHING RIGHT!
AND I CAN DO IT AGAIN!
NG-22: ELAINE IS LEAVING.
CONCLUDING INSPECTION ROUTINE--
WE HOPE YOU HAVE ENJOYED YOUR TOUR OF E.D.E.N., THE SEEDS OF A BRIGHTER FUTURE.
WE LOOK FORWARD TO BRINGING A PIECE OF PARADISE TO YOUR LIFE.

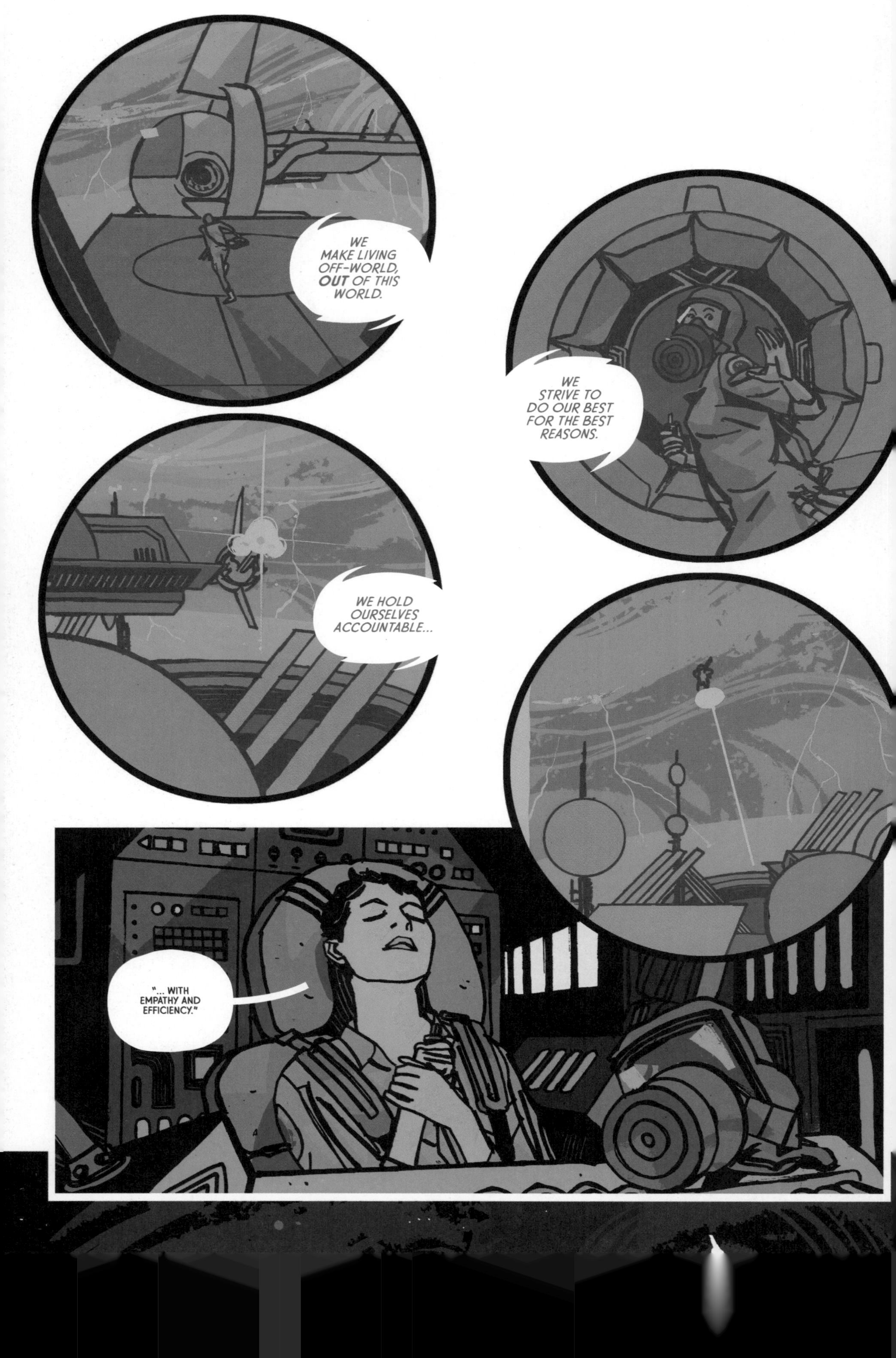
WE MAKE LIVING OFF-WORLD, **OUT** OF THIS WORLD.
WE STRIVE TO DO OUR BEST FOR THE BEST REASONS.
WE HOLD OURSELVES ACCOUNTABLE...
"... WITH EMPATHY AND EFFICIENCY."

THE FATHER OF ALL THINGS

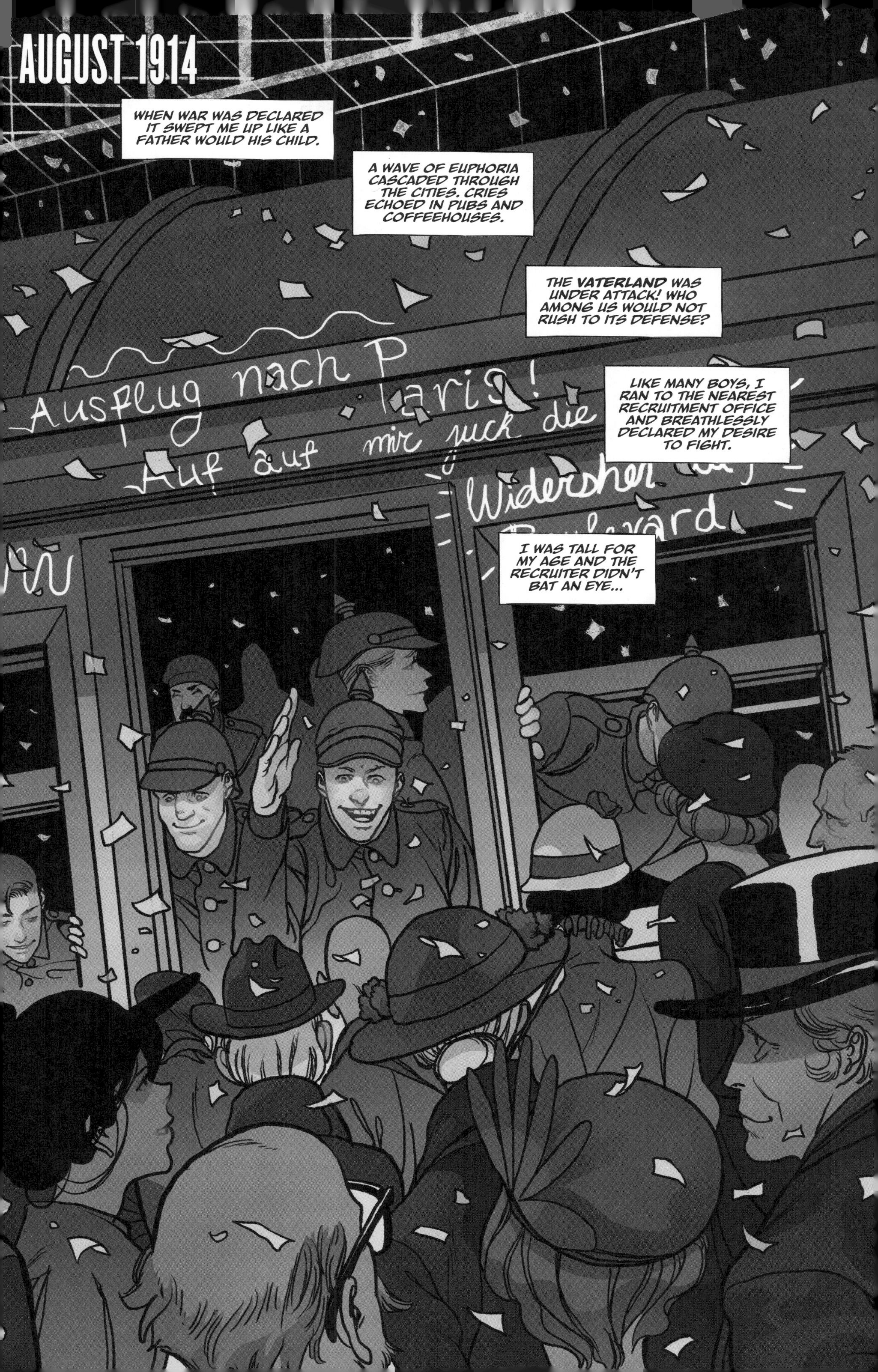
AUGUST 1914
WHEN WAR WAS DECLARED IT SWEPT ME UP LIKE A FATHER WOULD HIS CHILD.
A WAVE OF EUPHORIA CASCADED THROUGH THE CITIES. CRIES ECHOED IN PUBS AND COFFEEHOUSES.
THE VATERLAND WAS UNDER ATTACK! WHO AMONG US WOULD NOT RUSH TO ITS DEFENSE?
LIKE MANY BOYS, I RAN TO THE NEAREST RECRUITMENT OFFICE AND BREATHLESSLY DECLARED MY DESIRE TO FIGHT.
I WAS TALL FOR MY AGE AND THE RECRUITER DIDN'T BAT AN EYE...
Ausflug nach Paris!
Auf auf mir juck die

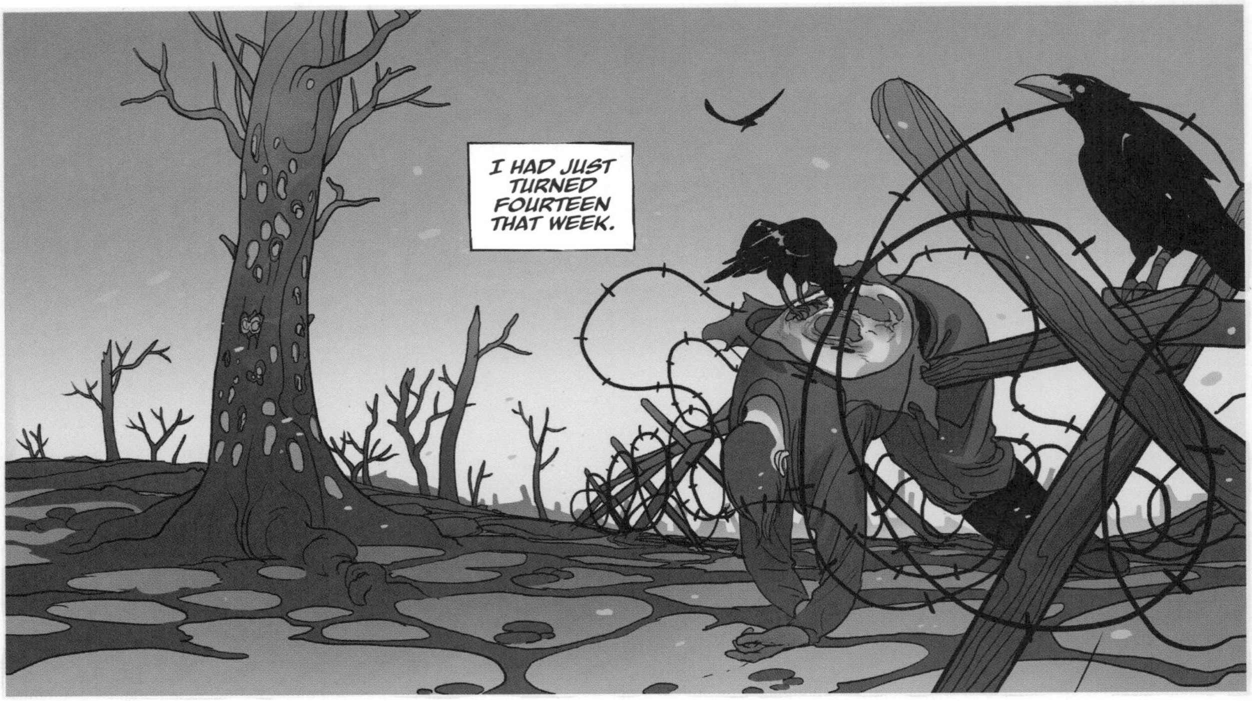
I HAD JUST TURNED FOURTEEN THAT WEEK.

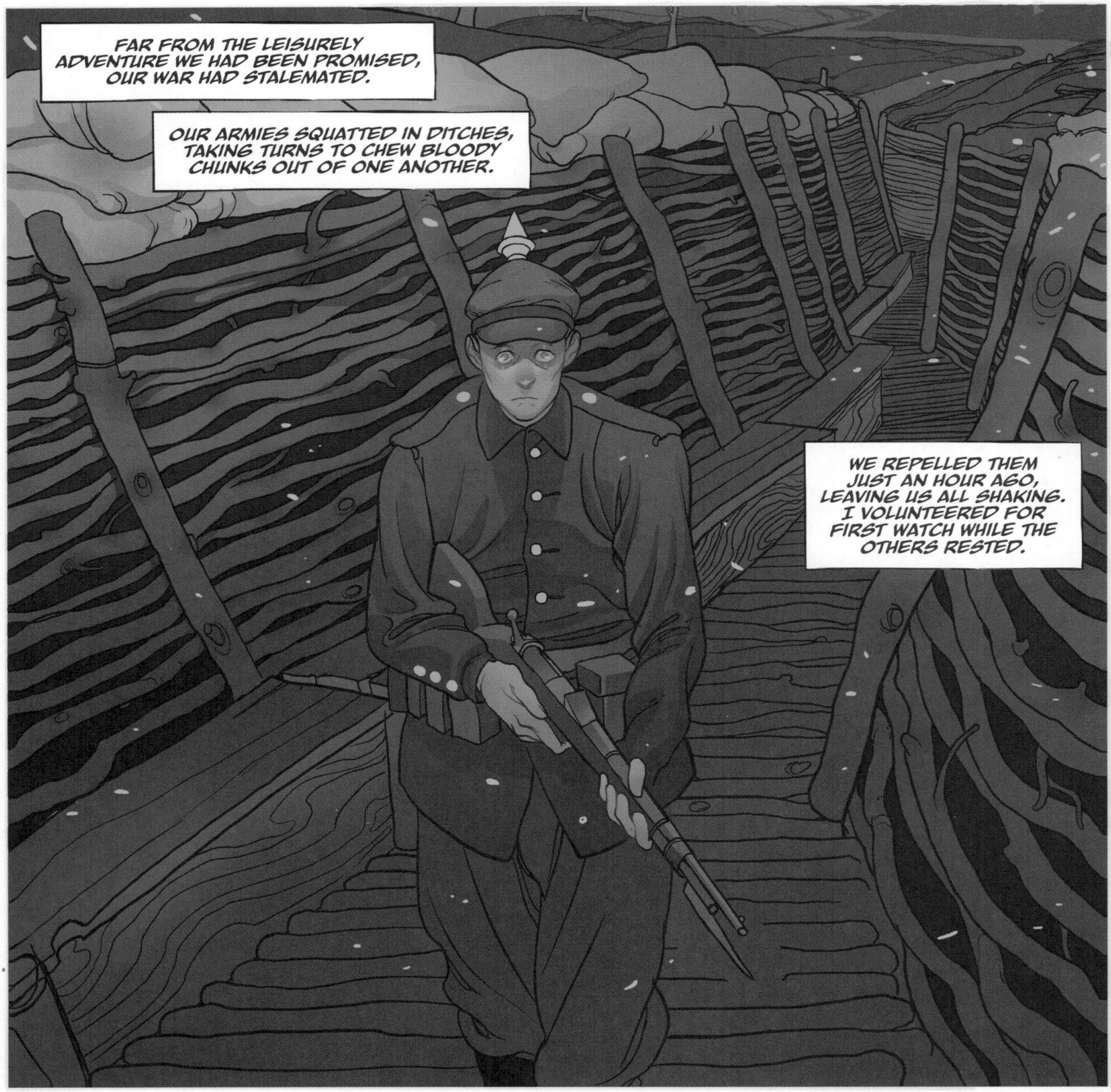
FAR FROM THE LEISURELY ADVENTURE WE HAD BEEN PROMISED, OUR WAR HAD STALEMATED.
OUR ARMIES SQUATTED IN DITCHES, TAKING TURNS TO CHEW BLOODY CHUNKS OUT OF ONE ANOTHER.
WE REPELLED THEM JUST AN HOUR AGO, LEAVING US ALL SHAKING. I VOLUNTEERED FOR FIRST WATCH WHILE THE OTHERS RESTED.

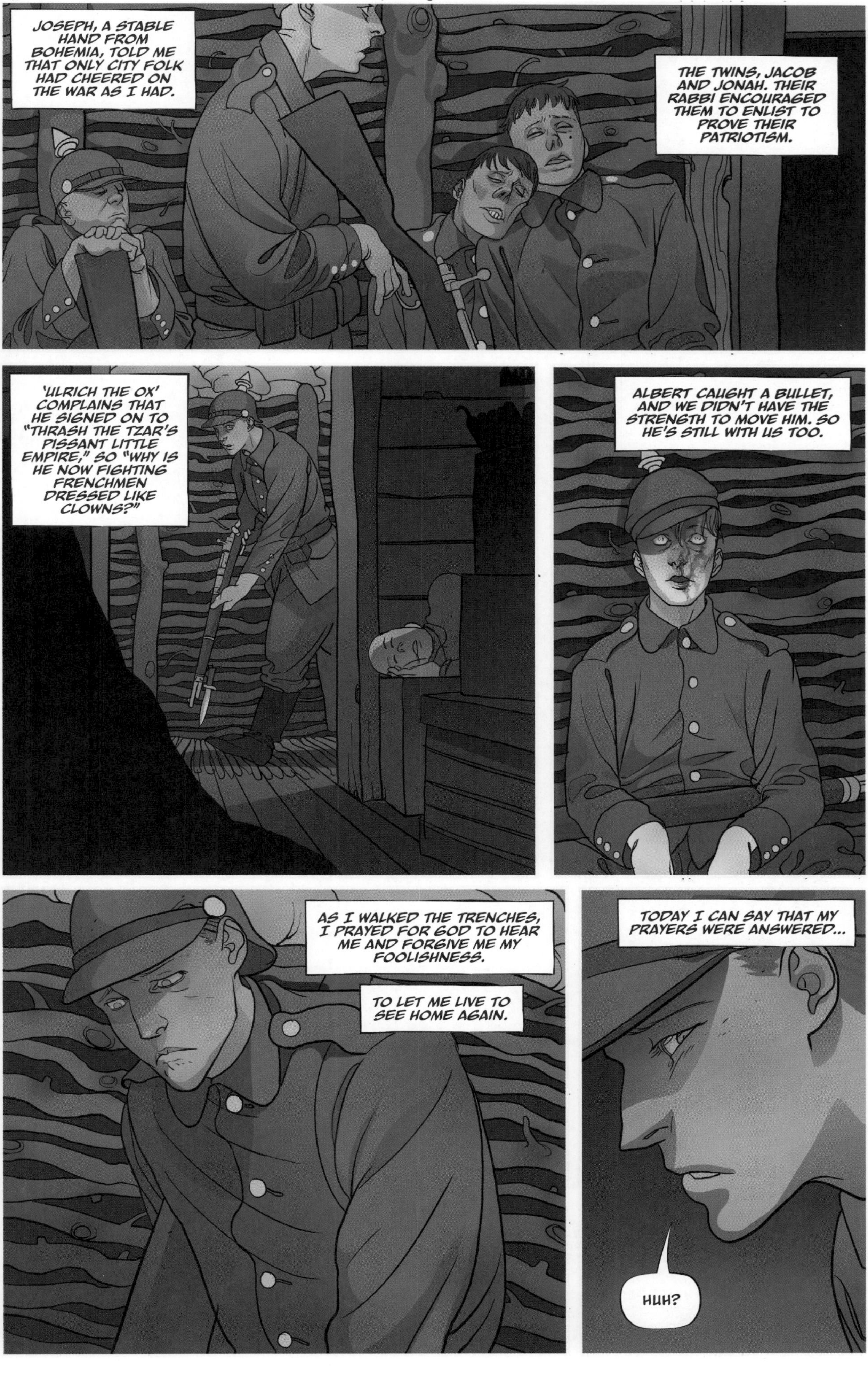
JOSEPH, A STABLE HAND FROM BOHEMIA, TOLD ME THAT ONLY CITY FOLK HAD CHEERED ON THE WAR AS I HAD.
THE TWINS, JACOB AND JONAH. THEIR RABBI ENCOURAGED THEM TO ENLIST TO PROVE THEIR PATRIOTISM.
'ULRICH THE OX' COMPLAINS THAT HE SIGNED ON TO "THRASH THE TZAR'S PISSANT LITTLE EMPIRE," SO "WHY IS HE NOW FIGHTING FRENCHMEN DRESSED LIKE CLOWNS?"
ALBERT CAUGHT A BULLET, AND WE DIDN'T HAVE THE STRENGTH TO MOVE HIM. SO HE'S STILL WITH US TOO.
AS I WALKED THE TRENCHES, I PRAYED FOR GOD TO HEAR ME AND FORGIVE ME MY FOOLISHNESS.
TO LET ME LIVE TO SEE HOME AGAIN.
TODAY I CAN SAY THAT MY PRAYERS WERE ANSWERED...
HUH?

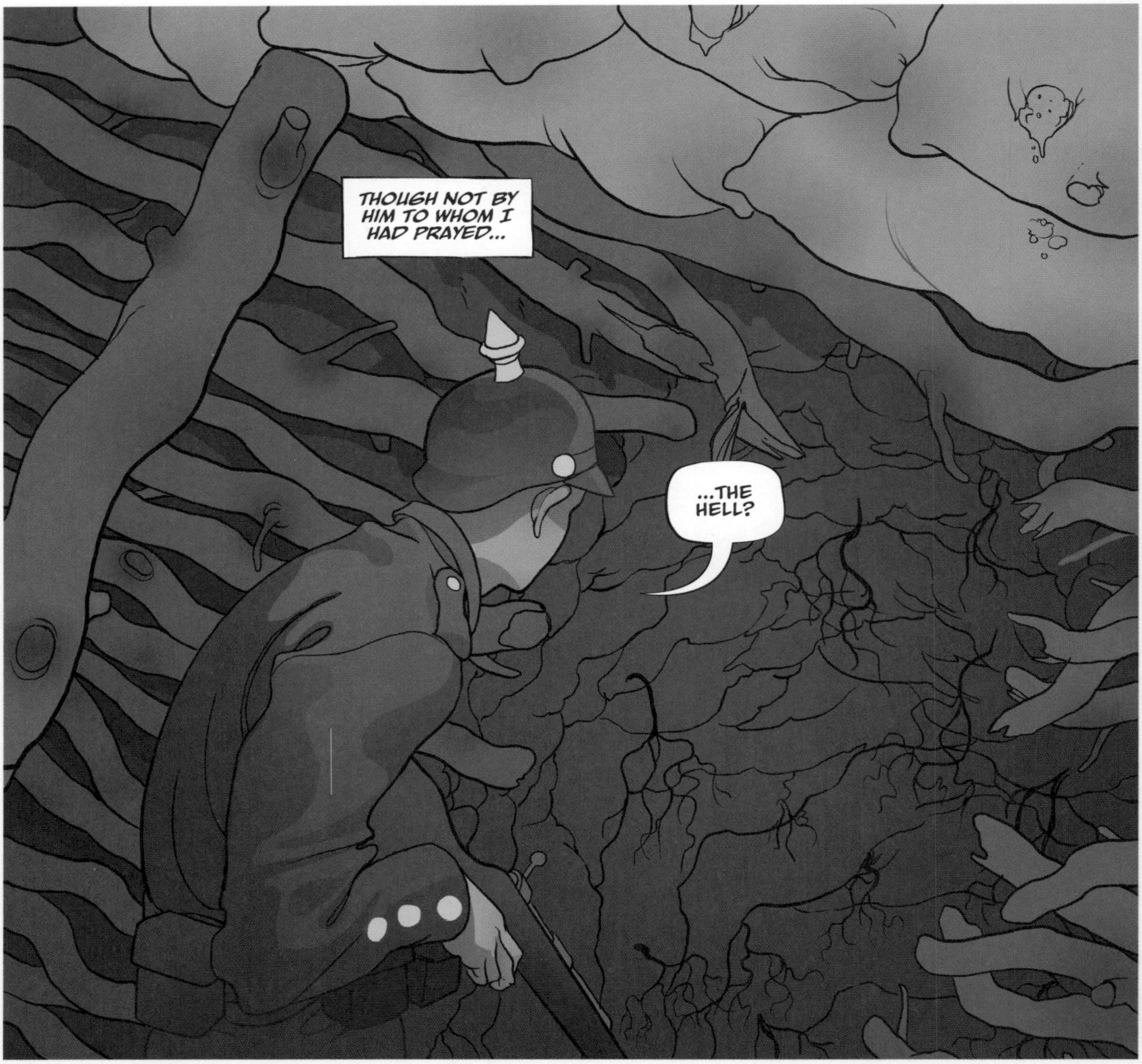
THOUGH NOT BY HIM TO WHOM I HAD PRAYED...
...THE HELL?

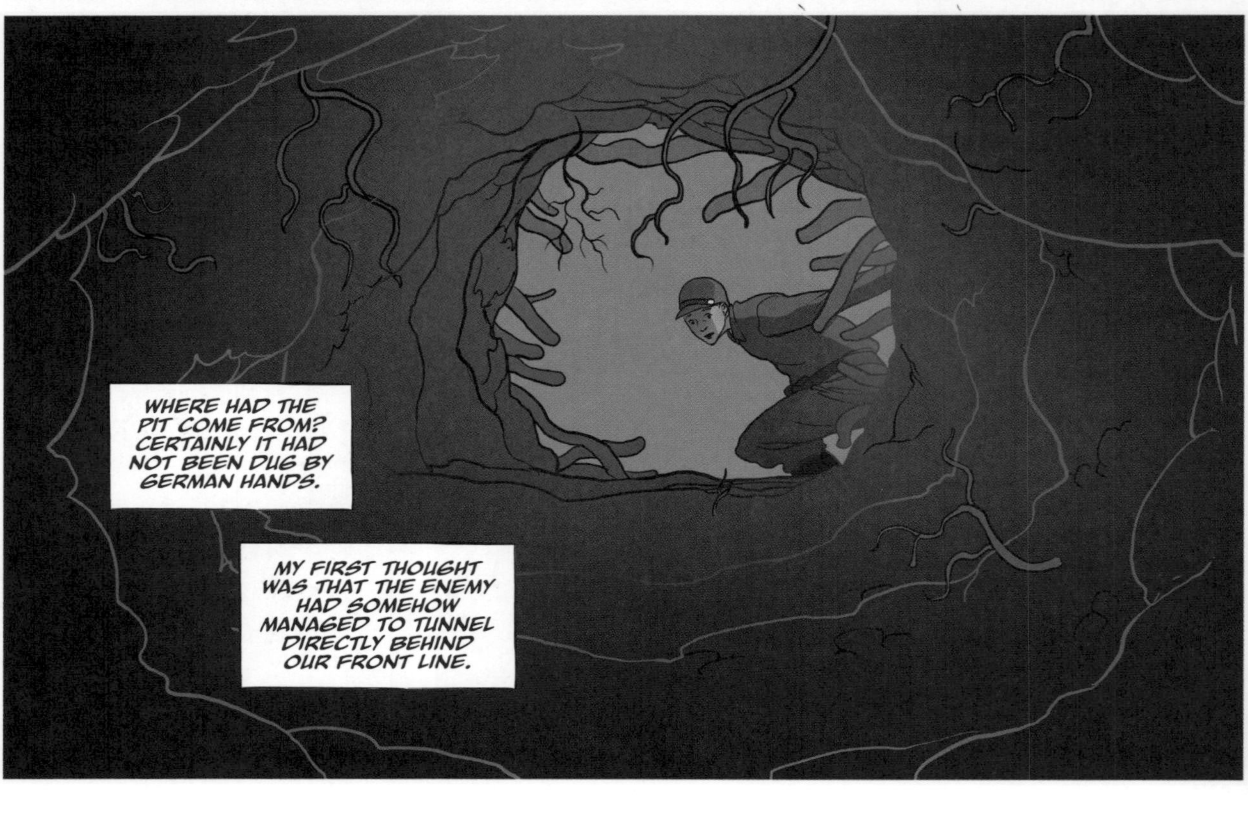
WHERE HAD THE PIT COME FROM? CERTAINLY IT HAD NOT BEEN DUG BY GERMAN HANDS.
MY FIRST THOUGHT WAS THAT THE ENEMY HAD SOMEHOW MANAGED TO TUNNEL DIRECTLY BEHIND OUR FRONT LINE.

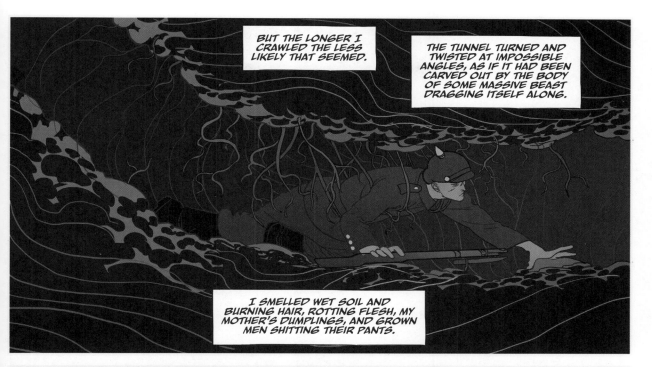

BUT THE LONGER I CRAWLED THE LESS LIKELY THAT SEEMED.

THE TUNNEL TURNED AND TWISTED AT IMPOSSIBLE ANGLES, AS IF IT HAD BEEN CARVED OUT BY THE BODY OF SOME MASSIVE BEAST DRAGGING ITSELF ALONG.

I SMELLED WET SOIL AND BURNING HAIR, ROTTING FLESH, MY MOTHER'S DUMPLINGS, AND GROWN MEN SHITTING THEIR PANTS.

I LOST TRACK OF TIME, BUT LIKE ALL THINGS, THE TUNNEL DID HAVE AN END.

YOU THERE! SHOW YOURSELF.

AND THERE IT WAS...

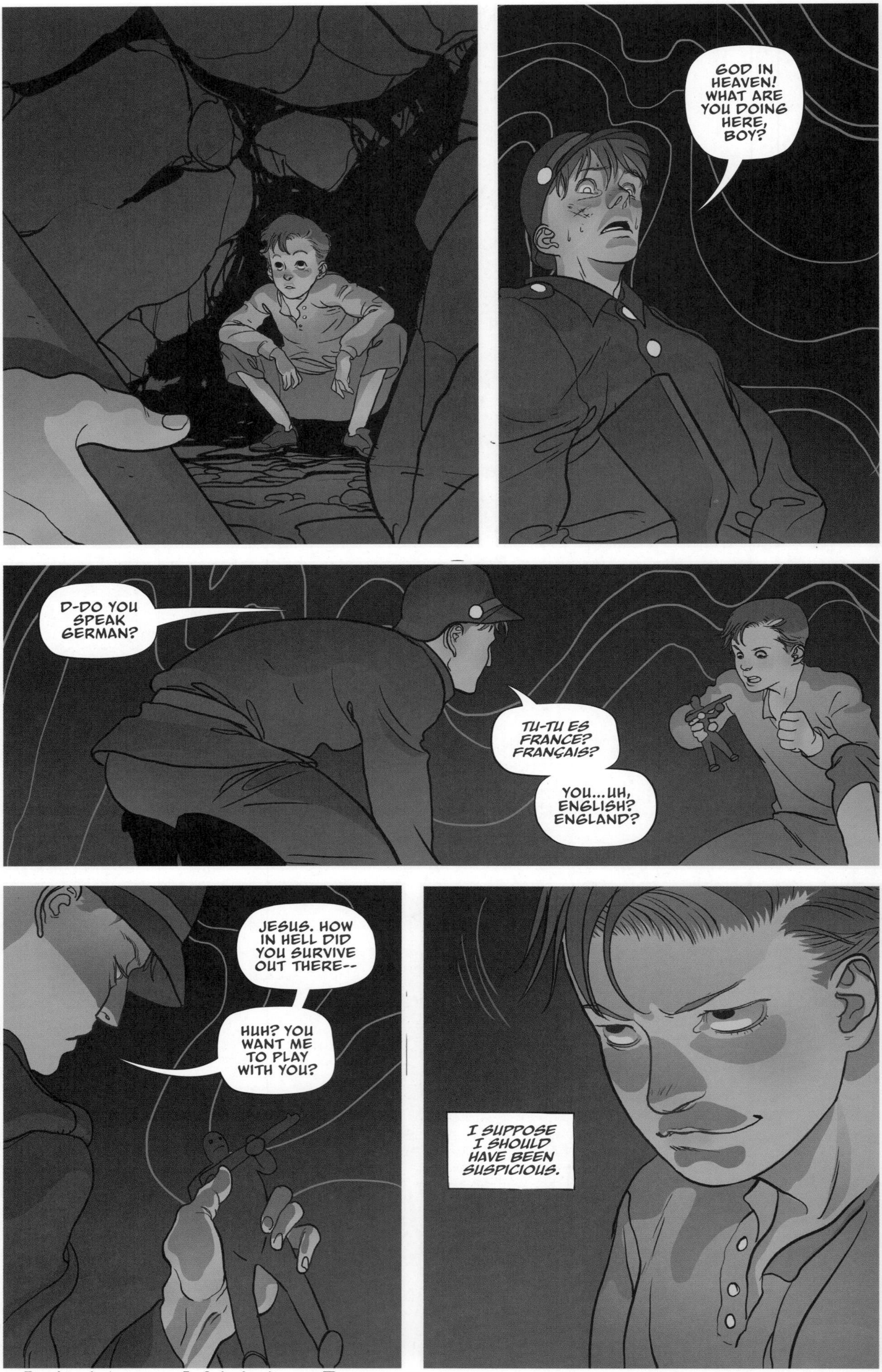
GOD IN HEAVEN! WHAT ARE YOU DOING HERE, BOY?
D-DO YOU SPEAK GERMAN?
TU-TU ES FRANCE? FRANÇAIS?
YOU...UH, ENGLISH? ENGLAND?
JESUS. HOW IN HELL DID YOU SURVIVE OUT THERE--
HUH? YOU WANT ME TO PLAY WITH YOU?
I SUPPOSE I SHOULD HAVE BEEN SUSPICIOUS.

BUT WAR HAD SHOWN ME STRANGER THINGS ALREADY.

AND SOMETHING ABOUT HIM MADE ME WANT TO PLEASE HIM.

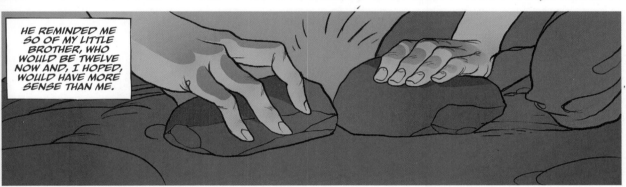

HE REMINDED ME SO OF MY LITTLE BROTHER, WHO WOULD BE TWELVE NOW AND, I HOPED, WOULD HAVE MORE SENSE THAN ME.

BOOM! HA HA HA.

HAHA. OH, MY LITTLE FRIEND. YOU DON'T KNOW HOW GOOD IT FEELS TO JUST PLAY.

I PRAY EVERY DAY THAT THIS WAR WILL END SO I CAN RETURN HOME.

I'D DO ANYTHING TO MAKE THAT HAPPEN.

ANYTHING?

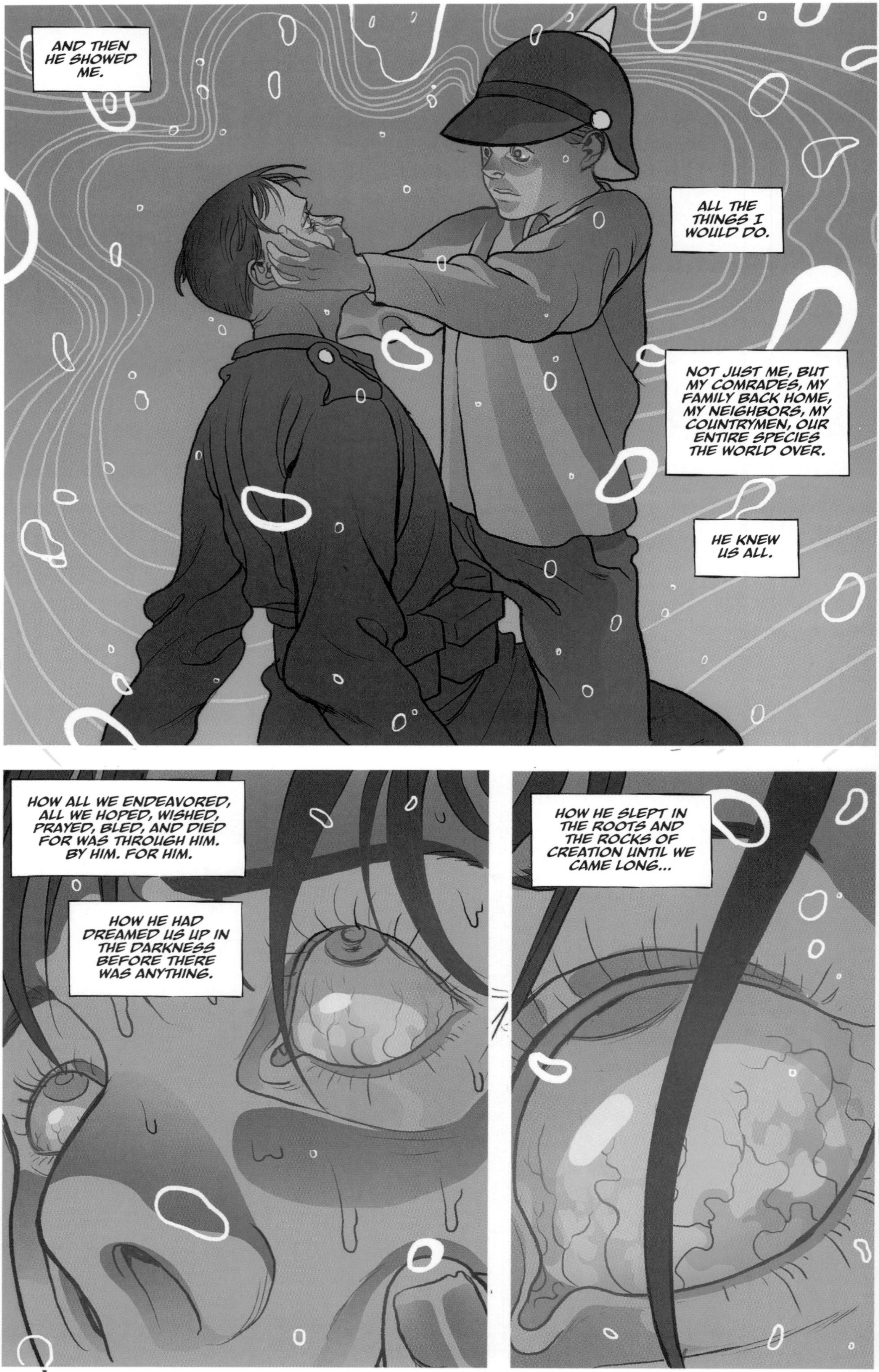
AND THEN HE SHOWED ME.
ALL THE THINGS I WOULD DO.
NOT JUST ME, BUT MY COMRADES, MY FAMILY BACK HOME, MY NEIGHBORS, MY COUNTRYMEN, OUR ENTIRE SPECIES THE WORLD OVER.
HE KNEW US ALL.
HOW ALL WE ENDEAVORED, ALL WE HOPED, WISHED, PRAYED, BLED, AND DIED FOR WAS THROUGH HIM. BY HIM. FOR HIM.
HOW HE HAD DREAMED US UP IN THE DARKNESS BEFORE THERE WAS ANYTHING.
HOW HE SLEPT IN THE ROOTS AND THE ROCKS OF CREATION UNTIL WE CAME LONG...

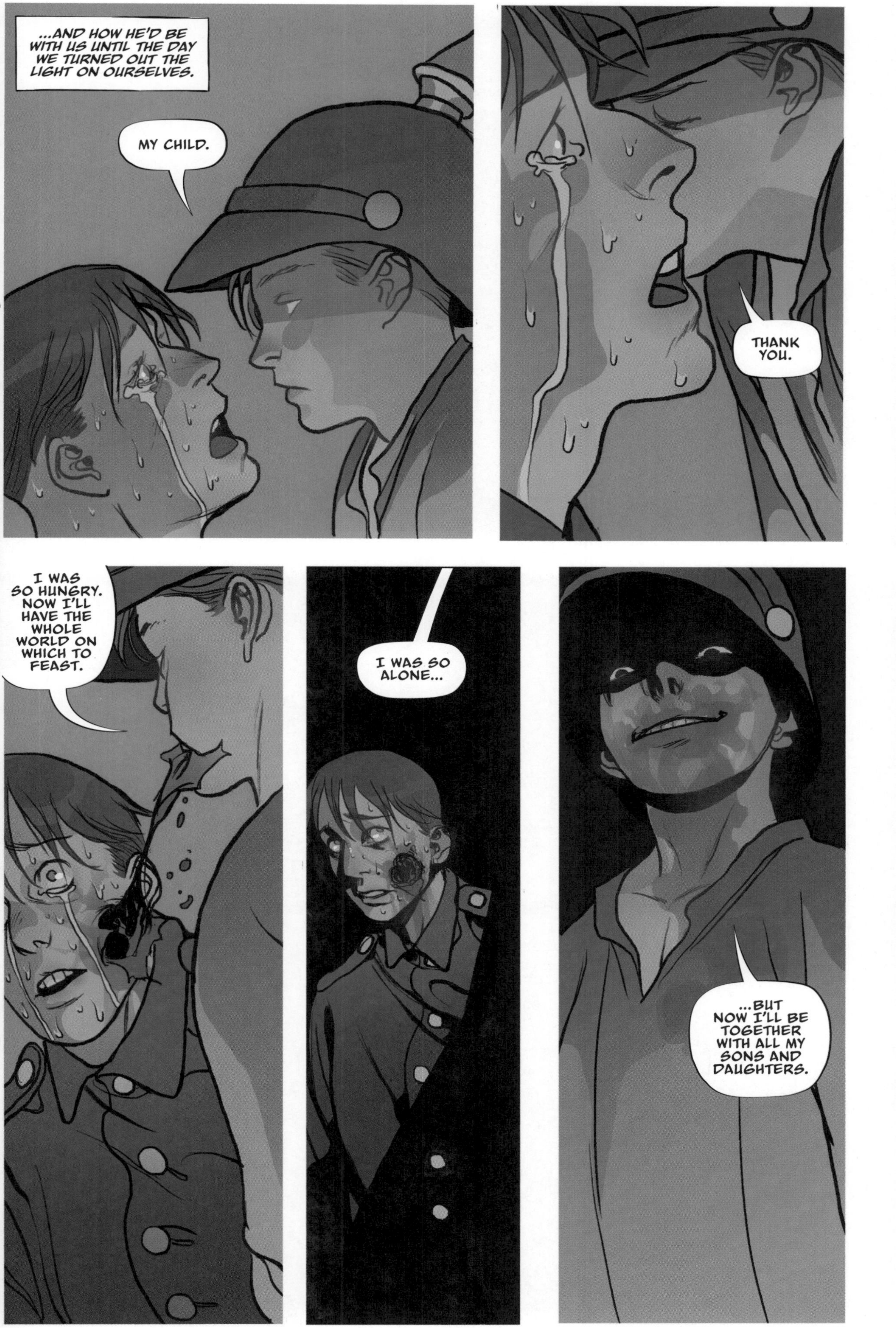
...AND HOW HE'D BE WITH US UNTIL THE DAY WE TURNED OUT THE LIGHT ON OURSELVES.
MY CHILD.
THANK YOU.
I WAS SO HUNGRY. NOW I'LL HAVE THE WHOLE WORLD ON WHICH TO FEAST.
I WAS SO ALONE...
...BUT NOW I'LL BE TOGETHER WITH ALL MY SONS AND DAUGHTERS.

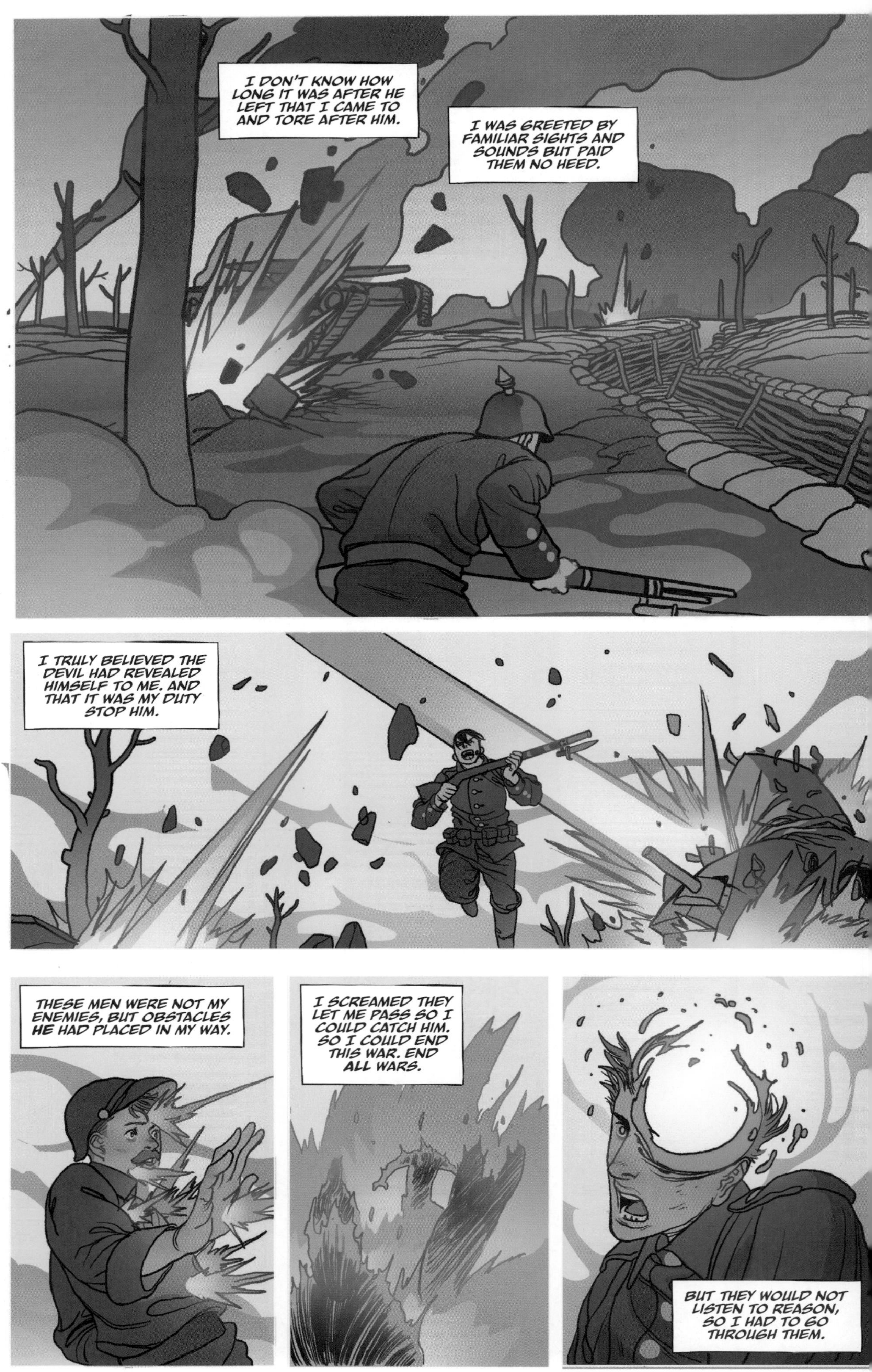
I DON'T KNOW HOW LONG IT WAS AFTER HE LEFT THAT I CAME TO AND TORE AFTER HIM.
I WAS GREETED BY FAMILIAR SIGHTS AND SOUNDS BUT PAID THEM NO HEED.
I TRULY BELIEVED THE DEVIL HAD REVEALED HIMSELF TO ME. AND THAT IT WAS MY DUTY STOP HIM.
THESE MEN WERE NOT MY ENEMIES, BUT OBSTACLES HE HAD PLACED IN MY WAY.
I SCREAMED THEY LET ME PASS SO I COULD CATCH HIM. SO I COULD END THIS WAR. END ALL WARS.
BUT THEY WOULD NOT LISTEN TO REASON, SO I HAD TO GO THROUGH THEM.

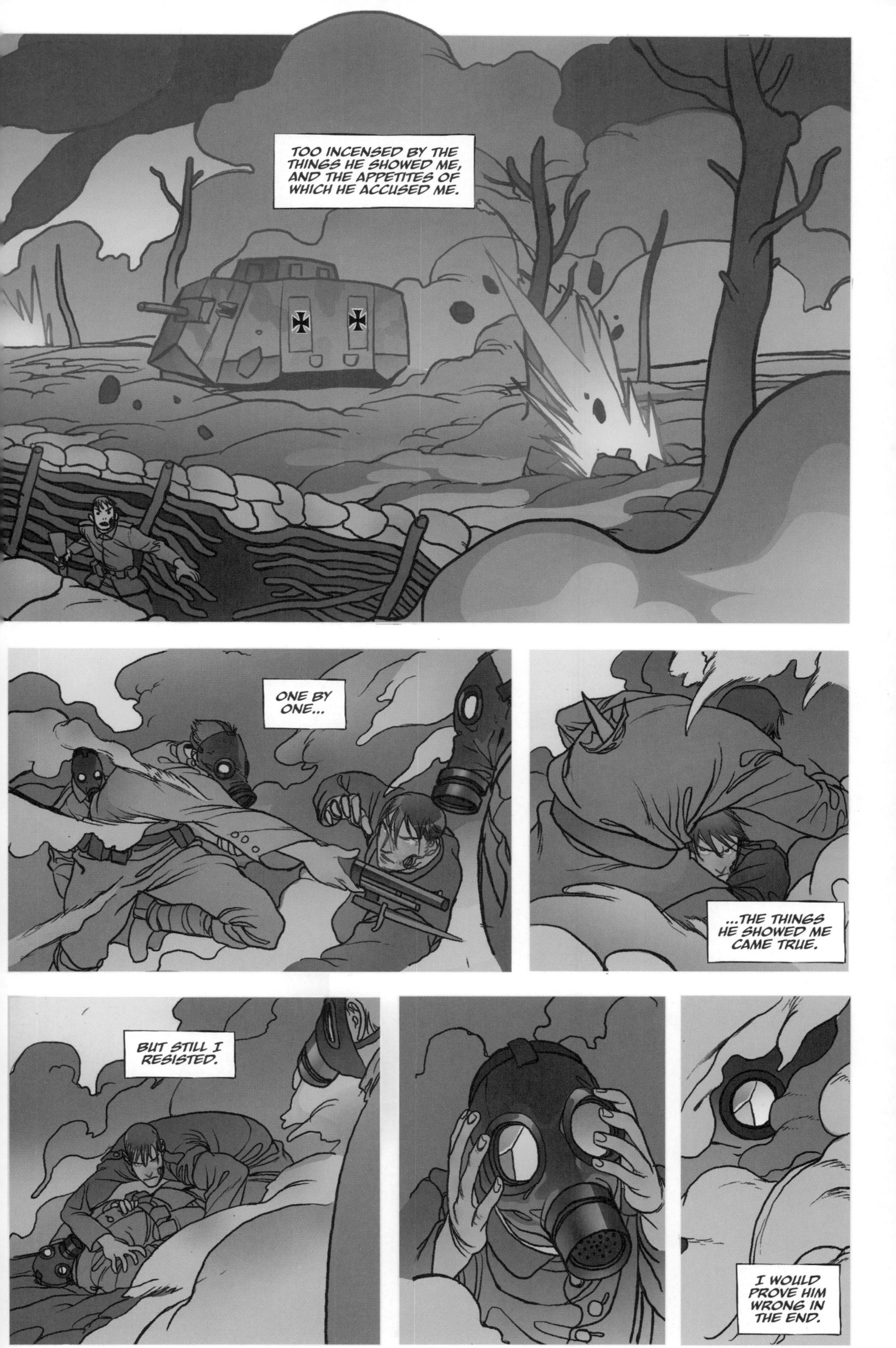
TOO INCENSED BY THE THINGS HE SHOWED ME, AND THE APPETITES OF WHICH HE ACCUSED ME.
ONE BY ONE...
...THE THINGS HE SHOWED ME CAME TRUE.
BUT STILL I RESISTED.
I WOULD PROVE HIM WRONG IN THE END.

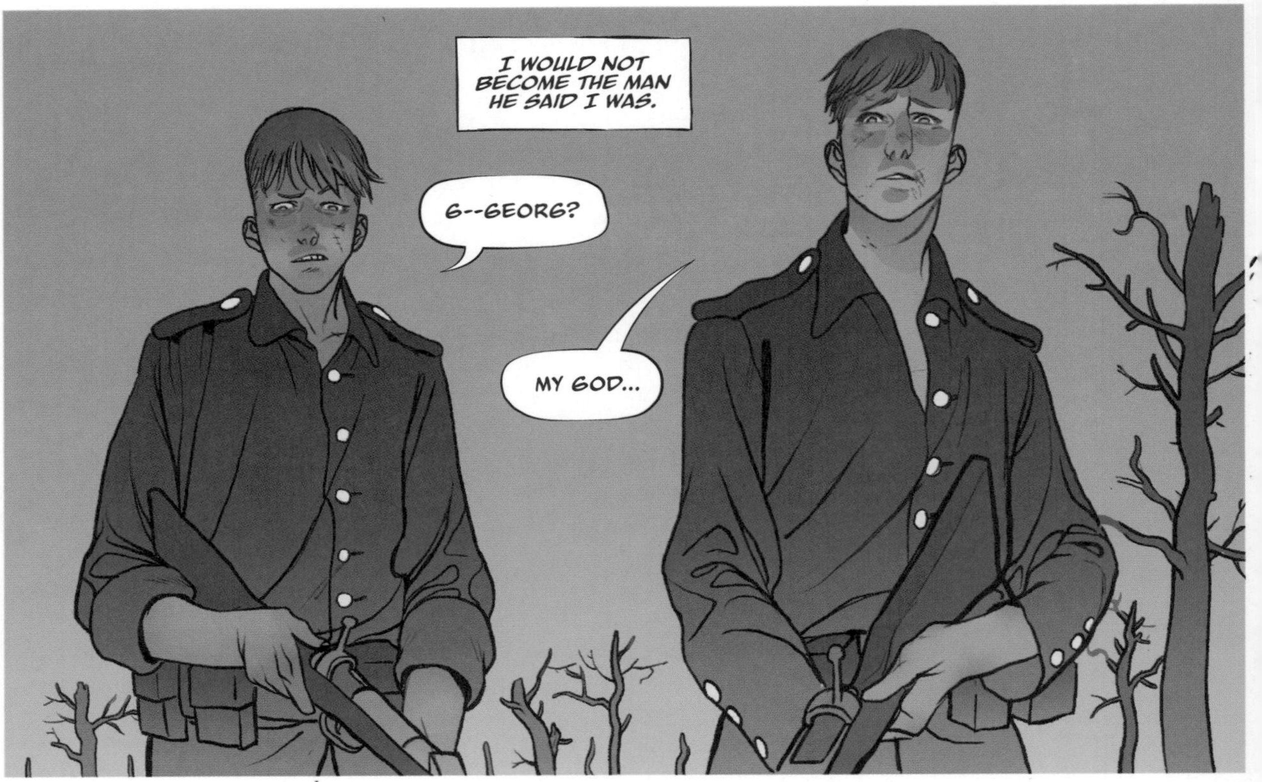
I WOULD NOT BECOME THE MAN HE SAID I WAS.
G--GEORG?
MY GOD...

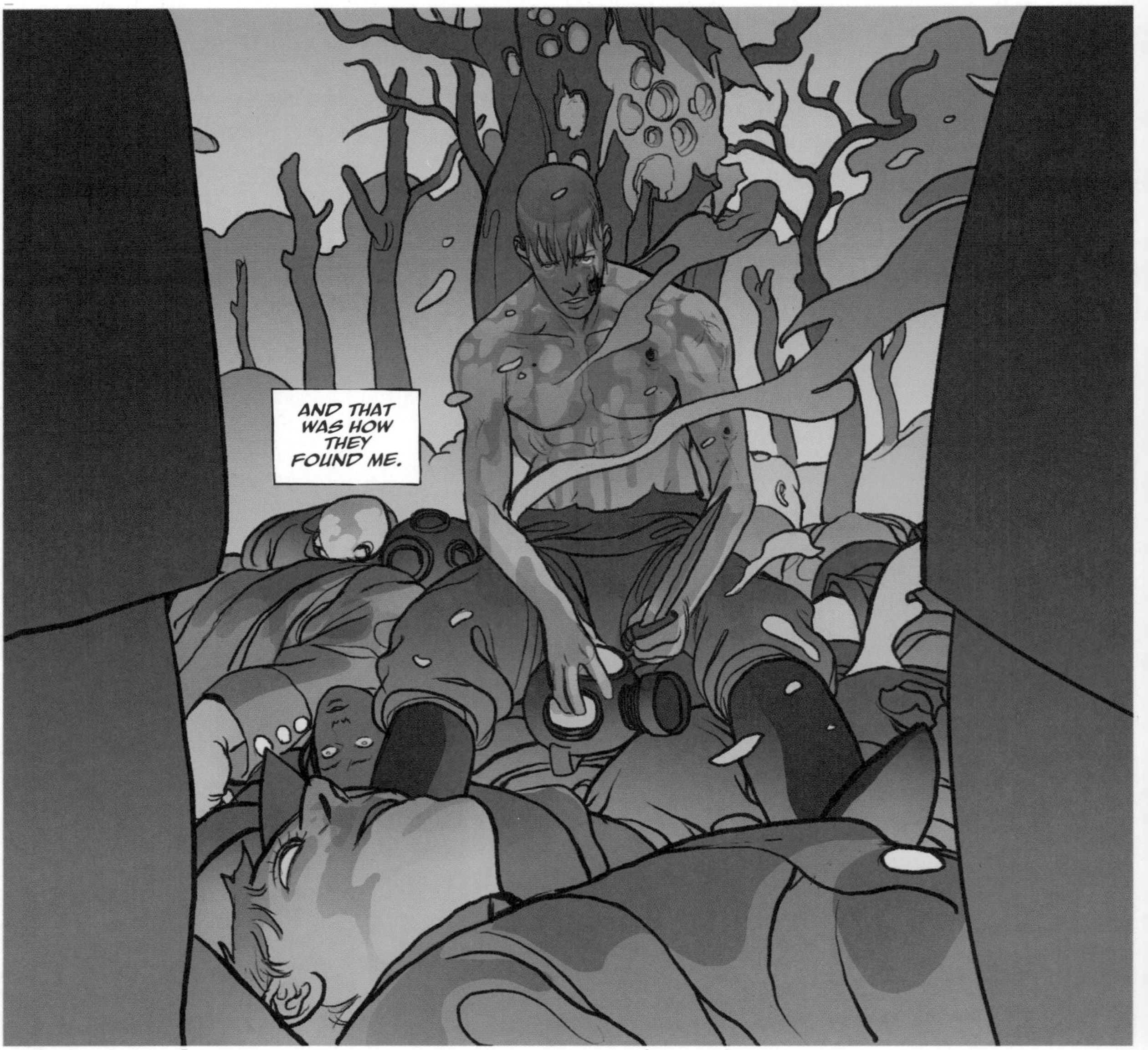
AND THAT WAS HOW THEY FOUND ME.

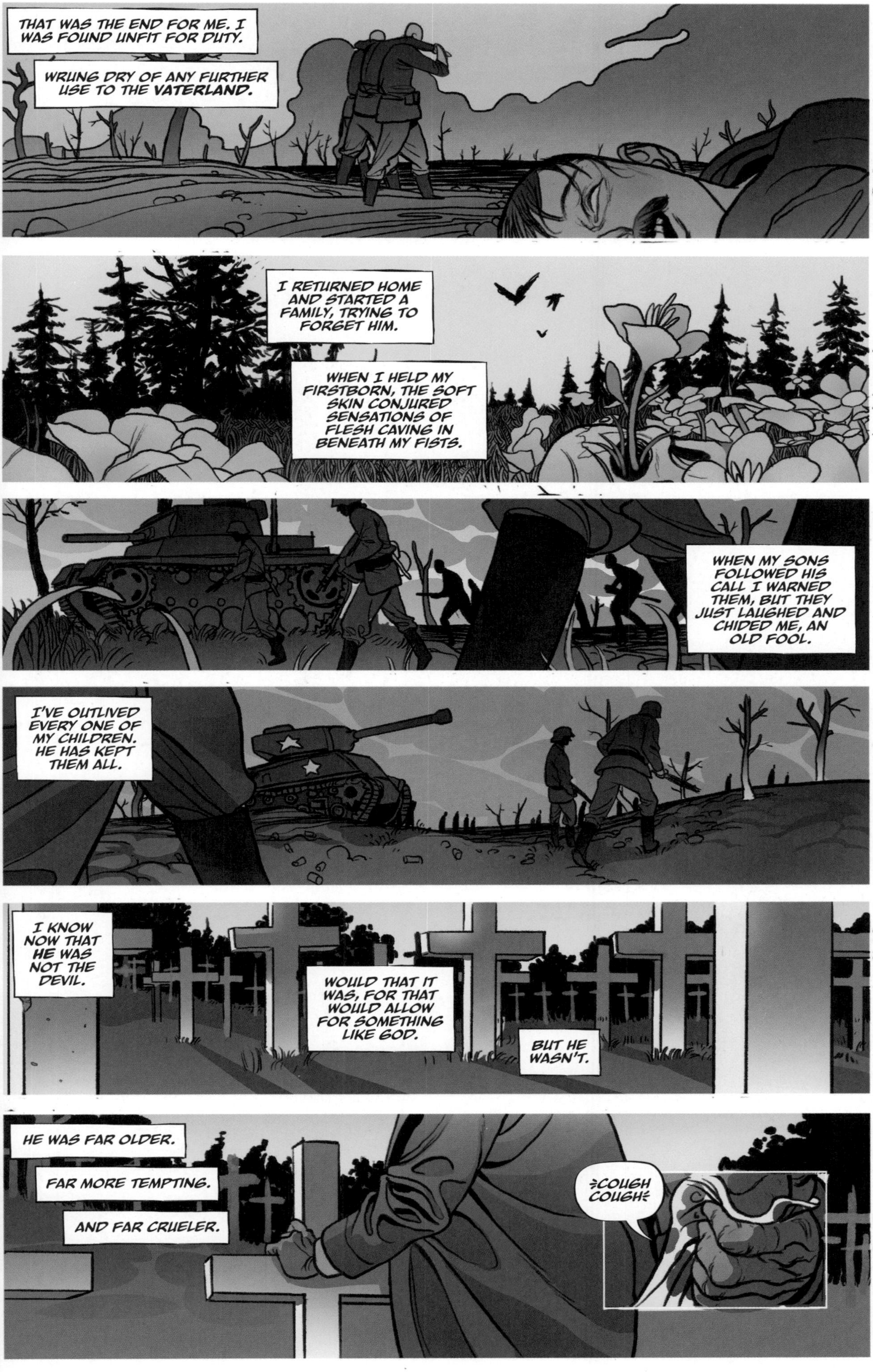
THAT WAS THE END FOR ME. I WAS FOUND UNFIT FOR DUTY.
WRUNG DRY OF ANY FURTHER USE TO THE VATERLAND.
I RETURNED HOME AND STARTED A FAMILY, TRYING TO FORGET HIM.
WHEN I HELD MY FIRSTBORN, THE SOFT SKIN CONJURED SENSATIONS OF FLESH CAVING IN BENEATH MY FISTS.
WHEN MY SONS FOLLOWED HIS CALL I WARNED THEM, BUT THEY JUST LAUGHED AND CHIDED ME, AN OLD FOOL.
I'VE OUTLIVED EVERY ONE OF MY CHILDREN. HE HAS KEPT THEM ALL.
I KNOW NOW THAT HE WAS NOT THE DEVIL.
WOULD THAT IT WAS, FOR THAT WOULD ALLOW FOR SOMETHING LIKE GOD.
BUT HE WASN'T.
HE WAS FAR OLDER.
FAR MORE TEMPTING.
AND FAR CRUELER.
COUGH COUGH

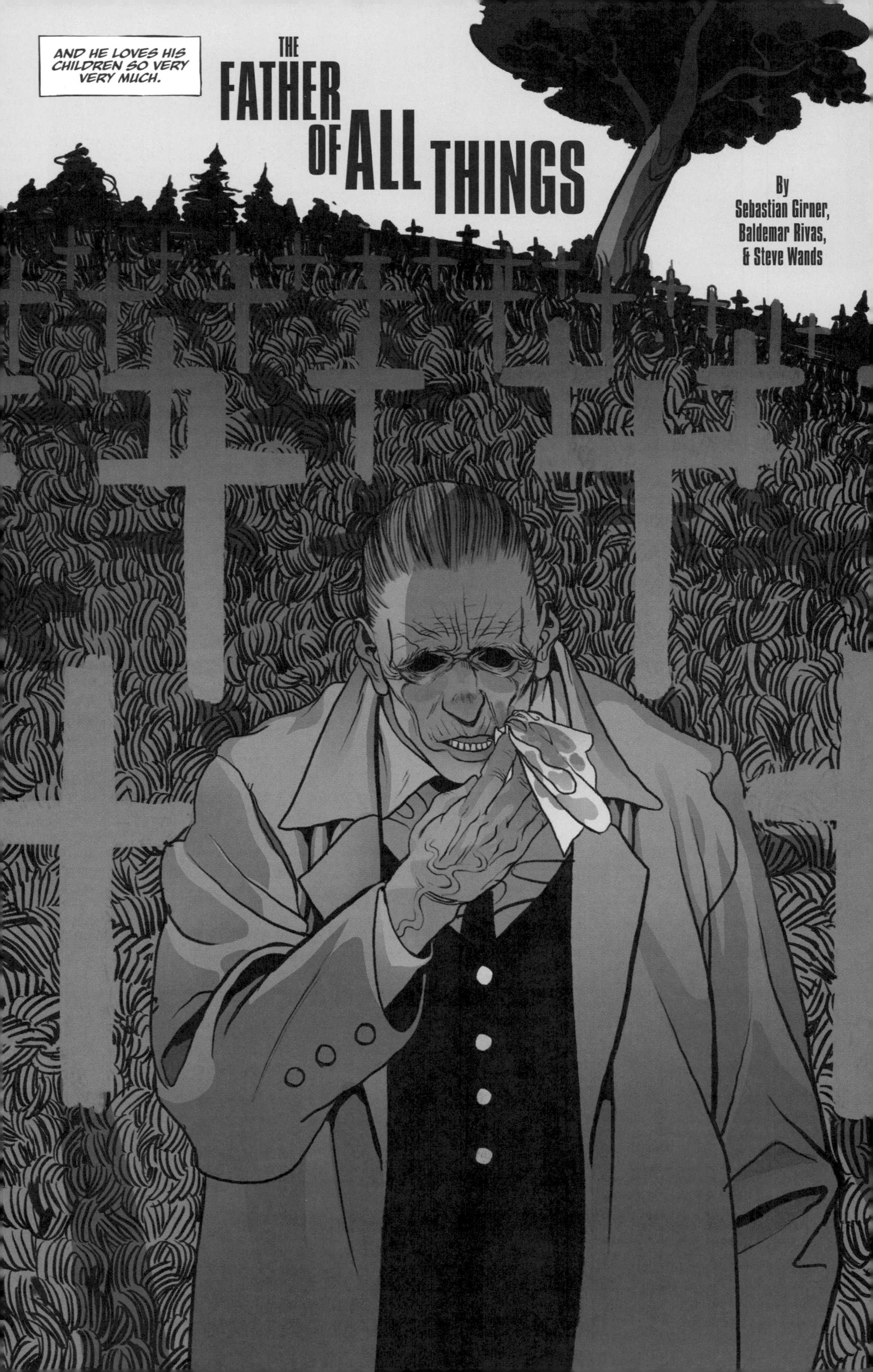
AND HE LOVES HIS CHILDREN SO VERY VERY MUCH.
THE FATHER OF ALL THINGS
By Sebastian Girner, Baldemar Rivas, & Steve Wands

NIGHT TRAIN

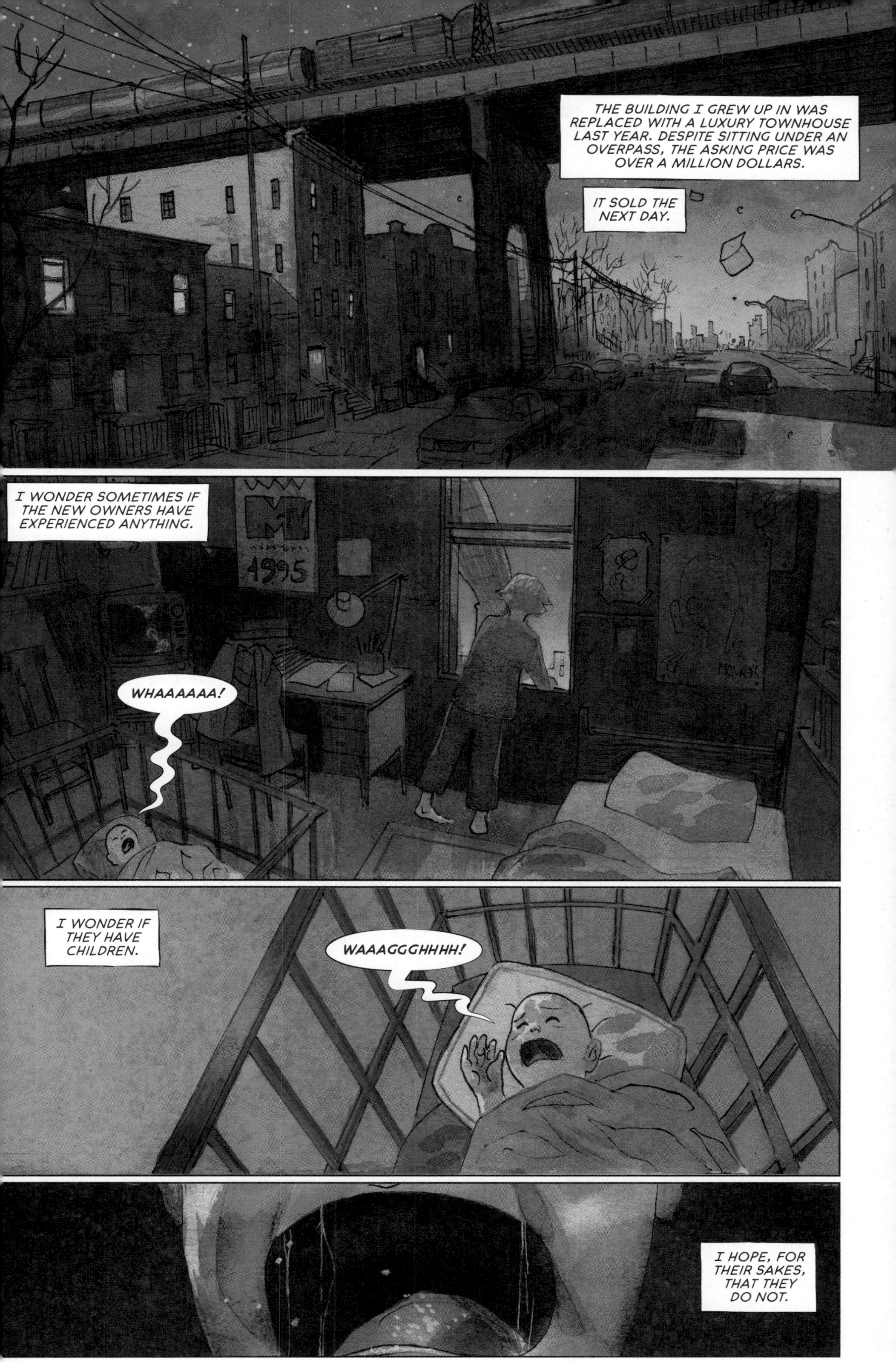
THE BUILDING I GREW UP IN WAS REPLACED WITH A LUXURY TOWNHOUSE LAST YEAR. DESPITE SITTING UNDER AN OVERPASS, THE ASKING PRICE WAS OVER A MILLION DOLLARS.
IT SOLD THE NEXT DAY.
I WONDER SOMETIMES IF THE NEW OWNERS HAVE EXPERIENCED ANYTHING.
MTV
1995
WHAAAAAA!
I WONDER IF THEY HAVE CHILDREN.
WAAAGGGHHHH!
I HOPE, FOR THEIR SAKES, THAT THEY DO NOT.

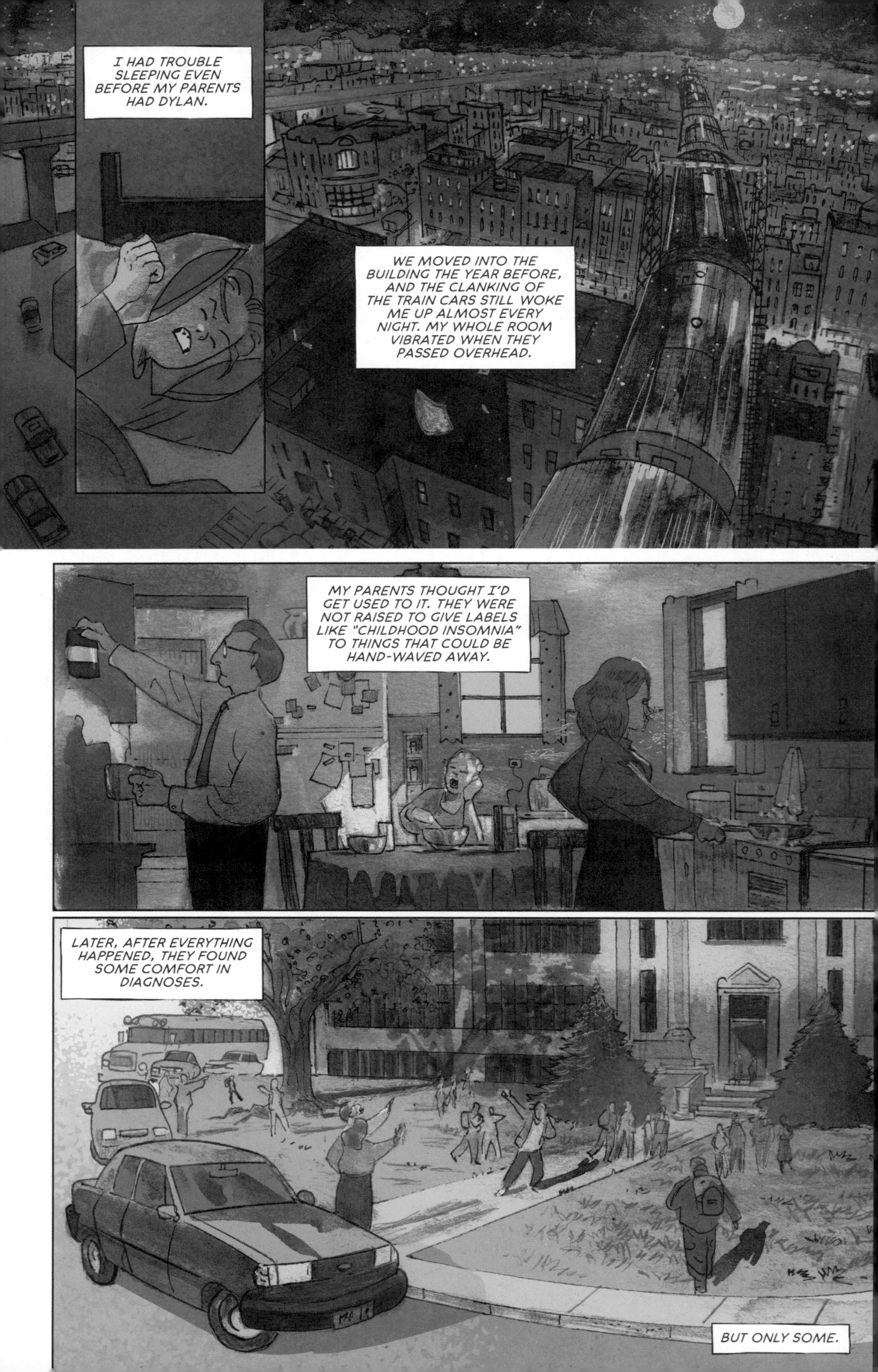
I HAD TROUBLE SLEEPING EVEN BEFORE MY PARENTS HAD DYLAN.
WE MOVED INTO THE BUILDING THE YEAR BEFORE, AND THE CLANKING OF THE TRAIN CARS STILL WOKE ME UP ALMOST EVERY NIGHT. MY WHOLE ROOM VIBRATED WHEN THEY PASSED OVERHEAD.
MY PARENTS THOUGHT I'D GET USED TO IT. THEY WERE NOT RAISED TO GIVE LABELS LIKE "CHILDHOOD INSOMNIA" TO THINGS THAT COULD BE HAND-WAVED AWAY.
LATER, AFTER EVERYTHING HAPPENED, THEY FOUND SOME COMFORT IN DIAGNOSES.
BUT ONLY SOME.

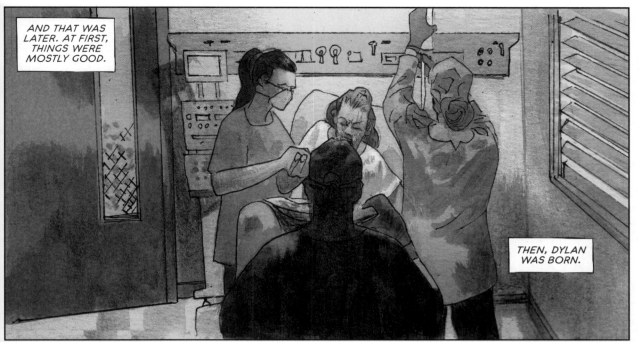

AND THAT WAS LATER. AT FIRST, THINGS WERE MOSTLY GOOD.

THEN, DYLAN WAS BORN.

BABY DYLAN DID NOT HAVE AN EASY BIRTH. HE WAS HEALTHY, BUT OUR MOM HAD COMPLICATIONS, AND DAD ENDED UP TAKING A LEAVE OF ABSENCE FROM WORK TO CARE FOR HER.

IT'S GOING TO SOUND LIKE I'M BLAMING DYLAN FOR EVERYTHING THAT HAPPENED, BUT I'M NOT. HE WAS JUST A BABY.

AND BECAUSE OF WHAT I DID, HE ALWAYS WILL BE.

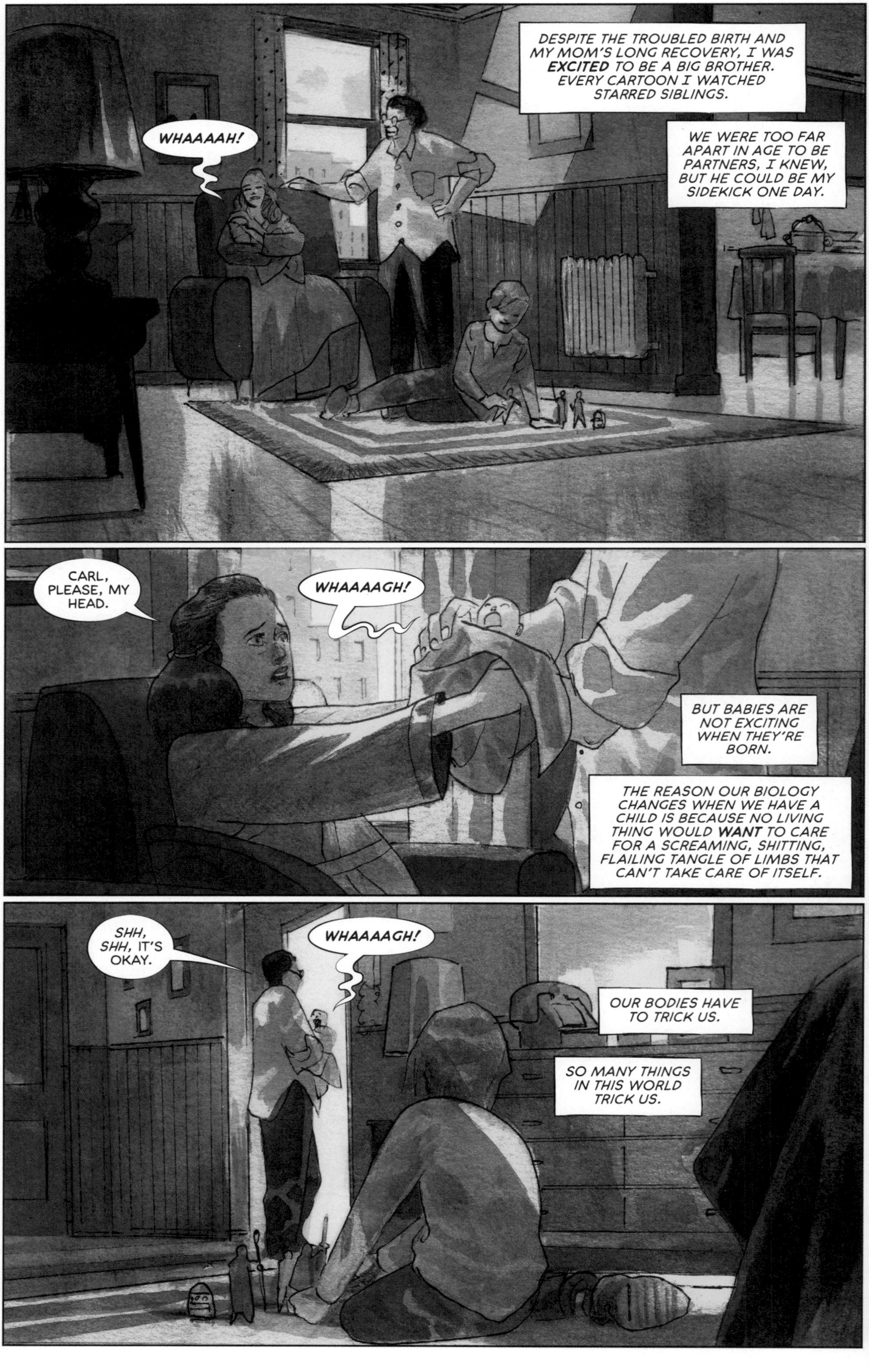
DESPITE THE TROUBLED BIRTH AND MY MOM'S LONG RECOVERY, I WAS **EXCITED** TO BE A BIG BROTHER. EVERY CARTOON I WATCHED STARRED SIBLINGS.
WHAAAAH!
WE WERE TOO FAR APART IN AGE TO BE PARTNERS, I KNEW, BUT HE COULD BE MY SIDEKICK ONE DAY.
CARL, PLEASE, MY HEAD.
WHAAAAGH!
BUT BABIES ARE NOT EXCITING WHEN THEY'RE BORN.
THE REASON OUR BIOLOGY CHANGES WHEN WE HAVE A CHILD IS BECAUSE NO LIVING THING WOULD **WANT** TO CARE FOR A SCREAMING, SHITTING, FLAILING TANGLE OF LIMBS THAT CAN'T TAKE CARE OF ITSELF.
SHH, SHH, IT'S OKAY.
WHAAAAGH!
OUR BODIES HAVE TO TRICK US.
SO MANY THINGS IN THIS WORLD TRICK US.

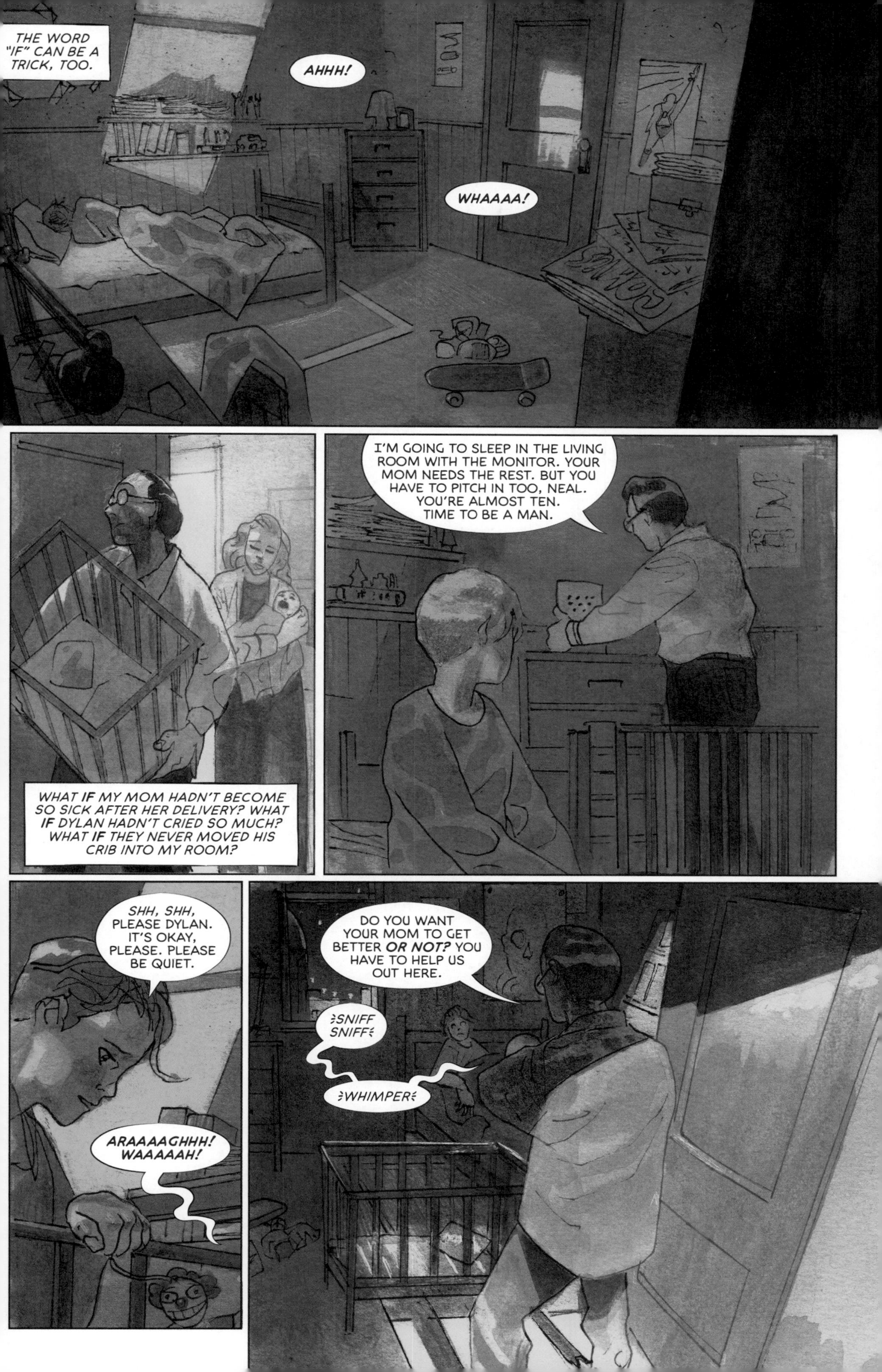
THE WORD "IF" CAN BE A TRICK, TOO.
AHHH!
WHAAAA!
COMICS
WHAT IF MY MOM HADN'T BECOME SO SICK AFTER HER DELIVERY? WHAT IF DYLAN HADN'T CRIED SO MUCH? WHAT IF THEY NEVER MOVED HIS CRIB INTO MY ROOM?
I'M GOING TO SLEEP IN THE LIVING ROOM WITH THE MONITOR. YOUR MOM NEEDS THE REST. BUT YOU HAVE TO PITCH IN TOO, NEAL. YOU'RE ALMOST TEN. TIME TO BE A MAN.
SHH, SHH, PLEASE DYLAN. IT'S OKAY, PLEASE. PLEASE BE QUIET.
ARAAAAGHHH! WAAAAAH!
DO YOU WANT YOUR MOM TO GET BETTER OR NOT? YOU HAVE TO HELP US OUT HERE.
SNIFF SNIFF
WHIMPER

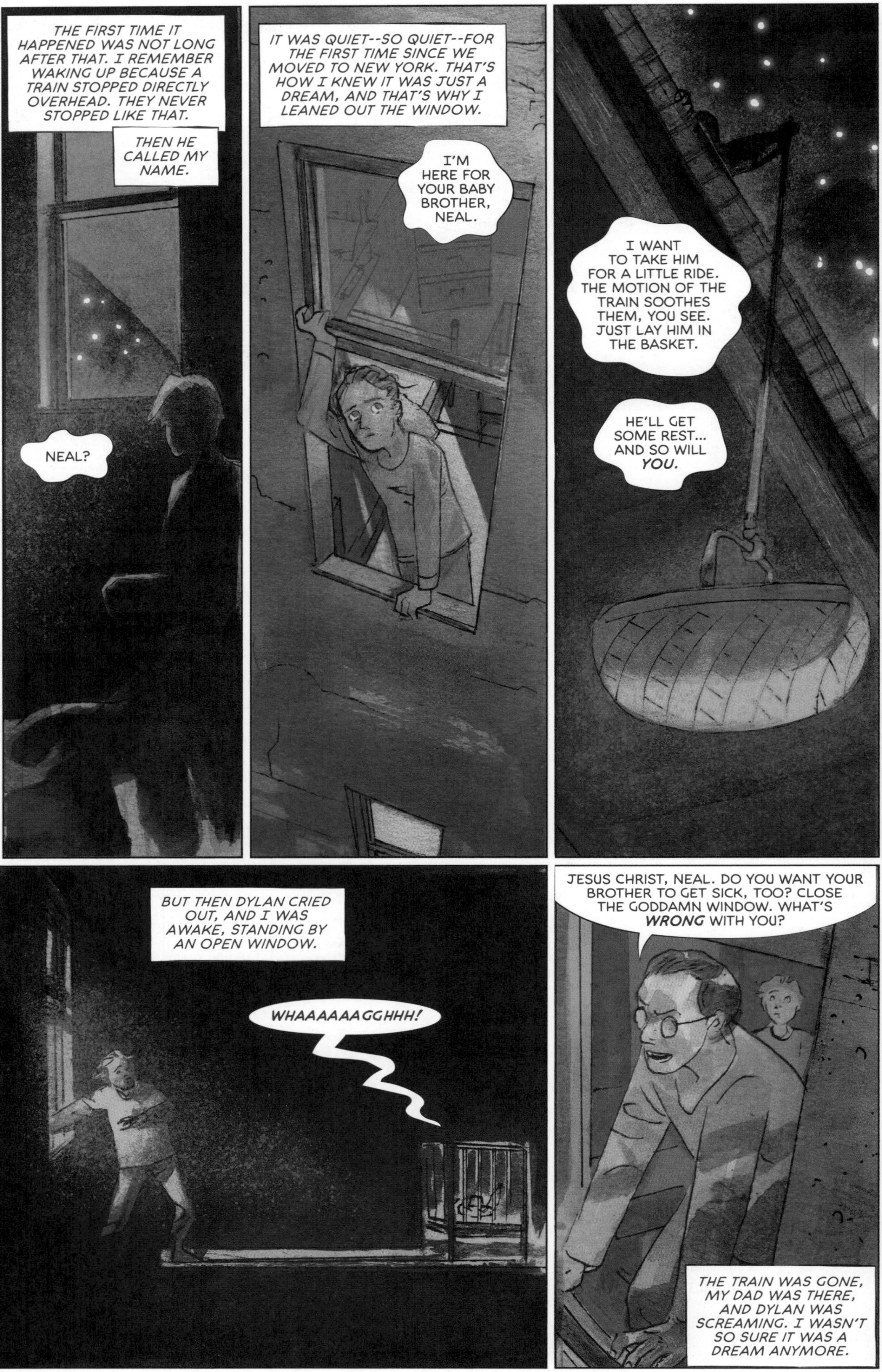
THE FIRST TIME IT HAPPENED WAS NOT LONG AFTER THAT. I REMEMBER WAKING UP BECAUSE A TRAIN STOPPED DIRECTLY OVERHEAD. THEY NEVER STOPPED LIKE THAT.
THEN HE CALLED MY NAME.
NEAL?
IT WAS QUIET--SO QUIET--FOR THE FIRST TIME SINCE WE MOVED TO NEW YORK. THAT'S HOW I KNEW IT WAS JUST A DREAM, AND THAT'S WHY I LEANED OUT THE WINDOW.
I'M HERE FOR YOUR BABY BROTHER, NEAL.
I WANT TO TAKE HIM FOR A LITTLE RIDE. THE MOTION OF THE TRAIN SOOTHES THEM, YOU SEE. JUST LAY HIM IN THE BASKET.
HE'LL GET SOME REST... AND SO WILL ***YOU.***
BUT THEN DYLAN CRIED OUT, AND I WAS AWAKE, STANDING BY AN OPEN WINDOW.
WHAAAAAAGGHHH!
JESUS CHRIST, NEAL. DO YOU WANT YOUR BROTHER TO GET SICK, TOO? CLOSE THE GODDAMN WINDOW. WHAT'S ***WRONG*** WITH YOU?
THE TRAIN WAS GONE, MY DAD WAS THERE, AND DYLAN WAS SCREAMING. I WASN'T SO SURE IT WAS A DREAM ANYMORE.

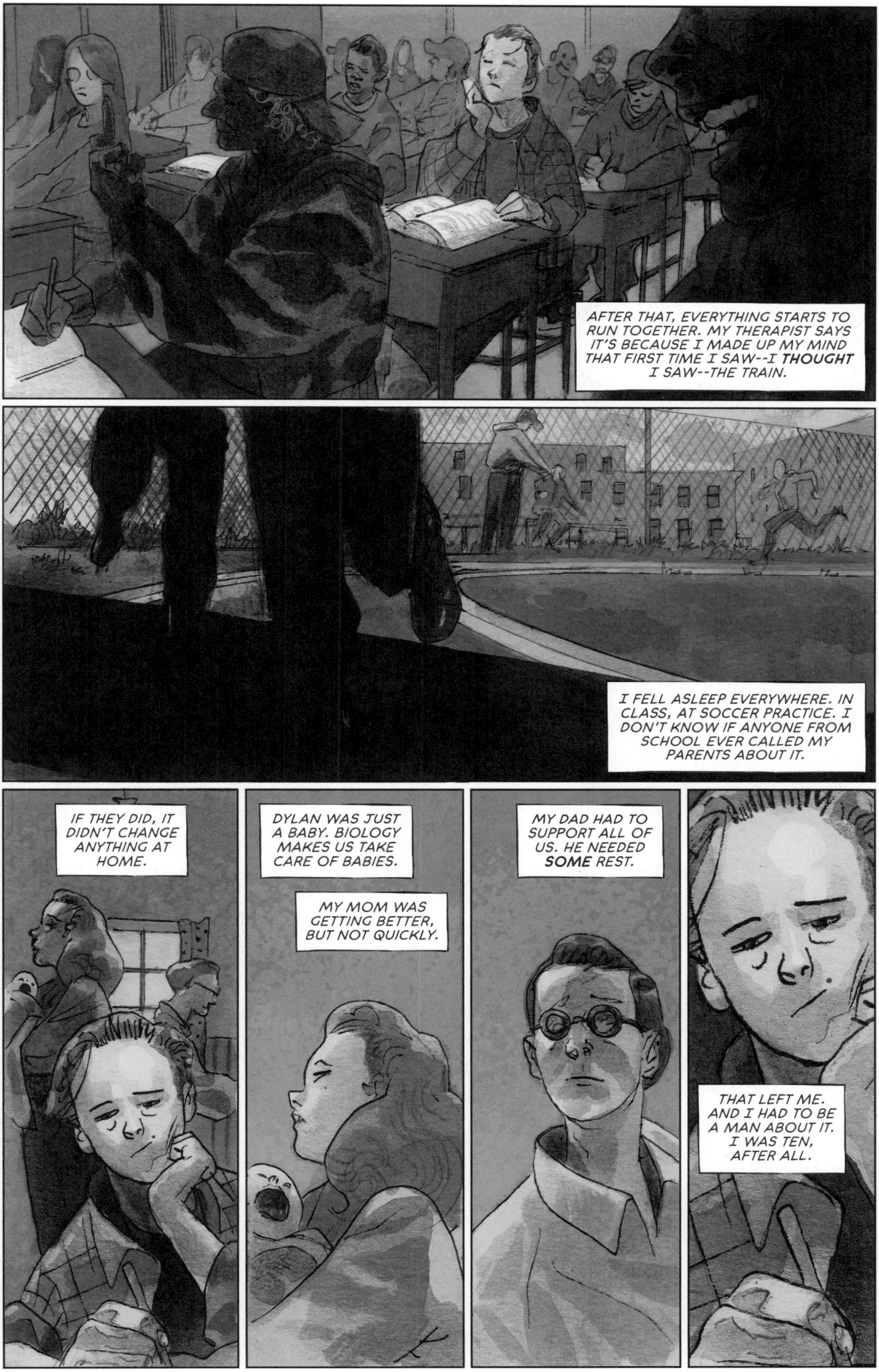
AFTER THAT, EVERYTHING STARTS TO RUN TOGETHER. MY THERAPIST SAYS IT'S BECAUSE I MADE UP MY MIND THAT FIRST TIME I SAW--I **THOUGHT** I SAW--THE TRAIN.
I FELL ASLEEP EVERYWHERE. IN CLASS, AT SOCCER PRACTICE. I DON'T KNOW IF ANYONE FROM SCHOOL EVER CALLED MY PARENTS ABOUT IT.
IF THEY DID, IT DIDN'T CHANGE ANYTHING AT HOME.
DYLAN WAS JUST A BABY. BIOLOGY MAKES US TAKE CARE OF BABIES.
MY MOM WAS GETTING BETTER, BUT NOT QUICKLY.
MY DAD HAD TO SUPPORT ALL OF US. HE NEEDED **SOME** REST.
THAT LEFT ME. AND I HAD TO BE A MAN ABOUT IT. I WAS TEN, AFTER ALL.

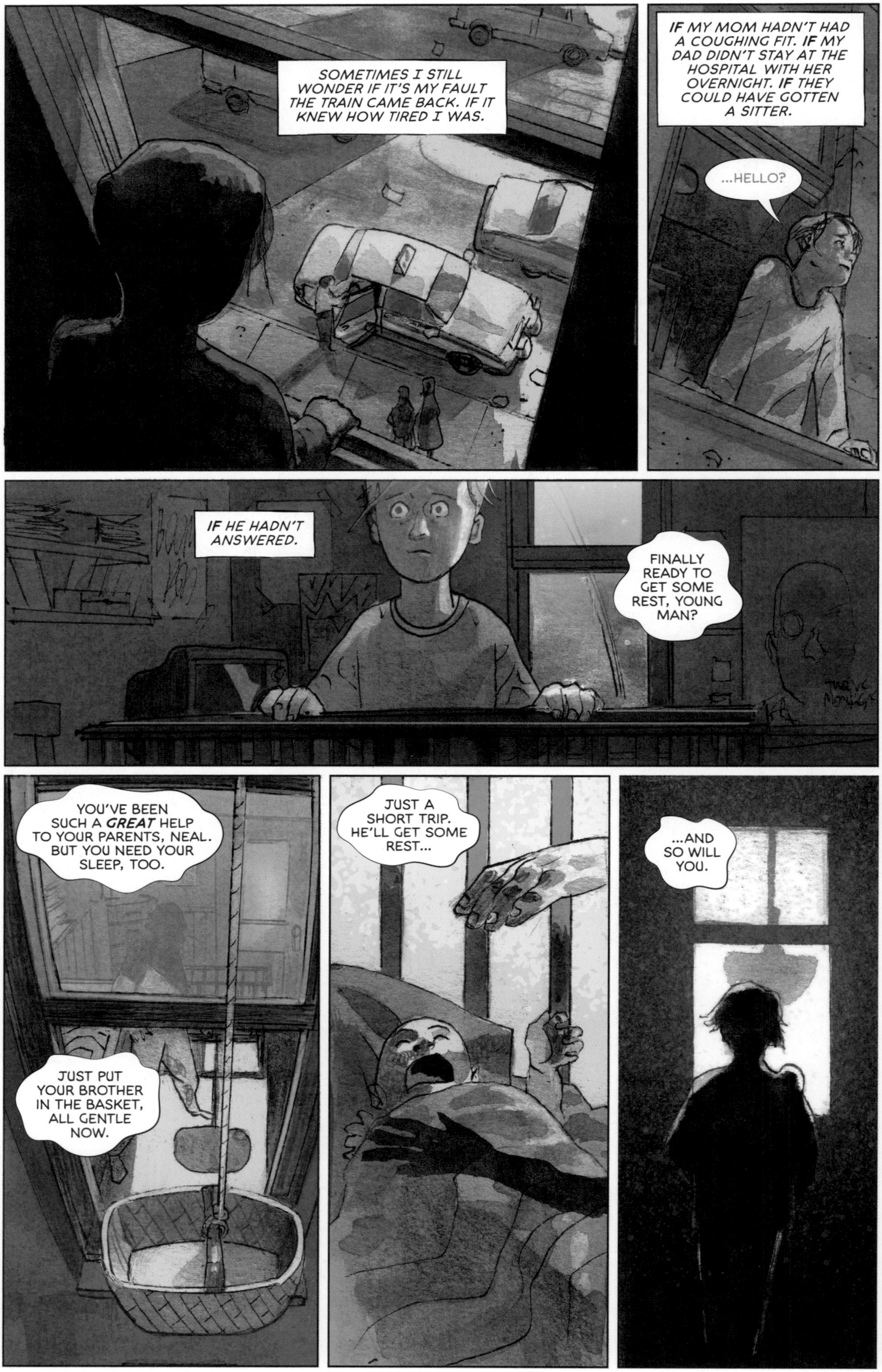
SOMETIMES I STILL WONDER IF IT'S MY FAULT THE TRAIN CAME BACK. IF IT KNEW HOW TIRED I WAS.
IF MY MOM HADN'T HAD A COUGHING FIT. IF MY DAD DIDN'T STAY AT THE HOSPITAL WITH HER OVERNIGHT. IF THEY COULD HAVE GOTTEN A SITTER.
...HELLO?
IF HE HADN'T ANSWERED.
FINALLY READY TO GET SOME REST, YOUNG MAN?
YOU'VE BEEN SUCH A GREAT HELP TO YOUR PARENTS, NEAL. BUT YOU NEED YOUR SLEEP, TOO.
JUST PUT YOUR BROTHER IN THE BASKET, ALL GENTLE NOW.
JUST A SHORT TRIP. HE'LL GET SOME REST...
...AND SO WILL YOU.

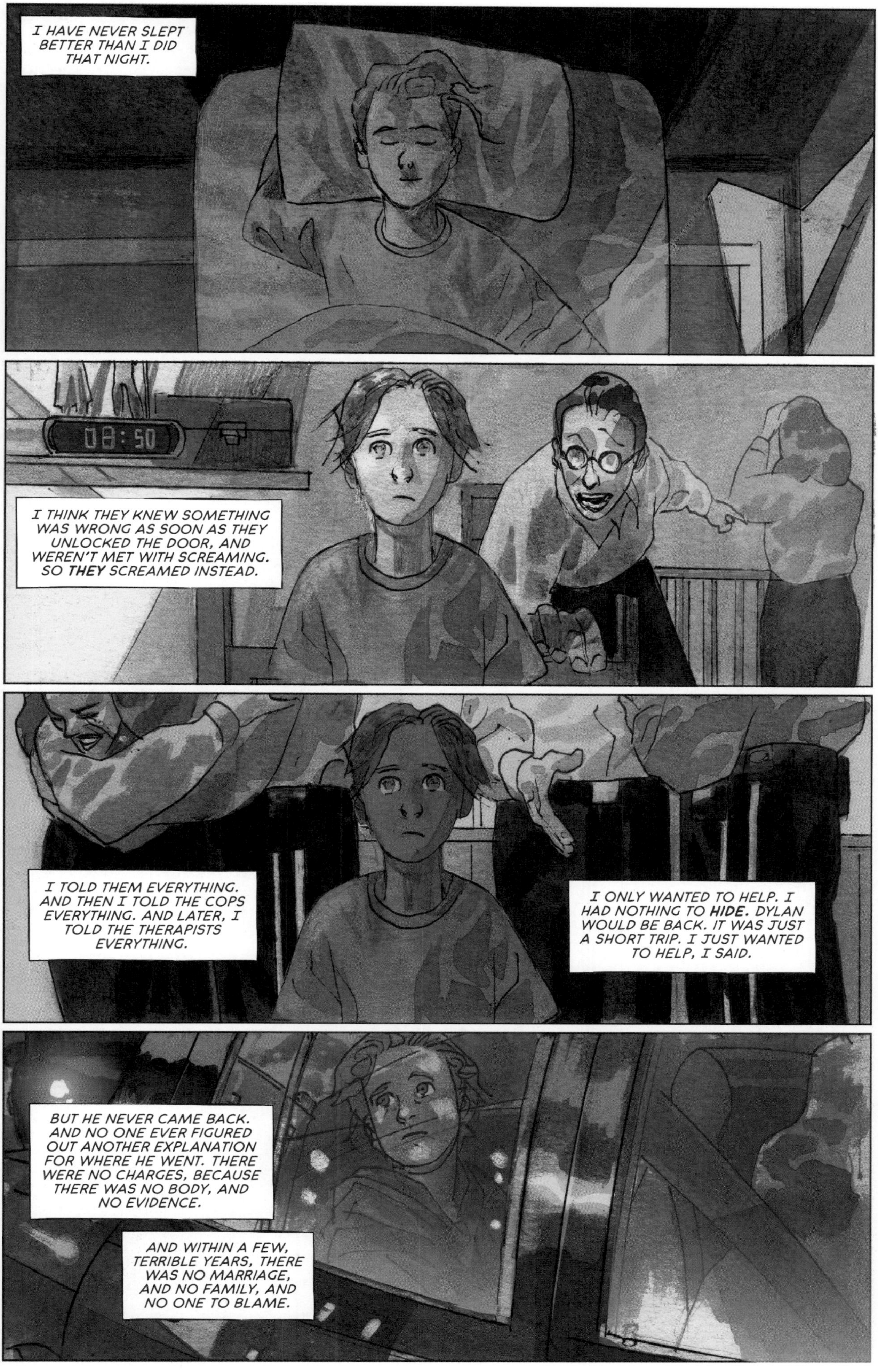
I HAVE NEVER SLEPT BETTER THAN I DID THAT NIGHT.
08:50
I THINK THEY KNEW SOMETHING WAS WRONG AS SOON AS THEY UNLOCKED THE DOOR, AND WEREN'T MET WITH SCREAMING. SO **THEY** SCREAMED INSTEAD.
I TOLD THEM EVERYTHING. AND THEN I TOLD THE COPS EVERYTHING. AND LATER, I TOLD THE THERAPISTS EVERYTHING.
I ONLY WANTED TO HELP. I HAD NOTHING TO **HIDE.** DYLAN WOULD BE BACK. IT WAS JUST A SHORT TRIP. I JUST WANTED TO HELP, I SAID.
BUT HE NEVER CAME BACK. AND NO ONE EVER FIGURED OUT ANOTHER EXPLANATION FOR WHERE HE WENT. THERE WERE NO CHARGES, BECAUSE THERE WAS NO BODY, AND NO EVIDENCE.
AND WITHIN A FEW, TERRIBLE YEARS, THERE WAS NO MARRIAGE, AND NO FAMILY, AND NO ONE TO BLAME.

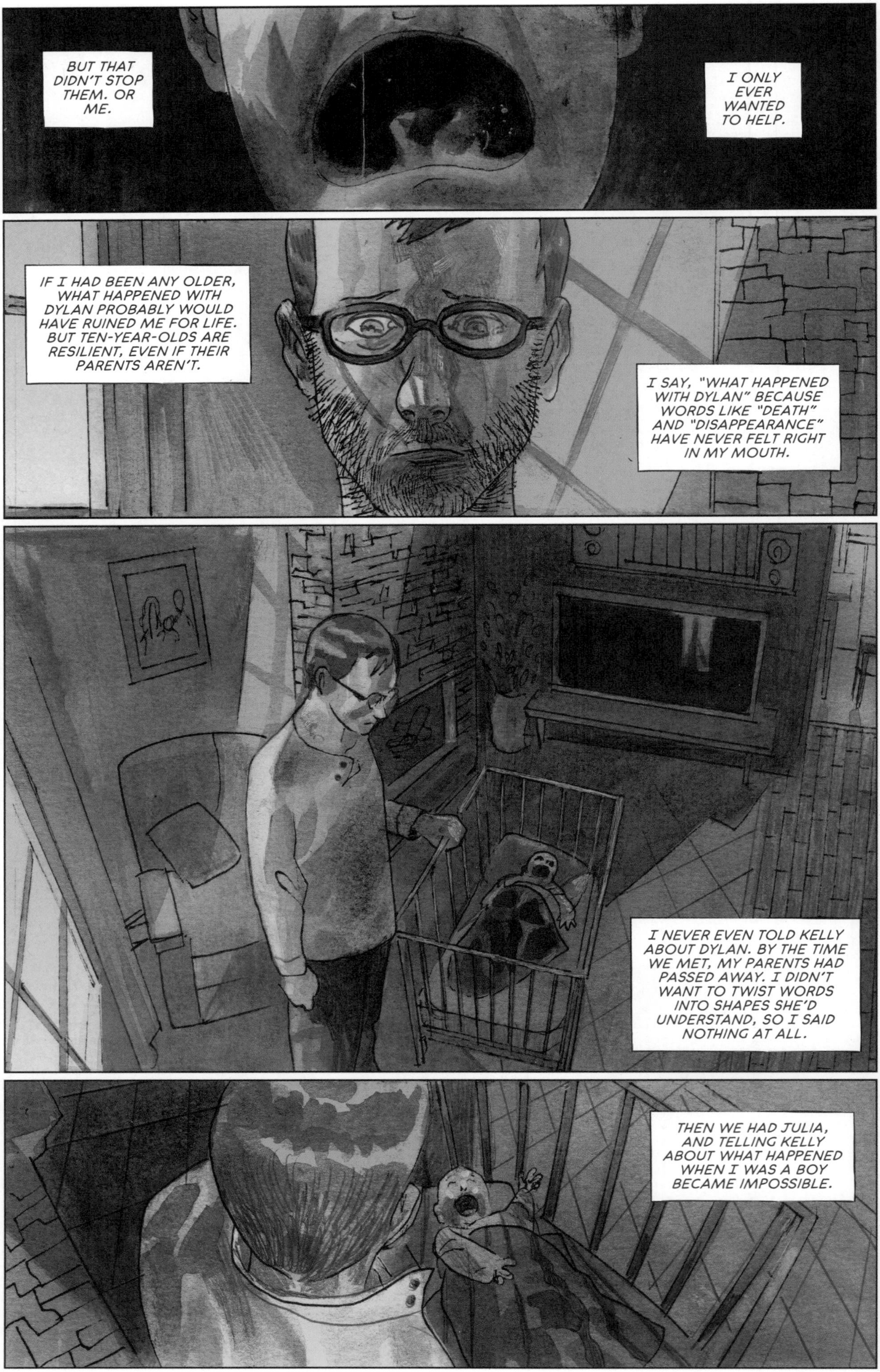
BUT THAT DIDN'T STOP THEM. OR ME.
I ONLY EVER WANTED TO HELP.
IF I HAD BEEN ANY OLDER, WHAT HAPPENED WITH DYLAN PROBABLY WOULD HAVE RUINED ME FOR LIFE. BUT TEN-YEAR-OLDS ARE RESILIENT, EVEN IF THEIR PARENTS AREN'T.
I SAY, "WHAT HAPPENED WITH DYLAN" BECAUSE WORDS LIKE "DEATH" AND "DISAPPEARANCE" HAVE NEVER FELT RIGHT IN MY MOUTH.
I NEVER EVEN TOLD KELLY ABOUT DYLAN. BY THE TIME WE MET, MY PARENTS HAD PASSED AWAY. I DIDN'T WANT TO TWIST WORDS INTO SHAPES SHE'D UNDERSTAND, SO I SAID NOTHING AT ALL.
THEN WE HAD JULIA, AND TELLING KELLY ABOUT WHAT HAPPENED WHEN I WAS A BOY BECAME IMPOSSIBLE.

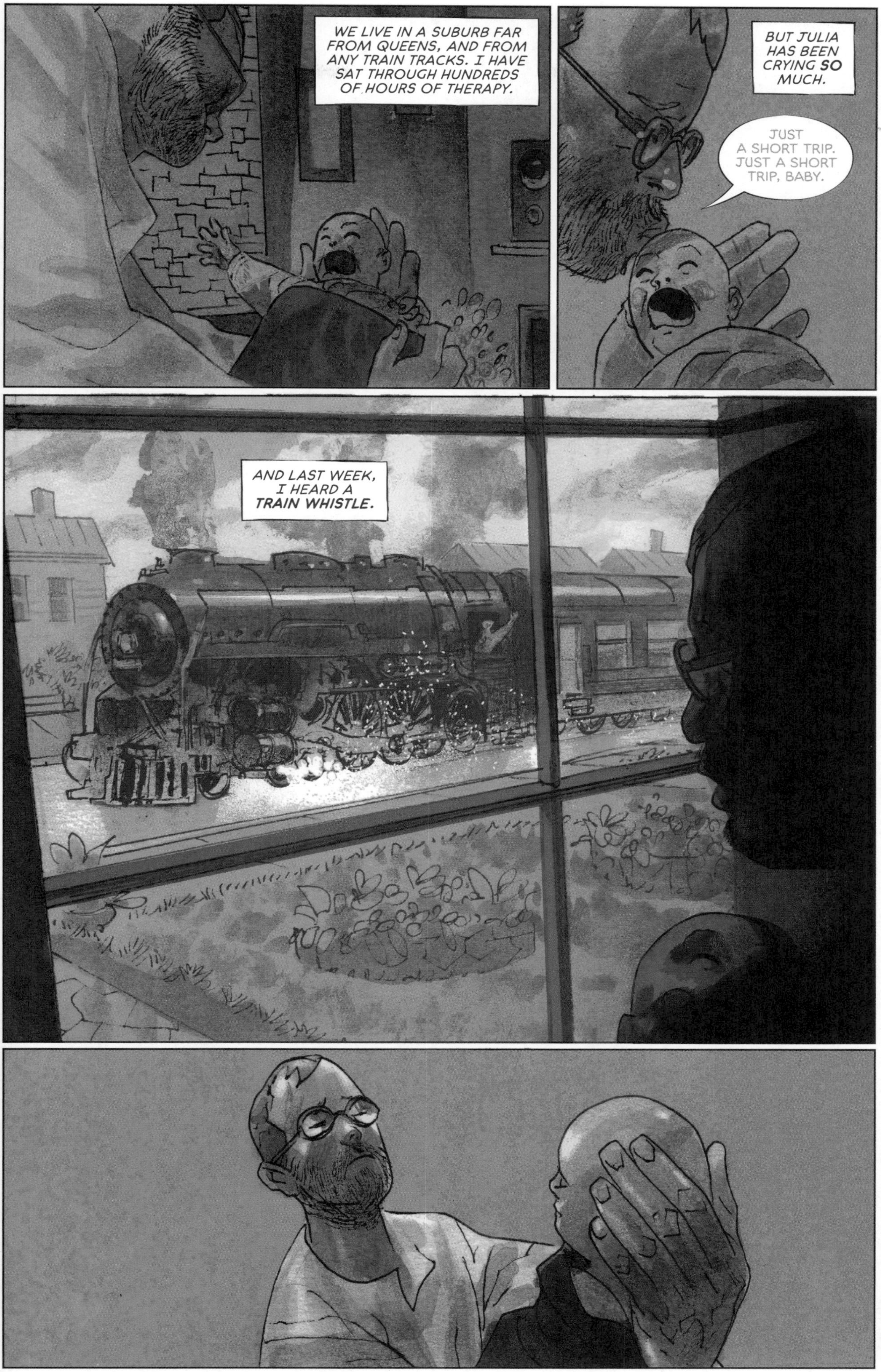
WE LIVE IN A SUBURB FAR FROM QUEENS, AND FROM ANY TRAIN TRACKS. I HAVE SAT THROUGH HUNDREDS OF HOURS OF THERAPY.
BUT JULIA HAS BEEN CRYING **SO** MUCH.
JUST A SHORT TRIP. JUST A SHORT TRIP, BABY.
AND LAST WEEK, I HEARD A **TRAIN WHISTLE.**

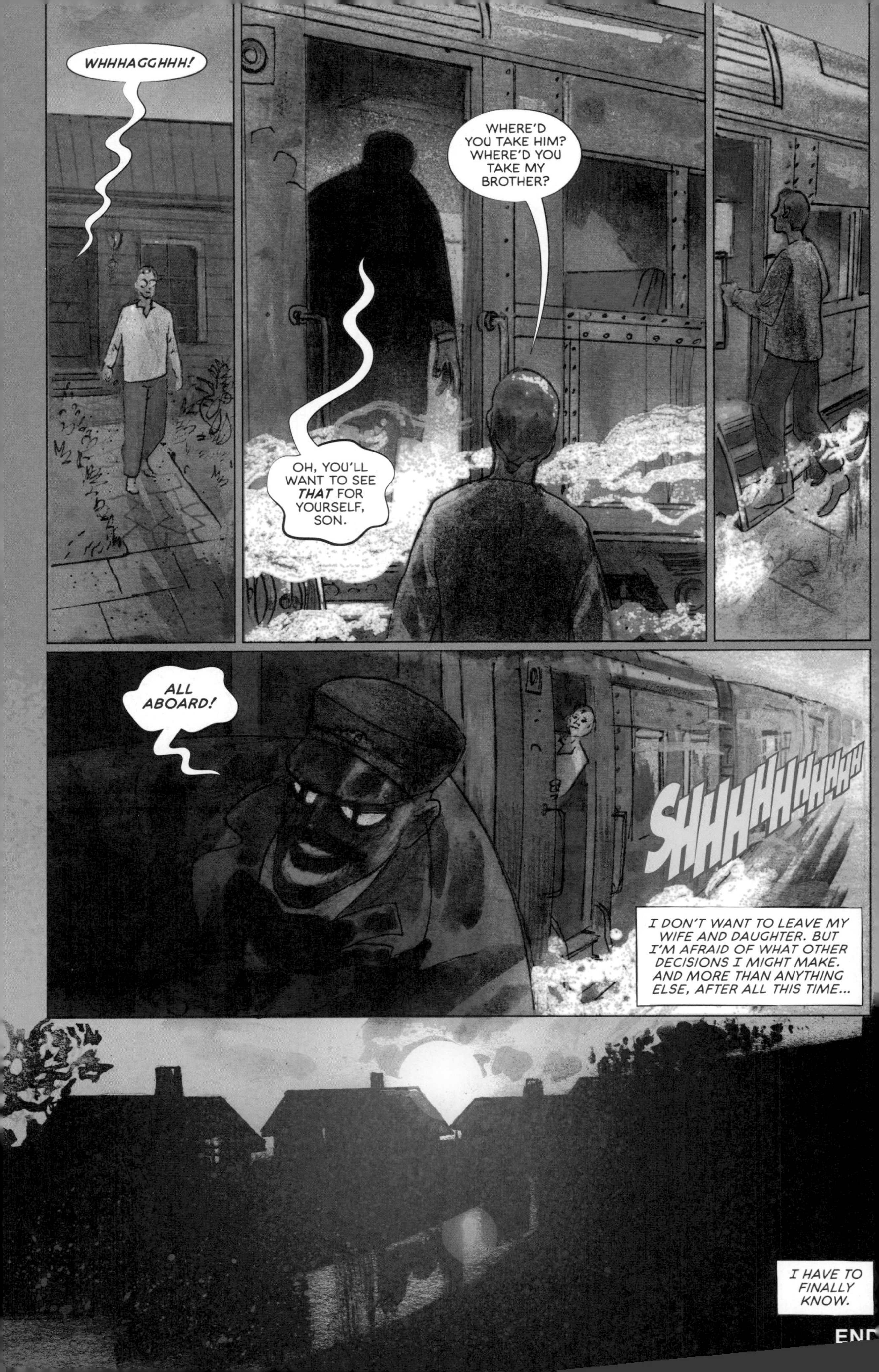
WHHHAGGHHH!
WHERE'D YOU TAKE HIM? WHERE'D YOU TAKE MY BROTHER?
OH, YOU'LL WANT TO SEE THAT FOR YOURSELF, SON.
ALL ABOARD!
SHHHHHHHHH
I DON'T WANT TO LEAVE MY WIFE AND DAUGHTER. BUT I'M AFRAID OF WHAT OTHER DECISIONS I MIGHT MAKE. AND MORE THAN ANYTHING ELSE, AFTER ALL THIS TIME...
I HAVE TO FINALLY KNOW.

ROOFSTOMPERS

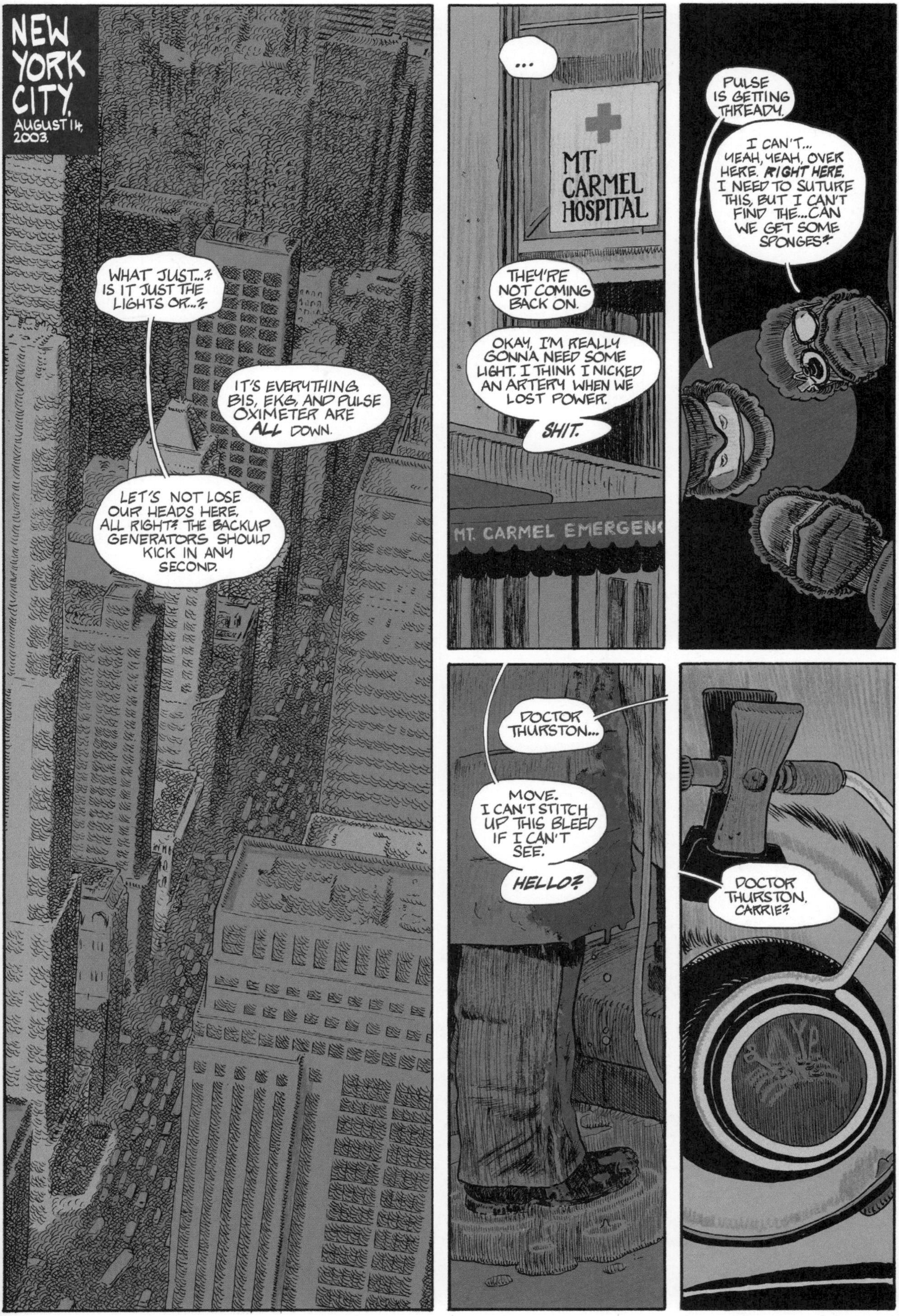
NEW YORK CITY.
AUGUST 14, 2003.
WHAT JUST...? IS IT JUST THE LIGHTS OR...?
IT'S EVERYTHING. BIS, EKG, AND PULSE OXIMETER ARE ALL DOWN.
LET'S NOT LOSE OUR HEADS HERE, ALL RIGHT? THE BACKUP GENERATORS SHOULD KICK IN ANY SECOND.
...
MT CARMEL HOSPITAL
THEY'RE NOT COMING BACK ON.
OKAY, I'M REALLY GONNA NEED SOME LIGHT. I THINK I NICKED AN ARTERY WHEN WE LOST POWER.
SHIT.
MT. CARMEL EMERGENC
PULSE IS GETTING THREADY.
I CAN'T... YEAH, YEAH, OVER HERE. RIGHT HERE. I NEED TO SUTURE THIS, BUT I CAN'T FIND THE...CAN WE GET SOME SPONGES?
DOCTOR THURSTON...
MOVE. I CAN'T STITCH UP THIS BLEED IF I CAN'T SEE.
HELLO?
DOCTOR THURSTON, CARRIE?

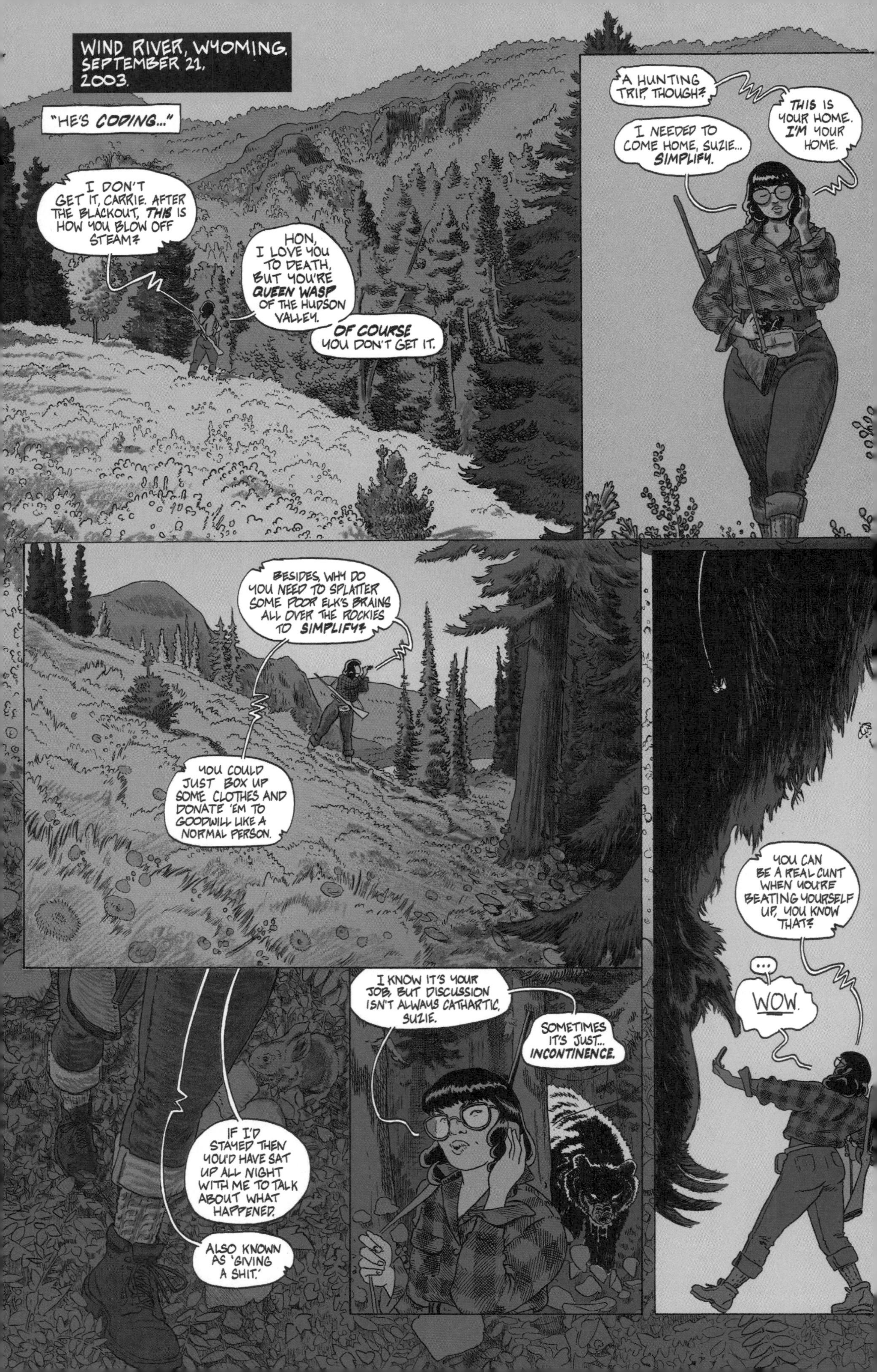
WIND RIVER, WYOMING. SEPTEMBER 21, 2003.
"HE'S CODING..."
I DON'T GET IT, CARRIE. AFTER THE BLACKOUT, THIS IS HOW YOU BLOW OFF STEAM?
HON, I LOVE YOU TO DEATH, BUT YOU'RE QUEEN WASP OF THE HUDSON VALLEY.
OF COURSE YOU DON'T GET IT.
A HUNTING TRIP, THOUGH?
I NEEDED TO COME HOME, SUZIE... SIMPLIFY.
THIS IS YOUR HOME. I'M YOUR HOME.
BESIDES, WHY DO YOU NEED TO SPLATTER SOME POOR ELK'S BRAINS ALL OVER THE ROCKIES TO SIMPLIFY?
YOU COULD JUST BOX UP SOME CLOTHES AND DONATE 'EM TO GOODWILL LIKE A NORMAL PERSON.
IF I'D STAYED THEN YOU'D HAVE SAT UP ALL NIGHT WITH ME TO TALK ABOUT WHAT HAPPENED.
ALSO KNOWN AS 'GIVING A SHIT.'
I KNOW IT'S YOUR JOB, BUT DISCUSSION ISN'T ALWAYS CATHARTIC, SUZIE.
SOMETIMES IT'S JUST... INCONTINENCE.
YOU CAN BE A REAL CUNT WHEN YOU'RE BEATING YOURSELF UP, YOU KNOW THAT?
...
WOW.

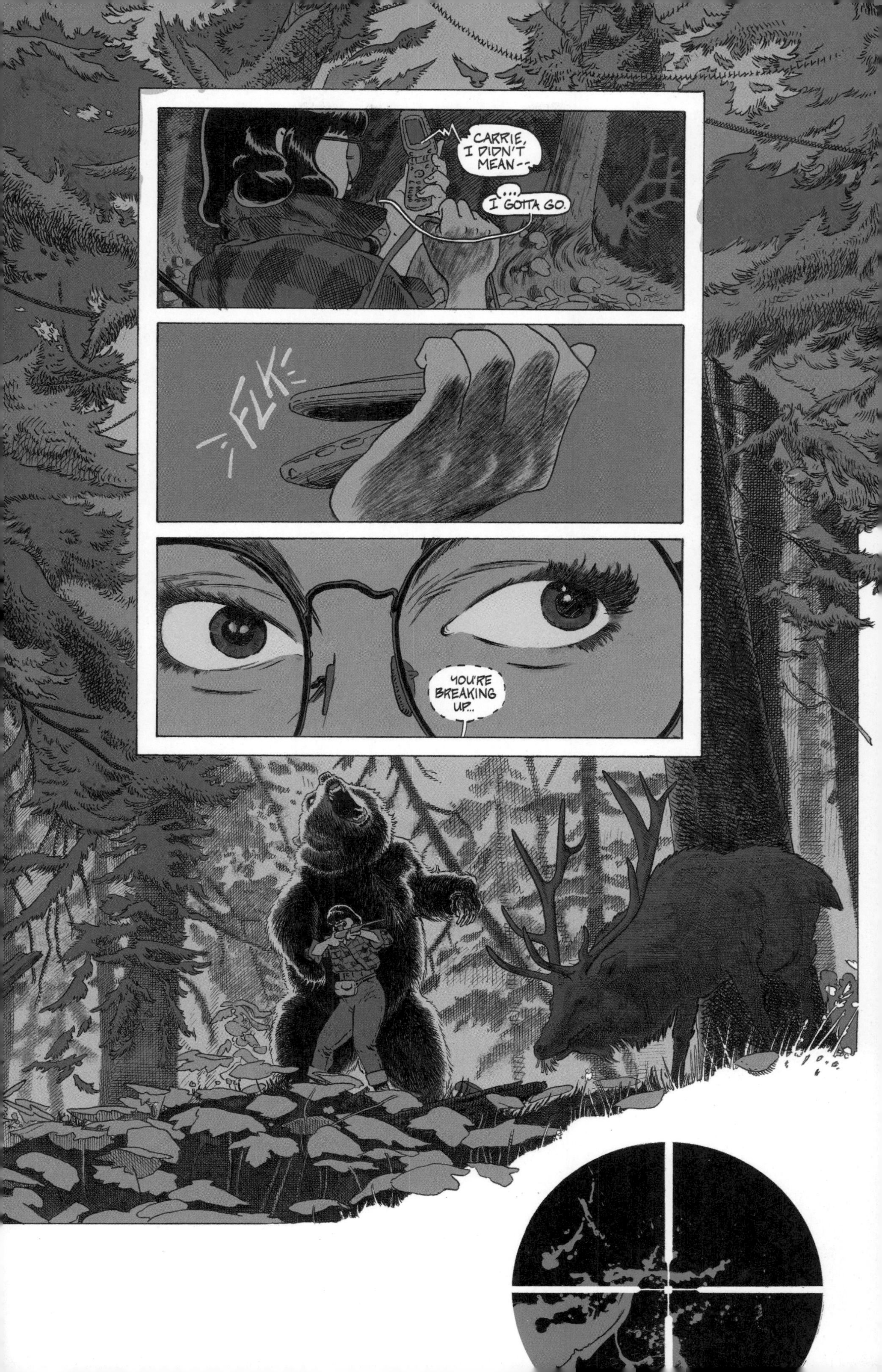
CARRIE, I DIDN'T MEAN--
...
I GOTTA GO.
FLK
YOU'RE BREAKING UP...

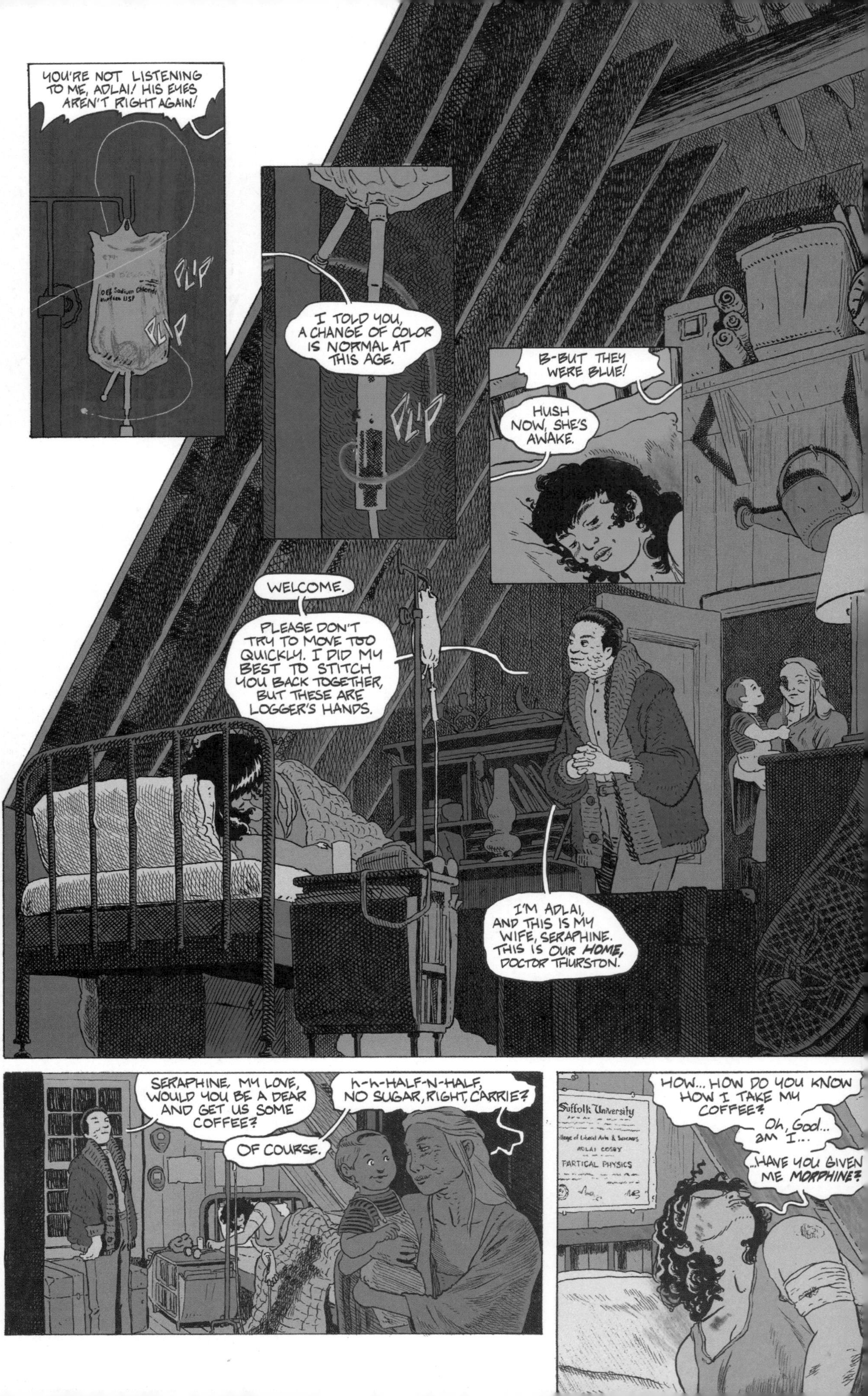
YOU'RE NOT LISTENING TO ME, ADLAI! HIS EYES AREN'T RIGHT AGAIN!
0.9% Sodium Chloride Injection USP
PLIP
PLIP
I TOLD YOU, A CHANGE OF COLOR IS NORMAL AT THIS AGE.
PLIP
B-BUT THEY WERE BLUE!
HUSH NOW, SHE'S AWAKE.
WELCOME.
PLEASE DON'T TRY TO MOVE TOO QUICKLY. I DID MY BEST TO STITCH YOU BACK TOGETHER, BUT THESE ARE LOGGER'S HANDS.
I'M ADLAI, AND THIS IS MY WIFE, SERAPHINE. THIS IS OUR HOME, DOCTOR THURSTON.
SERAPHINE, MY LOVE, WOULD YOU BE A DEAR AND GET US SOME COFFEE?
OF COURSE.
H-H-HALF-N-HALF, NO SUGAR, RIGHT, CARRIE?
HOW... HOW DO YOU KNOW HOW I TAKE MY COFFEE?
Oh, God... am I...
...HAVE YOU GIVEN ME MORPHINE?
Suffolk University
College of Liberal Arts & Sciences
ADLAI COSBY
PARTICAL PHYSICS

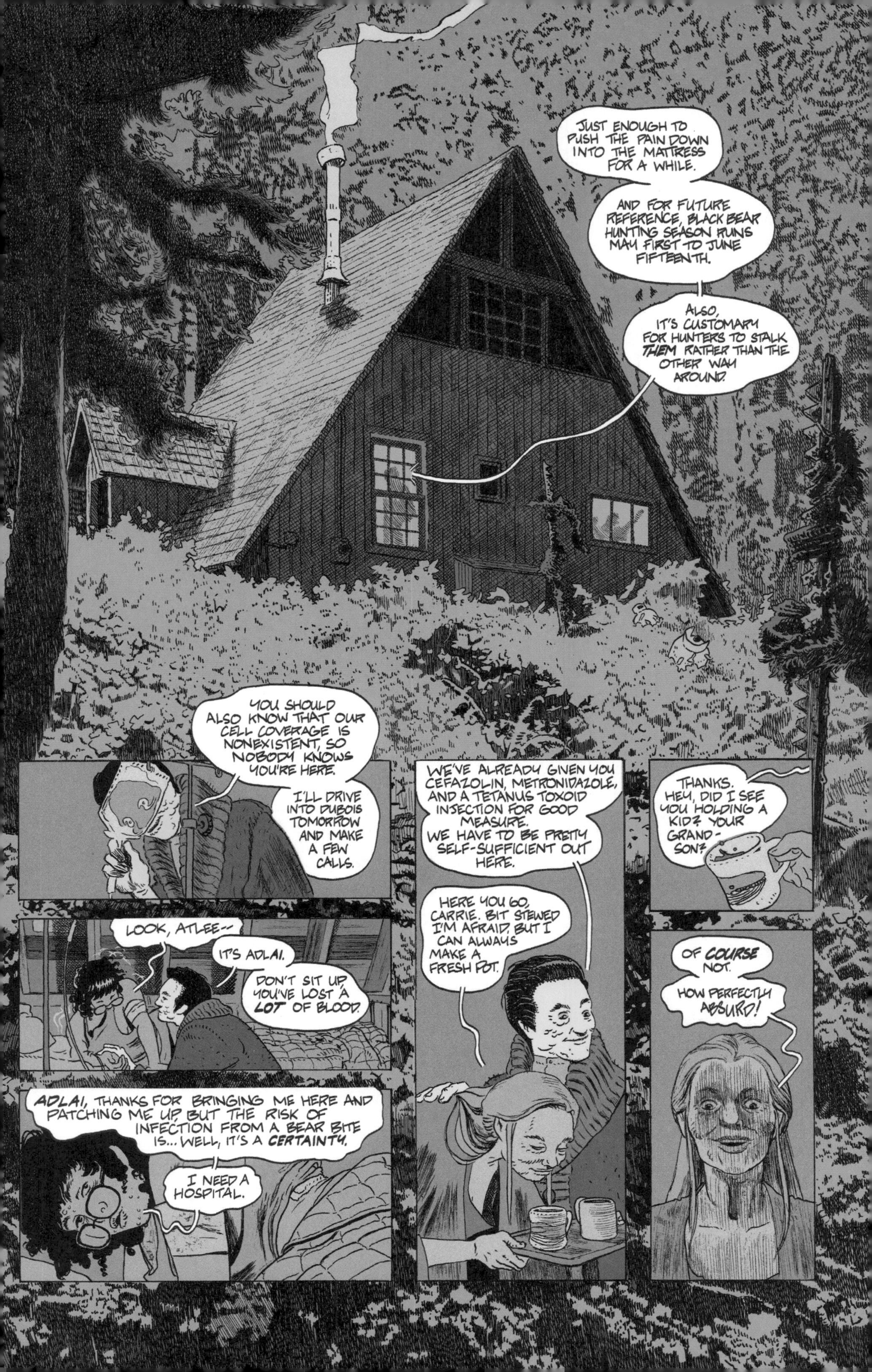
JUST ENOUGH TO PUSH THE PAIN DOWN INTO THE MATTRESS FOR A WHILE.
AND FOR FUTURE REFERENCE, BLACK BEAR HUNTING SEASON RUNS MAY FIRST TO JUNE FIFTEENTH.
ALSO, IT'S CUSTOMARY FOR HUNTERS TO STALK THEM RATHER THAN THE OTHER WAY AROUND.
YOU SHOULD ALSO KNOW THAT OUR CELL COVERAGE IS NONEXISTENT, SO NOBODY KNOWS YOU'RE HERE.
I'LL DRIVE INTO DUBOIS TOMORROW AND MAKE A FEW CALLS.
LOOK, ATLEE--
IT'S ADLAI.
DON'T SIT UP, YOU'VE LOST A LOT OF BLOOD.
ADLAI, THANKS FOR BRINGING ME HERE AND PATCHING ME UP, BUT THE RISK OF INFECTION FROM A BEAR BITE IS... WELL, IT'S A CERTAINTY.
I NEED A HOSPITAL.
WE'VE ALREADY GIVEN YOU CEFAZOLIN, METRONIDAZOLE, AND A TETANUS TOXOID INJECTION FOR GOOD MEASURE.
WE HAVE TO BE PRETTY SELF-SUFFICIENT OUT HERE.
HERE YOU GO, CARRIE. BIT STEWED I'M AFRAID, BUT I CAN ALWAYS MAKE A FRESH POT.
THANKS. HEY, DID I SEE YOU HOLDING A KID? YOUR GRAND-SON?
OF COURSE NOT.
HOW PERFECTLY ABSURD!

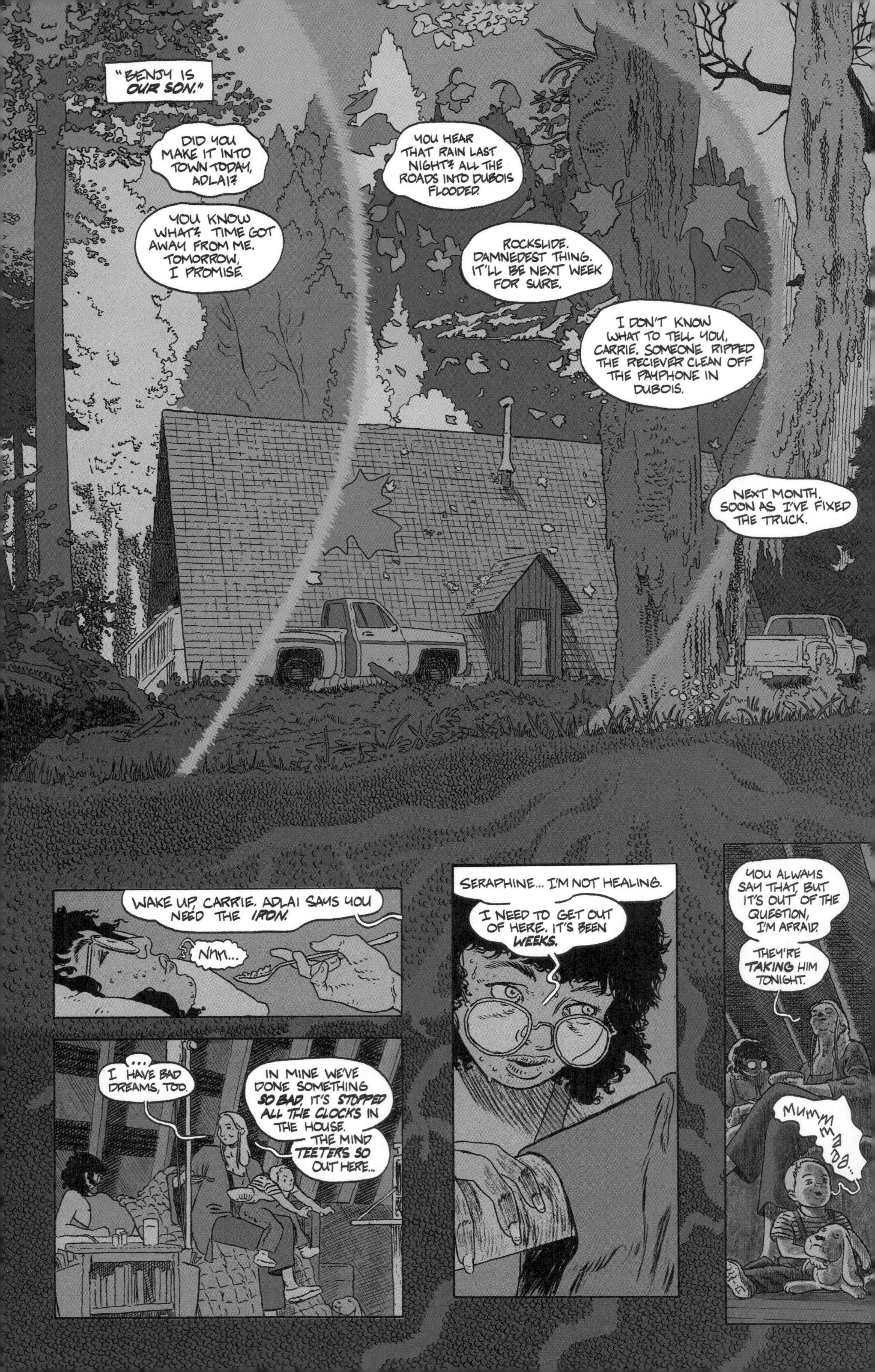
"BENJY IS OUR SON."
DID YOU MAKE IT INTO TOWN TODAY, ADLAI?
YOU KNOW WHAT? TIME GOT AWAY FROM ME. TOMORROW, I PROMISE.
YOU HEAR THAT RAIN LAST NIGHT? ALL THE ROADS INTO DUBOIS FLOODED.
ROCKSLIDE. DAMNEDEST THING. IT'LL BE NEXT WEEK FOR SURE.
I DON'T KNOW WHAT TO TELL YOU, CARRIE. SOMEONE RIPPED THE RECIEVER CLEAN OFF THE PAYPHONE IN DUBOIS.
NEXT MONTH. SOON AS I'VE FIXED THE TRUCK.
WAKE UP, CARRIE. ADLAI SAYS YOU NEED THE IRON.
NNN...
...
I HAVE BAD DREAMS, TOO.
IN MINE WE'VE DONE SOMETHING SO BAD, IT'S STOPPED ALL THE CLOCKS IN THE HOUSE.
THE MIND TEETERS SO OUT HERE...
SERAPHINE... I'M NOT HEALING.
I NEED TO GET OUT OF HERE. IT'S BEEN WEEKS.
YOU ALWAYS SAY THAT, BUT IT'S OUT OF THE QUESTION, I'M AFRAID.
THEY'RE TAKING HIM TONIGHT.
MUMMADA...

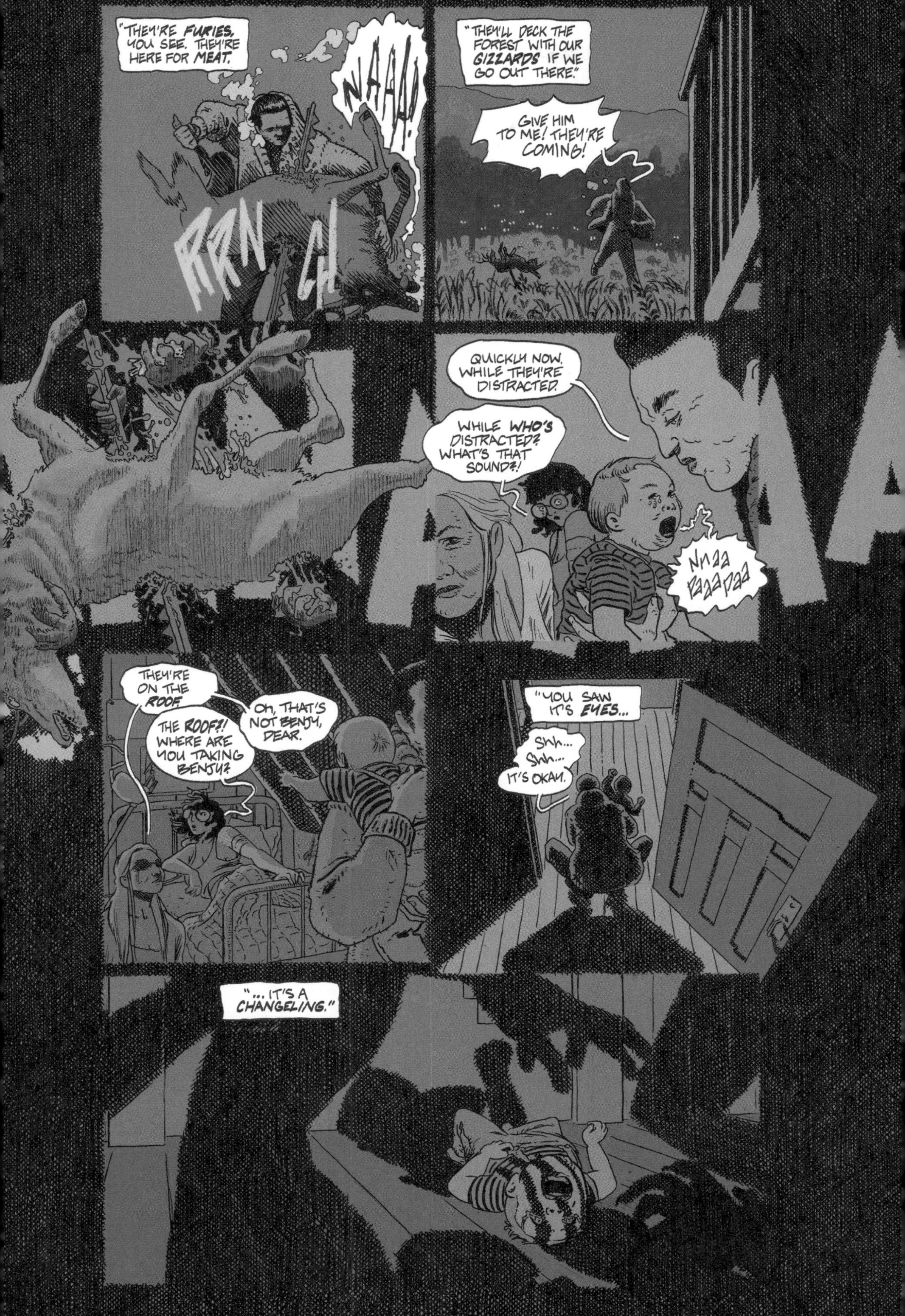

"THEY'RE FURIES, YOU SEE. THEY'RE HERE FOR MEAT.
NAAA!
RRN
CH
"THEY'LL DECK THE FOREST WITH OUR GIZZARDS IF WE GO OUT THERE."
GIVE HIM TO ME! THEY'RE COMING!
QUICKLY NOW. WHILE THEY'RE DISTRACTED.
WHILE WHO'S DISTRACTED? WHAT'S THAT SOUND?!
NNAA PAAAPAA
THEY'RE ON THE ROOF.
THE ROOF?! WHERE ARE YOU TAKING BENJY?
OH, THAT'S NOT BENJY, DEAR.
"YOU SAW IT'S EYES...
SHH... SHH... IT'S OKAY.
"... IT'S A CHANGELING."

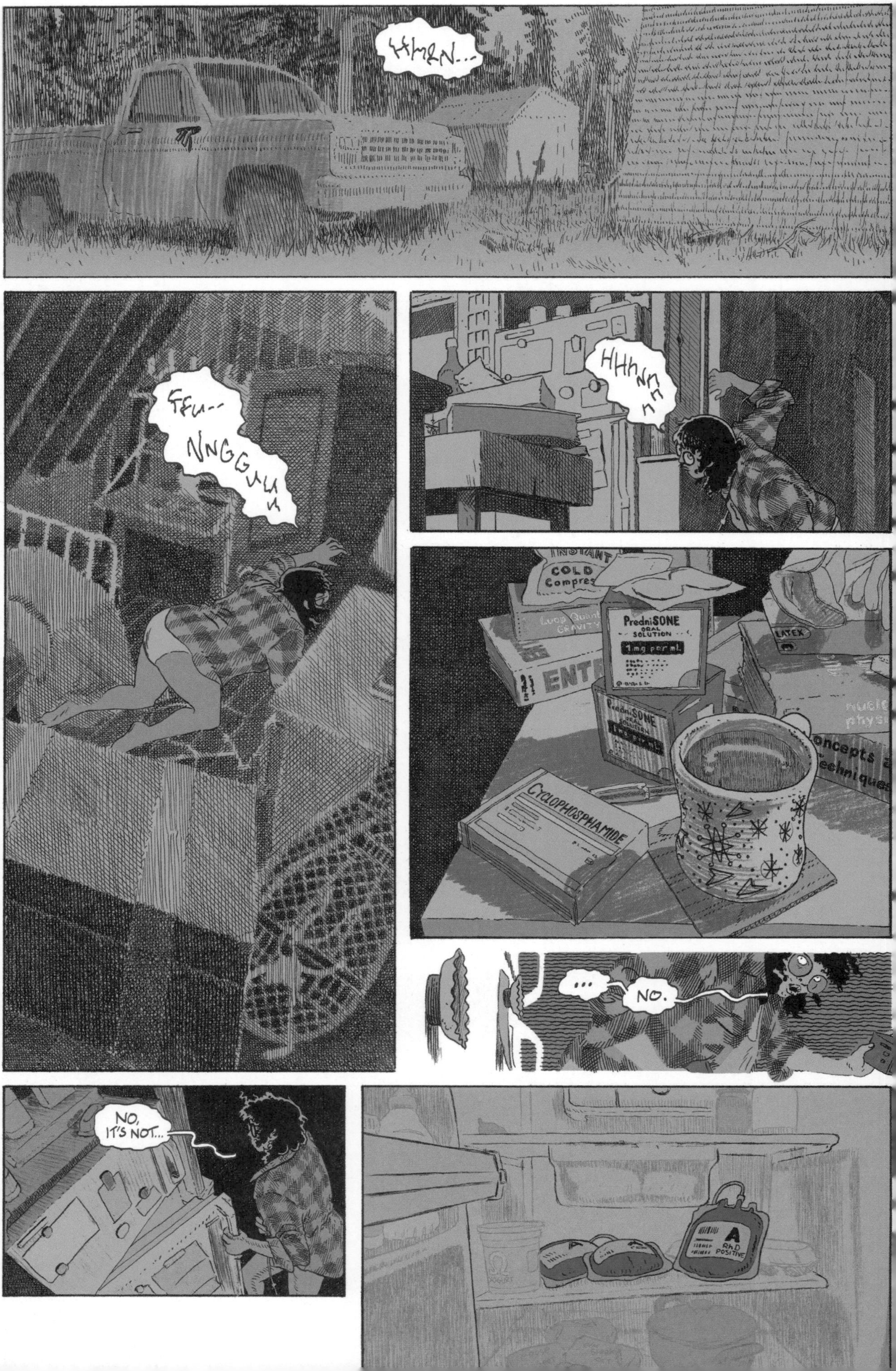
HMRN...
FFU-- NNGGUUU
HHhnnnn
INSTANT COLD Compress
PredniSONE ORAL SOLUTION 1 mg per mL
PredniSONE
LATEX
CYCLOPHOSPHAMIDE
... NO.
NO, IT'S NOT...
A RhD POSITIVE

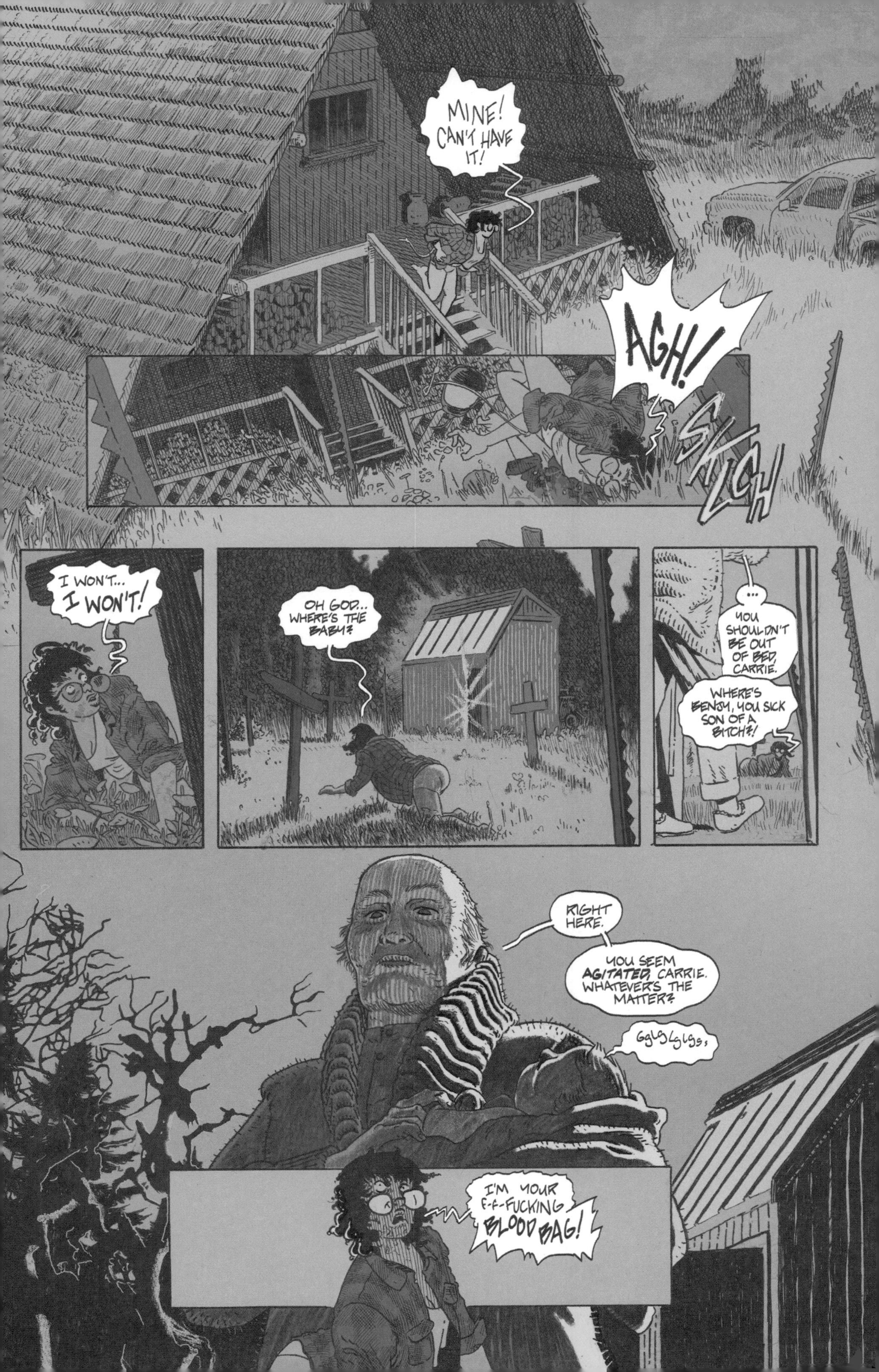
MINE! CAN'T HAVE IT!
AGH!
SKLCH
I WON'T... I WON'T!
OH GOD... WHERE'S THE BABY?
...
YOU SHOULDN'T BE OUT OF BED, CARRIE.
WHERE'S BENJY, YOU SICK SON OF A BITCH?!
RIGHT HERE.
YOU SEEM AGITATED, CARRIE. WHATEVER'S THE MATTER?
Gglglglgs,
I'M YOUR F-F-FUCKING BLOOD BAG!

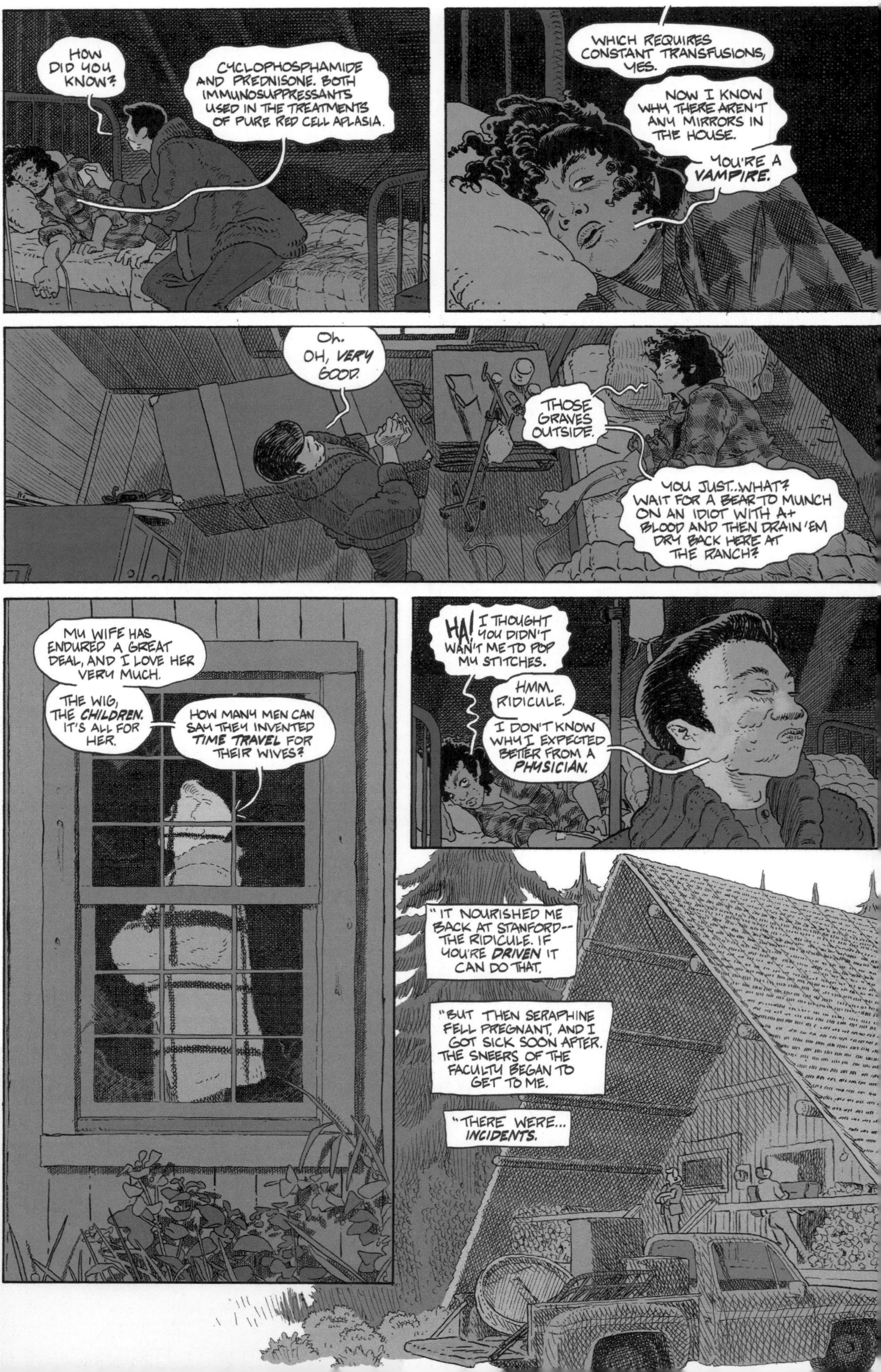
HOW DID YOU KNOW?
CYCLOPHOSPHAMIDE AND PREDNISONE. BOTH IMMUNOSUPPRESSANTS USED IN THE TREATMENTS OF PURE RED CELL APLASIA.
WHICH REQUIRES CONSTANT TRANSFUSIONS, YES.
NOW I KNOW WHY THERE AREN'T ANY MIRRORS IN THE HOUSE.
YOU'RE A VAMPIRE.
Oh. OH, VERY GOOD.
THOSE GRAVES OUTSIDE.
YOU JUST...WHAT? WAIT FOR A BEAR TO MUNCH ON AN IDIOT WITH A+ BLOOD AND THEN DRAIN 'EM DRY BACK HERE AT THE RANCH?
MY WIFE HAS ENDURED A GREAT DEAL, AND I LOVE HER VERY MUCH.
THE WIG, THE CHILDREN. IT'S ALL FOR HER.
HOW MANY MEN CAN SAY THEY INVENTED TIME TRAVEL FOR THEIR WIVES?
HA! I THOUGHT YOU DIDN'T WANT ME TO POP MY STITCHES.
HMM. RIDICULE.
I DON'T KNOW WHY I EXPECTED BETTER FROM A PHYSICIAN.
"IT NOURISHED ME BACK AT STANFORD-- THE RIDICULE. IF YOU'RE DRIVEN IT CAN DO THAT.
"BUT THEN SERAPHINE FELL PREGNANT, AND I GOT SICK SOON AFTER. THE SNEERS OF THE FACULTY BEGAN TO GET TO ME.
"THERE WERE... INCIDENTS.

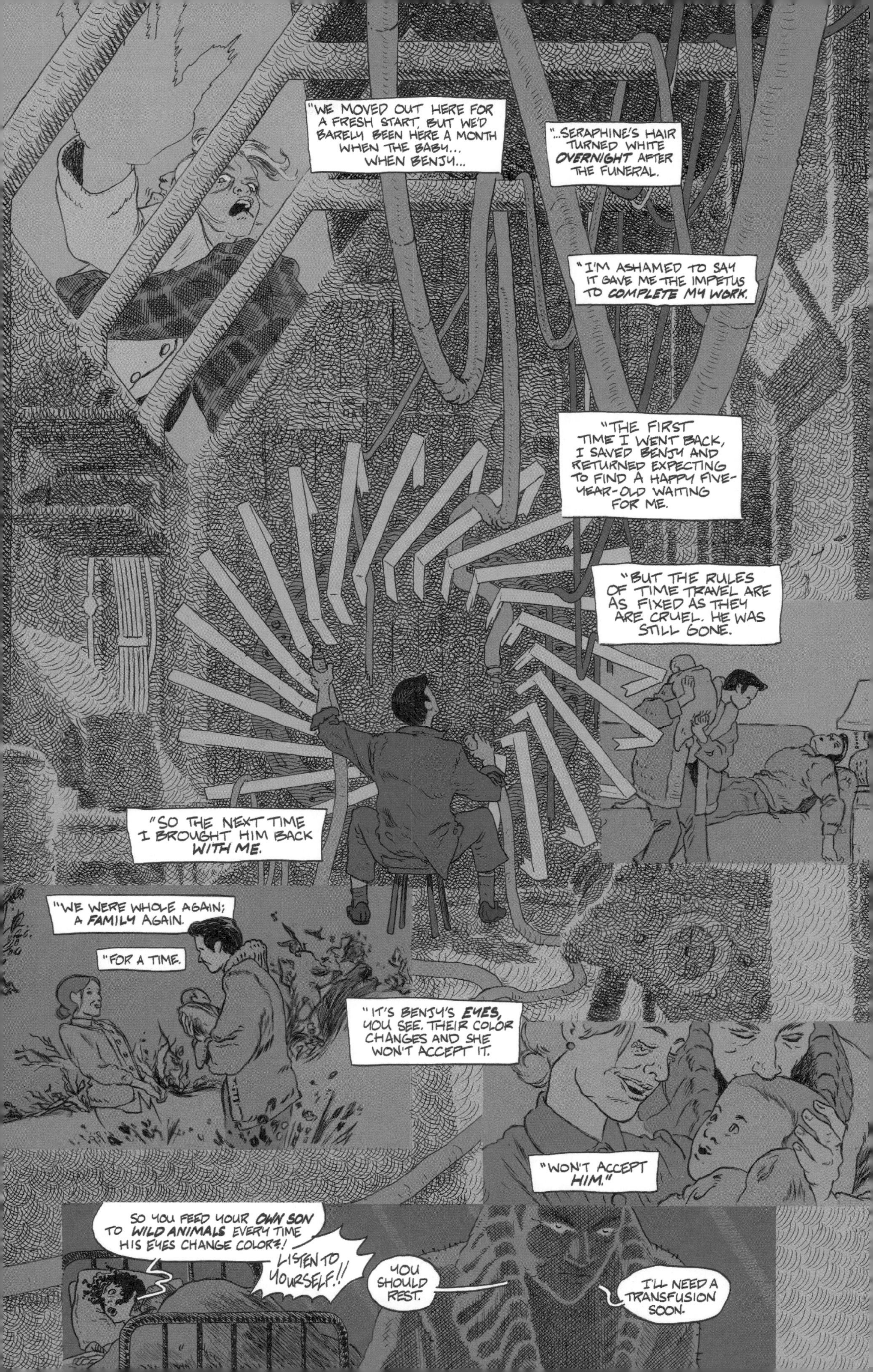
"WE MOVED OUT HERE FOR A FRESH START, BUT WE'D BARELY BEEN HERE A MONTH WHEN THE BABY... WHEN BENJY...
"...SERAPHINE'S HAIR TURNED WHITE OVERNIGHT AFTER THE FUNERAL.
"I'M ASHAMED TO SAY IT GAVE ME THE IMPETUS TO COMPLETE MY WORK.
"THE FIRST TIME I WENT BACK, I SAVED BENJY AND RETURNED EXPECTING TO FIND A HAPPY FIVE-YEAR-OLD WAITING FOR ME.
"BUT THE RULES OF TIME TRAVEL ARE AS FIXED AS THEY ARE CRUEL. HE WAS STILL GONE.
"SO THE NEXT TIME I BROUGHT HIM BACK WITH ME.
"WE WERE WHOLE AGAIN; A FAMILY AGAIN.
"FOR A TIME.
"IT'S BENJY'S EYES, YOU SEE. THEIR COLOR CHANGES AND SHE WON'T ACCEPT IT.
"WON'T ACCEPT HIM."
SO YOU FEED YOUR OWN SON TO WILD ANIMALS EVERY TIME HIS EYES CHANGE COLOR?!
LISTEN TO YOURSELF!!
YOU SHOULD REST.
I'LL NEED A TRANSFUSION SOON.

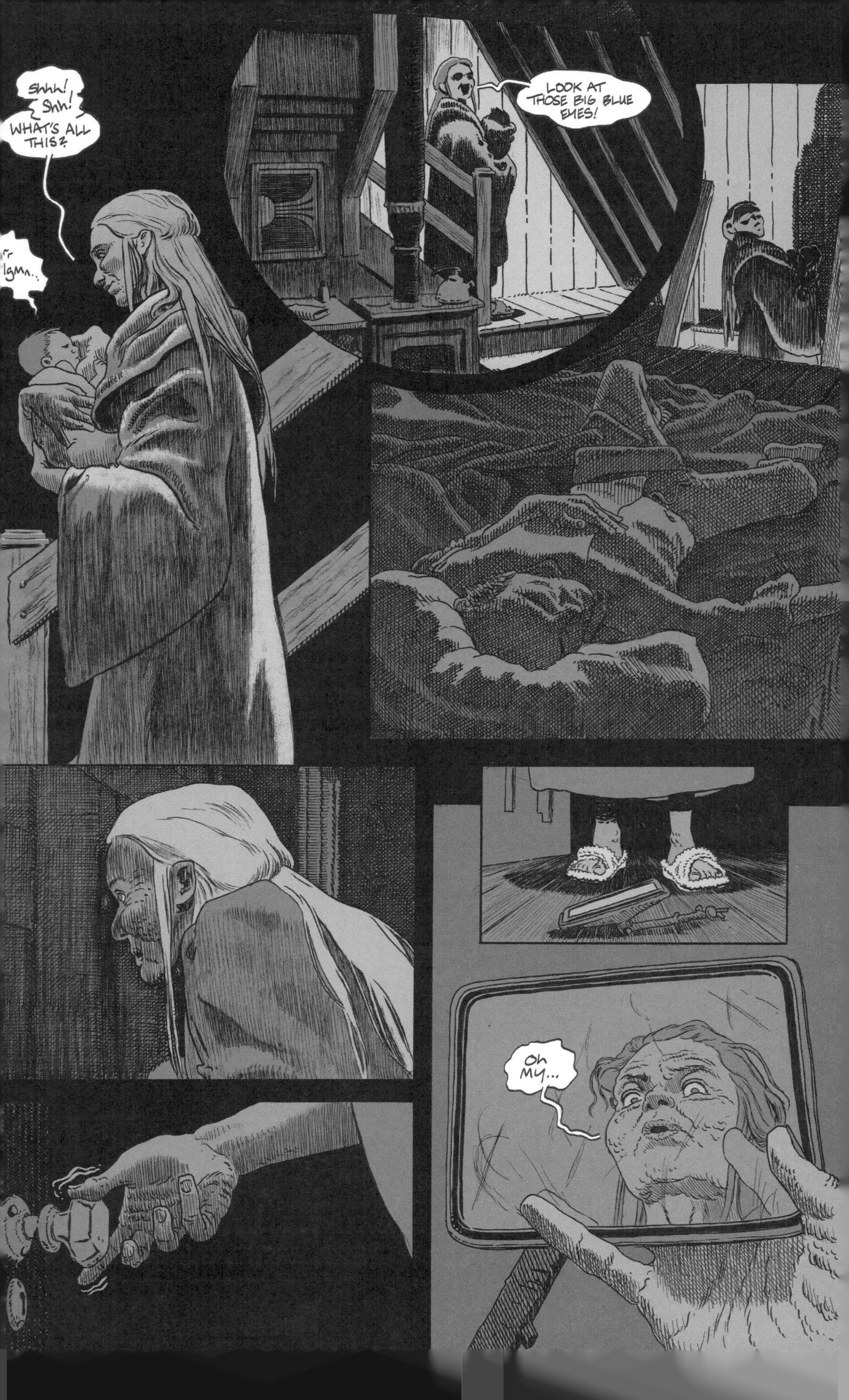
Shhh! Shh! WHAT'S ALL THIS?
LOOK AT THOSE BIG BLUE EYES!
Oh MY...

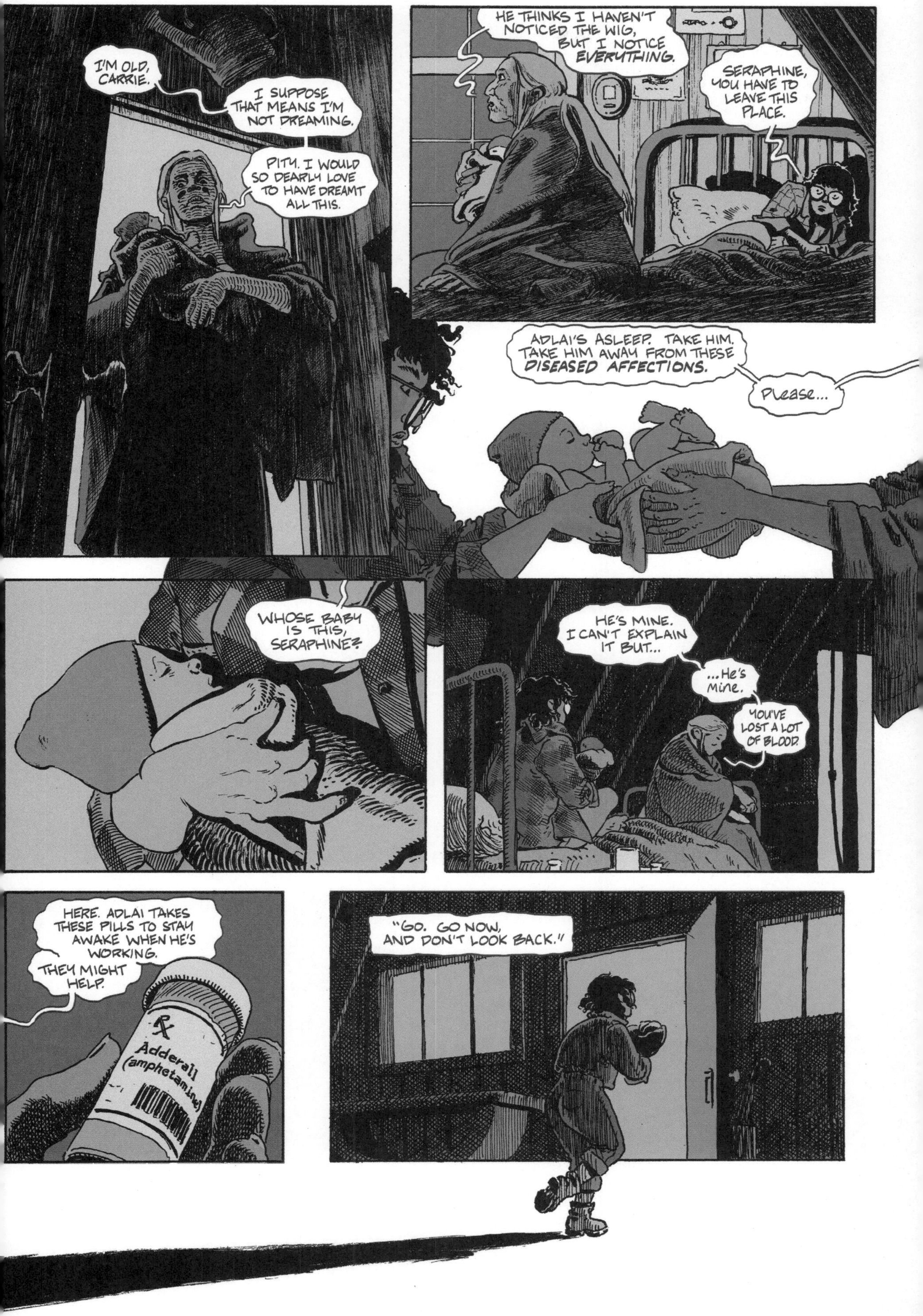
I'M OLD, CARRIE.
I SUPPOSE THAT MEANS I'M NOT DREAMING.
PITY. I WOULD SO DEARLY LOVE TO HAVE DREAMT ALL THIS.
HE THINKS I HAVEN'T NOTICED THE WIG, BUT I NOTICE EVERYTHING.
SERAPHINE, YOU HAVE TO LEAVE THIS PLACE.
ADLAI'S ASLEEP. TAKE HIM. TAKE HIM AWAY FROM THESE DISEASED AFFECTIONS.
Please...
WHOSE BABY IS THIS, SERAPHINE?
HE'S MINE. I CAN'T EXPLAIN IT BUT...
...He's mine.
YOU'VE LOST A LOT OF BLOOD.
HERE. ADLAI TAKES THESE PILLS TO STAY AWAKE WHEN HE'S WORKING.
THEY MIGHT HELP.
Rx
Adderall (amphetamine)
"GO. GO NOW, AND DON'T LOOK BACK."

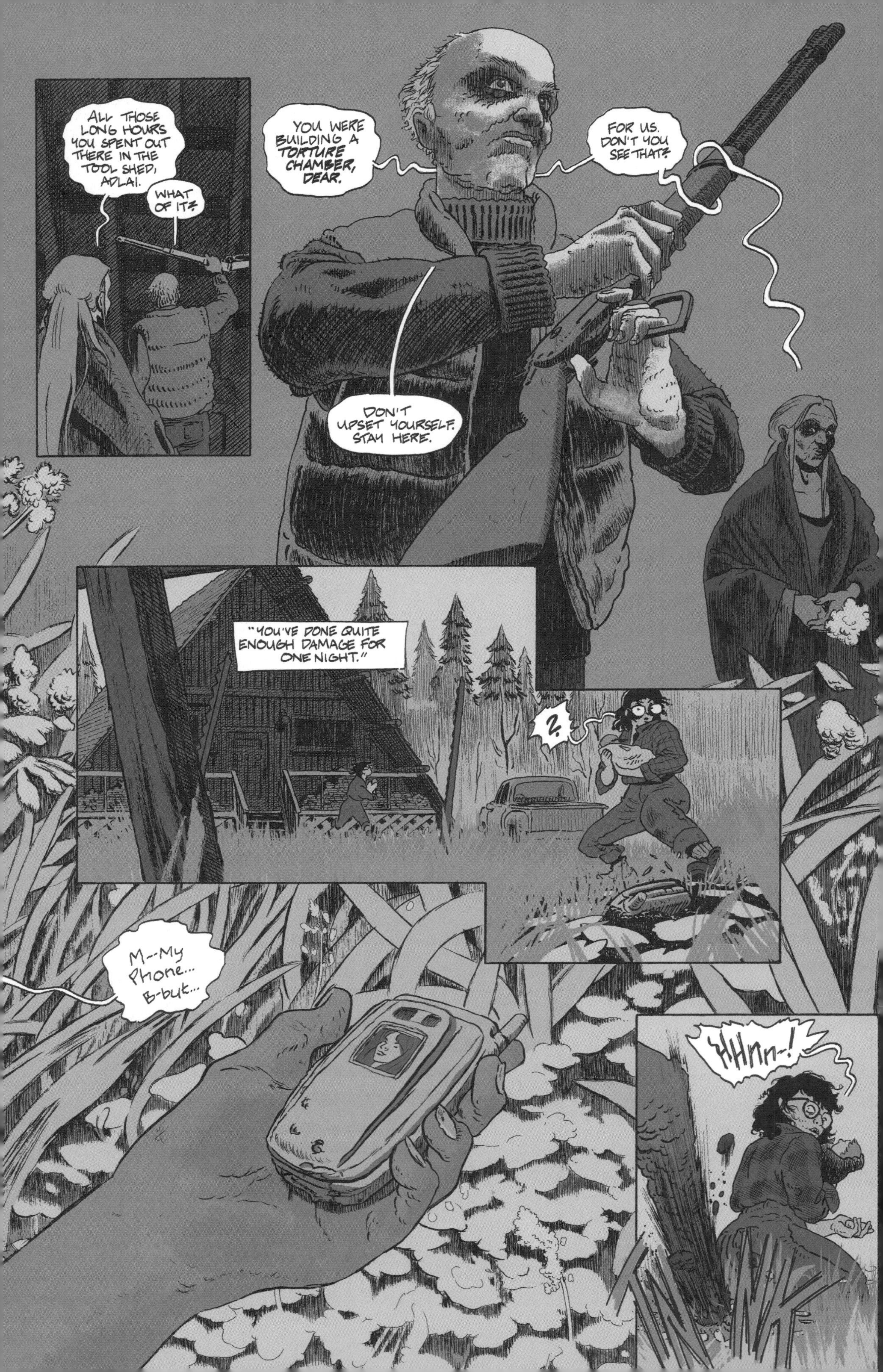
ALL THOSE LONG HOURS YOU SPENT OUT THERE IN THE TOOL SHED, ADLAI.
WHAT OF IT?
YOU WERE BUILDING A TORTURE CHAMBER, DEAR.
FOR US. DON'T YOU SEE THAT?
DON'T UPSET YOURSELF. STAY HERE.
"YOU'VE DONE QUITE ENOUGH DAMAGE FOR ONE NIGHT."
?
M--My Phone... B-but...
HHnn-!

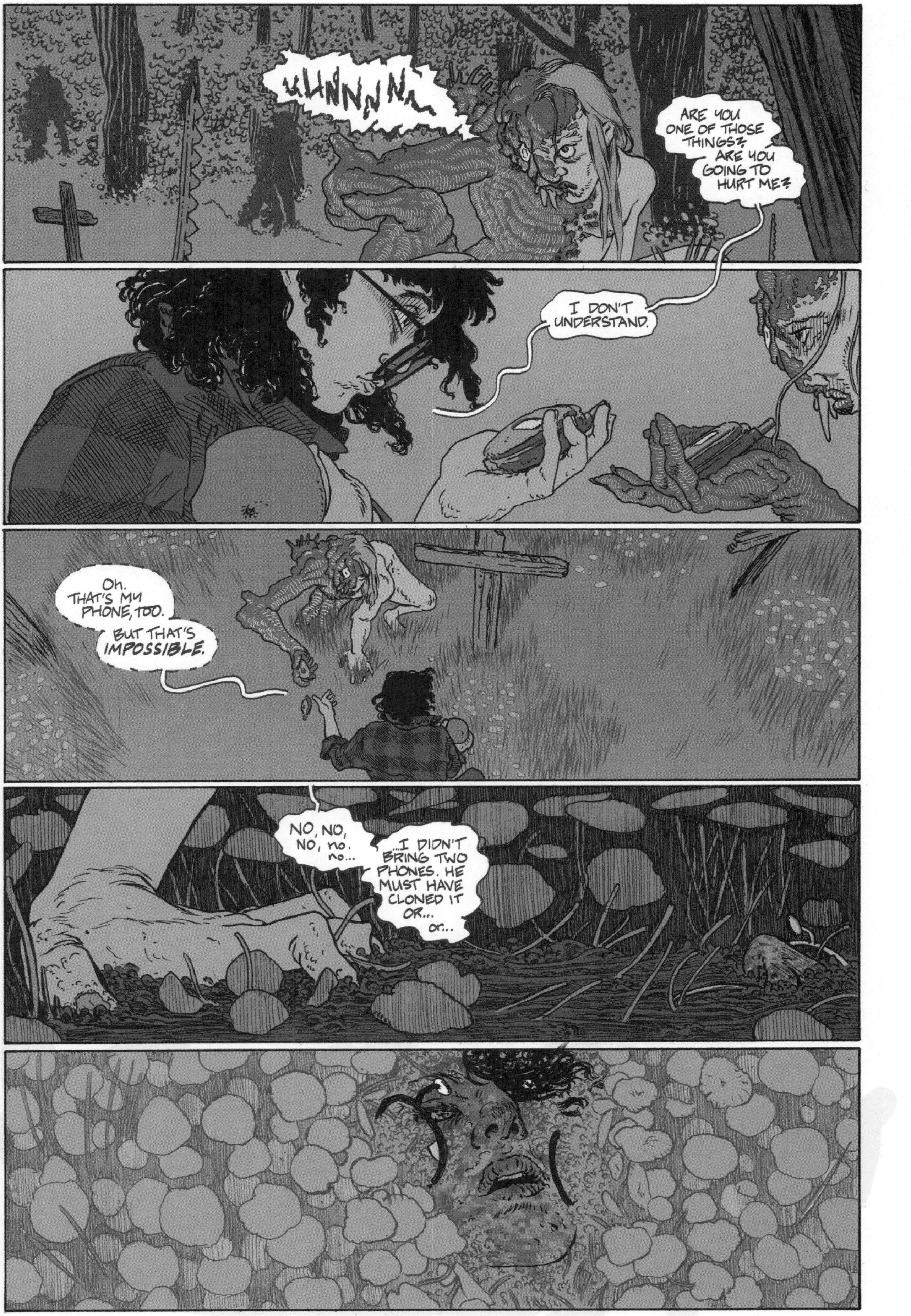

UHNNNN
ARE YOU ONE OF THOSE THINGS?! ARE YOU GOING TO HURT ME?!
I DON'T UNDERSTAND.
Oh. THAT'S MY PHONE, TOO.
BUT THAT'S IMPOSSIBLE.
NO, NO, NO, no. no...
...I DIDN'T BRING TWO PHONES. HE MUST HAVE CLONED IT OR... or...

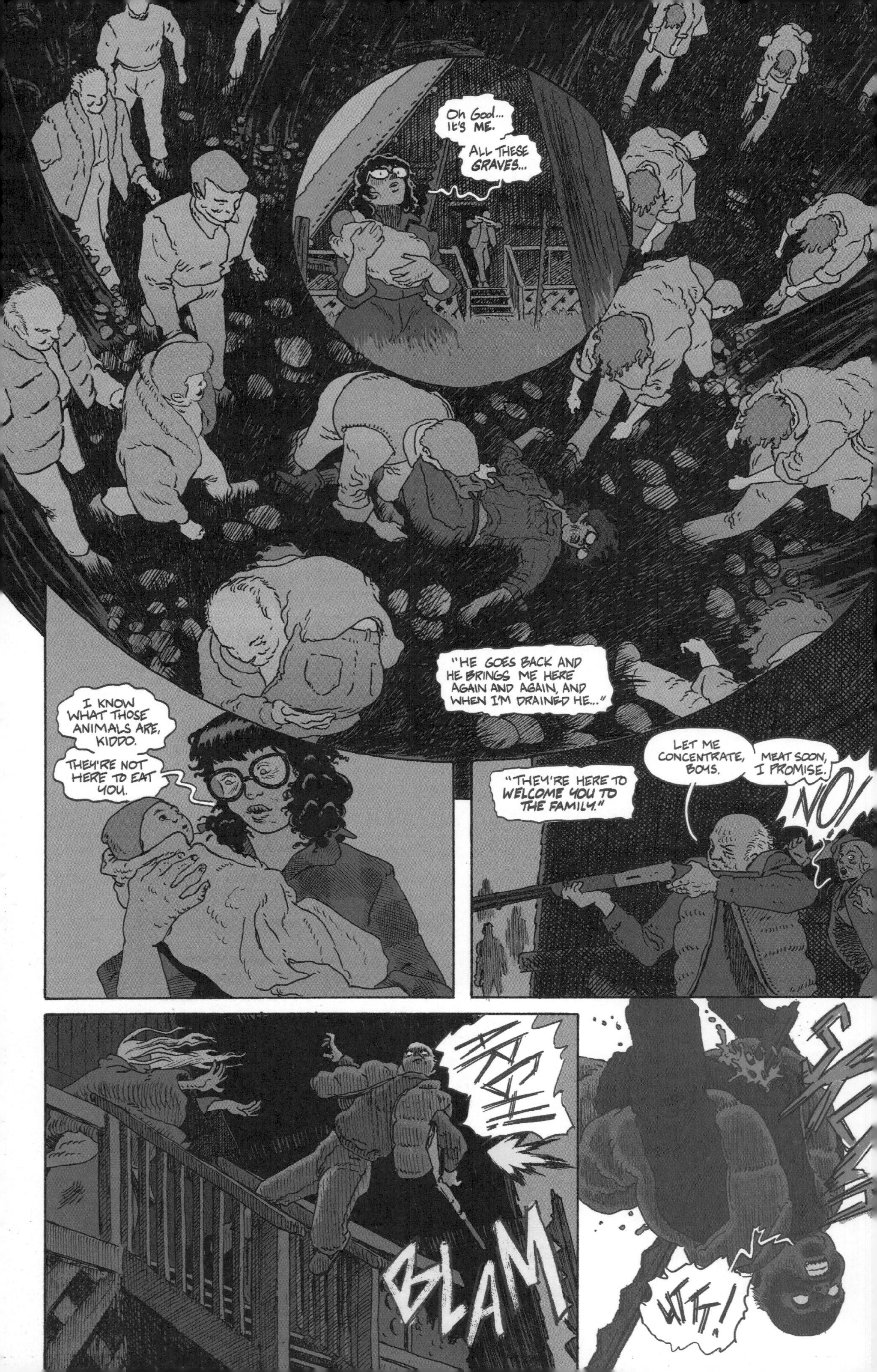
Oh God... It's ME.
ALL THESE GRAVES...
"HE GOES BACK AND HE BRINGS ME HERE AGAIN AND AGAIN, AND WHEN I'M DRAINED HE..."
I KNOW WHAT THOSE ANIMALS ARE, KIDDO.
THEY'RE NOT HERE TO EAT YOU.
"THEY'RE HERE TO WELCOME YOU TO THE FAMILY."
LET ME CONCENTRATE, BOYS.
MEAT SOON, I PROMISE.
NO!
BLAM
UTTT!

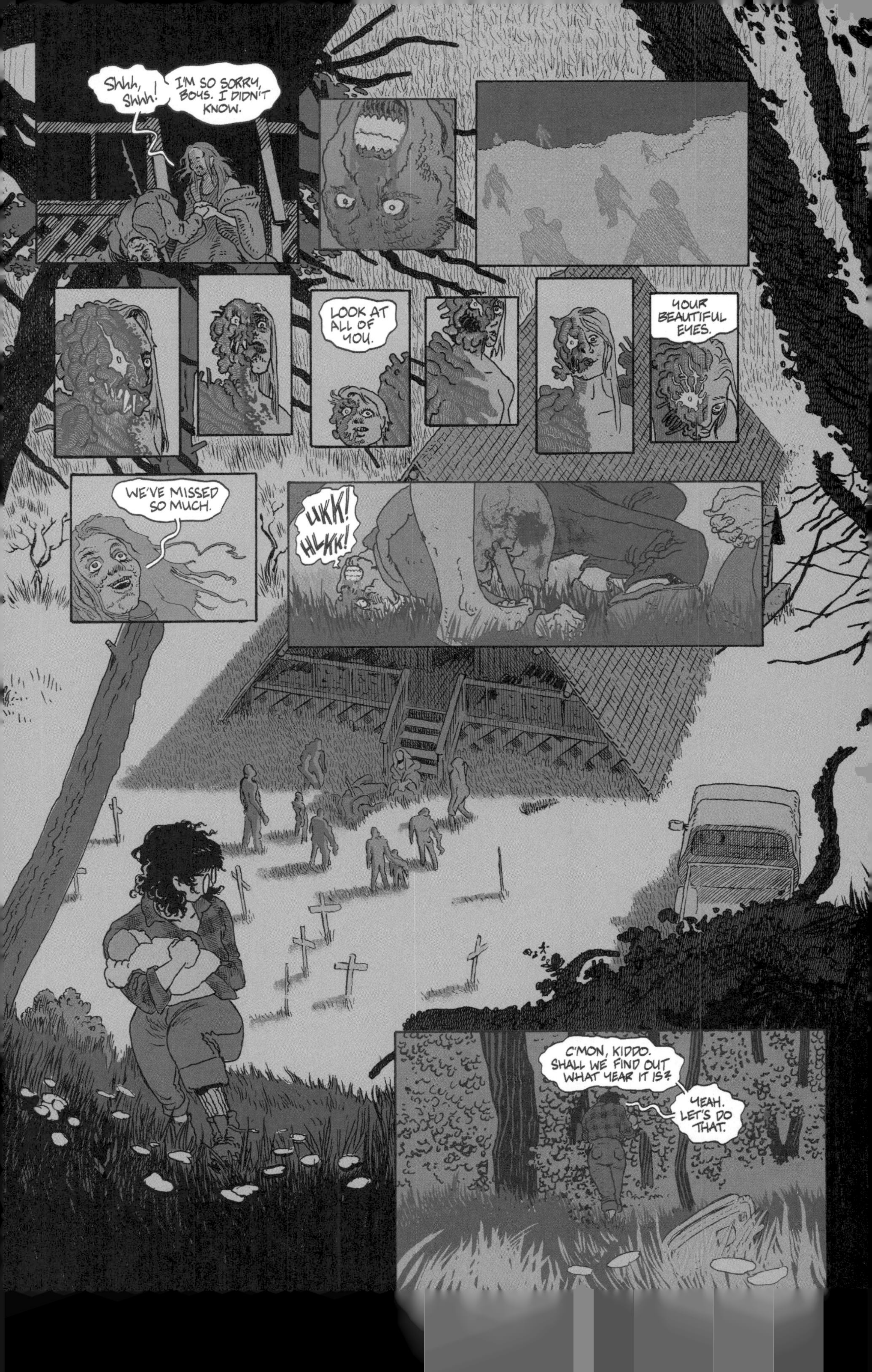
Shhh, Shhh!
I'M SO SORRY, BOYS. I DIDN'T KNOW.
LOOK AT ALL OF YOU.
YOUR BEAUTIFUL EYES.
WE'VE MISSED SO MUCH.
UKK! HLKK!
C'MON, KIDDO. SHALL WE FIND OUT WHAT YEAR IT IS?
YEAH. LET'S DO THAT.

RIVER OF SIN

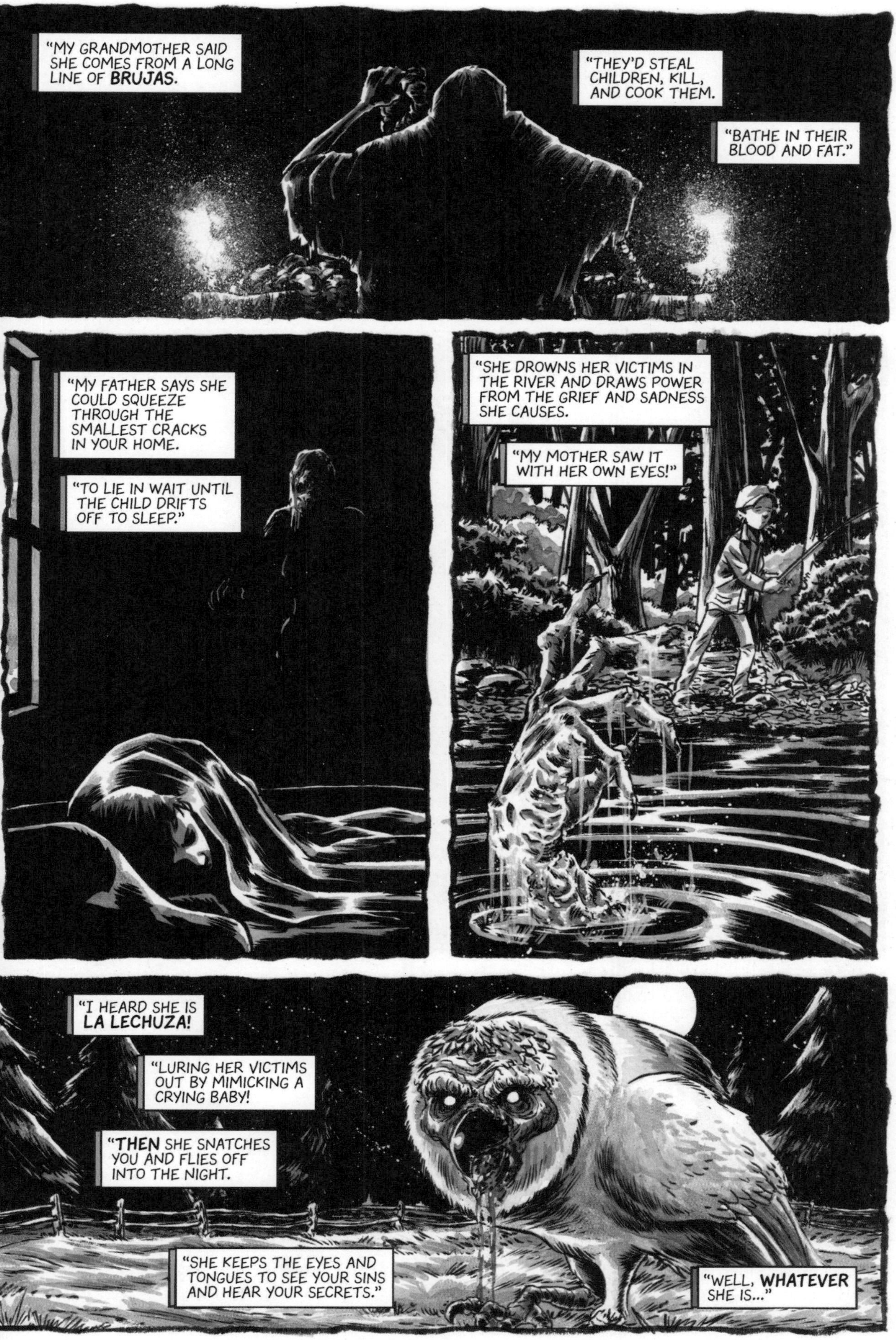
"MY GRANDMOTHER SAID SHE COMES FROM A LONG LINE OF **BRUJAS**.
"THEY'D STEAL CHILDREN, KILL, AND COOK THEM.
"BATHE IN THEIR BLOOD AND FAT."
"MY FATHER SAYS SHE COULD SQUEEZE THROUGH THE SMALLEST CRACKS IN YOUR HOME.
"TO LIE IN WAIT UNTIL THE CHILD DRIFTS OFF TO SLEEP."
"SHE DROWNS HER VICTIMS IN THE RIVER AND DRAWS POWER FROM THE GRIEF AND SADNESS SHE CAUSES.
"MY MOTHER SAW IT WITH HER OWN EYES!"
"I HEARD SHE IS **LA LECHUZA!**
"LURING HER VICTIMS OUT BY MIMICKING A CRYING BABY!
"**THEN** SHE SNATCHES YOU AND FLIES OFF INTO THE NIGHT.
"SHE KEEPS THE EYES AND TONGUES TO SEE YOUR SINS AND HEAR YOUR SECRETS."
"WELL, **WHATEVER** SHE IS..."

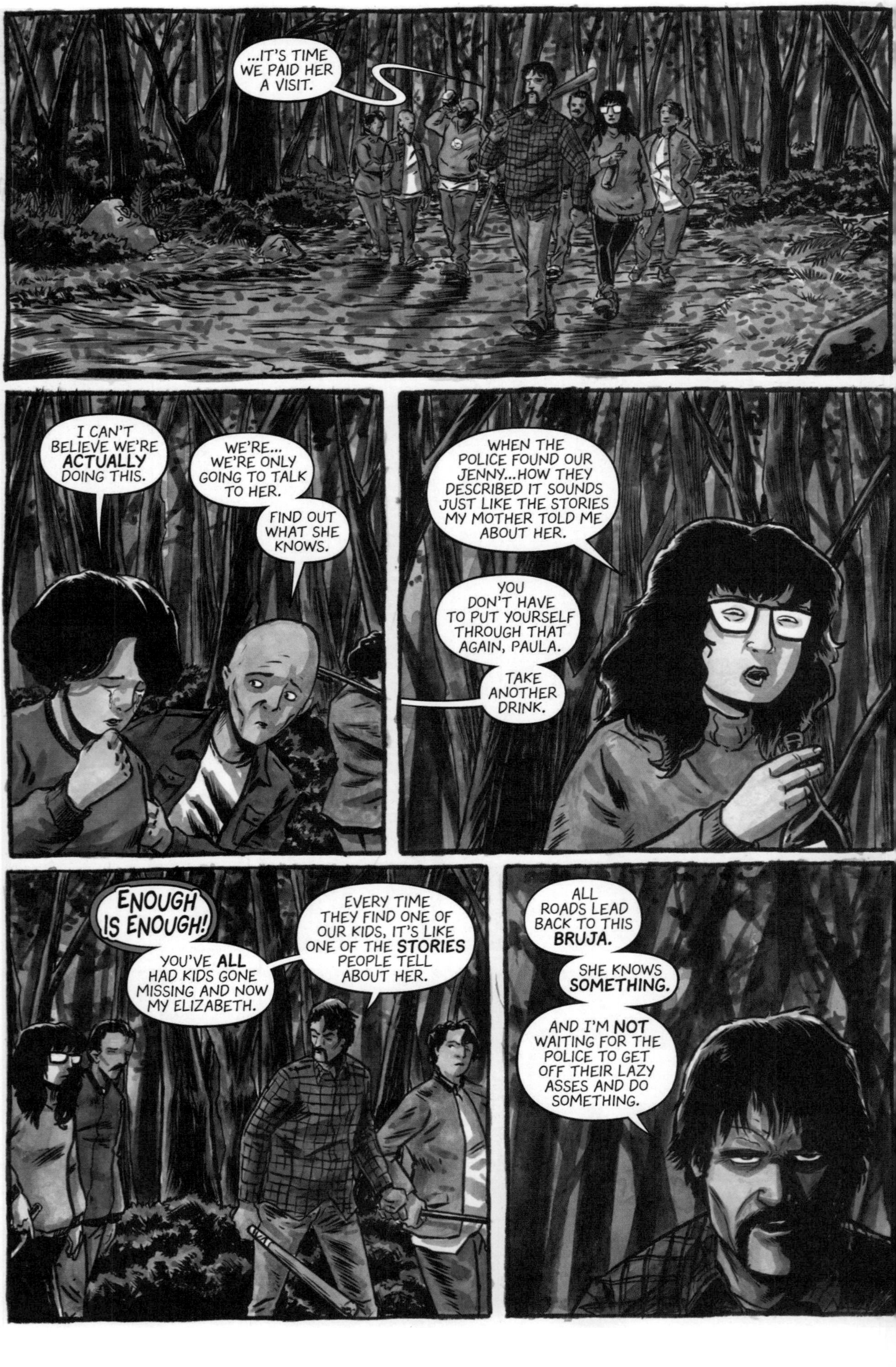
...IT'S TIME WE PAID HER A VISIT.
I CAN'T BELIEVE WE'RE ACTUALLY DOING THIS.
WE'RE... WE'RE ONLY GOING TO TALK TO HER.
FIND OUT WHAT SHE KNOWS.
WHEN THE POLICE FOUND OUR JENNY...HOW THEY DESCRIBED IT SOUNDS JUST LIKE THE STORIES MY MOTHER TOLD ME ABOUT HER.
YOU DON'T HAVE TO PUT YOURSELF THROUGH THAT AGAIN, PAULA.
TAKE ANOTHER DRINK.
ENOUGH IS ENOUGH!
YOU'VE ALL HAD KIDS GONE MISSING AND NOW MY ELIZABETH.
EVERY TIME THEY FIND ONE OF OUR KIDS, IT'S LIKE ONE OF THE STORIES PEOPLE TELL ABOUT HER.
ALL ROADS LEAD BACK TO THIS BRUJA.
SHE KNOWS SOMETHING.
AND I'M NOT WAITING FOR THE POLICE TO GET OFF THEIR LAZY ASSES AND DO SOMETHING.

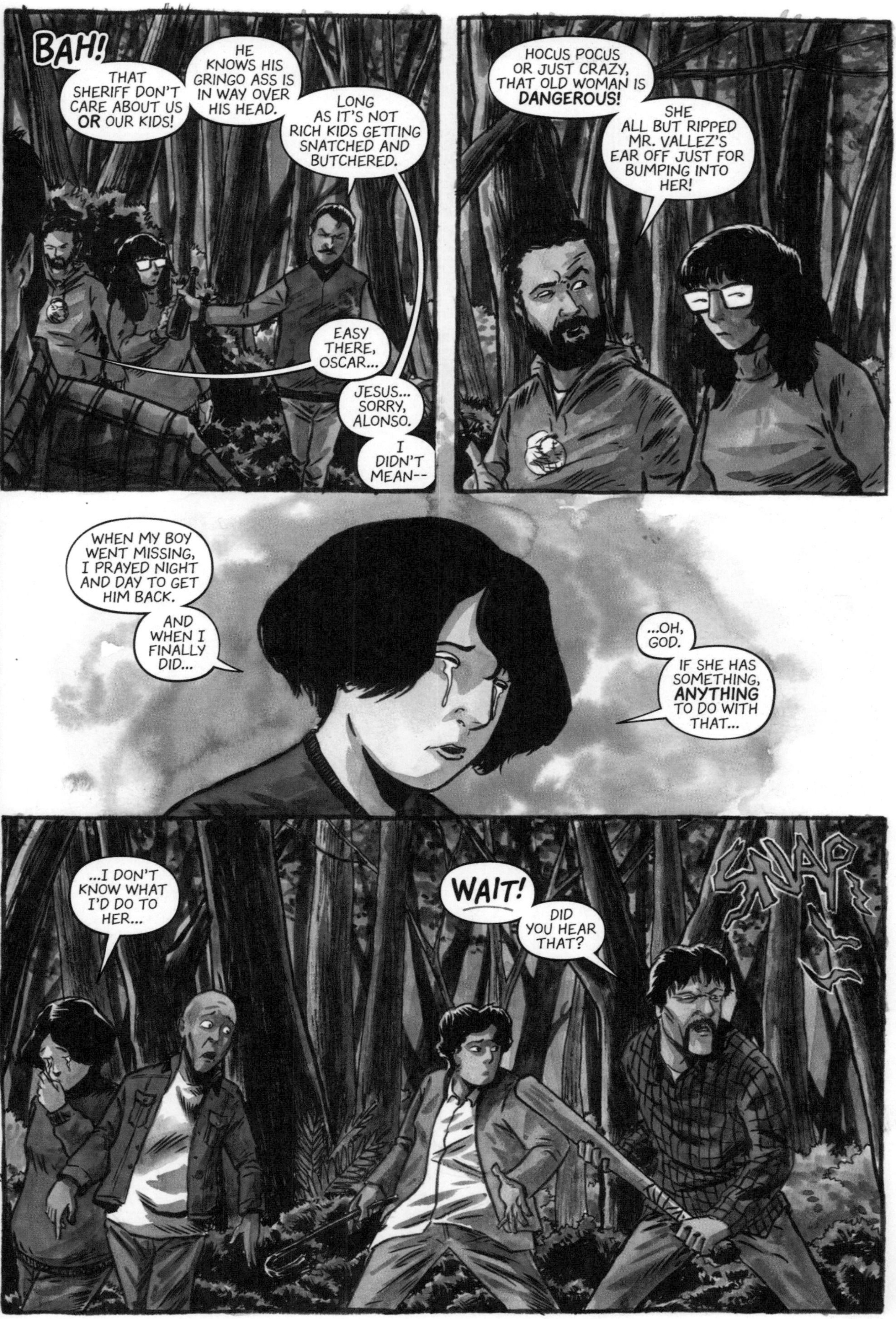
BAH!
THAT SHERIFF DON'T CARE ABOUT US OR OUR KIDS!
HE KNOWS HIS GRINGO ASS IS IN WAY OVER HIS HEAD.
LONG AS IT'S NOT RICH KIDS GETTING SNATCHED AND BUTCHERED.
EASY THERE, OSCAR...
JESUS... SORRY, ALONSO.
I DIDN'T MEAN--
HOCUS POCUS OR JUST CRAZY, THAT OLD WOMAN IS DANGEROUS!
SHE ALL BUT RIPPED MR. VALLEZ'S EAR OFF JUST FOR BUMPING INTO HER!
WHEN MY BOY WENT MISSING, I PRAYED NIGHT AND DAY TO GET HIM BACK.
AND WHEN I FINALLY DID...
...OH, GOD.
IF SHE HAS SOMETHING, ANYTHING TO DO WITH THAT...
...I DON'T KNOW WHAT I'D DO TO HER...
WAIT!
DID YOU HEAR THAT?
SNAP!

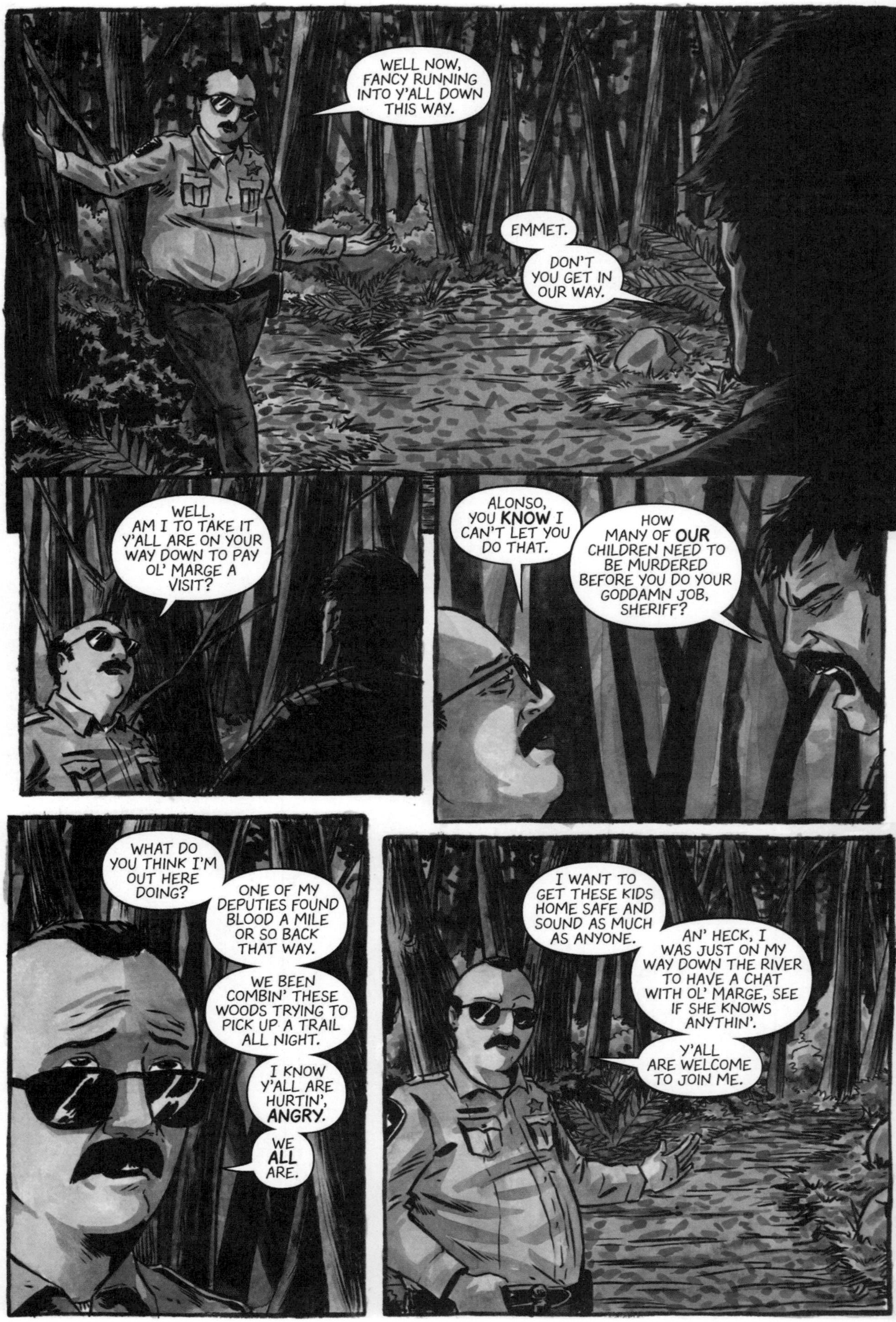
WELL NOW, FANCY RUNNING INTO Y'ALL DOWN THIS WAY.
EMMET.
DON'T YOU GET IN OUR WAY.
WELL, AM I TO TAKE IT Y'ALL ARE ON YOUR WAY DOWN TO PAY OL' MARGE A VISIT?
ALONSO, YOU **KNOW** I CAN'T LET YOU DO THAT.
HOW MANY OF **OUR** CHILDREN NEED TO BE MURDERED BEFORE YOU DO YOUR GODDAMN JOB, SHERIFF?
WHAT DO YOU THINK I'M OUT HERE DOING?
ONE OF MY DEPUTIES FOUND BLOOD A MILE OR SO BACK THAT WAY.
WE BEEN COMBIN' THESE WOODS TRYING TO PICK UP A TRAIL ALL NIGHT.
I KNOW Y'ALL ARE HURTIN', **ANGRY**.
WE **ALL** ARE.
I WANT TO GET THESE KIDS HOME SAFE AND SOUND AS MUCH AS ANYONE.
AN' HECK, I WAS JUST ON MY WAY DOWN THE RIVER TO HAVE A CHAT WITH OL' MARGE, SEE IF SHE KNOWS ANYTHIN'.
Y'ALL ARE WELCOME TO JOIN ME.

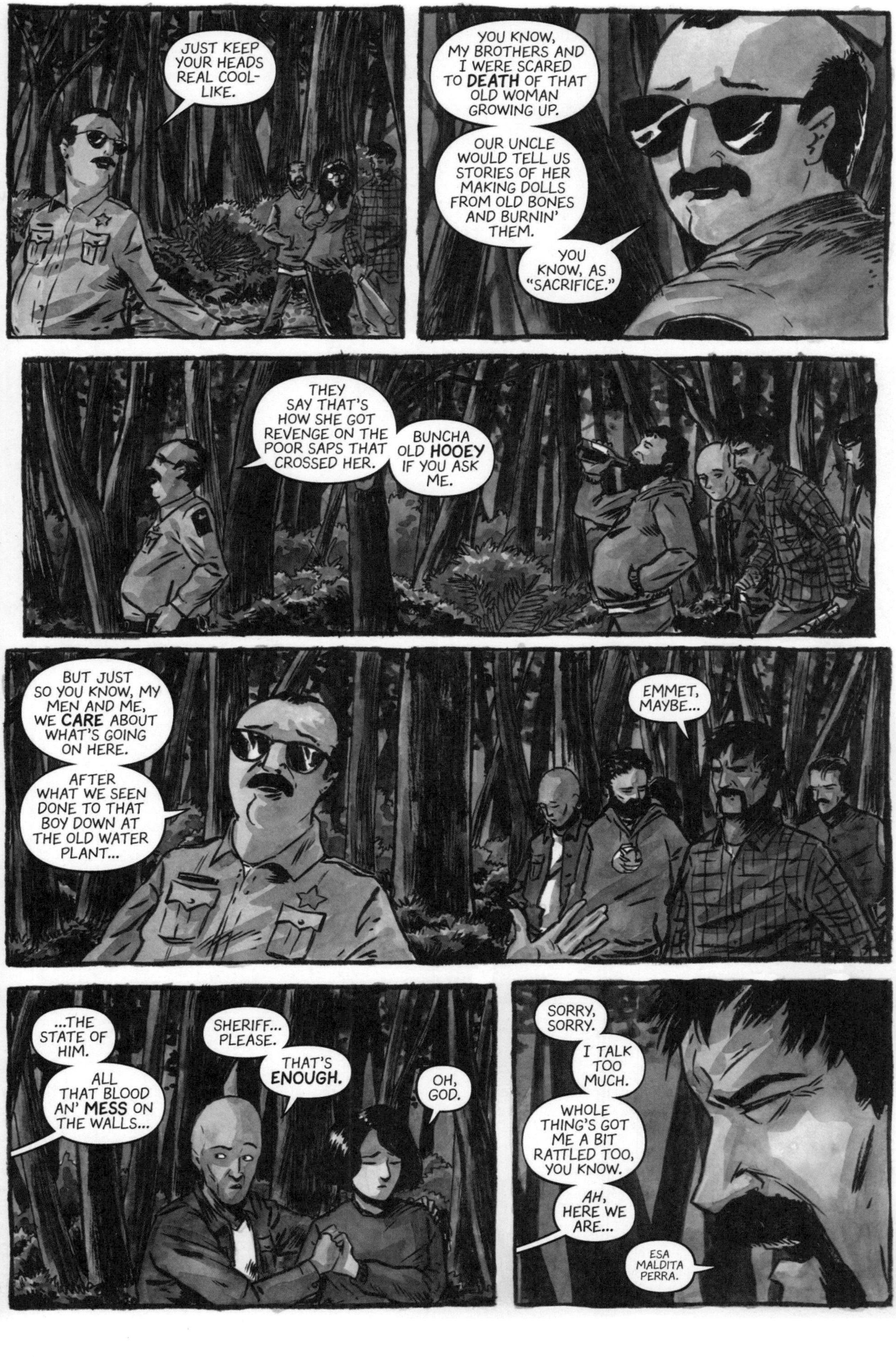
JUST KEEP YOUR HEADS REAL COOL-LIKE.
YOU KNOW, MY BROTHERS AND I WERE SCARED TO **DEATH** OF THAT OLD WOMAN GROWING UP.
OUR UNCLE WOULD TELL US STORIES OF HER MAKING DOLLS FROM OLD BONES AND BURNIN' THEM.
YOU KNOW, AS "SACRIFICE."
THEY SAY THAT'S HOW SHE GOT REVENGE ON THE POOR SAPS THAT CROSSED HER.
BUNCHA OLD **HOOEY** IF YOU ASK ME.
BUT JUST SO YOU KNOW, MY MEN AND ME, WE **CARE** ABOUT WHAT'S GOING ON HERE.
AFTER WHAT WE SEEN DONE TO THAT BOY DOWN AT THE OLD WATER PLANT...
EMMET, MAYBE...
...THE STATE OF HIM.
ALL THAT BLOOD AN' **MESS** ON THE WALLS...
SHERIFF... PLEASE.
THAT'S **ENOUGH.**
OH, GOD.
SORRY, SORRY.
I TALK TOO MUCH.
WHOLE THING'S GOT ME A BIT RATTLED TOO, YOU KNOW.
AH, HERE WE ARE...
ESA MALDITA PERRA.

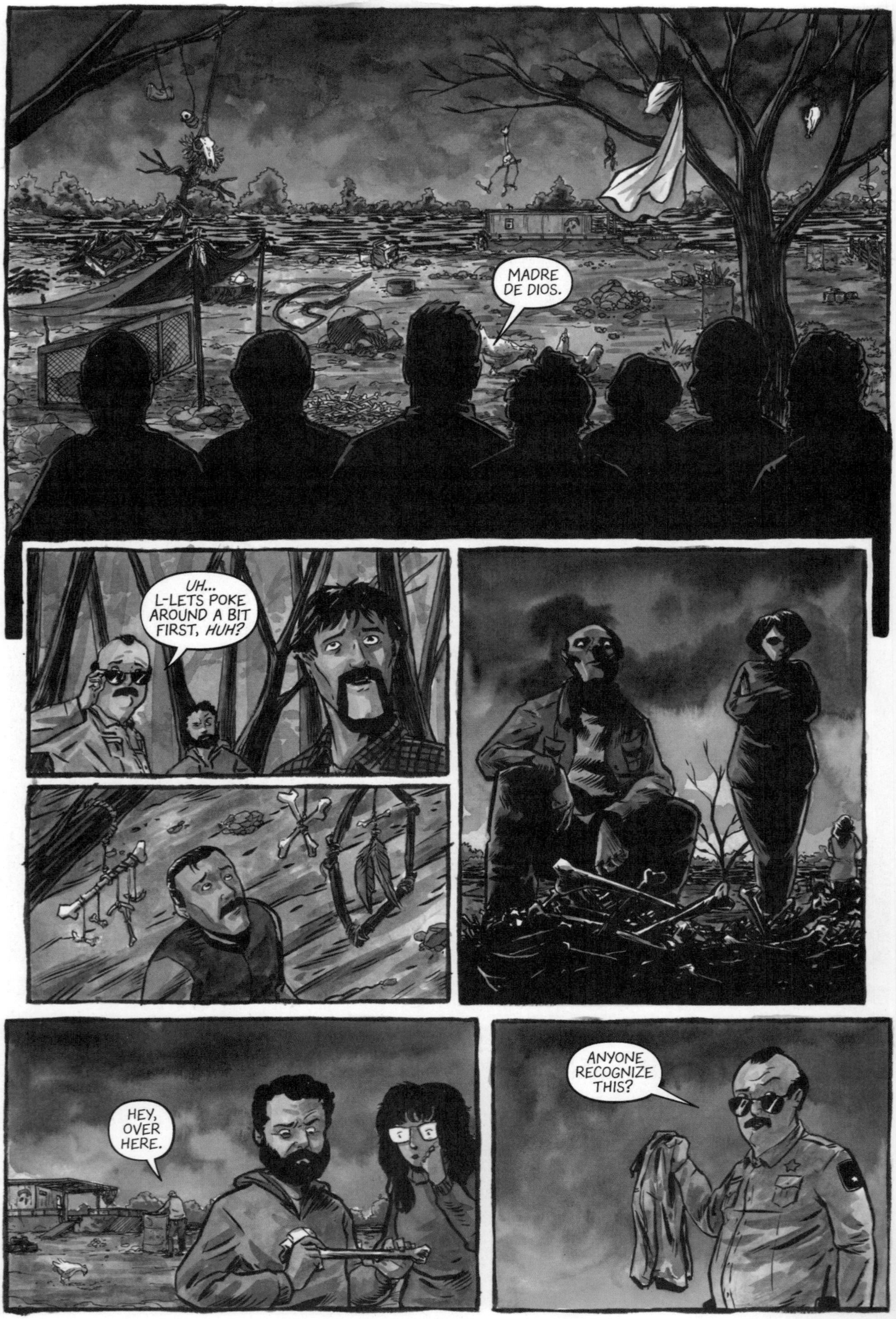
MADRE DE DIOS.
UH... L-LETS POKE AROUND A BIT FIRST, *HUH?*
HEY, OVER HERE.
ANYONE RECOGNIZE THIS?

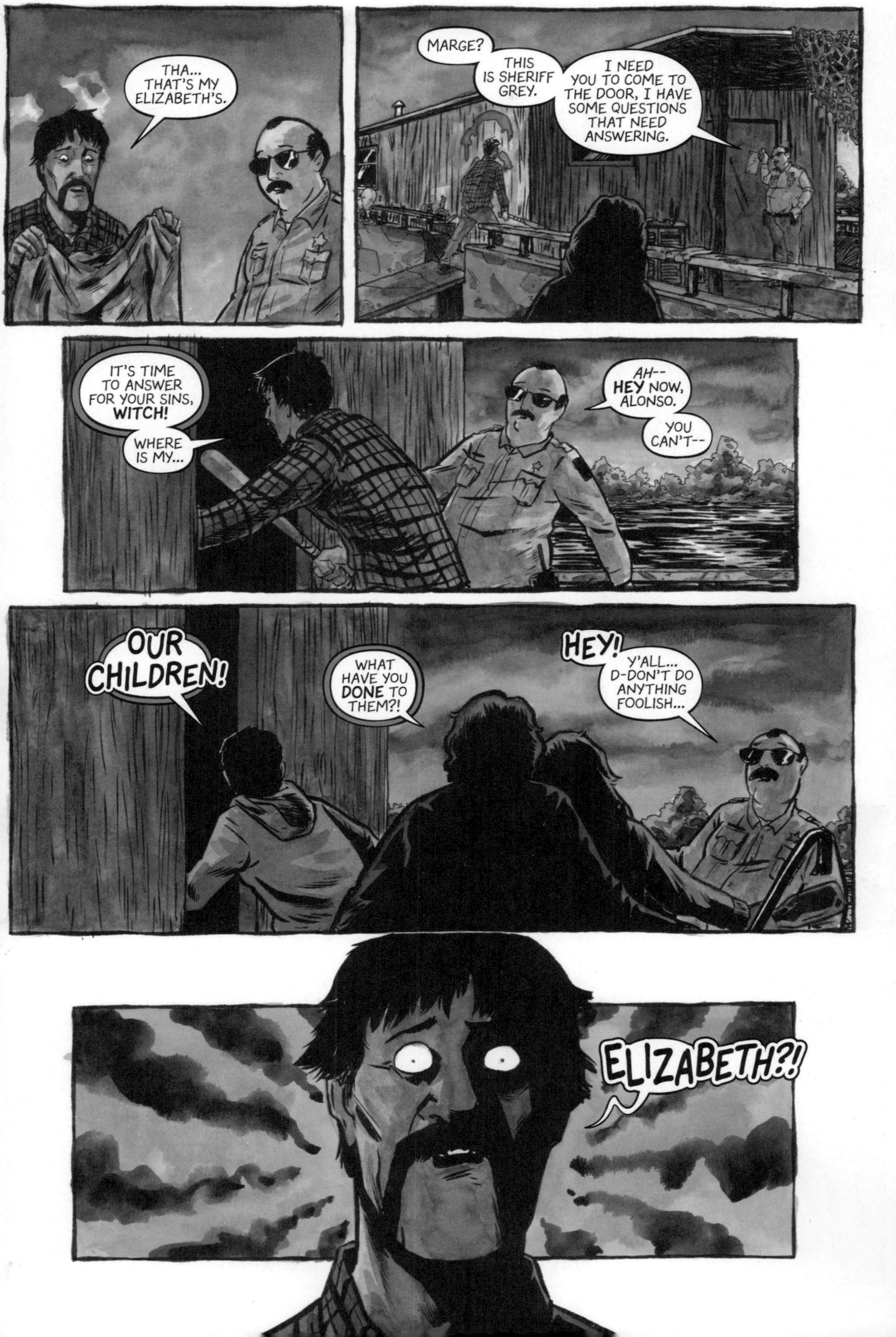
THA... THAT'S MY ELIZABETH'S.
MARGE?
THIS IS SHERIFF GREY.
I NEED YOU TO COME TO THE DOOR, I HAVE SOME QUESTIONS THAT NEED ANSWERING.
IT'S TIME TO ANSWER FOR YOUR SINS, **WITCH!**
WHERE IS MY...
AH-- **HEY** NOW, ALONSO.
YOU CAN'T--
OUR CHILDREN!
WHAT HAVE YOU **DONE** TO THEM?!
HEY!
Y'ALL... D-DON'T DO ANYTHING FOOLISH...
ELIZABETH?!

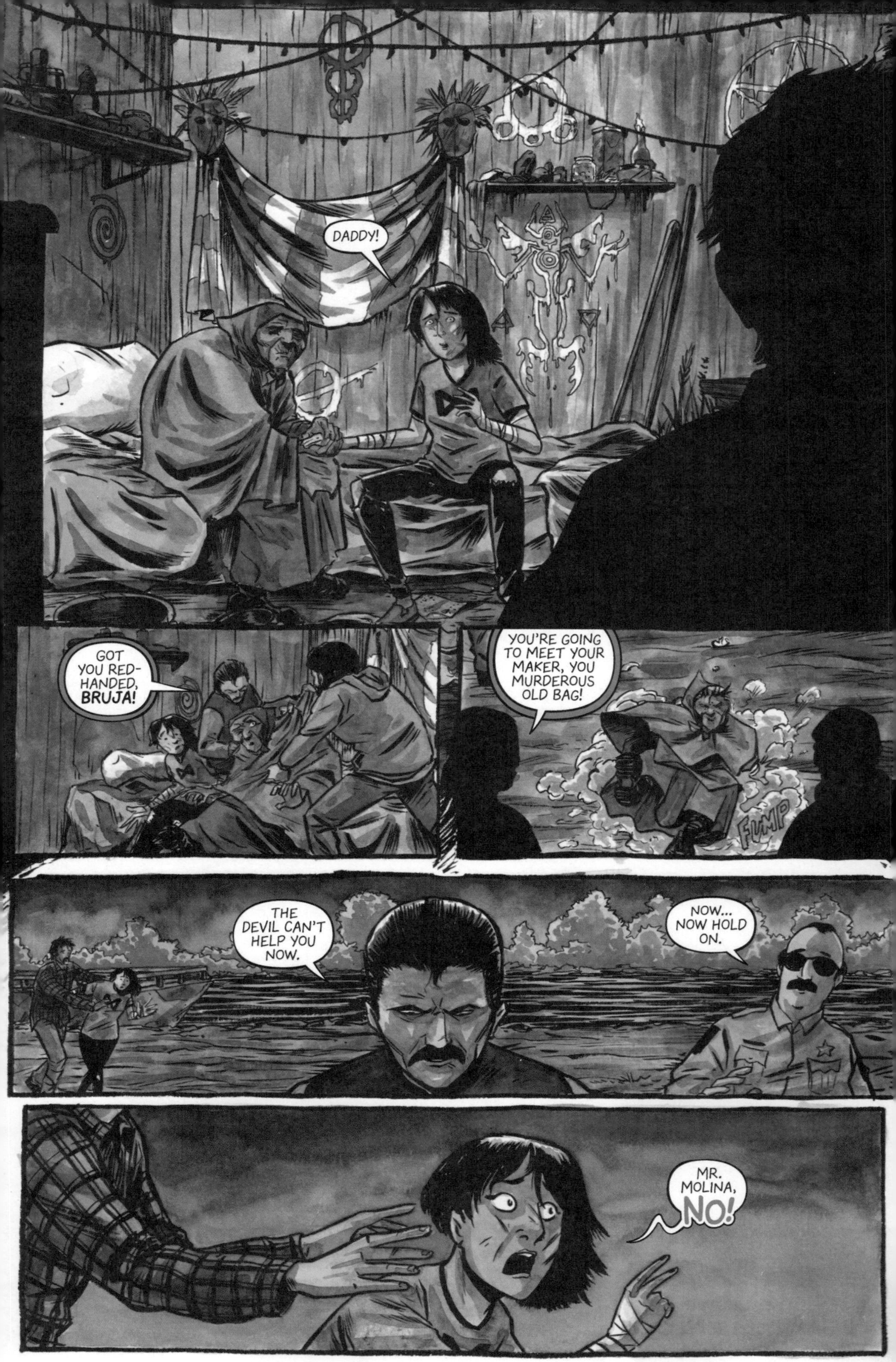

DADDY!
GOT YOU RED-HANDED, BRUJA!
YOU'RE GOING TO MEET YOUR MAKER, YOU MURDEROUS OLD BAG!
FUMP
THE DEVIL CAN'T HELP YOU NOW.
NOW... NOW HOLD ON.
MR. MOLINA, NO!

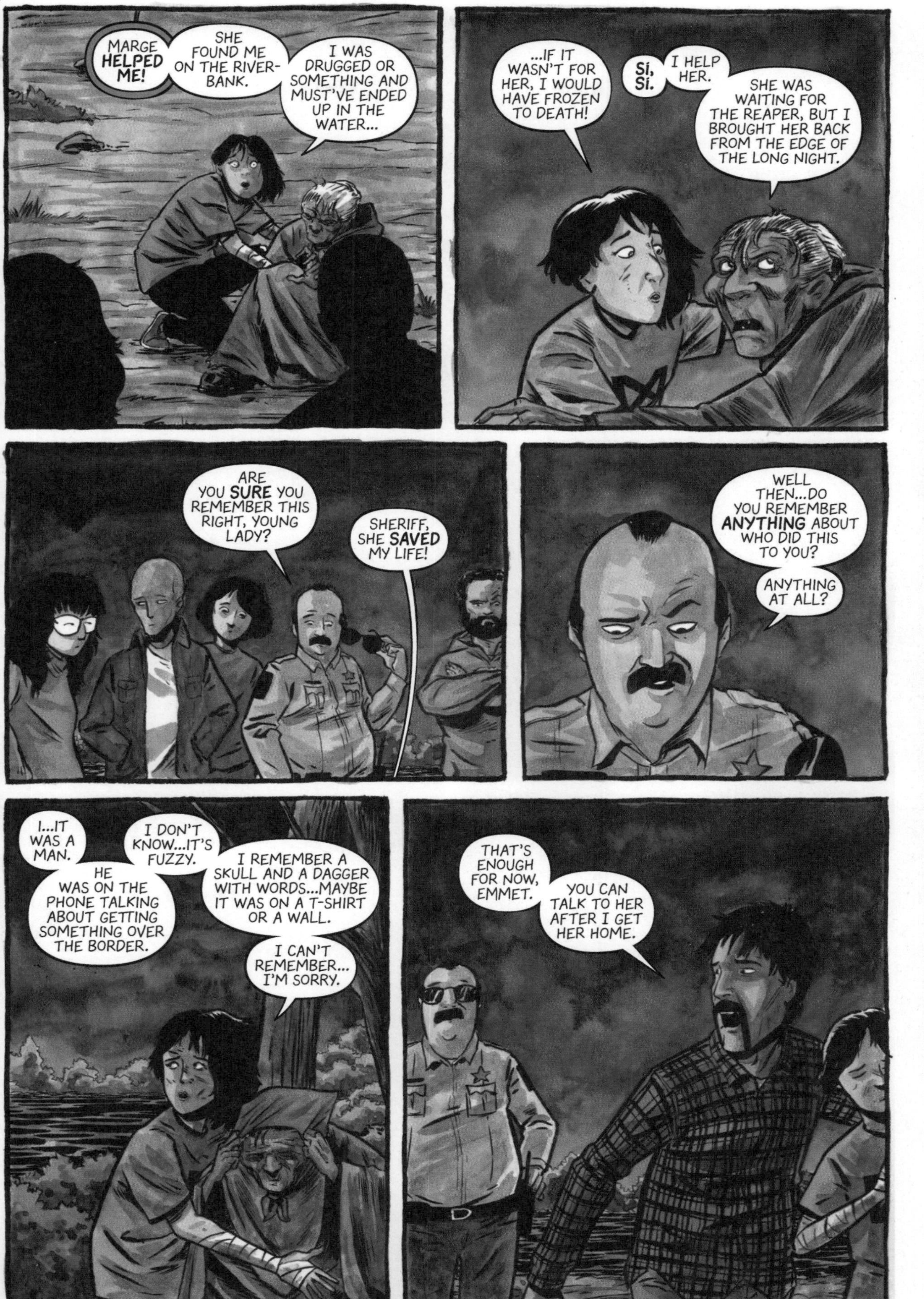
MARGE **HELPED** **ME!**
SHE FOUND ME ON THE RIVER-BANK.
I WAS DRUGGED OR SOMETHING AND MUST'VE ENDED UP IN THE WATER...
...IF IT WASN'T FOR HER, I WOULD HAVE FROZEN TO DEATH!
SÍ, SÍ.
I HELP HER.
SHE WAS WAITING FOR THE REAPER, BUT I BROUGHT HER BACK FROM THE EDGE OF THE LONG NIGHT.
ARE YOU **SURE** YOU REMEMBER THIS RIGHT, YOUNG LADY?
SHERIFF, SHE **SAVED** MY LIFE!
WELL THEN...DO YOU REMEMBER **ANYTHING** ABOUT WHO DID THIS TO YOU?
ANYTHING AT ALL?
I...IT WAS A MAN.
I DON'T KNOW...IT'S FUZZY.
HE WAS ON THE PHONE TALKING ABOUT GETTING SOMETHING OVER THE BORDER.
I REMEMBER A SKULL AND A DAGGER WITH WORDS...MAYBE IT WAS ON A T-SHIRT OR A WALL.
I CAN'T REMEMBER... I'M SORRY.
THAT'S ENOUGH FOR NOW, EMMET.
YOU CAN TALK TO HER AFTER I GET HER HOME.

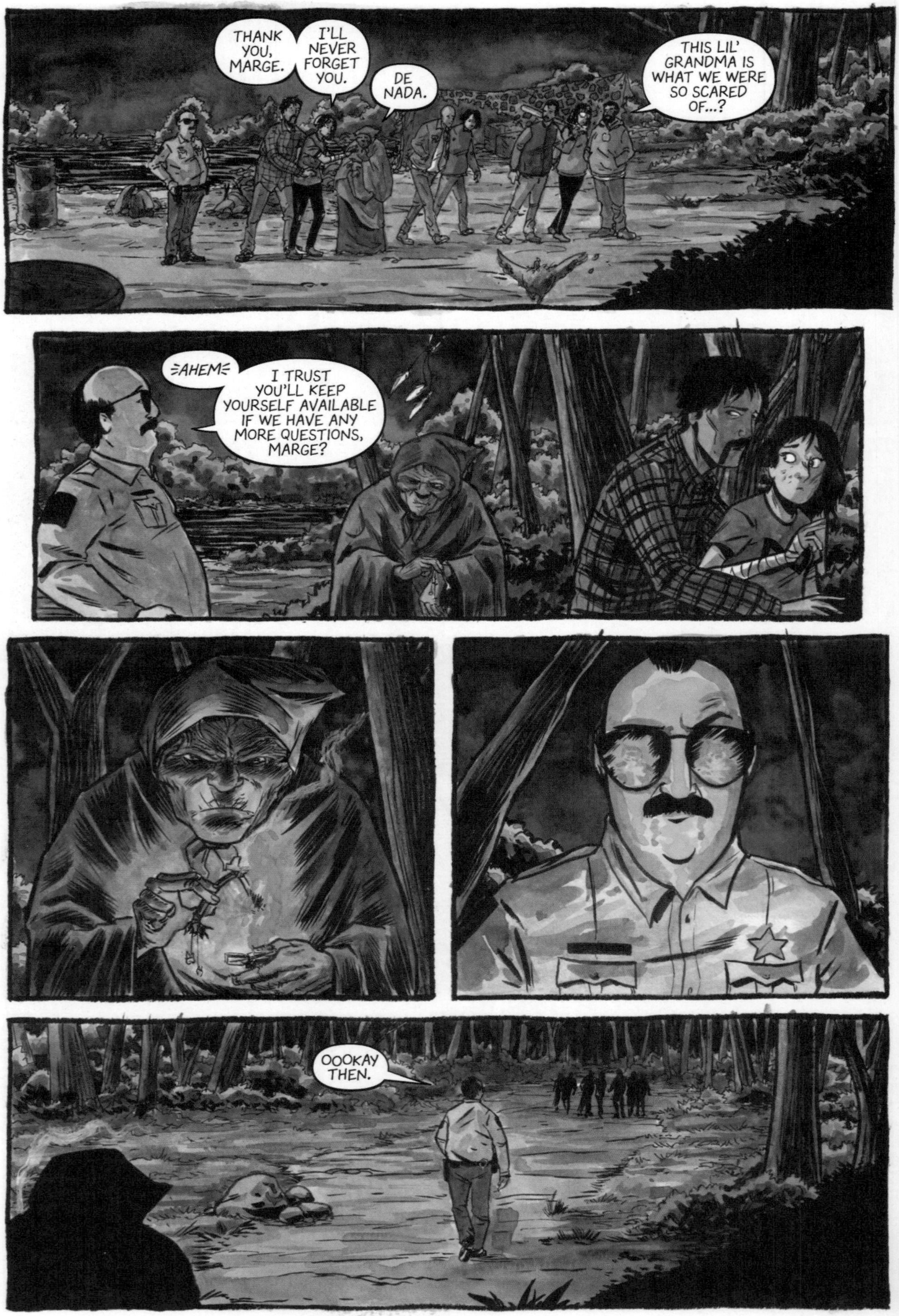
THANK YOU, MARGE.
I'LL NEVER FORGET YOU.
DE NADA.
THIS LIL' GRANDMA IS WHAT WE WERE SO SCARED OF...?
AHEM
I TRUST YOU'LL KEEP YOURSELF AVAILABLE IF WE HAVE ANY MORE QUESTIONS, MARGE?
OOOKAY THEN.

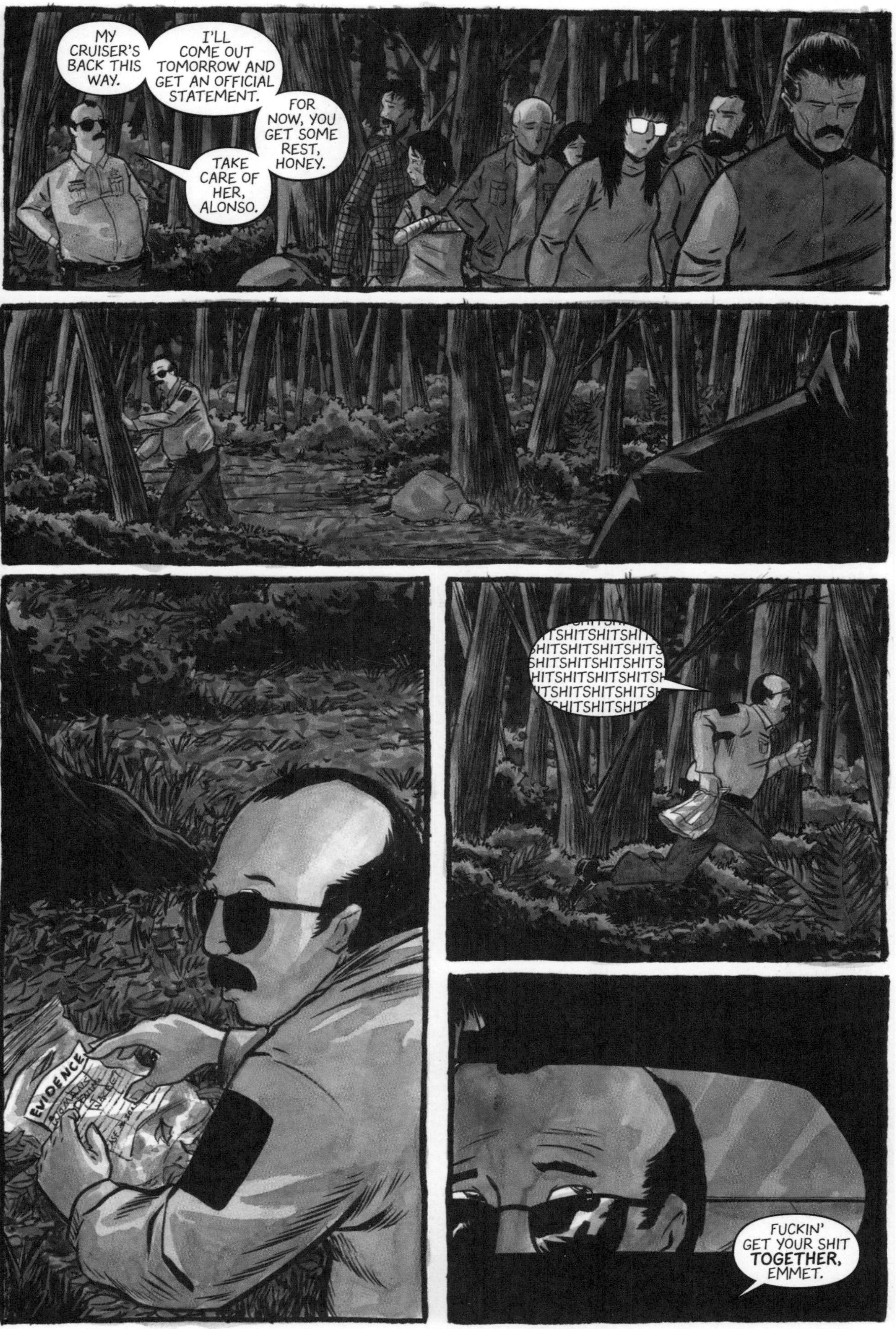

MY CRUISER'S BACK THIS WAY.
I'LL COME OUT TOMORROW AND GET AN OFFICIAL STATEMENT.
FOR NOW, YOU GET SOME REST, HONEY.
TAKE CARE OF HER, ALONSO.
EVIDENCE
SHITSHITSHITSHITSHITSHITSHITSHITSHITSHITSHITSHITSHITSHIT
FUCKIN' GET YOUR SHIT **TOGETHER,** EMMET.

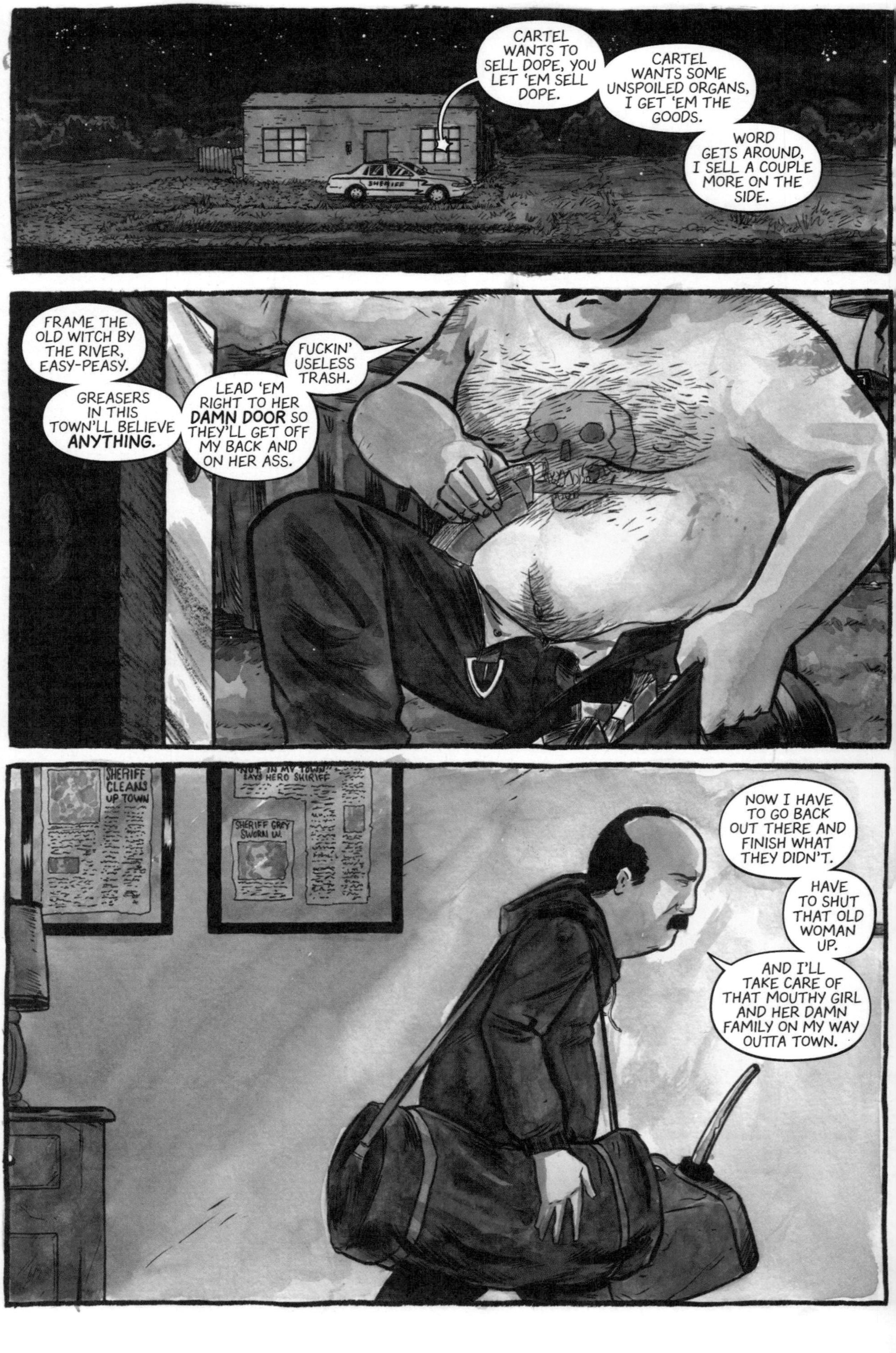
CARTEL WANTS TO SELL DOPE, YOU LET 'EM SELL DOPE.
CARTEL WANTS SOME UNSPOILED ORGANS, I GET 'EM THE GOODS.
WORD GETS AROUND, I SELL A COUPLE MORE ON THE SIDE.
SHERIFF
FRAME THE OLD WITCH BY THE RIVER, EASY-PEASY.
GREASERS IN THIS TOWN'LL BELIEVE **ANYTHING.**
FUCKIN' USELESS TRASH.
LEAD 'EM RIGHT TO HER **DAMN DOOR** SO THEY'LL GET OFF MY BACK AND ON HER ASS.
SHERIFF CLEANS UP TOWN
SAYS HERO SHIRIFF
SHERIFF GREY SWORN IN.
NOW I HAVE TO GO BACK OUT THERE AND FINISH WHAT THEY DIDN'T.
HAVE TO SHUT THAT OLD WOMAN UP.
AND I'LL TAKE CARE OF THAT MOUTHY GIRL AND HER DAMN FAMILY ON MY WAY OUTTA TOWN.

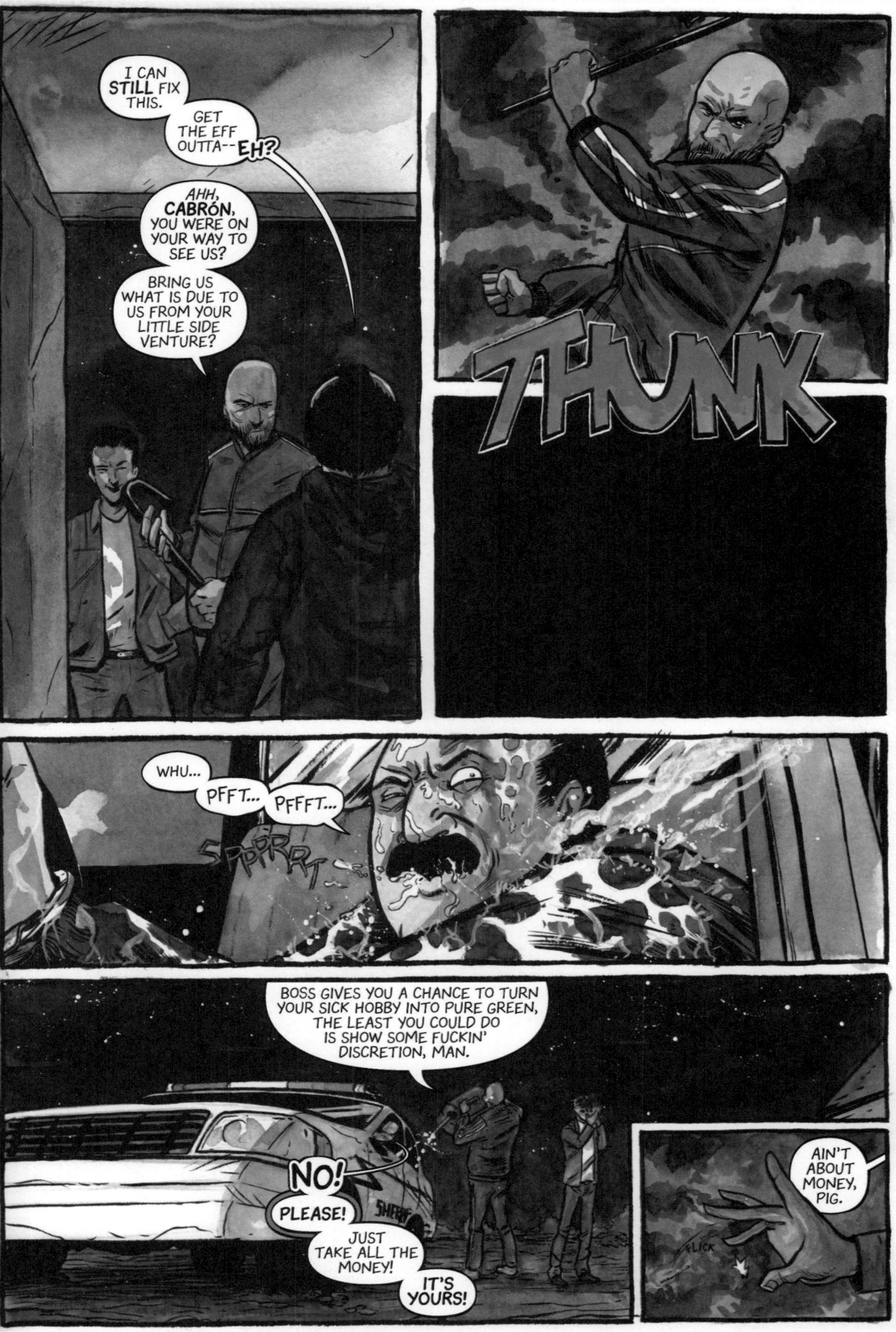
I CAN STILL FIX THIS.
GET THE EFF OUTTA--EH?
AHH, CABRÓN, YOU WERE ON YOUR WAY TO SEE US?
BRING US WHAT IS DUE TO US FROM YOUR LITTLE SIDE VENTURE?
THUNK
WHU...
PFFT...
PFFFT...
SPPPRRT
BOSS GIVES YOU A CHANCE TO TURN YOUR SICK HOBBY INTO PURE GREEN, THE LEAST YOU COULD DO IS SHOW SOME FUCKIN' DISCRETION, MAN.
NO!
PLEASE!
JUST TAKE ALL THE MONEY!
IT'S YOURS!
AIN'T ABOUT MONEY, PIG.
FLICK

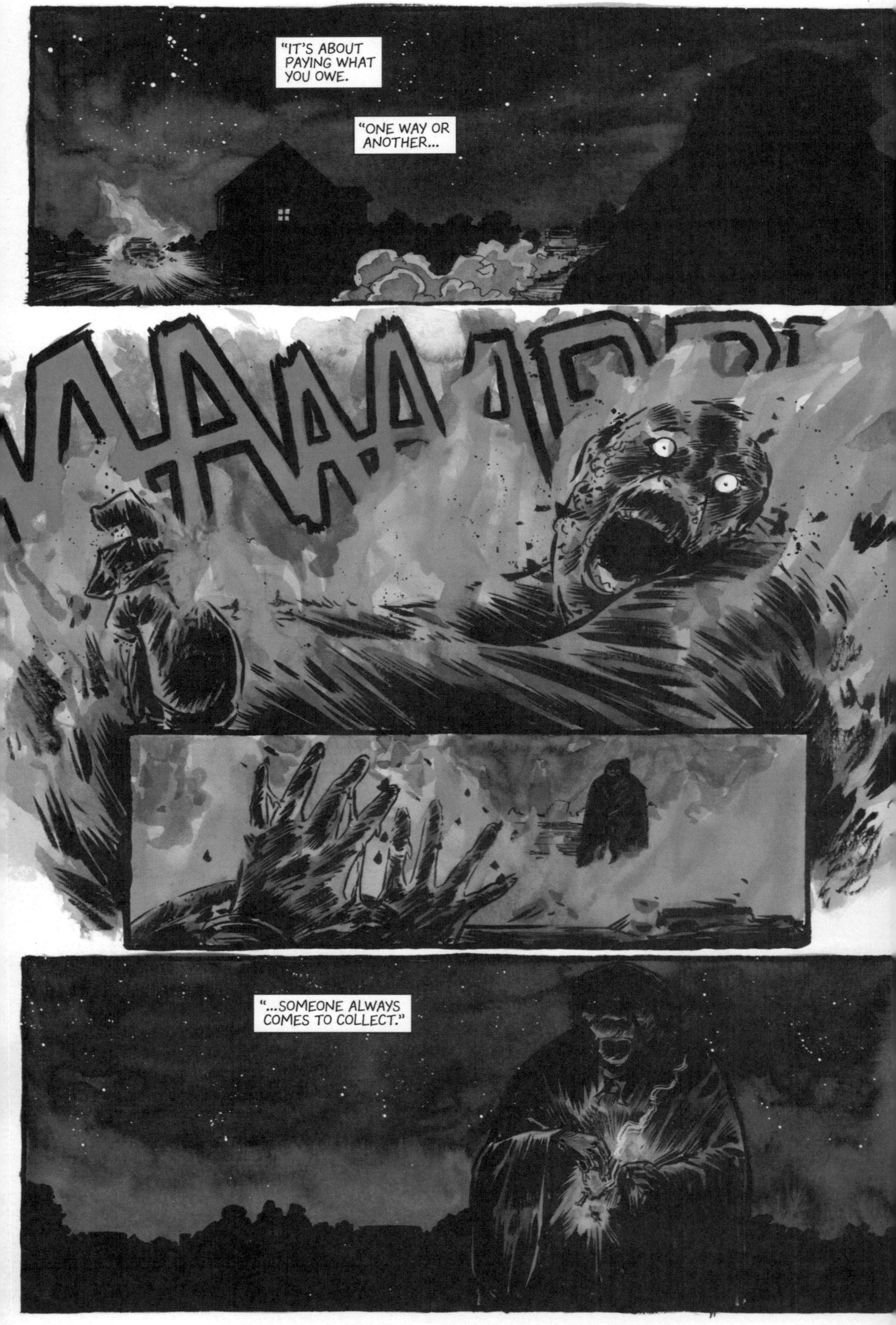
"IT'S ABOUT PAYING WHAT YOU OWE.
"ONE WAY OR ANOTHER...
"...SOMEONE ALWAYS COMES TO COLLECT."

DAME FROM THE DARK

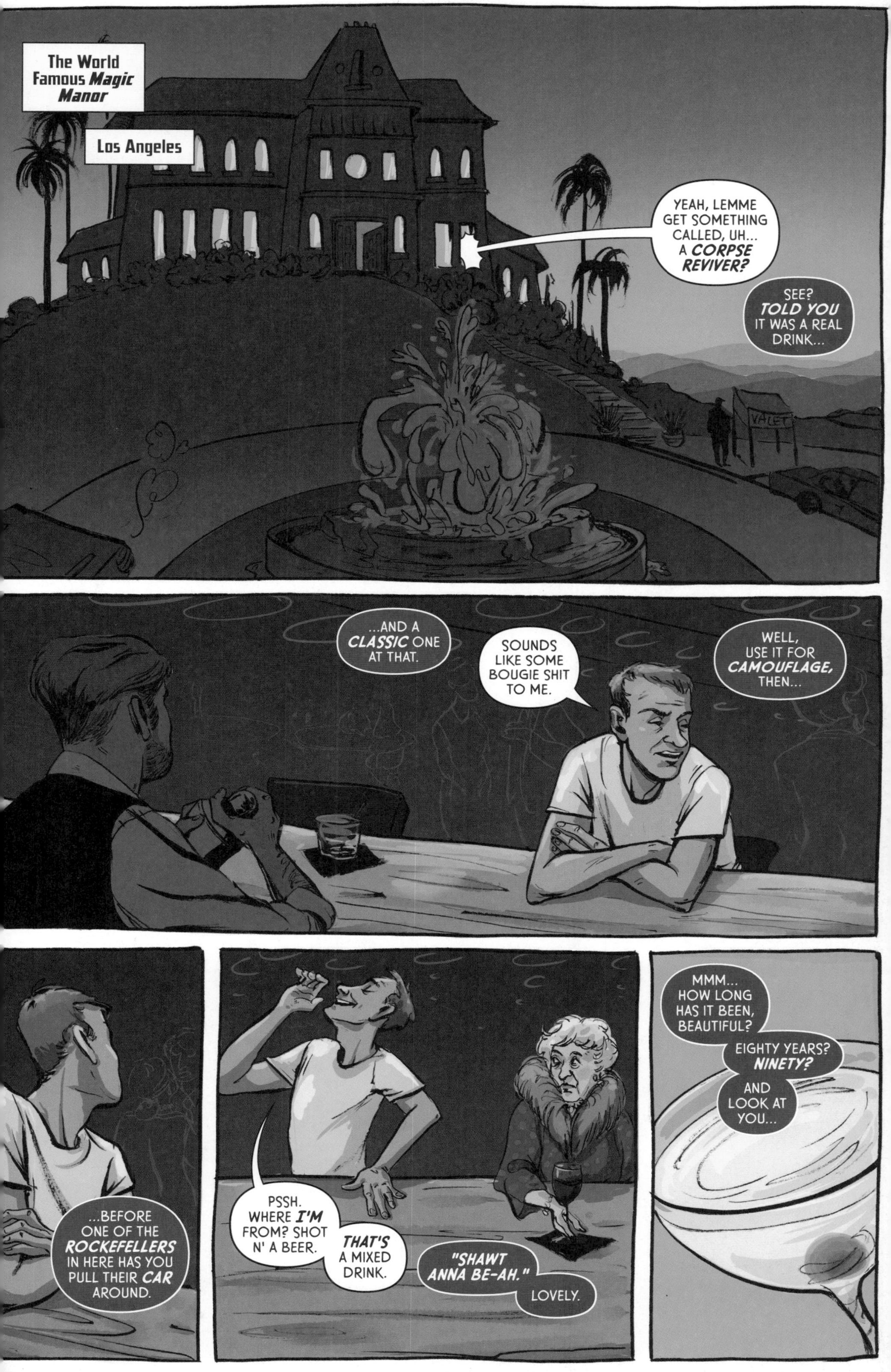

The World Famous Magic Manor
Los Angeles
YEAH, LEMME GET SOMETHING CALLED, UH... A CORPSE REVIVER?
SEE? TOLD YOU IT WAS A REAL DRINK...
...AND A CLASSIC ONE AT THAT.
SOUNDS LIKE SOME BOUGIE SHIT TO ME.
WELL, USE IT FOR CAMOUFLAGE, THEN...
...BEFORE ONE OF THE ROCKEFELLERS IN HERE HAS YOU PULL THEIR CAR AROUND.
PSSH. WHERE I'M FROM? SHOT N' A BEER.
THAT'S A MIXED DRINK.
"SHAWT ANNA BE-AH."
LOVELY.
MMM... HOW LONG HAS IT BEEN, BEAUTIFUL?
EIGHTY YEARS? NINETY?
AND LOOK AT YOU...
VALET

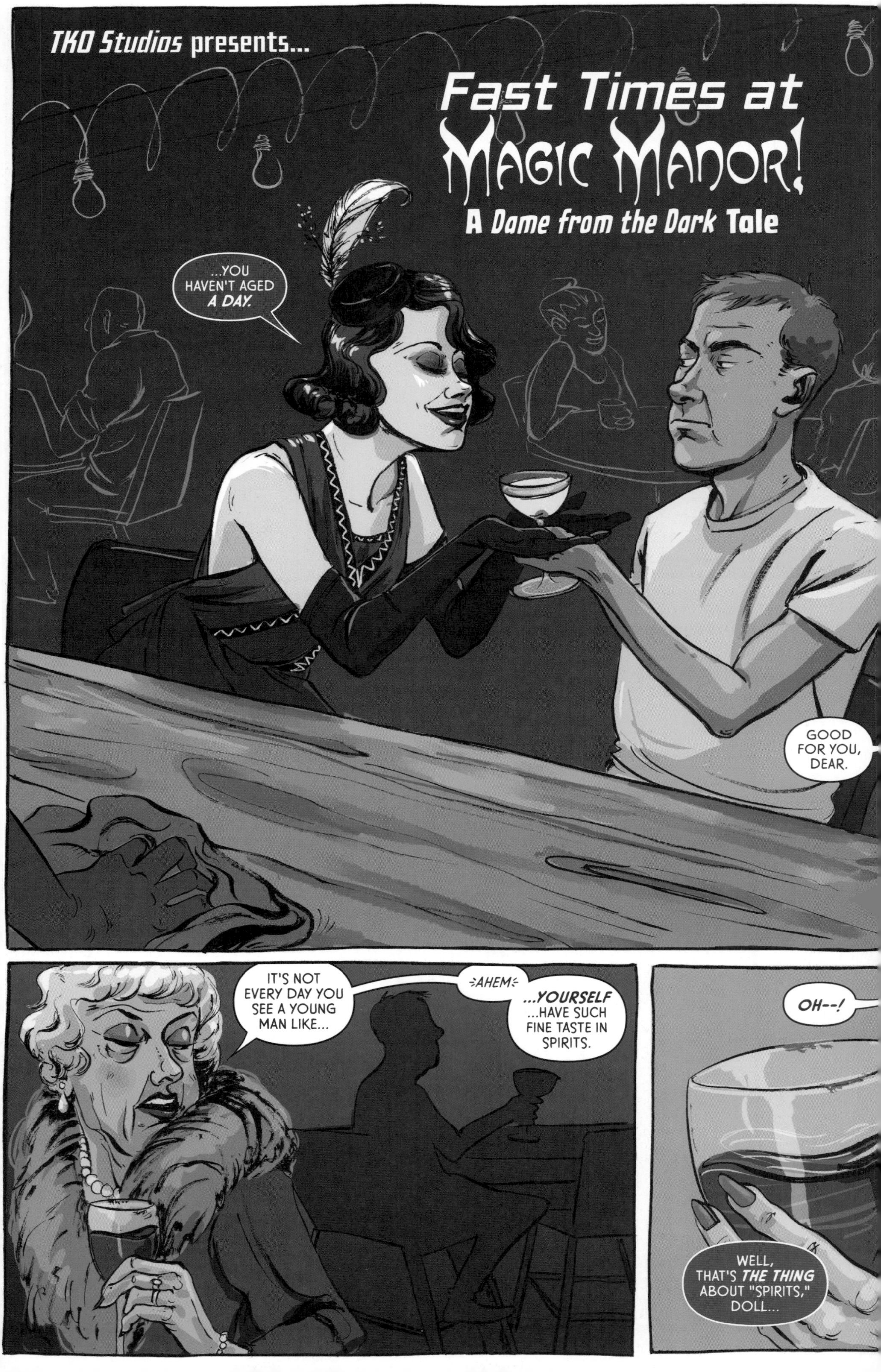
TKO Studios presents...
Fast Times at
Magic Manor!
A Dame from the Dark Tale
...YOU HAVEN'T AGED A DAY.
GOOD FOR YOU, DEAR.
IT'S NOT EVERY DAY YOU SEE A YOUNG MAN LIKE...
AHEM
...YOURSELF ...HAVE SUCH FINE TASTE IN SPIRITS.
OH--!
WELL, THAT'S THE THING ABOUT "SPIRITS," DOLL...

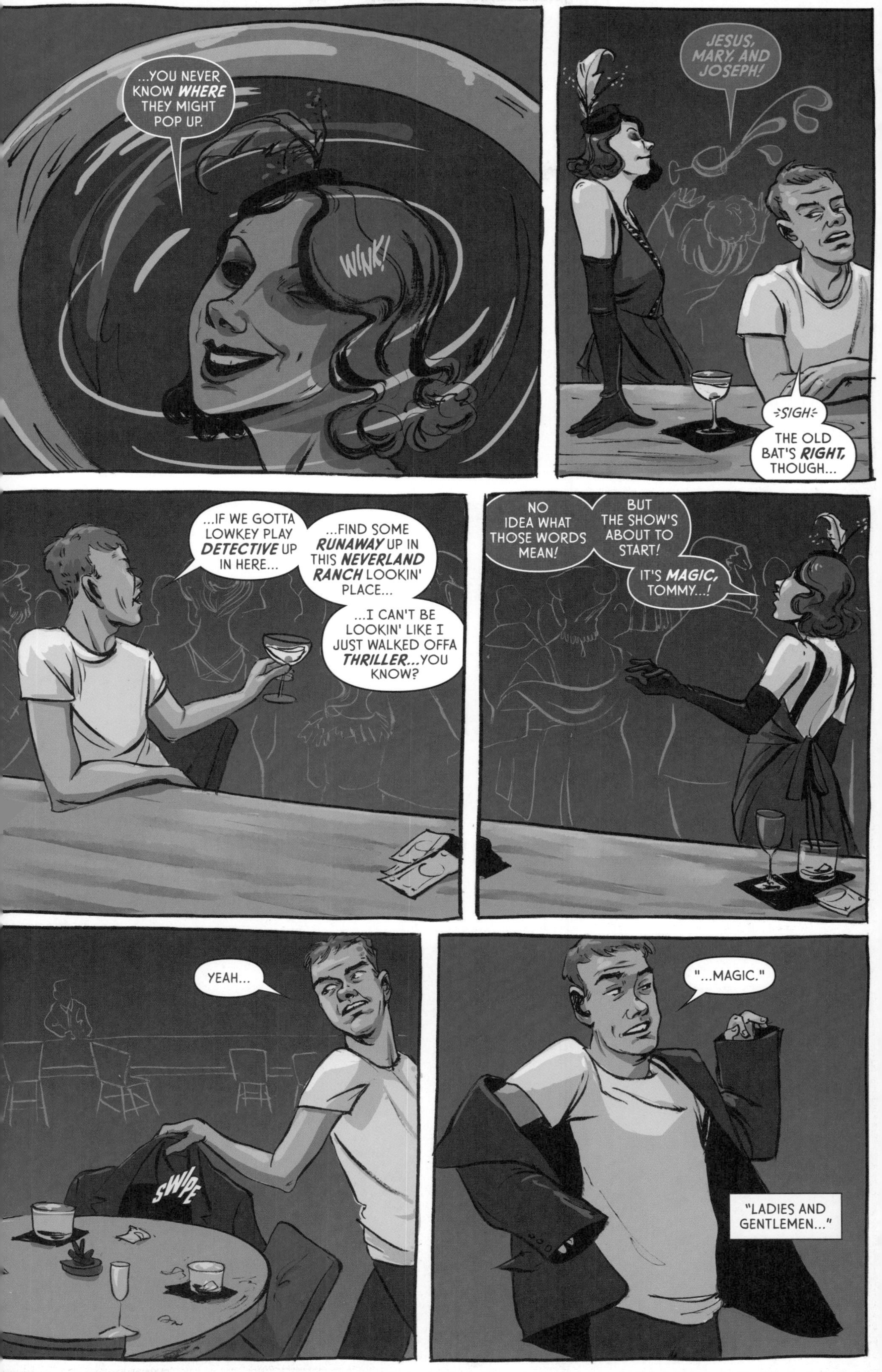
...YOU NEVER KNOW WHERE THEY MIGHT POP UP.
WINK!
JESUS, MARY, AND JOSEPH!
-SIGH-
THE OLD BAT'S RIGHT, THOUGH...
...IF WE GOTTA LOWKEY PLAY DETECTIVE UP IN HERE...
...FIND SOME RUNAWAY UP IN THIS NEVERLAND RANCH LOOKIN' PLACE...
...I CAN'T BE LOOKIN' LIKE I JUST WALKED OFFA THRILLER...YOU KNOW?
NO IDEA WHAT THOSE WORDS MEAN!
BUT THE SHOW'S ABOUT TO START!
IT'S MAGIC, TOMMY...!
YEAH...
SWIPE
"...MAGIC."
"LADIES AND GENTLEMEN..."

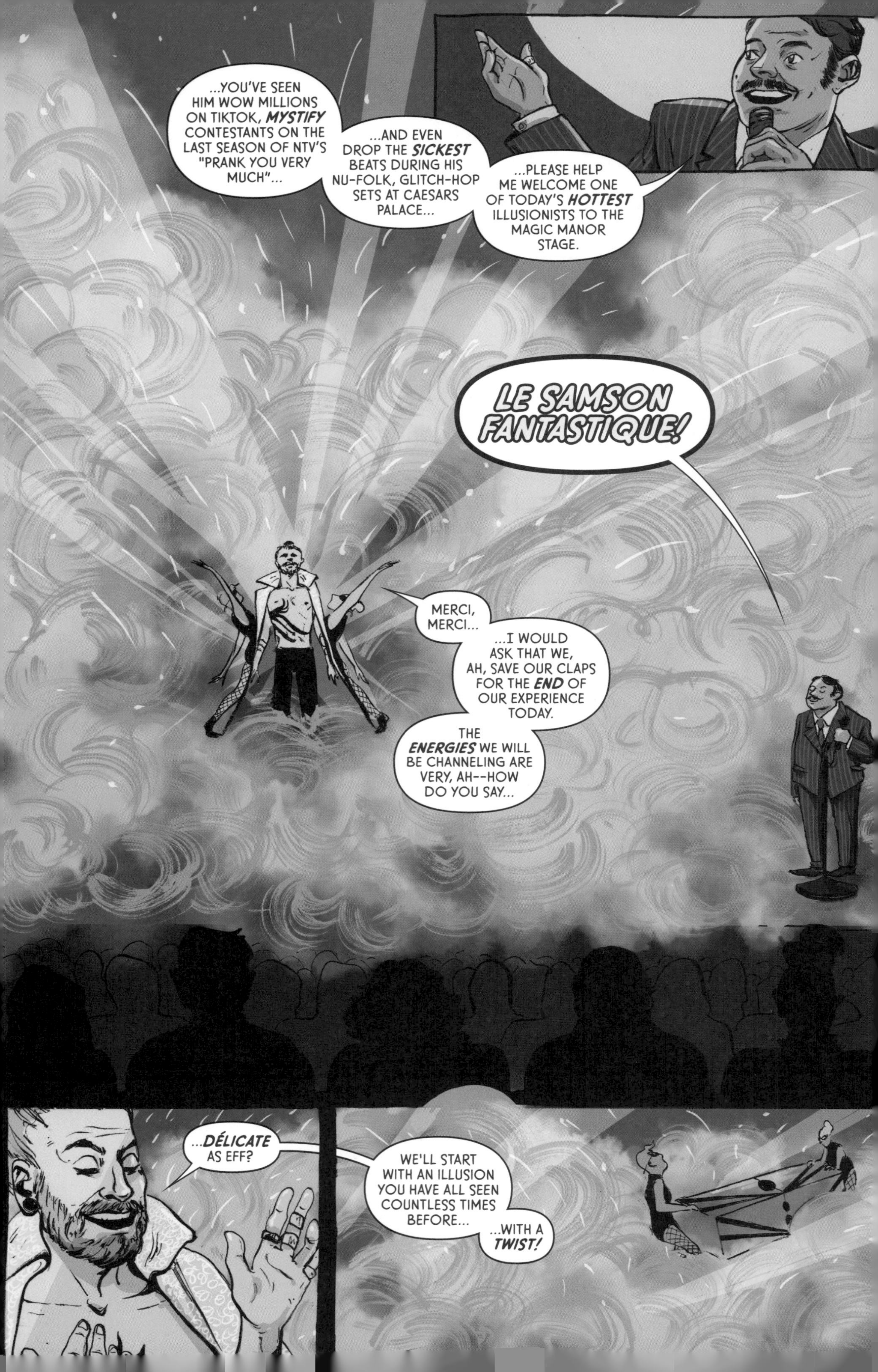
...YOU'VE SEEN HIM WOW MILLIONS ON TIKTOK, MYSTIFY CONTESTANTS ON THE LAST SEASON OF NTV'S "PRANK YOU VERY MUCH"...
...AND EVEN DROP THE SICKEST BEATS DURING HIS NU-FOLK, GLITCH-HOP SETS AT CAESARS PALACE...
...PLEASE HELP ME WELCOME ONE OF TODAY'S HOTTEST ILLUSIONISTS TO THE MAGIC MANOR STAGE.
LE SAMSON FANTASTIQUE!
MERCI, MERCI...
...I WOULD ASK THAT WE, AH, SAVE OUR CLAPS FOR THE END OF OUR EXPERIENCE TODAY.
THE ENERGIES WE WILL BE CHANNELING ARE VERY, AH--HOW DO YOU SAY...
...DÉLICATE AS EFF?
WE'LL START WITH AN ILLUSION YOU HAVE ALL SEEN COUNTLESS TIMES BEFORE...
...WITH A TWIST!

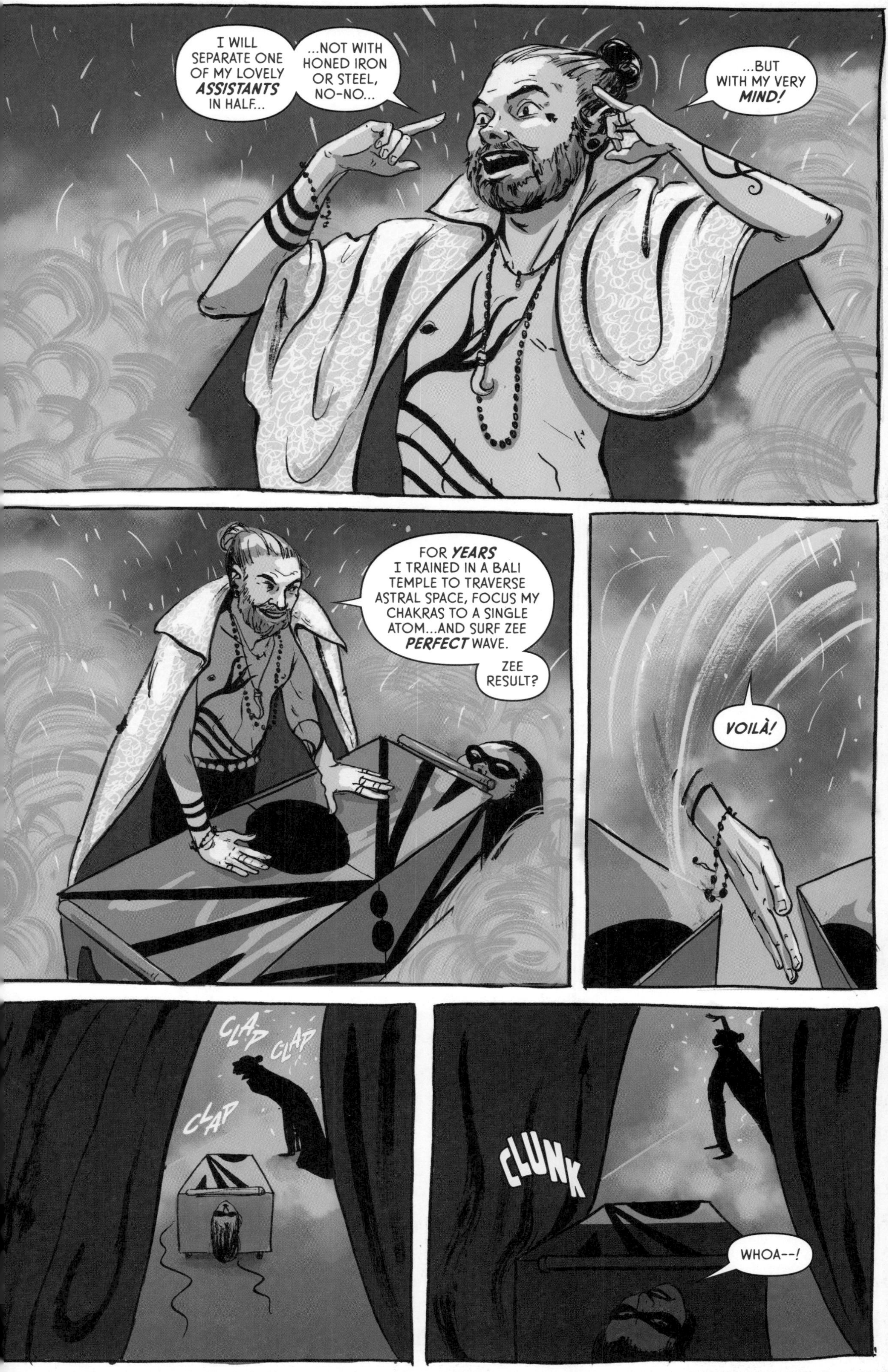
I WILL SEPARATE ONE OF MY LOVELY *ASSISTANTS* IN HALF...
...NOT WITH HONED IRON OR STEEL, NO-NO...
...BUT WITH MY VERY *MIND!*
FOR *YEARS* I TRAINED IN A BALI TEMPLE TO TRAVERSE ASTRAL SPACE, FOCUS MY CHAKRAS TO A SINGLE ATOM...AND SURF ZEE *PERFECT* WAVE.
ZEE RESULT?
VOILÀ!
CLAP CLAP
CLAP
CLUNK
WHOA--!

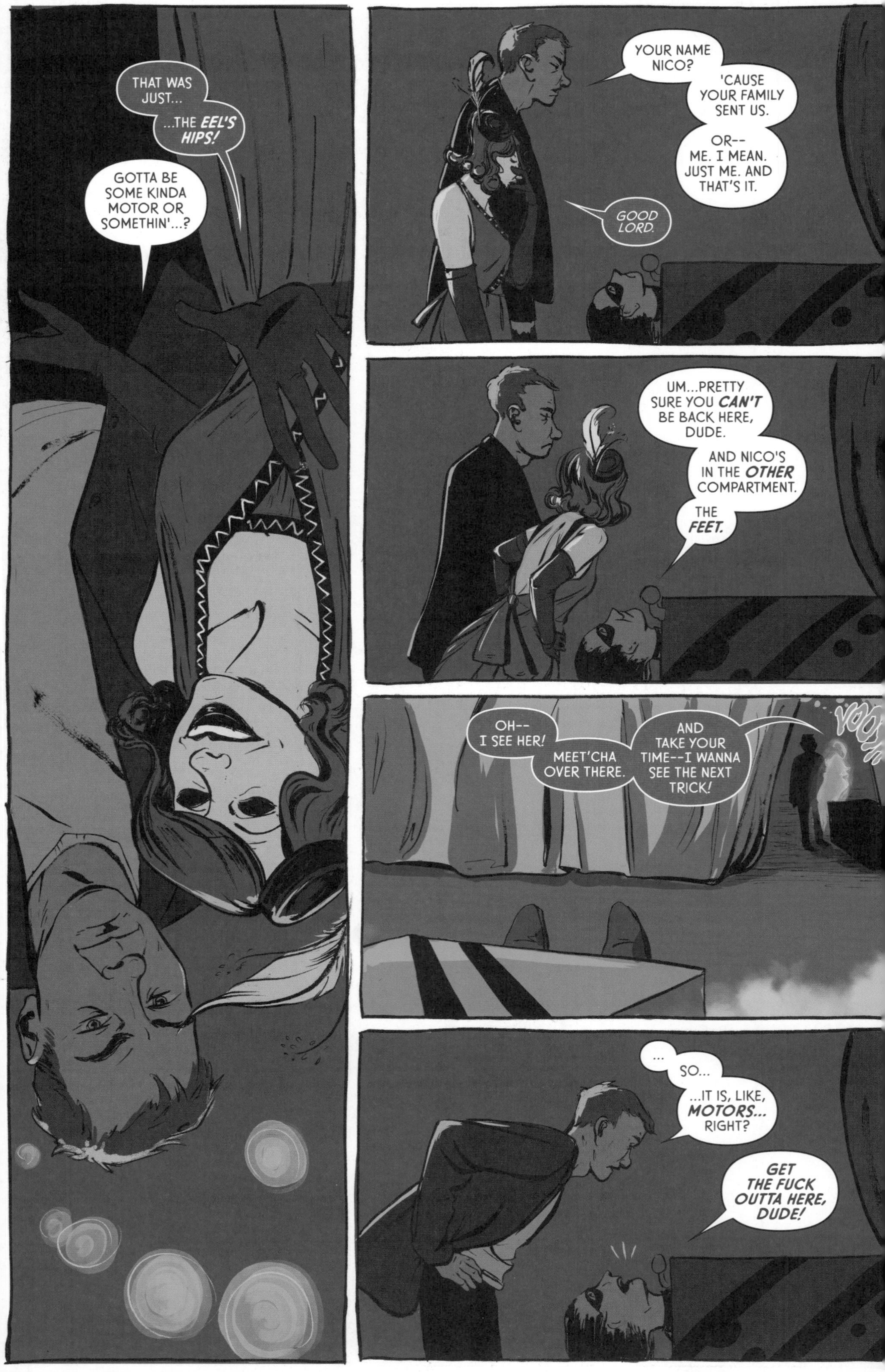
THAT WAS JUST...
...THE EEL'S HIPS!
GOTTA BE SOME KINDA MOTOR OR SOMETHIN'...?
YOUR NAME NICO?
'CAUSE YOUR FAMILY SENT US.
OR-- ME. I MEAN. JUST ME. AND THAT'S IT.
GOOD LORD.
UM...PRETTY SURE YOU CAN'T BE BACK HERE, DUDE.
AND NICO'S IN THE OTHER COMPARTMENT.
THE FEET.
OH-- I SEE HER!
MEET'CHA OVER THERE.
AND TAKE YOUR TIME--I WANNA SEE THE NEXT TRICK!
...
SO...
...IT IS, LIKE, MOTORS... RIGHT?
GET THE FUCK OUTTA HERE, DUDE!

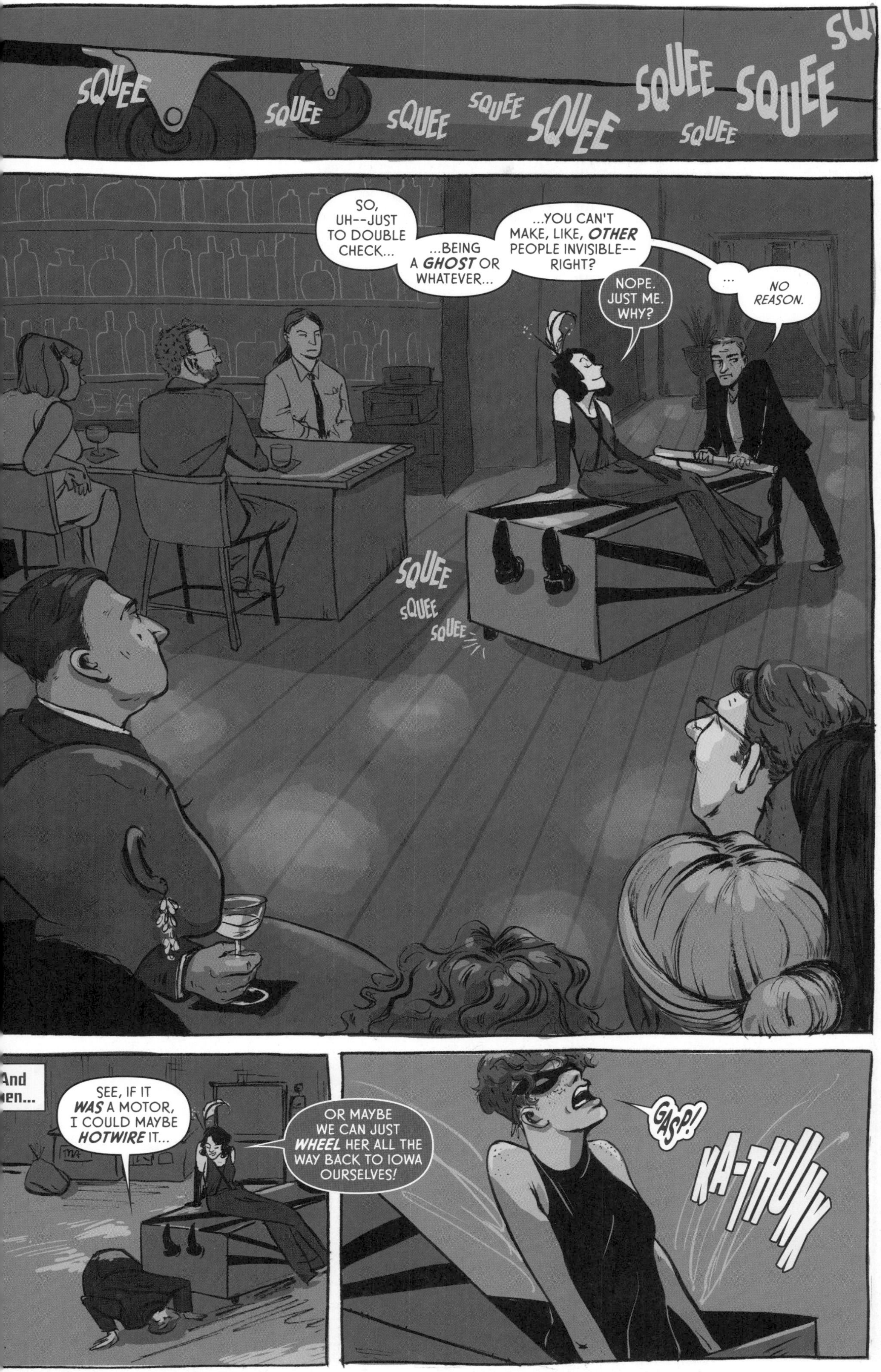
SQUEE
SQUEE
SQUEE
SQUEE
SQUEE
SQUEE
SQUEE
SQUEE
SO, UH--JUST TO DOUBLE CHECK...
...BEING A GHOST OR WHATEVER...
...YOU CAN'T MAKE, LIKE, OTHER PEOPLE INVISIBLE-- RIGHT?
NOPE. JUST ME. WHY?
...
NO REASON.
SQUEE
SQUEE
SQUEE
And then...
SEE, IF IT WAS A MOTOR, I COULD MAYBE HOTWIRE IT...
OR MAYBE WE CAN JUST WHEEL HER ALL THE WAY BACK TO IOWA OURSELVES!
GASP!
KA-THUNK

WHOA-- HEY!

NICO, RIGHT?

WHO-- WHO ARE YOU?

WAIT, *WHERE AM I?!*

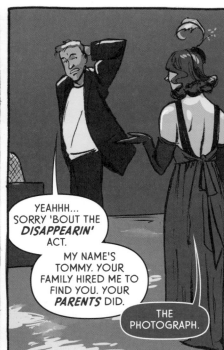

YEAHHH... SORRY 'BOUT THE *DISAPPEARIN'* ACT.

MY NAME'S TOMMY. YOUR FAMILY HIRED ME TO FIND YOU. YOUR *PARENTS* DID.

THE PHOTOGRAPH.

MY PARENTS...?

NO. THEY WOULDN'T DO THIS.

THEY *DISOWNED* ME. YEARS AGO.

YEAH, THEY DIDN'T REALLY SAY ANYTHING 'BOUT THAT.

JUST THAT, YANNO, THEY'RE SORRY...

...AND THEY *MISSED* YOU.

UMM...

...I DON'T LIKE THE LOOKS OF *THIS.*

WHAT THE--

whap!

--OW, SHIT.

YEAH, SO... MAYBE A CHANGE IN SCENERY WOULDN'T BE SUCH A *BAD* THING?

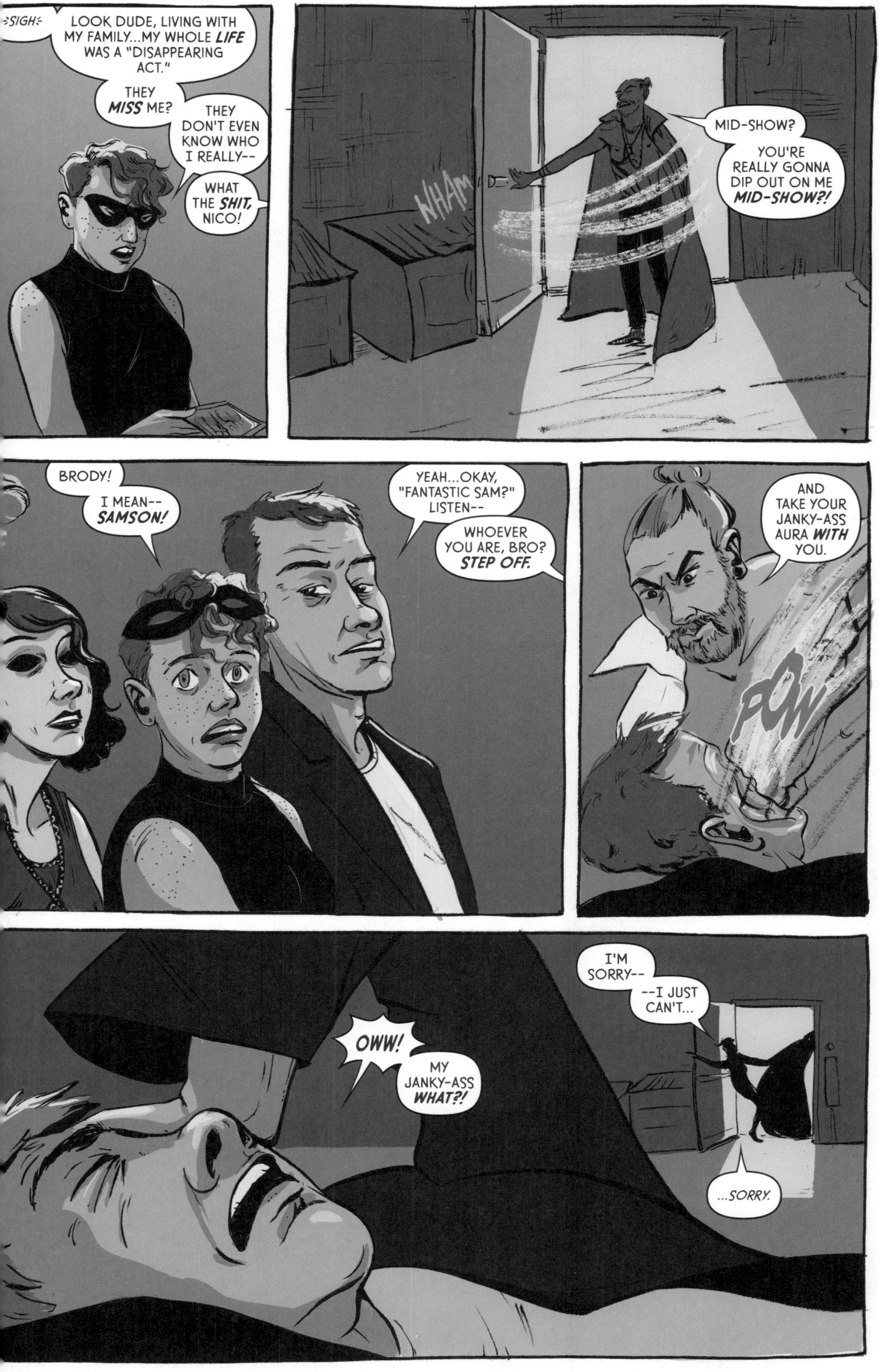

≈SIGH≈
LOOK DUDE, LIVING WITH MY FAMILY...MY WHOLE *LIFE* WAS A "DISAPPEARING ACT."
THEY *MISS* ME?
THEY DON'T EVEN KNOW WHO I REALLY--
WHAT THE *SHIT,* NICO!
WHAM
MID-SHOW?
YOU'RE REALLY GONNA DIP OUT ON ME *MID-SHOW?!*
BRODY!
I MEAN-- *SAMSON!*
YEAH...OKAY, "FANTASTIC SAM?" LISTEN--
WHOEVER YOU ARE, BRO? *STEP OFF.*
AND TAKE YOUR JANKY-ASS AURA *WITH* YOU.
POW
OWW!
MY JANKY-ASS *WHAT?!*
I'M SORRY--
--I JUST CAN'T...
...SORRY.

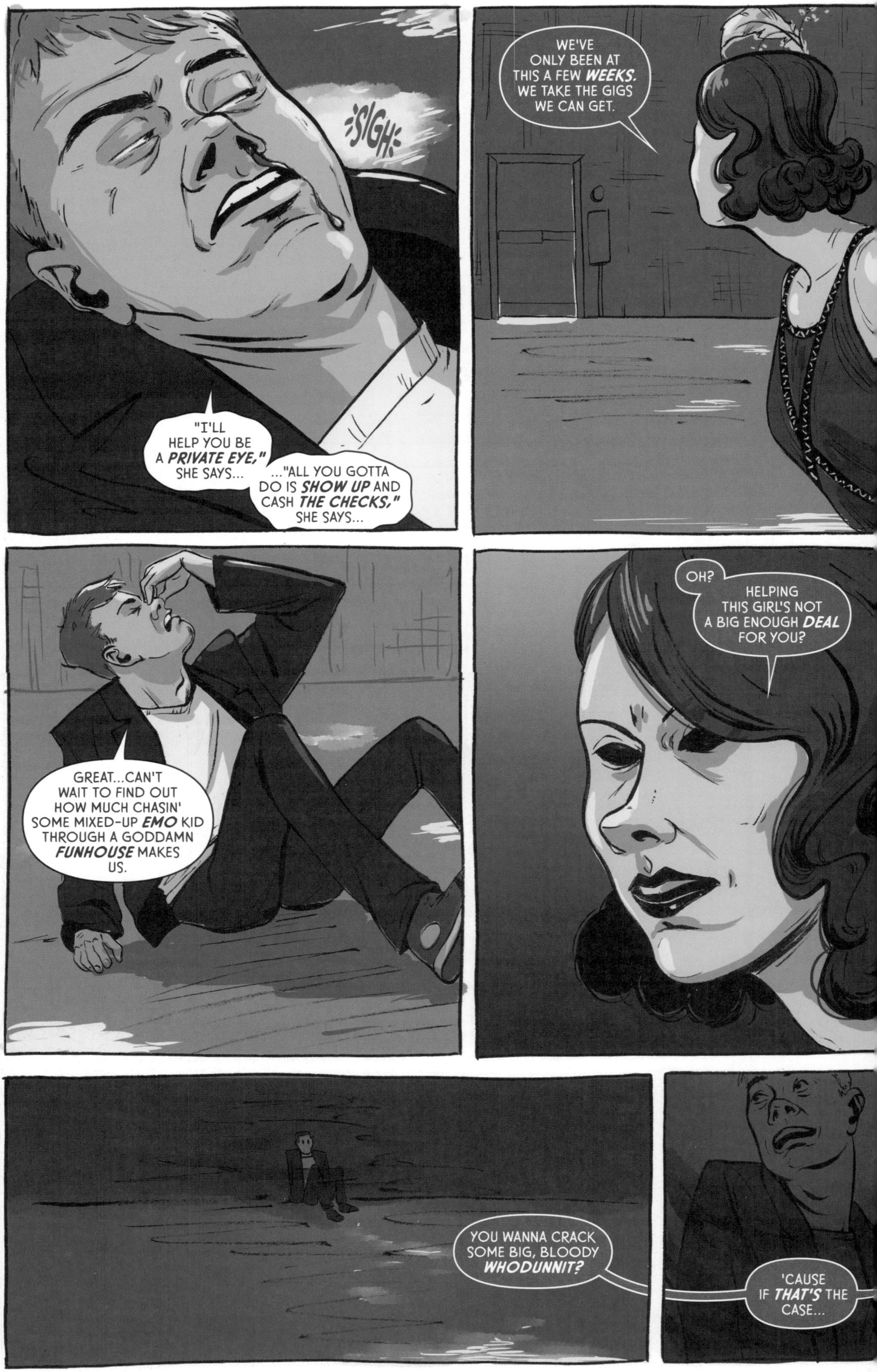
SIGH
"I'LL HELP YOU BE A PRIVATE EYE," SHE SAYS...
..."ALL YOU GOTTA DO IS SHOW UP AND CASH THE CHECKS," SHE SAYS...
WE'VE ONLY BEEN AT THIS A FEW WEEKS. WE TAKE THE GIGS WE CAN GET.
GREAT...CAN'T WAIT TO FIND OUT HOW MUCH CHASIN' SOME MIXED-UP EMO KID THROUGH A GODDAMN FUNHOUSE MAKES US.
OH?
HELPING THIS GIRL'S NOT A BIG ENOUGH DEAL FOR YOU?
YOU WANNA CRACK SOME BIG, BLOODY WHODUNNIT?
'CAUSE IF THAT'S THE CASE...

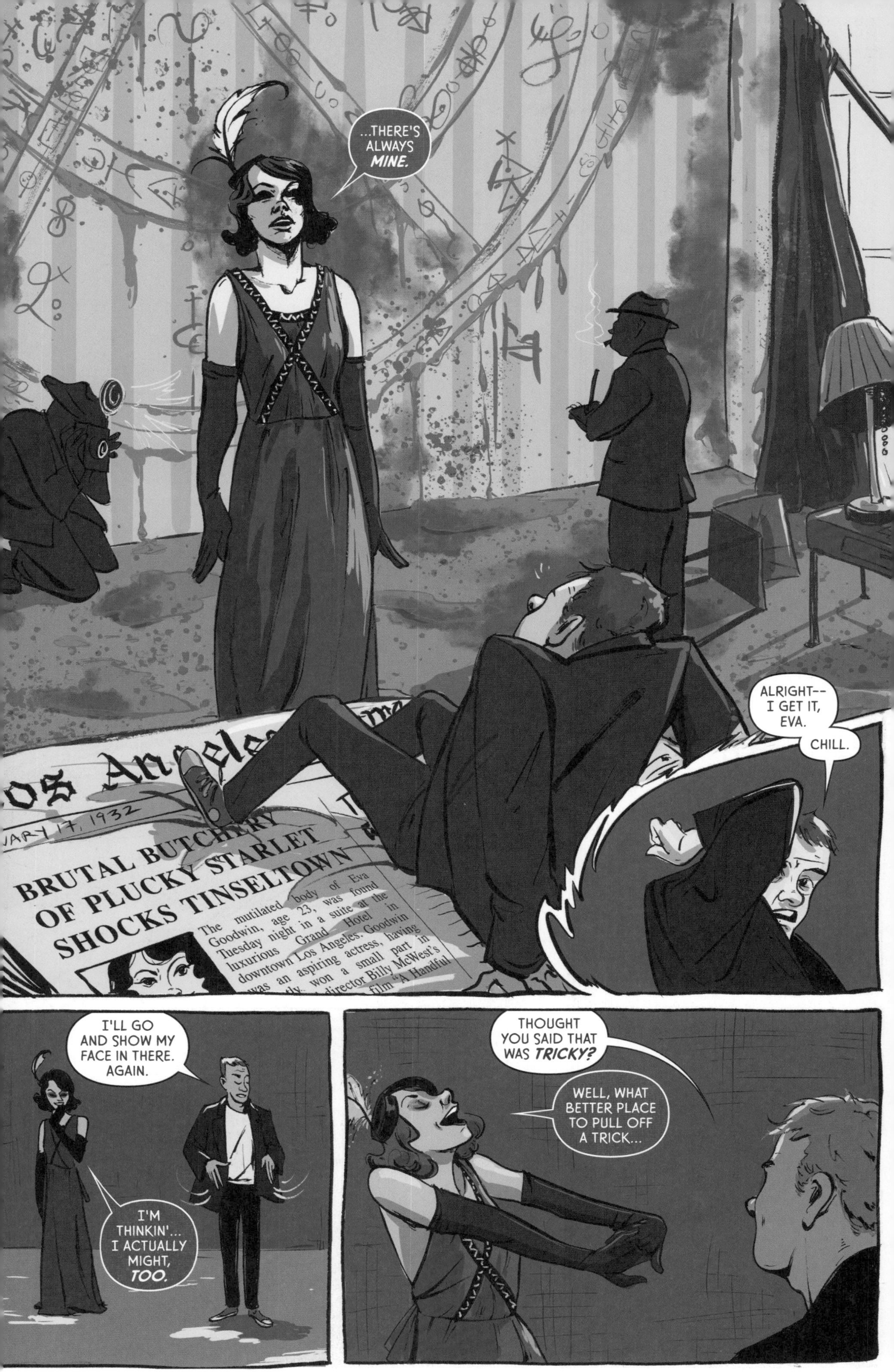

...THERE'S ALWAYS *MINE.*
ARY 17, 1932
BRUTAL BUTCHERY OF PLUCKY STARLET SHOCKS TINSELTOWN
The mutilated body of Eva Goodwin, age 23, was found Tuesday night in a suite at the luxurious Grand Hotel in downtown Los Angeles. Goodwin was an aspiring actress, having won a small part in director Billy McWest's film "A Handful
ALRIGHT-- I GET IT, EVA.
CHILL.
I'LL GO AND SHOW MY FACE IN THERE. AGAIN.
I'M THINKIN'... I ACTUALLY MIGHT, *TOO.*
THOUGHT YOU SAID THAT WAS *TRICKY?*
WELL, WHAT BETTER PLACE TO PULL OFF A TRICK...

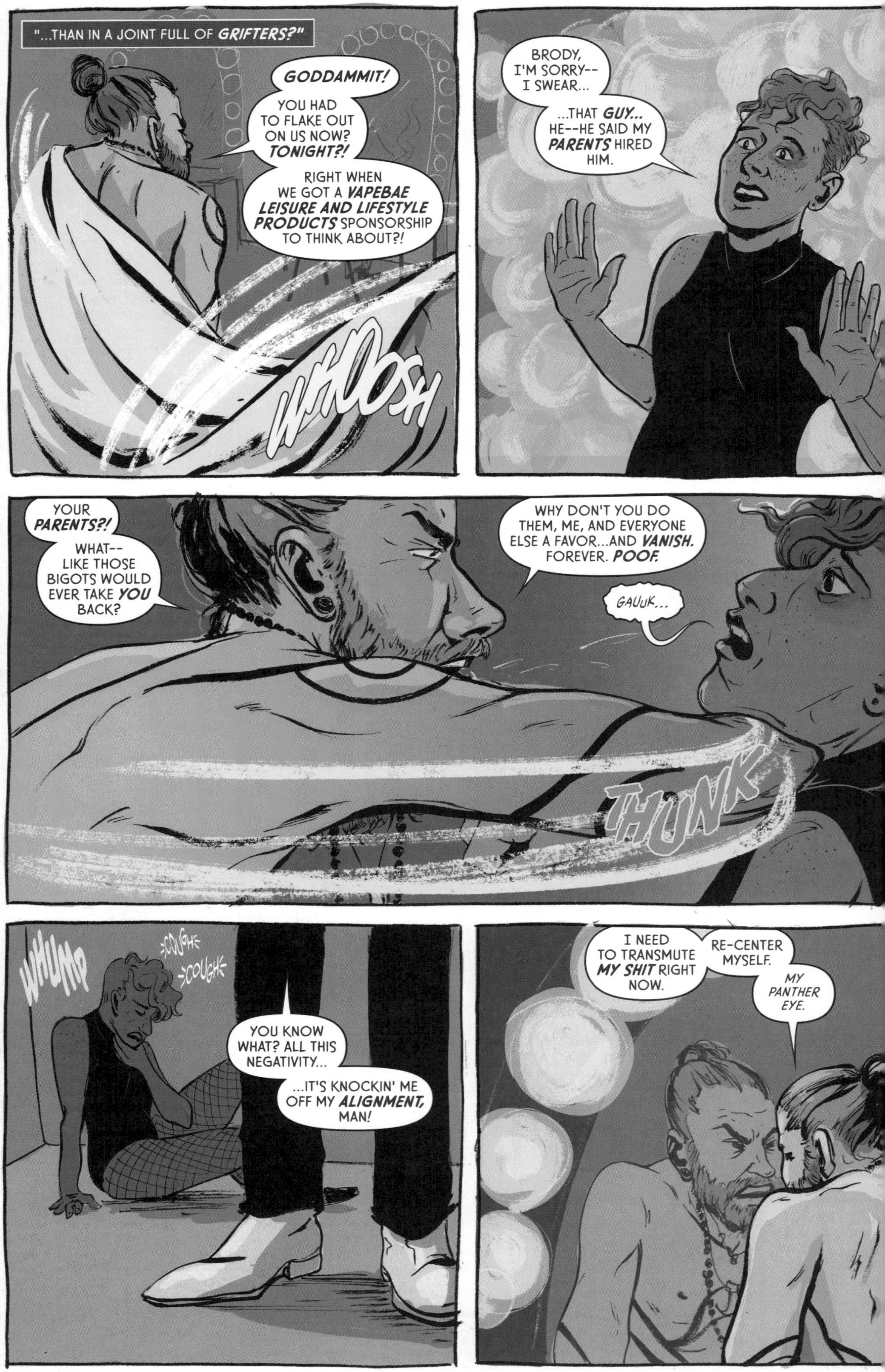
"...THAN IN A JOINT FULL OF GRIFTERS?"
GODDAMMIT!
YOU HAD TO FLAKE OUT ON US NOW? TONIGHT?!
RIGHT WHEN WE GOT A VAPEBAE LEISURE AND LIFESTYLE PRODUCTS SPONSORSHIP TO THINK ABOUT?!
WHOOSH
BRODY, I'M SORRY-- I SWEAR...
...THAT GUY... HE--HE SAID MY PARENTS HIRED HIM.
YOUR PARENTS?! WHAT-- LIKE THOSE BIGOTS WOULD EVER TAKE YOU BACK?
WHY DON'T YOU DO THEM, ME, AND EVERYONE ELSE A FAVOR...AND VANISH. FOREVER. POOF.
GAUUK...
THUNK
WHUMP
COUGH
COUGH
YOU KNOW WHAT? ALL THIS NEGATIVITY...
...IT'S KNOCKIN' ME OFF MY ALIGNMENT, MAN!
I NEED TO TRANSMUTE MY SHIT RIGHT NOW.
RE-CENTER MYSELF.
MY PANTHER EYE.

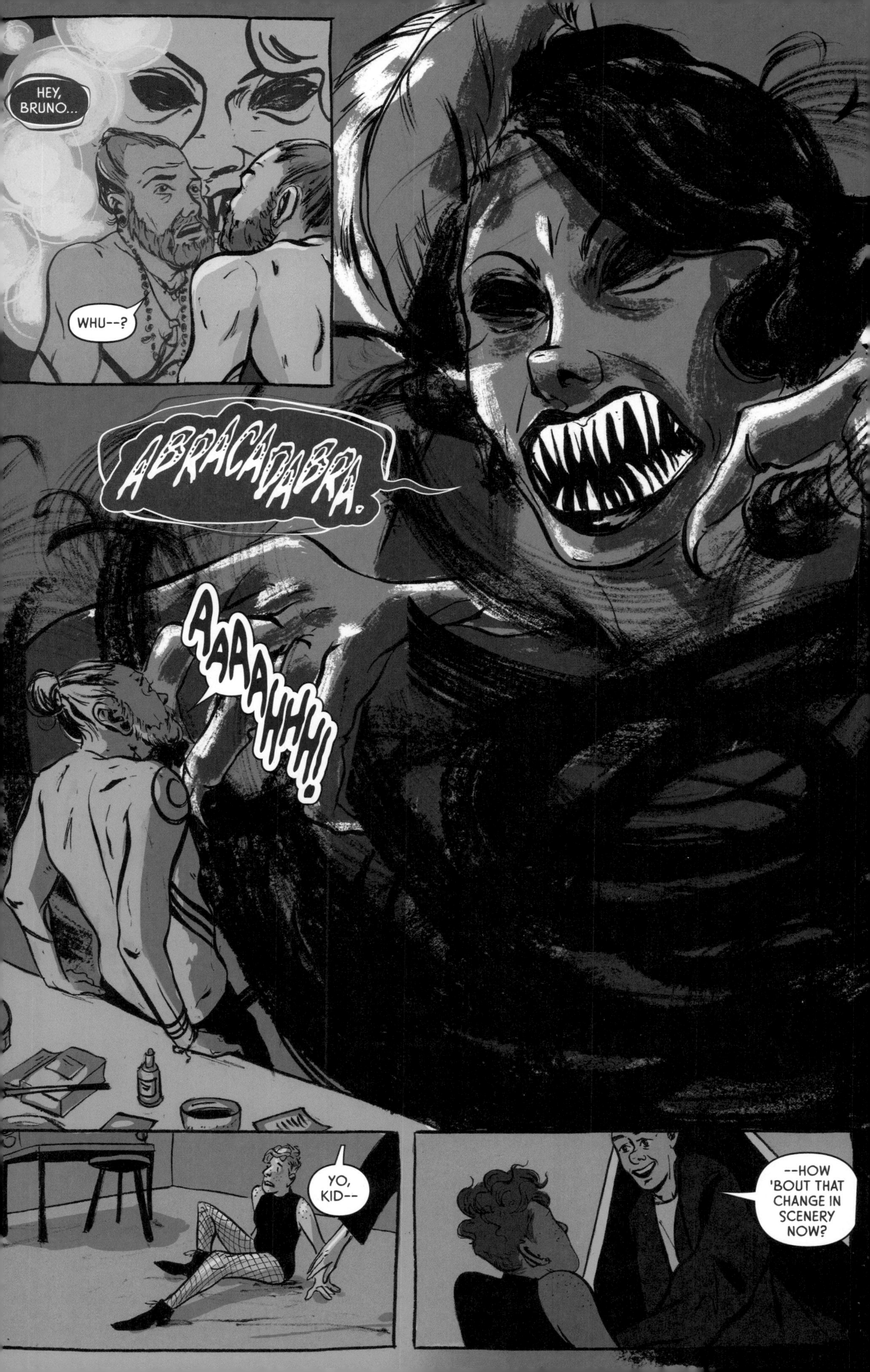
HEY, BRUNO...
WHU--?
ABRACADABRA.
AAAAHHH!
YO, KID--
--HOW 'BOUT THAT CHANGE IN SCENERY NOW?

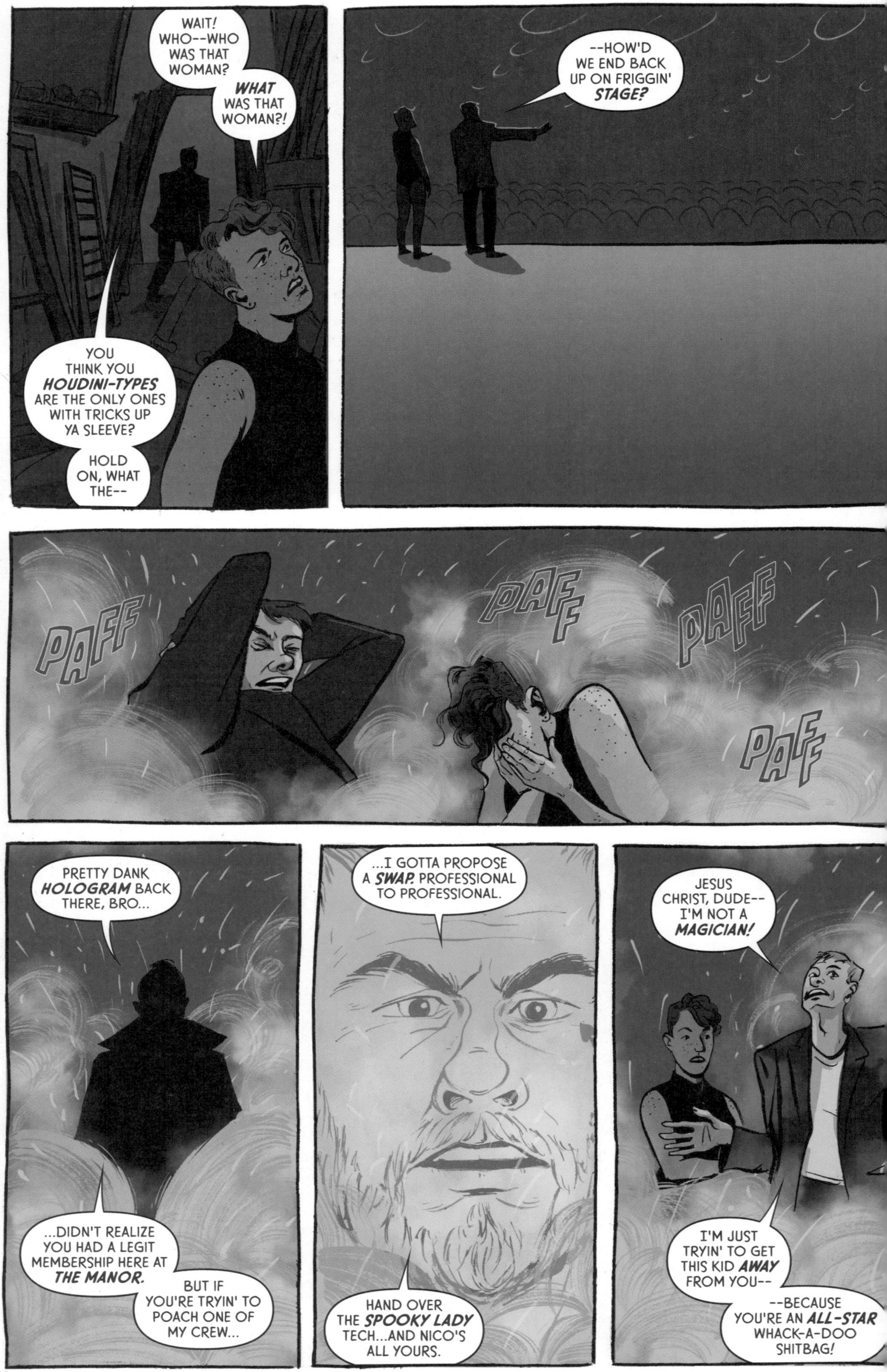
WAIT! WHO--WHO WAS THAT WOMAN?
WHAT WAS THAT WOMAN?!
YOU THINK YOU HOUDINI-TYPES ARE THE ONLY ONES WITH TRICKS UP YA SLEEVE?
HOLD ON, WHAT THE--
--HOW'D WE END BACK UP ON FRIGGIN' STAGE?
PAFF
PAFF
PAFF
PAFF
PRETTY DANK HOLOGRAM BACK THERE, BRO...
...DIDN'T REALIZE YOU HAD A LEGIT MEMBERSHIP HERE AT THE MANOR.
BUT IF YOU'RE TRYIN' TO POACH ONE OF MY CREW...
...I GOTTA PROPOSE A SWAP. PROFESSIONAL TO PROFESSIONAL.
HAND OVER THE SPOOKY LADY TECH...AND NICO'S ALL YOURS.
JESUS CHRIST, DUDE-- I'M NOT A MAGICIAN!
I'M JUST TRYIN' TO GET THIS KID AWAY FROM YOU--
--BECAUSE YOU'RE AN ALL-STAR WHACK-A-DOO SHITBAG!

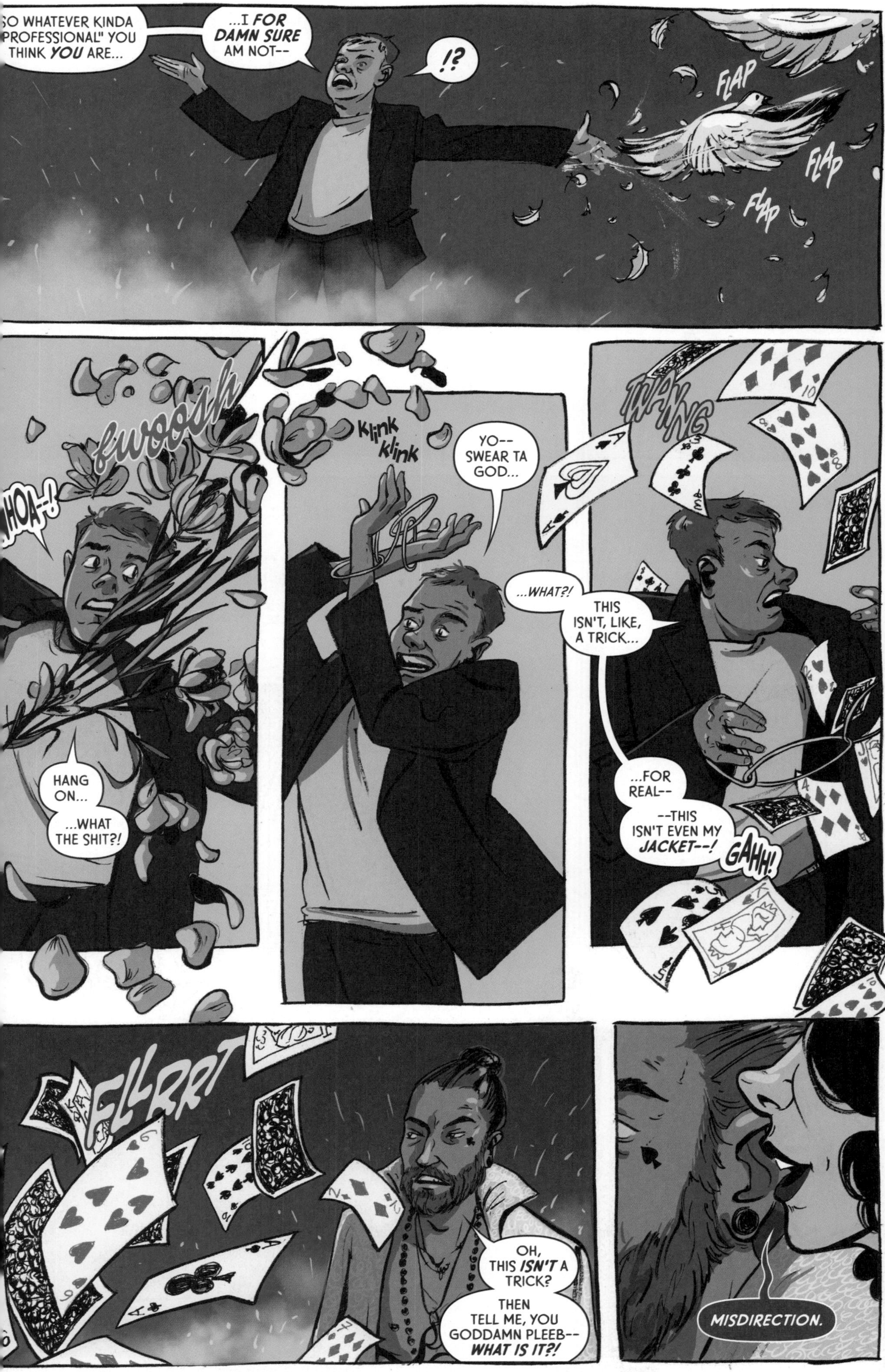
SO WHATEVER KINDA "PROFESSIONAL" YOU THINK *YOU* ARE...
...I ***FOR DAMN SURE*** AM NOT--
!?
FLAP
FLAP
FLAP
fwoosh
WHOA--!
HANG ON...
...WHAT THE SHIT?!
klink klink
YO-- SWEAR TA GOD...
TWANG
...*WHAT?!*
THIS ISN'T, LIKE, A TRICK...
...FOR REAL--
--THIS ISN'T EVEN MY ***JACKET--!***
GAHH!
FLLRRRT
OH, THIS ***ISN'T*** A TRICK?
THEN TELL ME, YOU GODDAMN PLEEB-- ***WHAT IS IT?!***
MISDIRECTION.

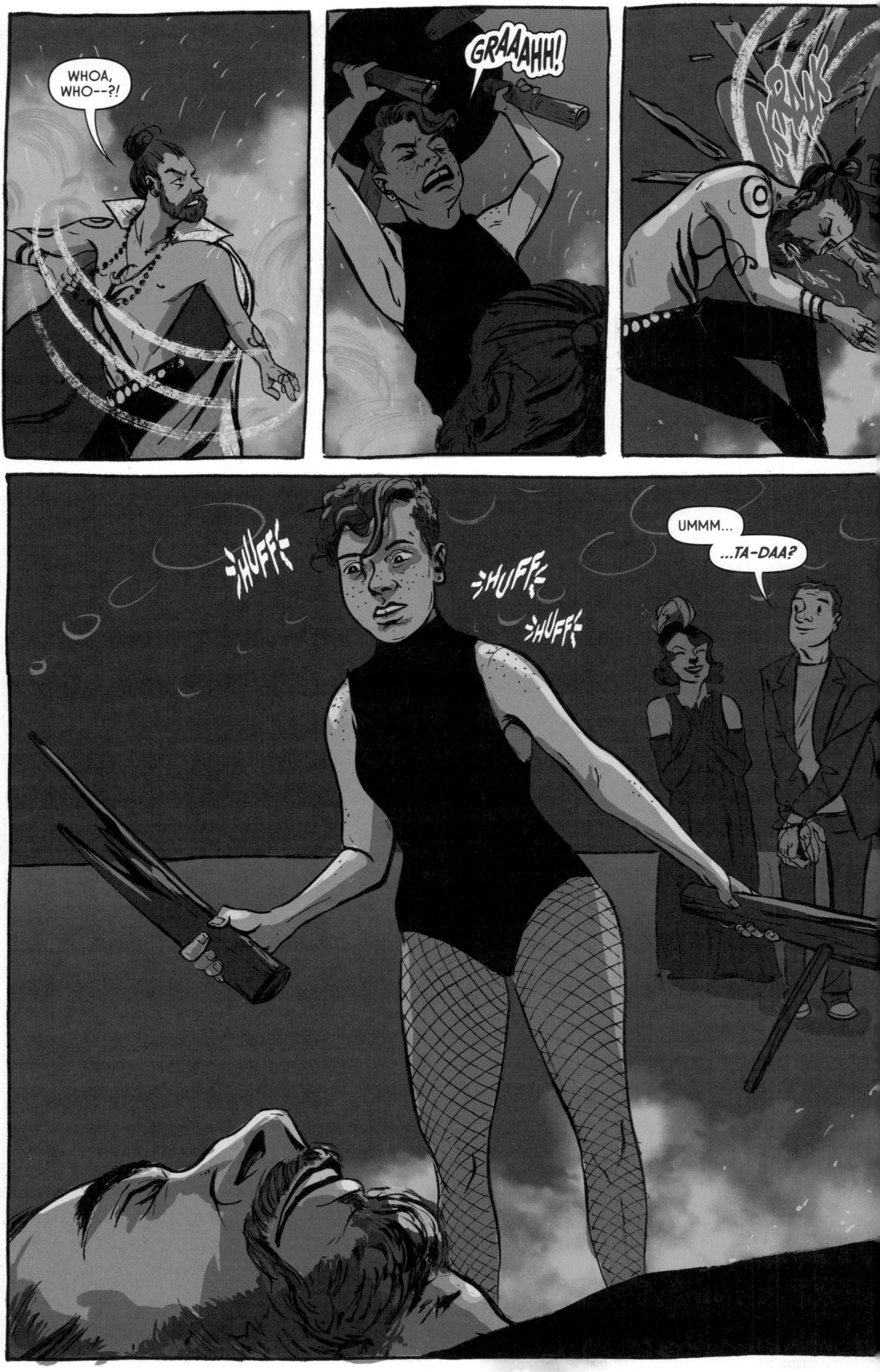
WHOA, WHO--?!
GRAAAHH!
KRAAK
HUFF
HUFF
HUFF
UMMM...
...TA-DAA?

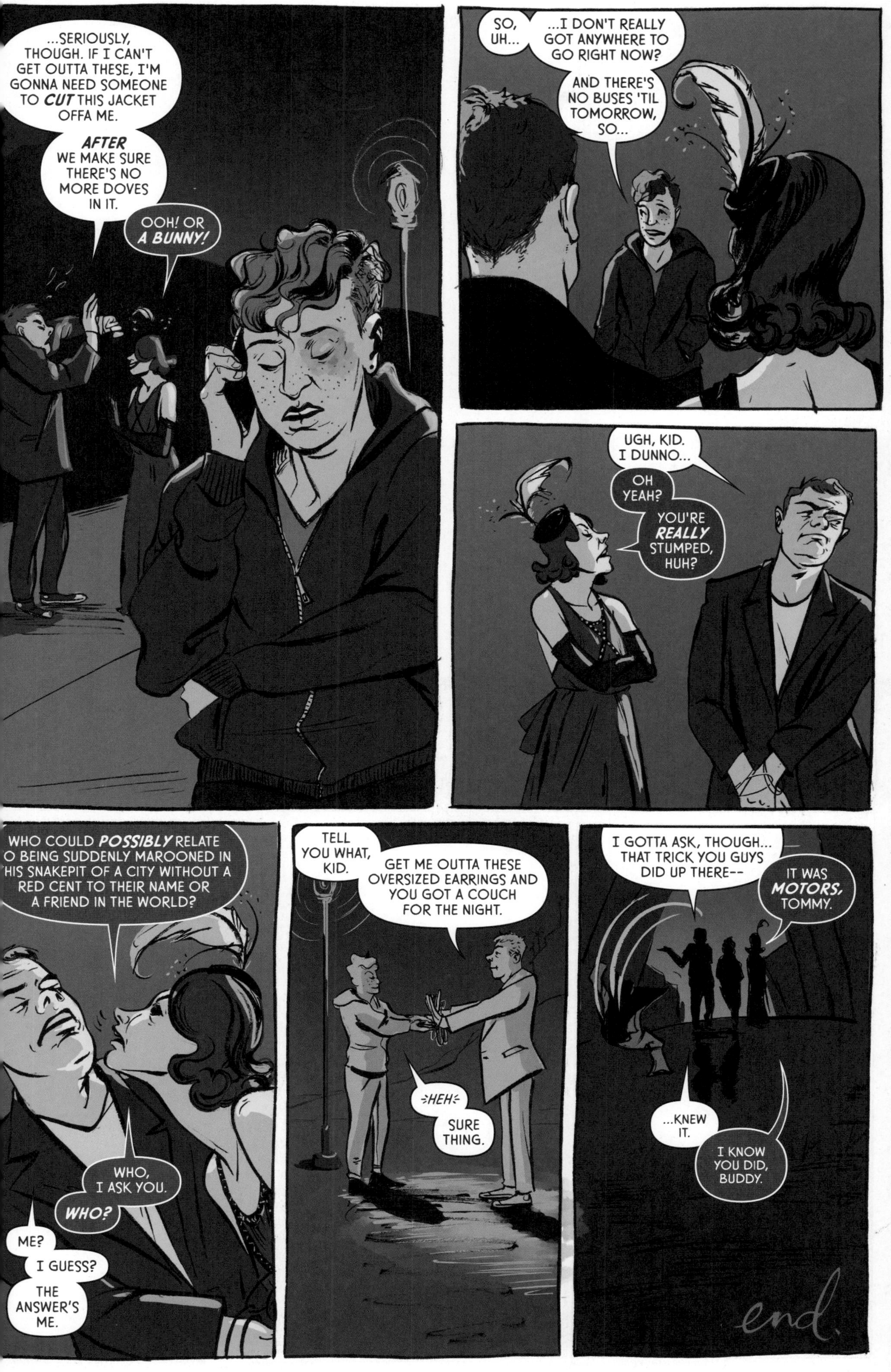
...SERIOUSLY, THOUGH. IF I CAN'T GET OUTTA THESE, I'M GONNA NEED SOMEONE TO CUT THIS JACKET OFFA ME.
AFTER WE MAKE SURE THERE'S NO MORE DOVES IN IT.
OOH! OR A BUNNY!
SO, UH...
...I DON'T REALLY GOT ANYWHERE TO GO RIGHT NOW?
AND THERE'S NO BUSES 'TIL TOMORROW, SO...
UGH, KID. I DUNNO...
OH YEAH?
YOU'RE REALLY STUMPED, HUH?
WHO COULD POSSIBLY RELATE O BEING SUDDENLY MAROONED IN HIS SNAKEPIT OF A CITY WITHOUT A RED CENT TO THEIR NAME OR A FRIEND IN THE WORLD?
WHO, I ASK YOU.
WHO?
ME?
I GUESS?
THE ANSWER'S ME.
TELL YOU WHAT, KID.
GET ME OUTTA THESE OVERSIZED EARRINGS AND YOU GOT A COUCH FOR THE NIGHT.
HEH
SURE THING.
I GOTTA ASK, THOUGH... THAT TRICK YOU GUYS DID UP THERE--
IT WAS MOTORS, TOMMY.
...KNEW IT.
I KNOW YOU DID, BUDDY.
end.

THE WALK

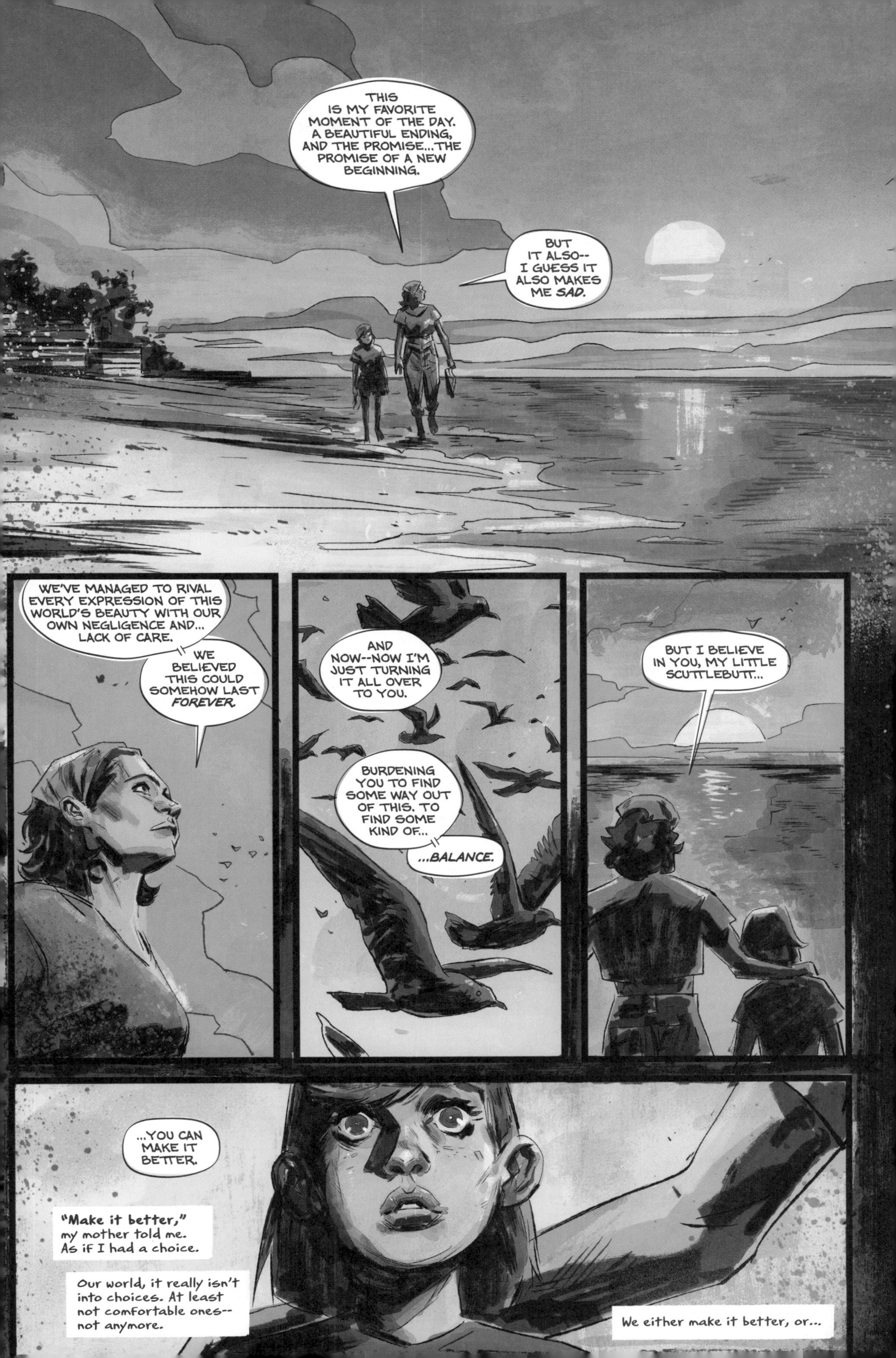
THIS IS MY FAVORITE MOMENT OF THE DAY. A BEAUTIFUL ENDING, AND THE PROMISE... THE PROMISE OF A NEW BEGINNING.
BUT IT ALSO-- I GUESS IT ALSO MAKES ME *SAD*.
WE'VE MANAGED TO RIVAL EVERY EXPRESSION OF THIS WORLD'S BEAUTY WITH OUR OWN NEGLIGENCE AND... LACK OF CARE.
WE BELIEVED THIS COULD SOMEHOW LAST *FOREVER*.
AND NOW--NOW I'M JUST TURNING IT ALL OVER TO YOU.
BURDENING YOU TO FIND SOME WAY OUT OF THIS. TO FIND SOME KIND OF...
...BALANCE.
BUT I BELIEVE IN YOU, MY LITTLE SCUTTLEBUTT...
...YOU CAN MAKE IT BETTER.
"Make it better," my mother told me. As if I had a choice.
Our world, it really isn't into choices. At least not comfortable ones-- not anymore.
We either make it better, or...

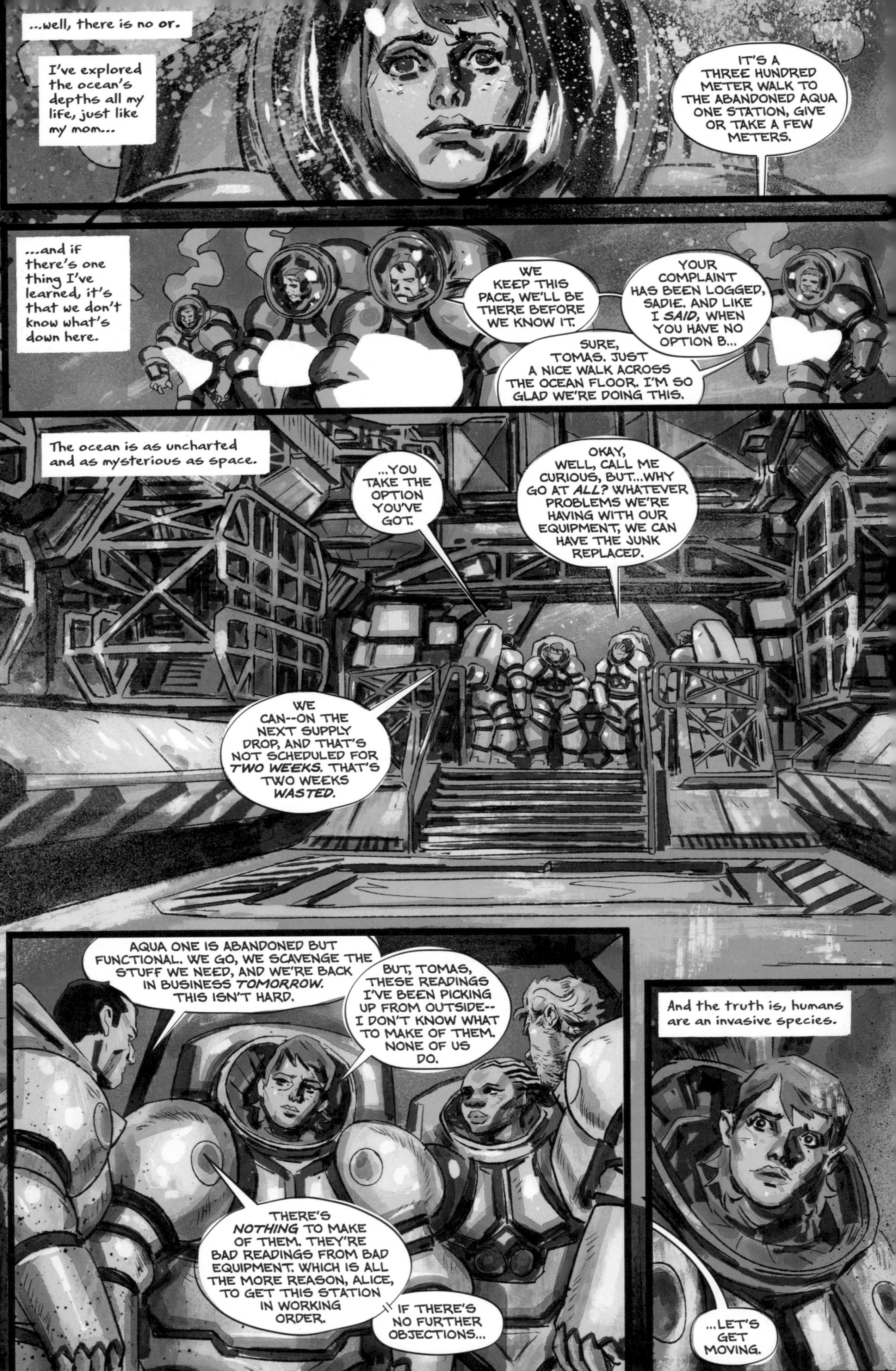
...well, there is no or.
I've explored the ocean's depths all my life, just like my mom...
IT'S A THREE HUNDRED METER WALK TO THE ABANDONED AQUA ONE STATION, GIVE OR TAKE A FEW METERS.
...and if there's one thing I've learned, it's that we don't know what's down here.
WE KEEP THIS PACE, WE'LL BE THERE BEFORE WE KNOW IT.
SURE, TOMAS. JUST A NICE WALK ACROSS THE OCEAN FLOOR. I'M SO GLAD WE'RE DOING THIS.
YOUR COMPLAINT HAS BEEN LOGGED, SADIE. AND LIKE I SAID, WHEN YOU HAVE NO OPTION B...
The ocean is as uncharted and as mysterious as space.
...YOU TAKE THE OPTION YOU'VE GOT.
OKAY, WELL, CALL ME CURIOUS, BUT...WHY GO AT ALL? WHATEVER PROBLEMS WE'RE HAVING WITH OUR EQUIPMENT, WE CAN HAVE THE JUNK REPLACED.
WE CAN--ON THE NEXT SUPPLY DROP, AND THAT'S NOT SCHEDULED FOR TWO WEEKS. THAT'S TWO WEEKS WASTED.
AQUA ONE IS ABANDONED BUT FUNCTIONAL. WE GO, WE SCAVENGE THE STUFF WE NEED, AND WE'RE BACK IN BUSINESS TOMORROW. THIS ISN'T HARD.
BUT, TOMAS, THESE READINGS I'VE BEEN PICKING UP FROM OUTSIDE-- I DON'T KNOW WHAT TO MAKE OF THEM. NONE OF US DO.
THERE'S NOTHING TO MAKE OF THEM. THEY'RE BAD READINGS FROM BAD EQUIPMENT. WHICH IS ALL THE MORE REASON, ALICE, TO GET THIS STATION IN WORKING ORDER.
IF THERE'S NO FURTHER OBJECTIONS...
And the truth is, humans are an invasive species.
...LET'S GET MOVING.

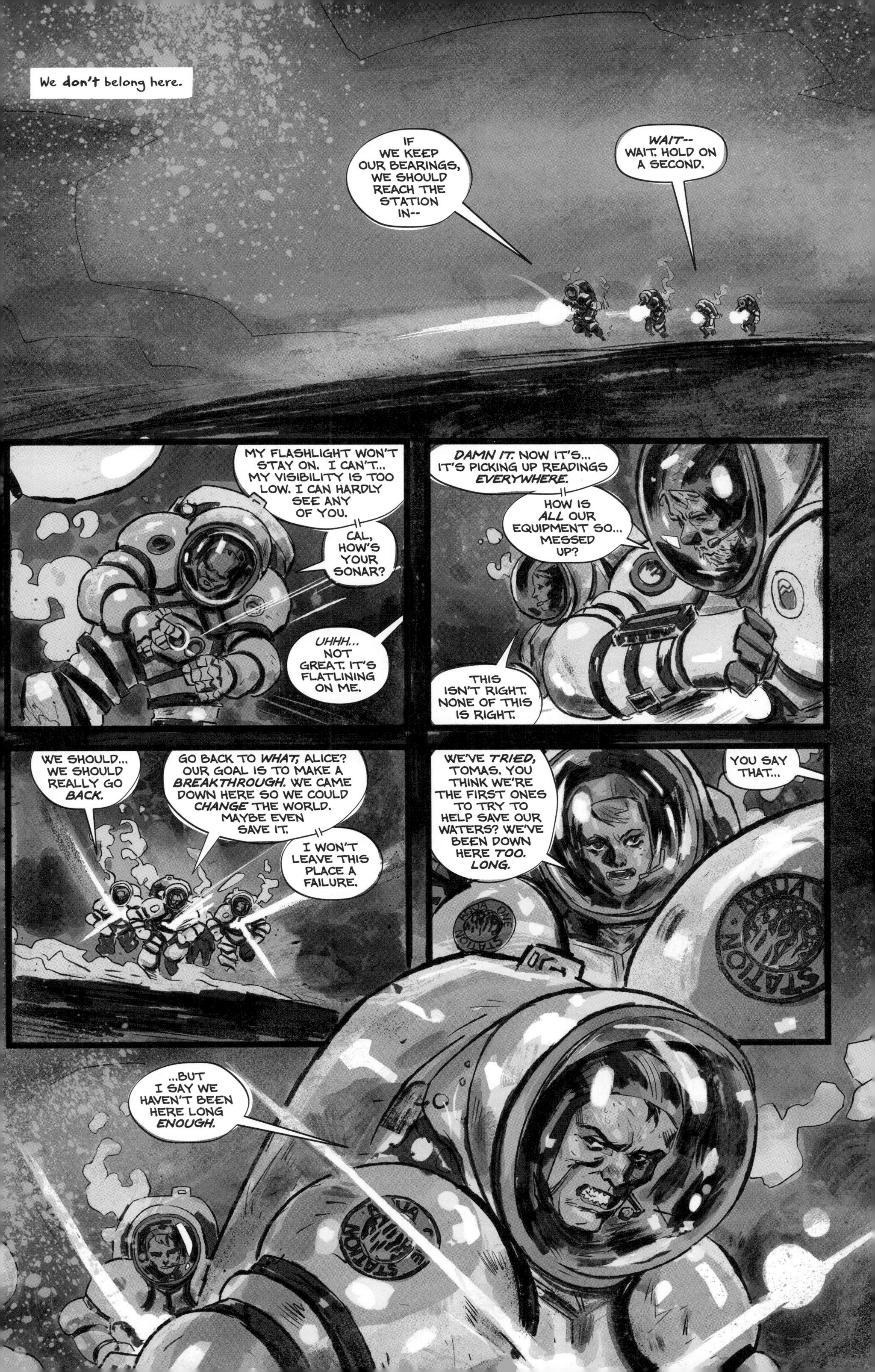
We don't belong here.
IF WE KEEP OUR BEARINGS, WE SHOULD REACH THE STATION IN--
WAIT-- WAIT. HOLD ON A SECOND.
MY FLASHLIGHT WON'T STAY ON. I CAN'T... MY VISIBILITY IS TOO LOW. I CAN HARDLY SEE ANY OF YOU.
CAL, HOW'S YOUR SONAR?
UHHH... NOT GREAT. IT'S FLATLINING ON ME.
DAMN IT. NOW IT'S... IT'S PICKING UP READINGS EVERYWHERE.
HOW IS ALL OUR EQUIPMENT SO... MESSED UP?
THIS ISN'T RIGHT. NONE OF THIS IS RIGHT.
WE SHOULD... WE SHOULD REALLY GO BACK.
GO BACK TO WHAT, ALICE? OUR GOAL IS TO MAKE A BREAKTHROUGH. WE CAME DOWN HERE SO WE COULD CHANGE THE WORLD. MAYBE EVEN SAVE IT.
I WON'T LEAVE THIS PLACE A FAILURE.
WE'VE TRIED, TOMAS. YOU THINK WE'RE THE FIRST ONES TO TRY TO HELP SAVE OUR WATERS? WE'VE BEEN DOWN HERE TOO. LONG.
YOU SAY THAT...
...BUT I SAY WE HAVEN'T BEEN HERE LONG ENOUGH.
AQUA ONE STATION

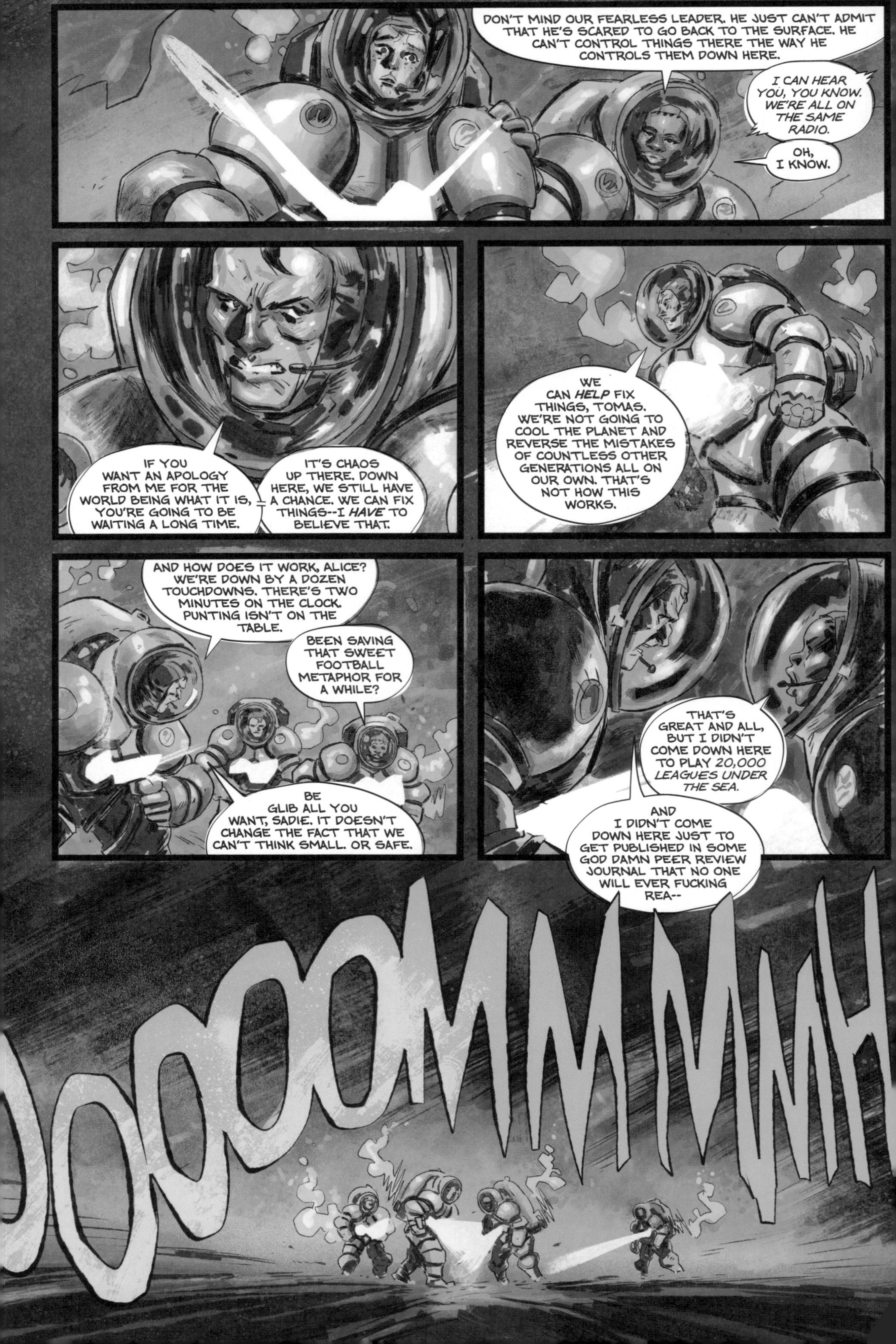
DON'T MIND OUR FEARLESS LEADER. HE JUST CAN'T ADMIT THAT HE'S SCARED TO GO BACK TO THE SURFACE. HE CAN'T CONTROL THINGS THERE THE WAY HE CONTROLS THEM DOWN HERE.
I CAN HEAR YOU, YOU KNOW. WE'RE ALL ON THE SAME RADIO.
OH, I KNOW.
IF YOU WANT AN APOLOGY FROM ME FOR THE WORLD BEING WHAT IT IS, YOU'RE GOING TO BE WAITING A LONG TIME.
IT'S CHAOS UP THERE. DOWN HERE, WE STILL HAVE A CHANCE. WE CAN FIX THINGS--I *HAVE* TO BELIEVE THAT.
WE CAN *HELP* FIX THINGS, TOMAS. WE'RE NOT GOING TO COOL THE PLANET AND REVERSE THE MISTAKES OF COUNTLESS OTHER GENERATIONS ALL ON OUR OWN. THAT'S NOT HOW THIS WORKS.
AND HOW DOES IT WORK, ALICE? WE'RE DOWN BY A DOZEN TOUCHDOWNS. THERE'S TWO MINUTES ON THE CLOCK. PUNTING ISN'T ON THE TABLE.
BEEN SAVING THAT SWEET FOOTBALL METAPHOR FOR A WHILE?
BE GLIB ALL YOU WANT, SADIE. IT DOESN'T CHANGE THE FACT THAT WE CAN'T THINK SMALL. OR SAFE.
THAT'S GREAT AND ALL, BUT I DIDN'T COME DOWN HERE TO PLAY *20,000 LEAGUES UNDER THE SEA.*
AND I DIDN'T COME DOWN HERE JUST TO GET PUBLISHED IN SOME GOD DAMN PEER REVIEW JOURNAL THAT NO ONE WILL EVER FUCKING REA--
OOOOOMMMMMH

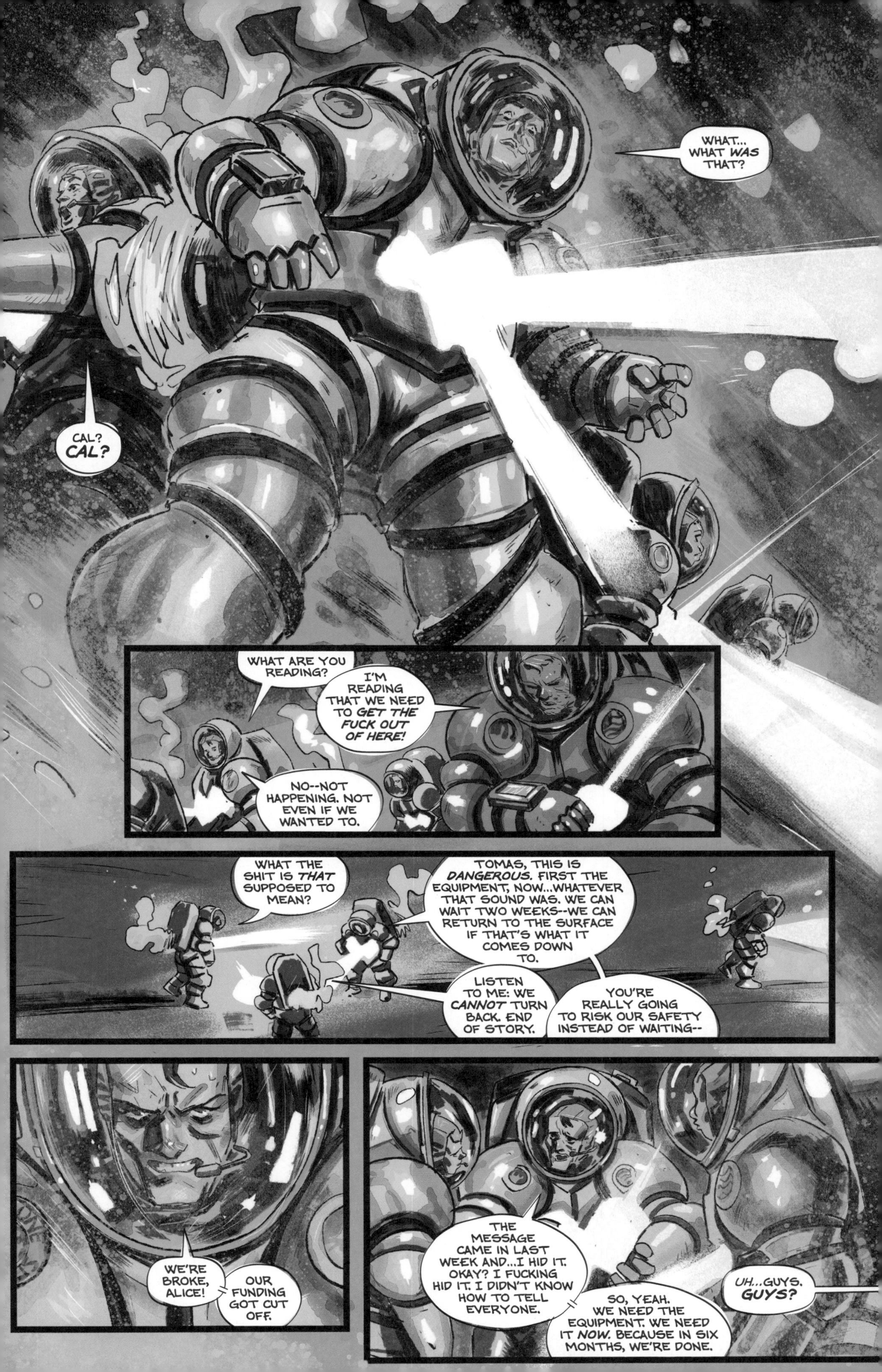
WHAT... WHAT *WAS* THAT?
CAL? **CAL?**
WHAT ARE YOU READING?
I'M READING THAT WE NEED TO *GET THE FUCK OUT OF HERE!*
NO--NOT HAPPENING. NOT EVEN IF WE WANTED TO.
WHAT THE SHIT IS *THAT* SUPPOSED TO MEAN?
TOMAS, THIS IS *DANGEROUS.* FIRST THE EQUIPMENT, NOW...WHATEVER THAT SOUND WAS. WE CAN WAIT TWO WEEKS--WE CAN RETURN TO THE SURFACE IF THAT'S WHAT IT COMES DOWN TO.
LISTEN TO ME: WE *CANNOT* TURN BACK. END OF STORY.
YOU'RE REALLY GOING TO RISK OUR SAFETY INSTEAD OF WAITING--
WE'RE BROKE, ALICE!
OUR FUNDING GOT CUT OFF.
THE MESSAGE CAME IN LAST WEEK AND...I HID IT. OKAY? I FUCKING HID IT. I DIDN'T KNOW HOW TO TELL EVERYONE.
SO, YEAH. WE NEED THE EQUIPMENT. WE NEED IT *NOW.* BECAUSE IN SIX MONTHS, WE'RE DONE.
UH...GUYS. ***GUYS?***

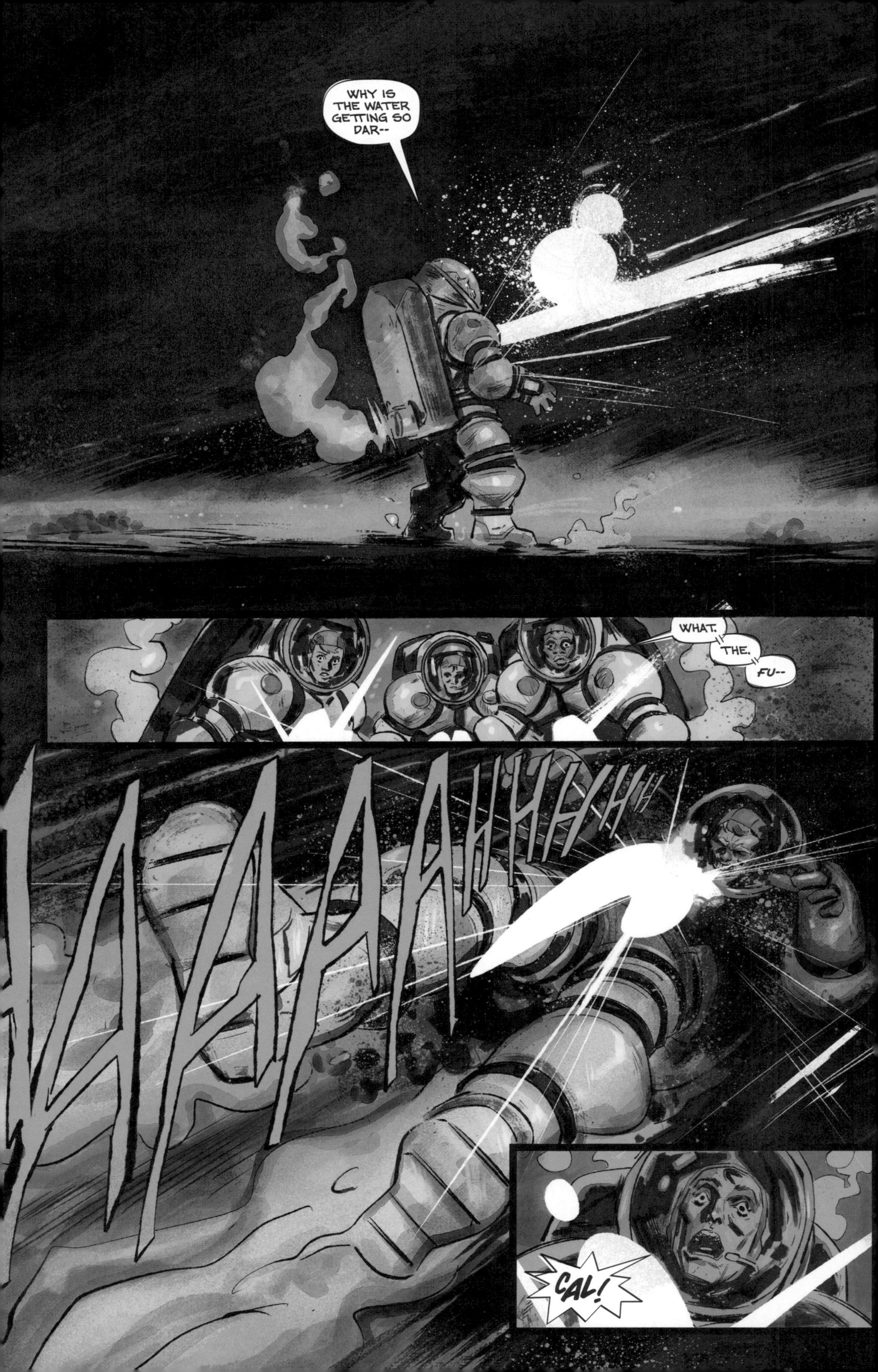
WHY IS THE WATER GETTING SO DAR--
WHAT.
THE.
FU--
WAAAAAHHHHH
CAL!

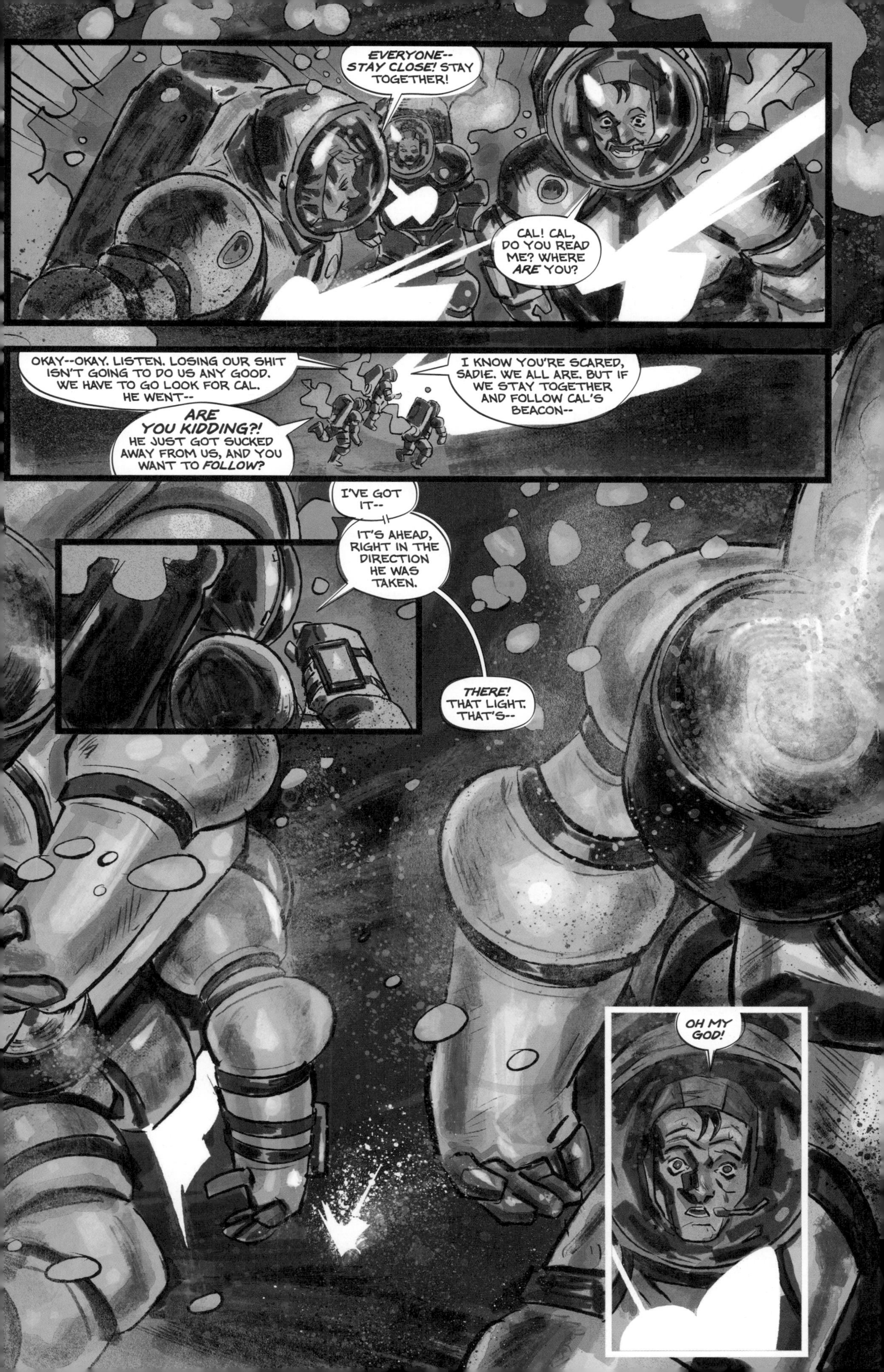
EVERYONE--
STAY CLOSE! STAY TOGETHER!
CAL! CAL, DO YOU READ ME? WHERE ARE YOU?
OKAY--OKAY. LISTEN. LOSING OUR SHIT ISN'T GOING TO DO US ANY GOOD. WE HAVE TO GO LOOK FOR CAL. HE WENT--
ARE YOU KIDDING?! HE JUST GOT SUCKED AWAY FROM US, AND YOU WANT TO FOLLOW?
I KNOW YOU'RE SCARED, SADIE. WE ALL ARE. BUT IF WE STAY TOGETHER AND FOLLOW CAL'S BEACON--
I'VE GOT IT--
IT'S AHEAD, RIGHT IN THE DIRECTION HE WAS TAKEN.
THERE! THAT LIGHT. THAT'S--
OH MY GOD!

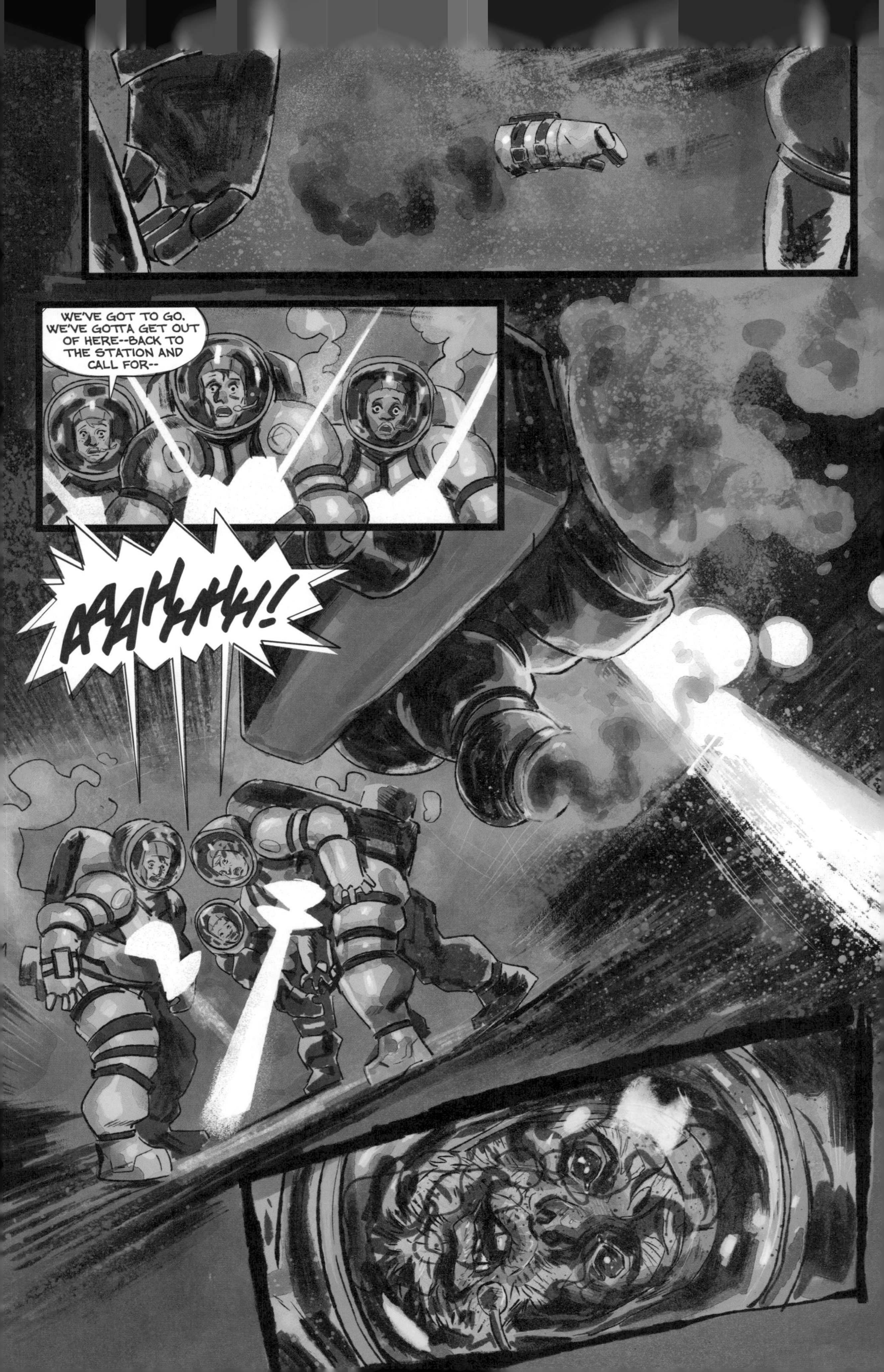
WE'VE GOT TO GO. WE'VE GOTTA GET OUT OF HERE--BACK TO THE STATION AND CALL FOR--
AAAHHHH!

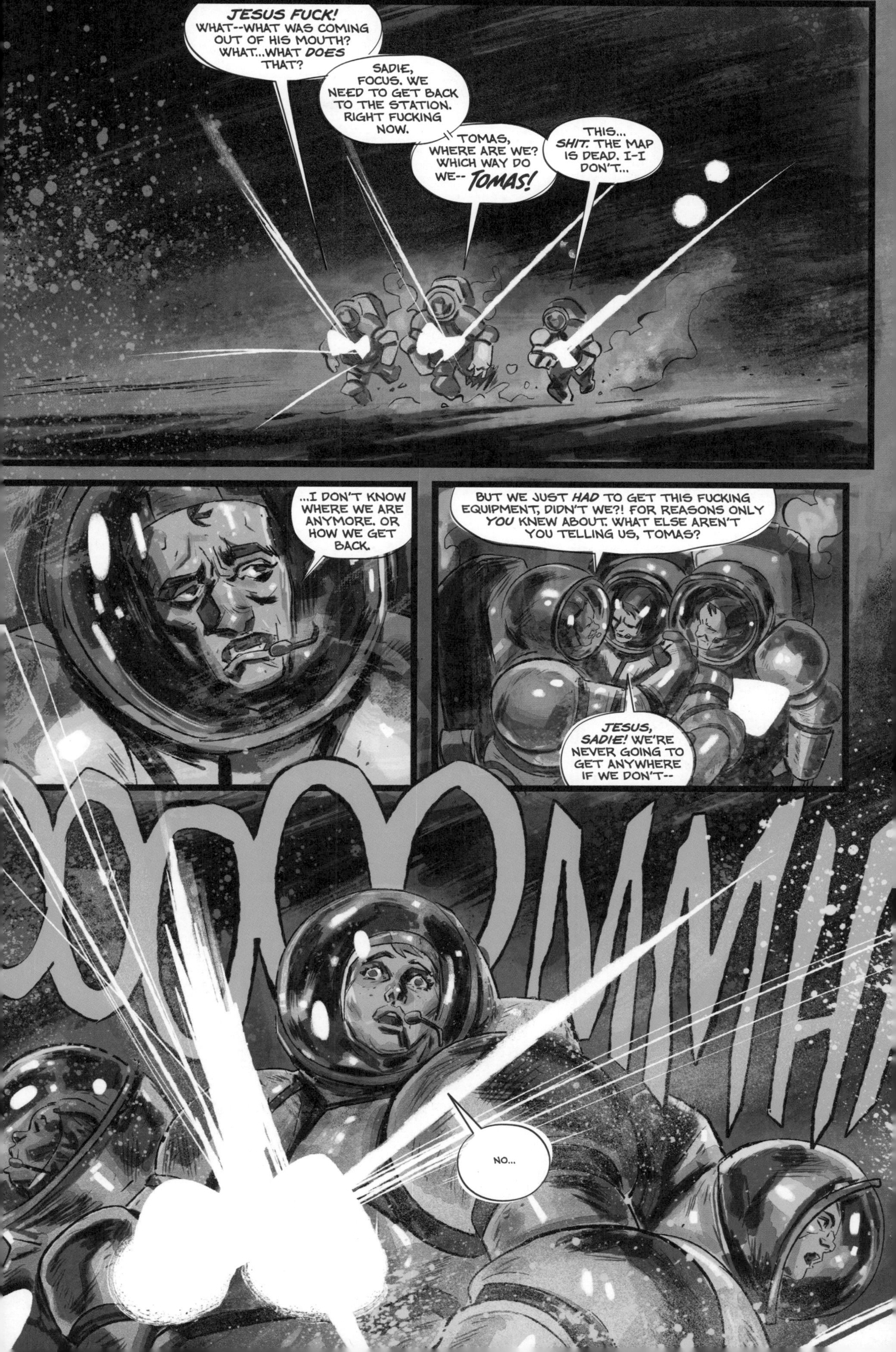
JESUS FUCK! WHAT--WHAT WAS COMING OUT OF HIS MOUTH? WHAT...WHAT DOES THAT?
SADIE, FOCUS. WE NEED TO GET BACK TO THE STATION. RIGHT FUCKING NOW.
TOMAS, WHERE ARE WE? WHICH WAY DO WE-- TOMAS!
THIS... SHIT. THE MAP IS DEAD. I-I DON'T...
...I DON'T KNOW WHERE WE ARE ANYMORE. OR HOW WE GET BACK.
BUT WE JUST HAD TO GET THIS FUCKING EQUIPMENT, DIDN'T WE?! FOR REASONS ONLY YOU KNEW ABOUT. WHAT ELSE AREN'T YOU TELLING US, TOMAS?
JESUS, SADIE! WE'RE NEVER GOING TO GET ANYWHERE IF WE DON'T--
OOOOMMH
NO...

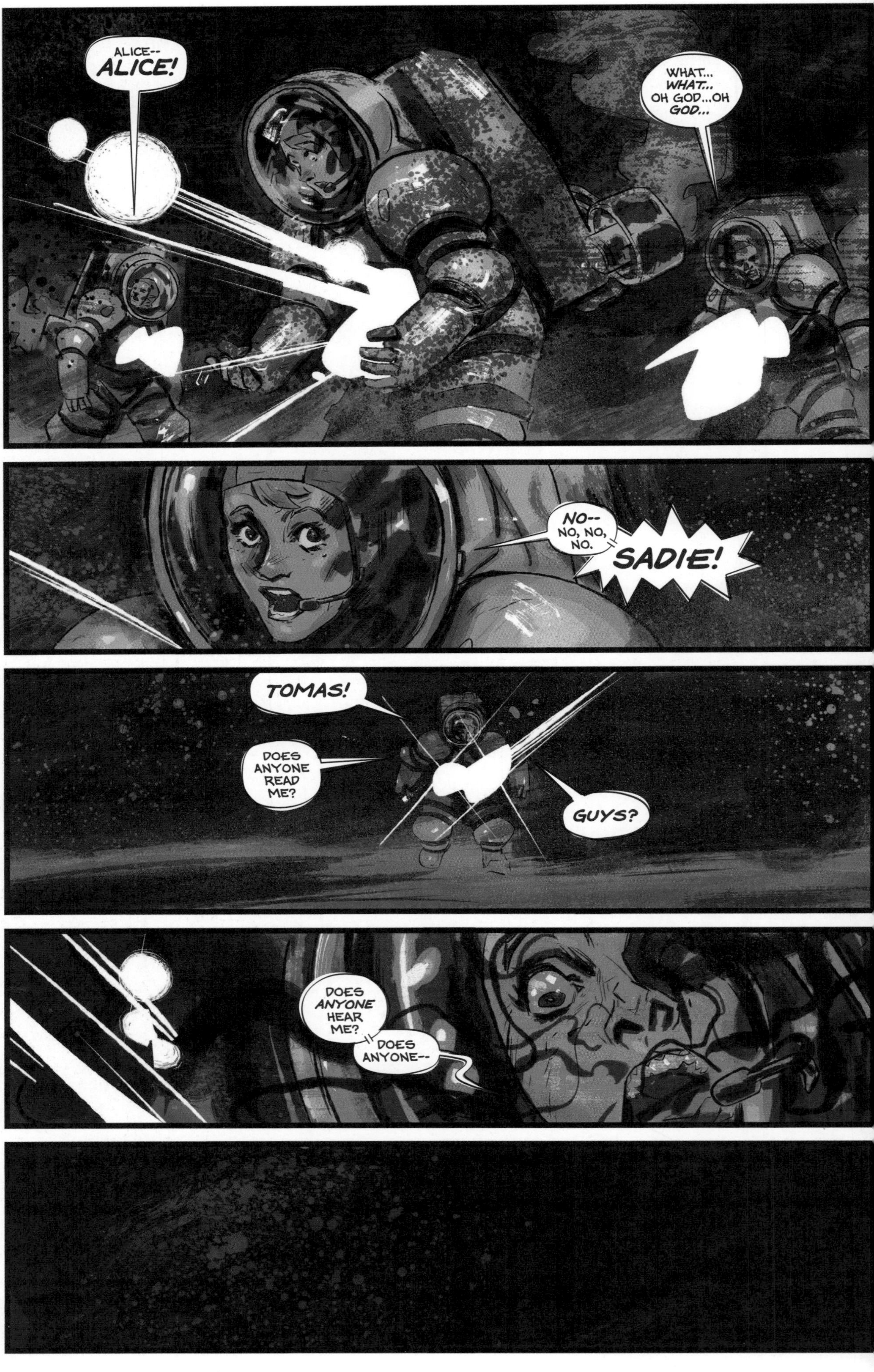

ALICE--
ALICE!
WHAT...
WHAT...
OH GOD...OH GOD...
NO--
NO, NO, NO.
SADIE!
TOMAS!
DOES ANYONE READ ME?
GUYS?
DOES ANYONE HEAR ME?
DOES ANYONE--

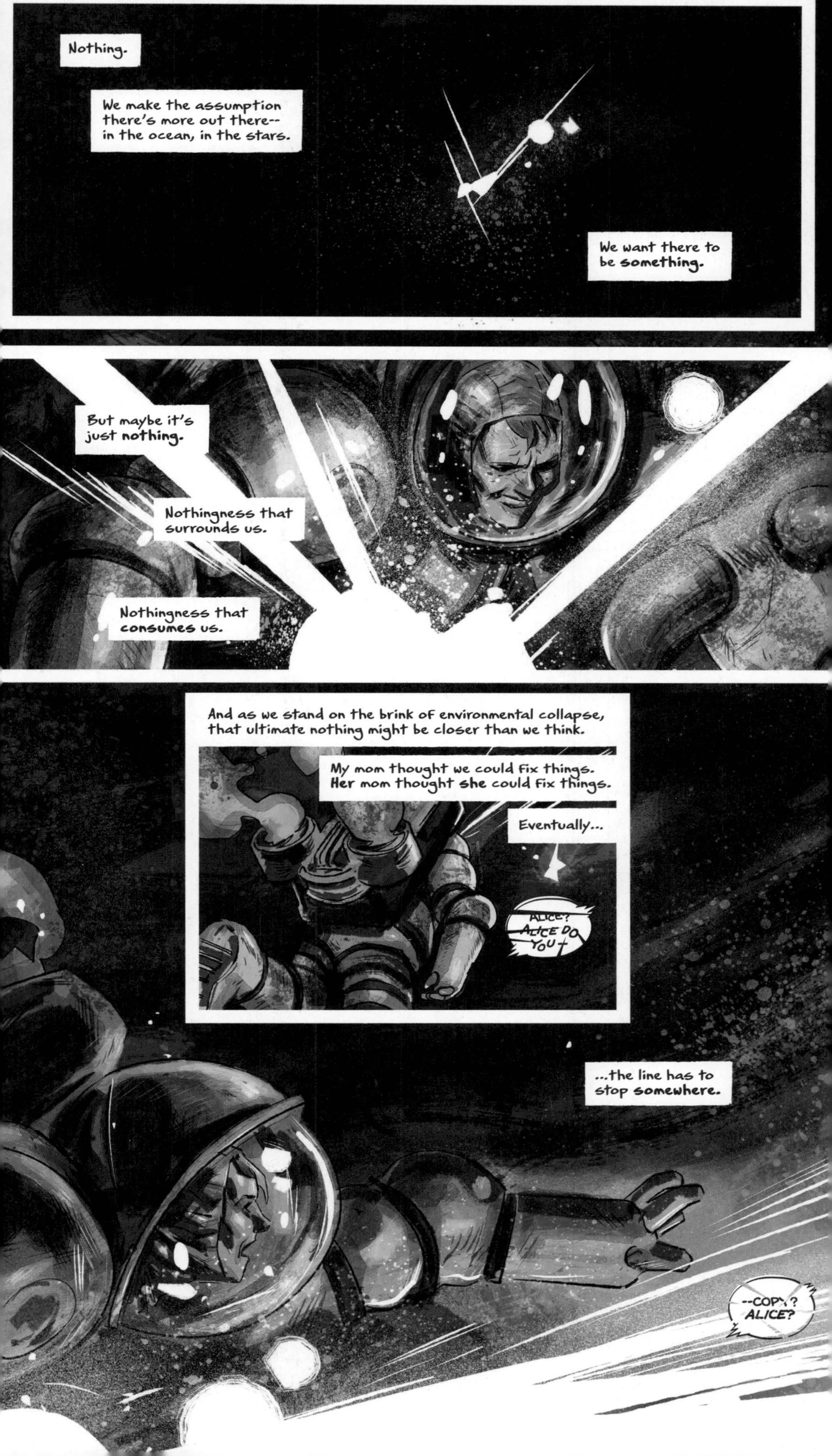
Nothing.
We make the assumption there's more out there-- in the ocean, in the stars.
We want there to be something.
But maybe it's just nothing.
Nothingness that surrounds us.
Nothingness that consumes us.
And as we stand on the brink of environmental collapse, that ultimate nothing might be closer than we think.
My mom thought we could fix things. Her mom thought she could fix things.
Eventually...
ALICE? ALICE DO YOU
...the line has to stop somewhere.
--COPY? ALICE?

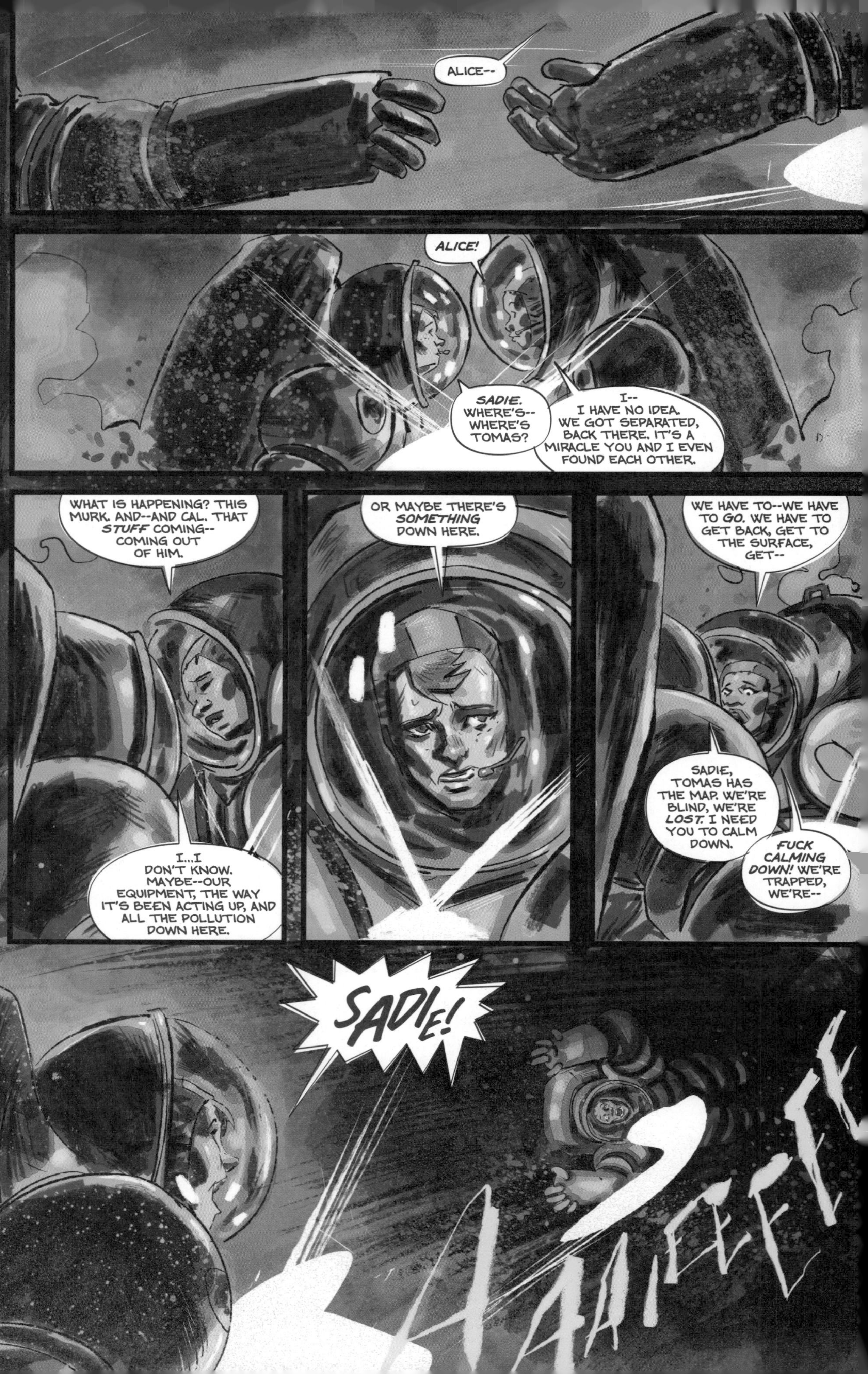
ALICE--
ALICE!
SADIE. WHERE'S-- WHERE'S TOMAS?
I-- I HAVE NO IDEA. WE GOT SEPARATED, BACK THERE. IT'S A MIRACLE YOU AND I EVEN FOUND EACH OTHER.
WHAT IS HAPPENING? THIS MURK. AND--AND CAL. THAT STUFF COMING-- COMING OUT OF HIM.
I...I DON'T KNOW. MAYBE--OUR EQUIPMENT, THE WAY IT'S BEEN ACTING UP, AND ALL THE POLLUTION DOWN HERE.
OR MAYBE THERE'S SOMETHING DOWN HERE.
WE HAVE TO--WE HAVE TO GO. WE HAVE TO GET BACK, GET TO THE SURFACE, GET--
SADIE, TOMAS HAS THE MAP. WE'RE BLIND, WE'RE LOST. I NEED YOU TO CALM DOWN.
FUCK CALMING DOWN! WE'RE TRAPPED, WE'RE--
SADIE!
AAIEEEE

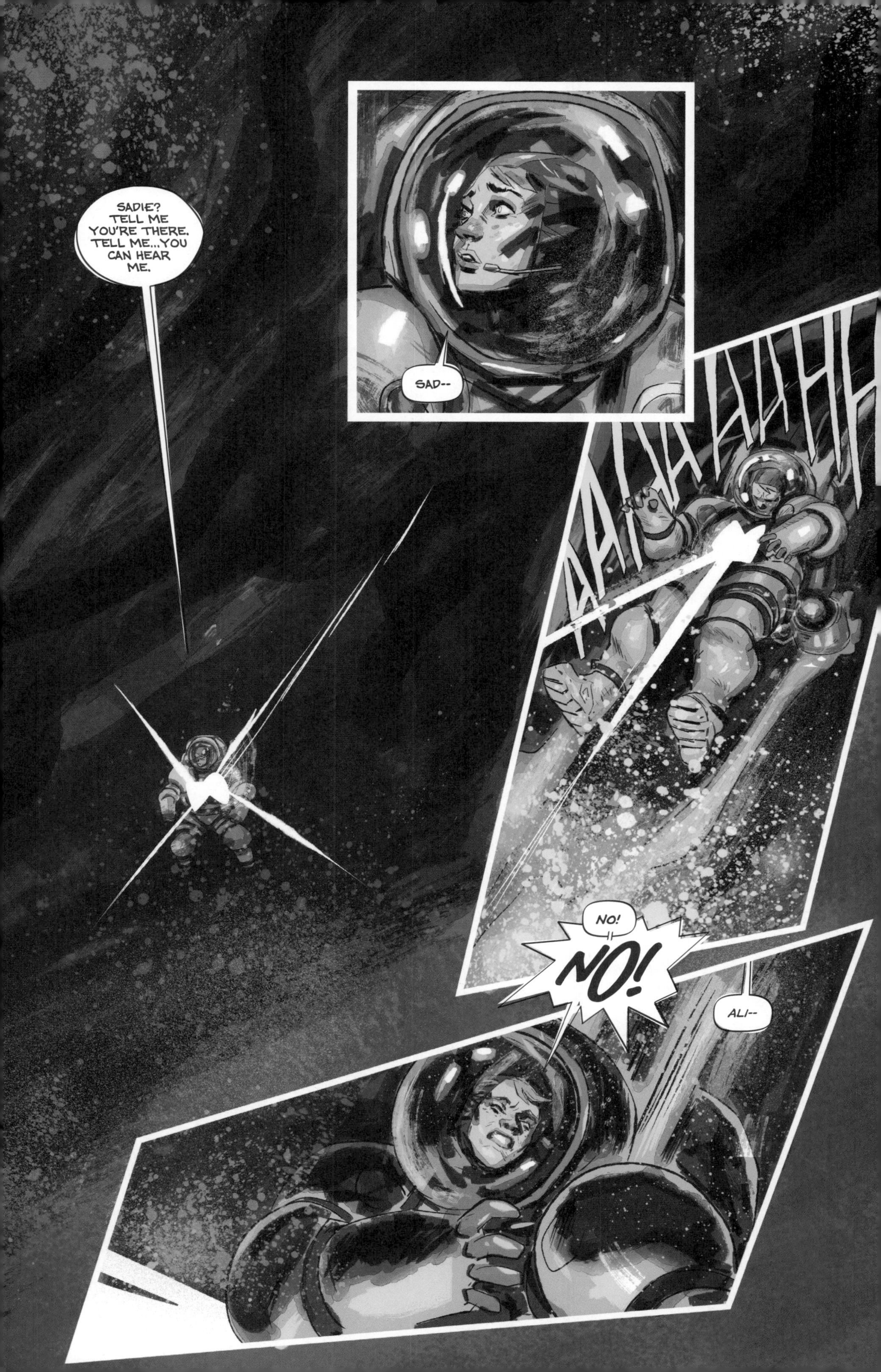
SADIE? TELL ME YOU'RE THERE. TELL ME...YOU CAN HEAR ME.
SAD--
AAAAAAAAHH
NO!
NO!
ALI--

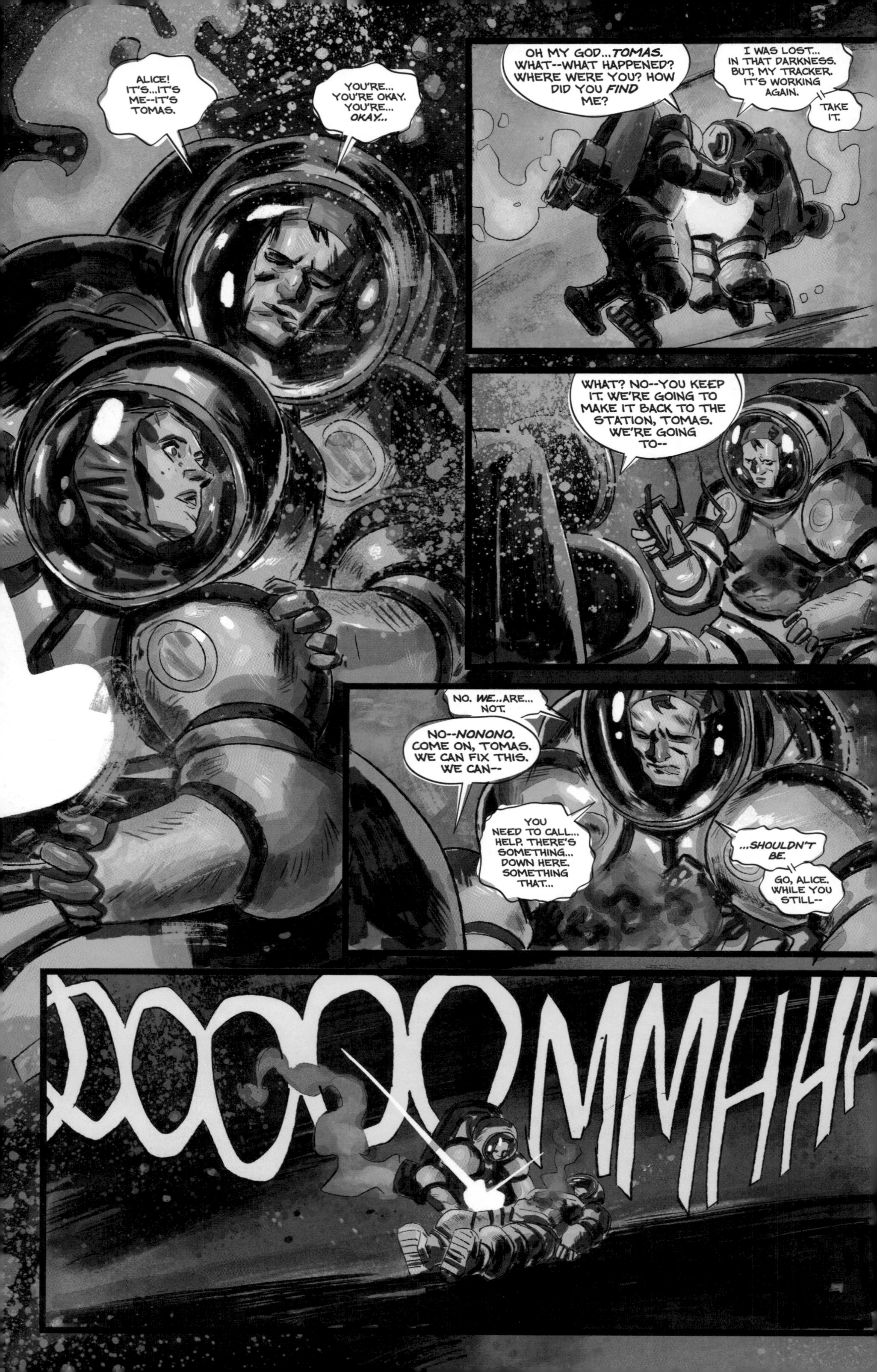
ALICE! IT'S...IT'S ME--IT'S TOMAS.
YOU'RE... YOU'RE OKAY. YOU'RE... OKAY...
OH MY GOD...TOMAS. WHAT--WHAT HAPPENED? WHERE WERE YOU? HOW DID YOU FIND ME?
I WAS LOST... IN THAT DARKNESS. BUT, MY TRACKER. IT'S WORKING AGAIN.
TAKE IT.
WHAT? NO--YOU KEEP IT. WE'RE GOING TO MAKE IT BACK TO THE STATION, TOMAS. WE'RE GOING TO--
NO. WE...ARE... NOT.
NO--NONONO. COME ON, TOMAS. WE CAN FIX THIS. WE CAN--
YOU NEED TO CALL... HELP. THERE'S SOMETHING... DOWN HERE. SOMETHING THAT...
...SHOULDN'T BE.
GO, ALICE. WHILE YOU STILL--
DOOOOMMHH

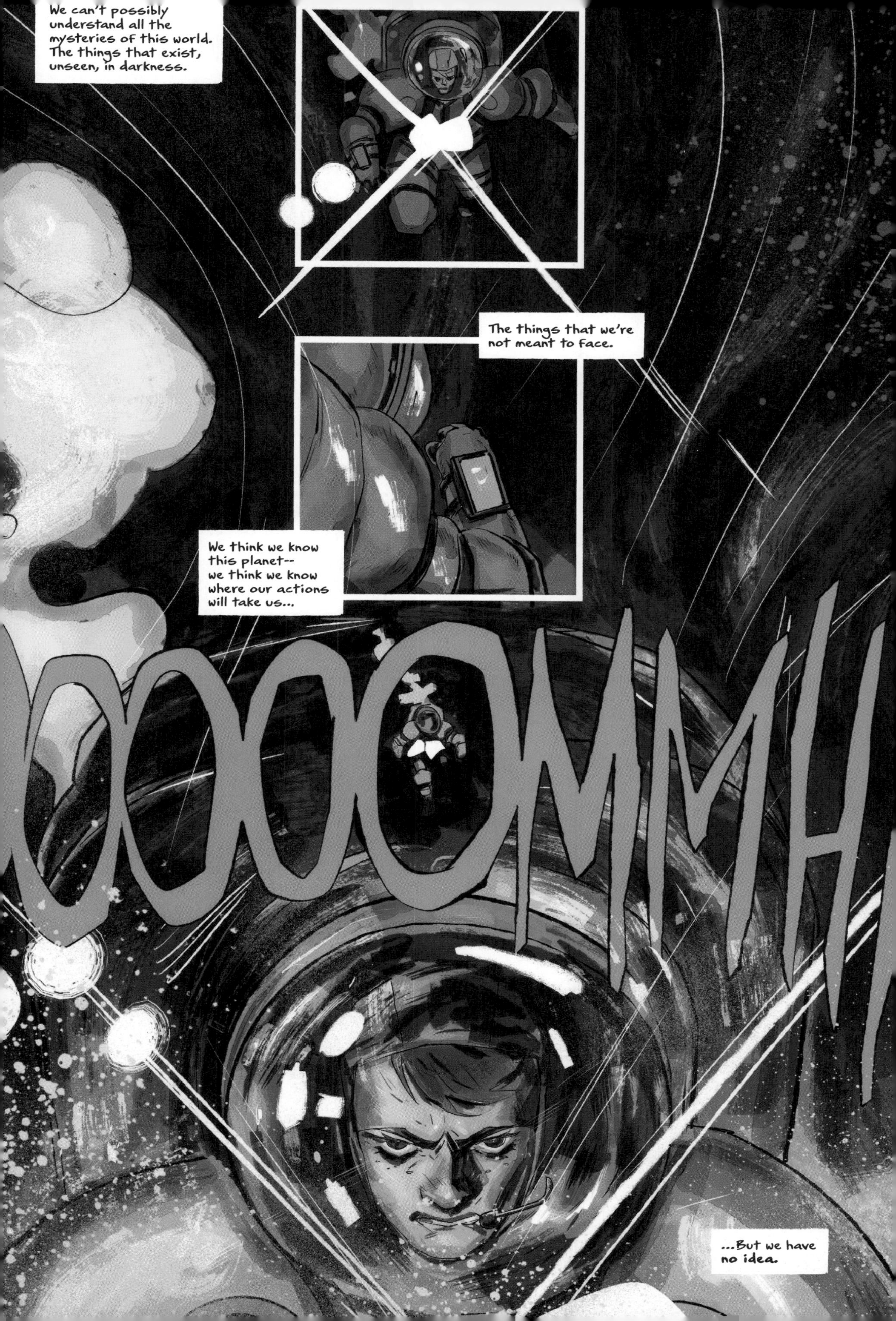
We can't possibly understand all the mysteries of this world. The things that exist, unseen, in darkness.
The things that we're not meant to face.
We think we know this planet-- we think we know where our actions will take us...
OOOOOMMH
...But we have no idea.

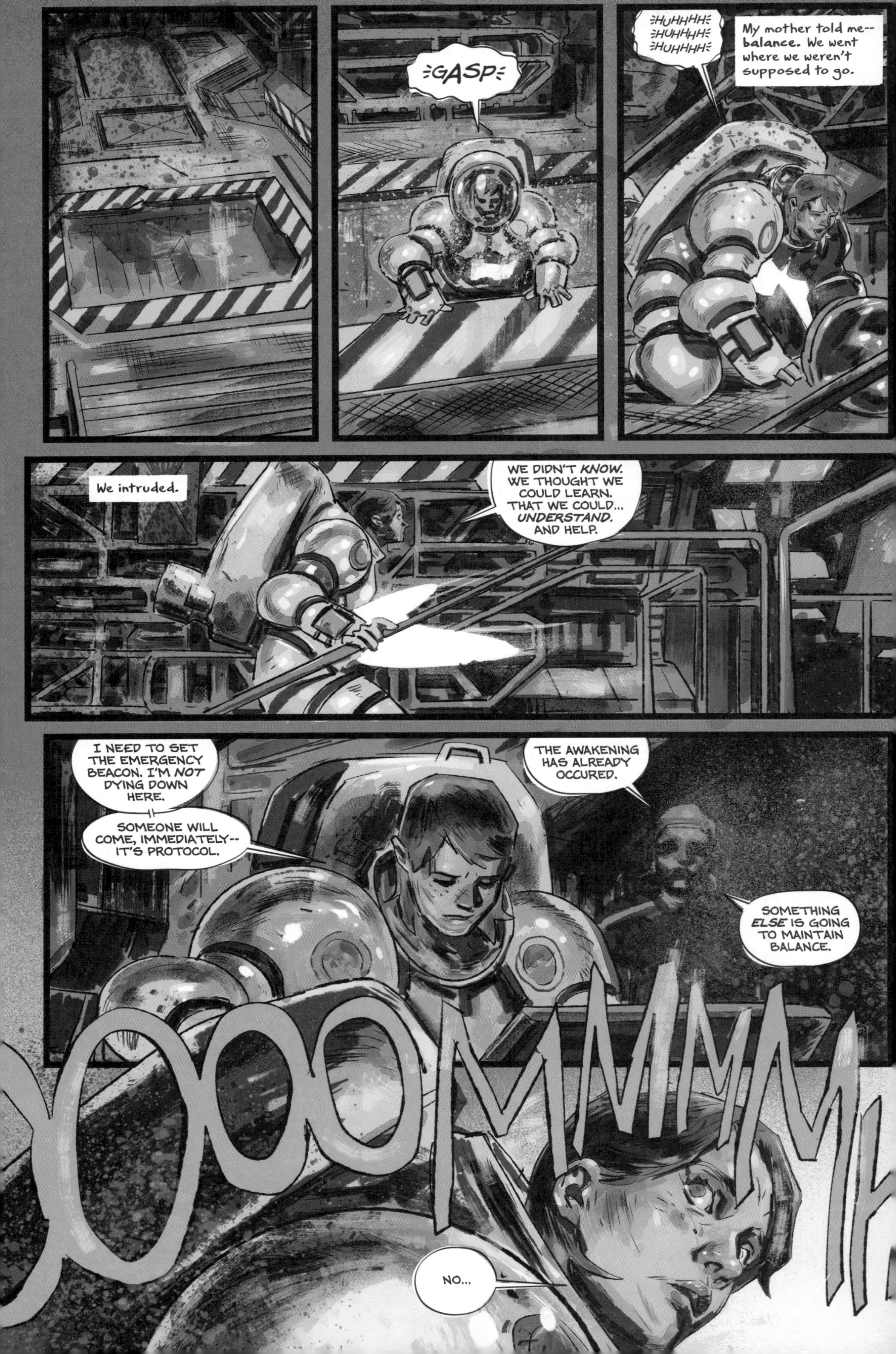
GASP
HUHHHH HUHHHH HUHHHH
My mother told me--balance. We went where we weren't supposed to go.
We intruded.
WE DIDN'T KNOW. WE THOUGHT WE COULD LEARN. THAT WE COULD... UNDERSTAND. AND HELP.
I NEED TO SET THE EMERGENCY BEACON. I'M NOT DYING DOWN HERE.
SOMEONE WILL COME, IMMEDIATELY--IT'S PROTOCOL.
THE AWAKENING HAS ALREADY OCCURED.
SOMETHING ELSE IS GOING TO MAINTAIN BALANCE.
OOOOMMMMH
NO...

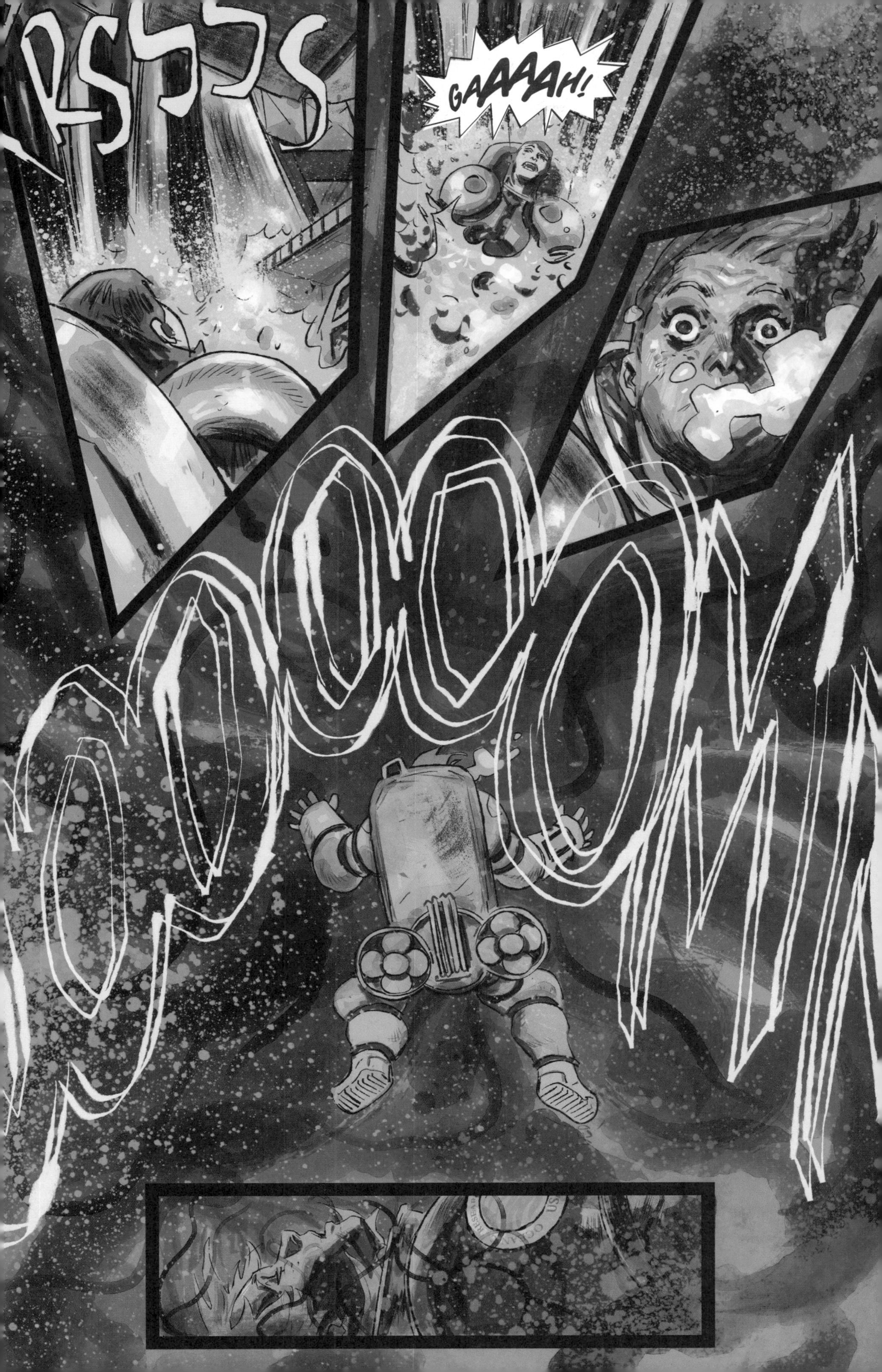
GAAAAH!

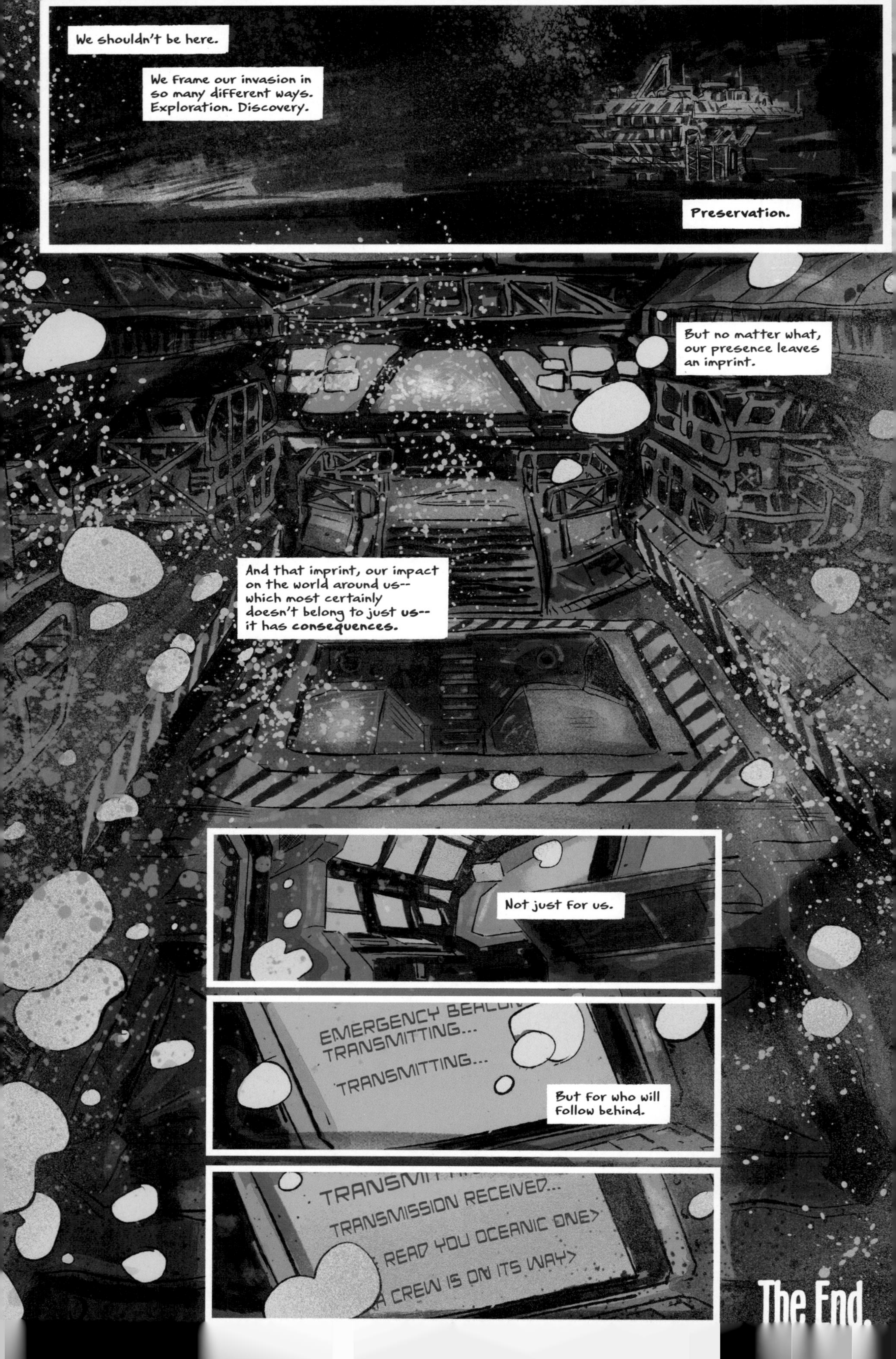
We shouldn't be here.
We frame our invasion in so many different ways. Exploration. Discovery.
Preservation.
But no matter what, our presence leaves an imprint.
And that imprint, our impact on the world around us-- which most certainly doesn't belong to just us-- it has consequences.
Not just for us.
EMERGENCY BEACON
TRANSMITTING...
TRANSMITTING...
But for who will follow behind.
TRANSMISSION RECEIVED...
READ YOU OCEANIC ONE>
CREW IS ON ITS WAY>
The End.

KILLIAMSBURG

THE BIGGEST BLIZZARD IN RECORDED HISTORY IS HITTING BROOKLYN TODAY.

IT'S FUUUUUUUUUU-UUUUUUUUU...

THE MAYOR HAS ORDERED AN EVACUATION OF BROOKLYN. NOT MANDATORY, BUT HIGHLY RECOMMENDED.

IT SEEMS LIKE MOST PEOPLE HAVE LEFT, BUT SOME STRAGGLERS HAVE STAYED BEHIND.

TO HAVE AN "EXPERIENCE."

...CCCKKKKKKKKK-IIIIINNNNGGG...

BUT PLEASE DON'T BE ONE OF THOSE PEOPLE. GO SOMEWHERE WARM. GO TO NEW JERSEY. GO TO CONNECTICUT.

...COOOOOLLLLLLLLLDDDDD.

HUH?

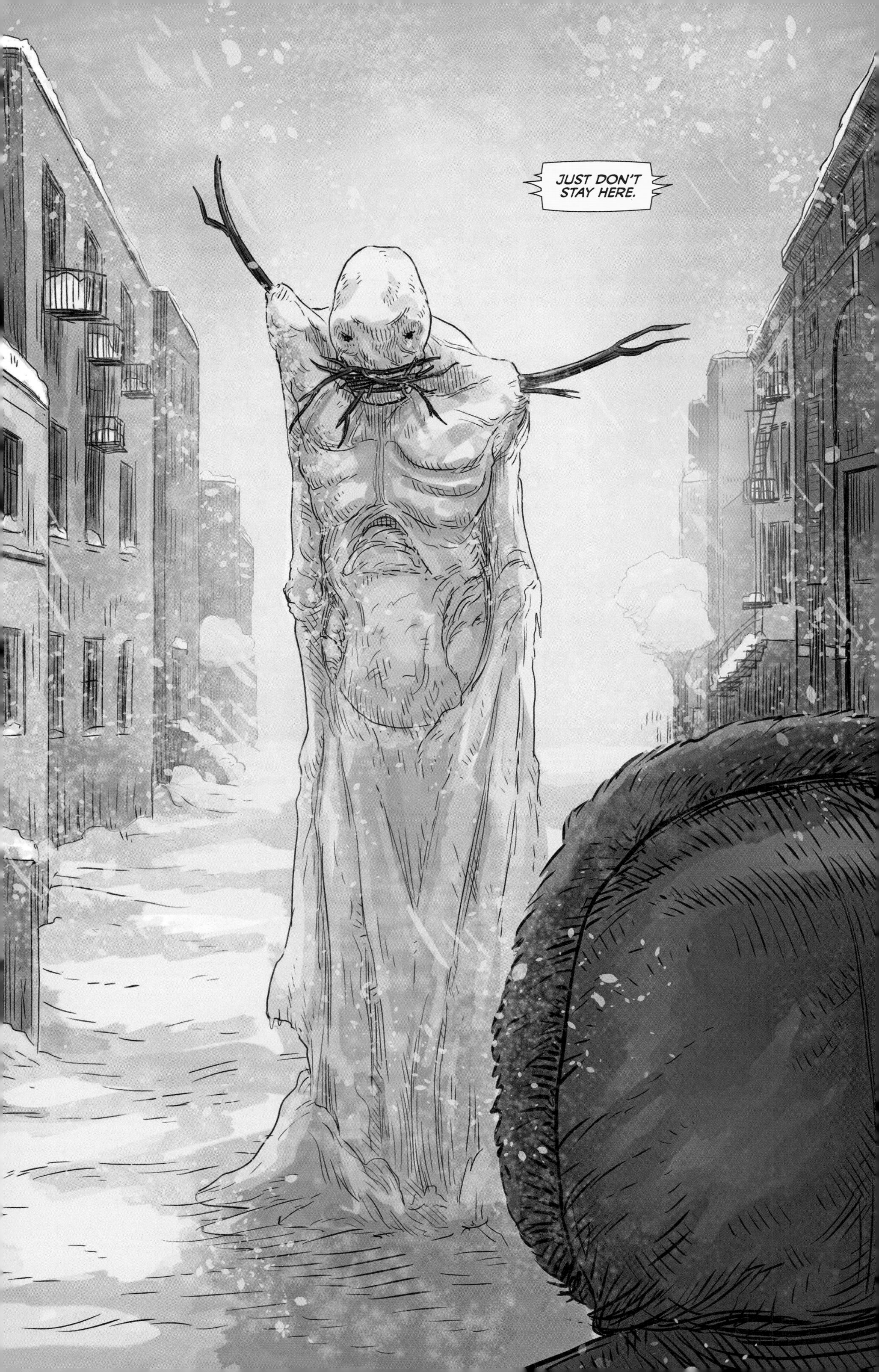
JUST DON'T STAY HERE.

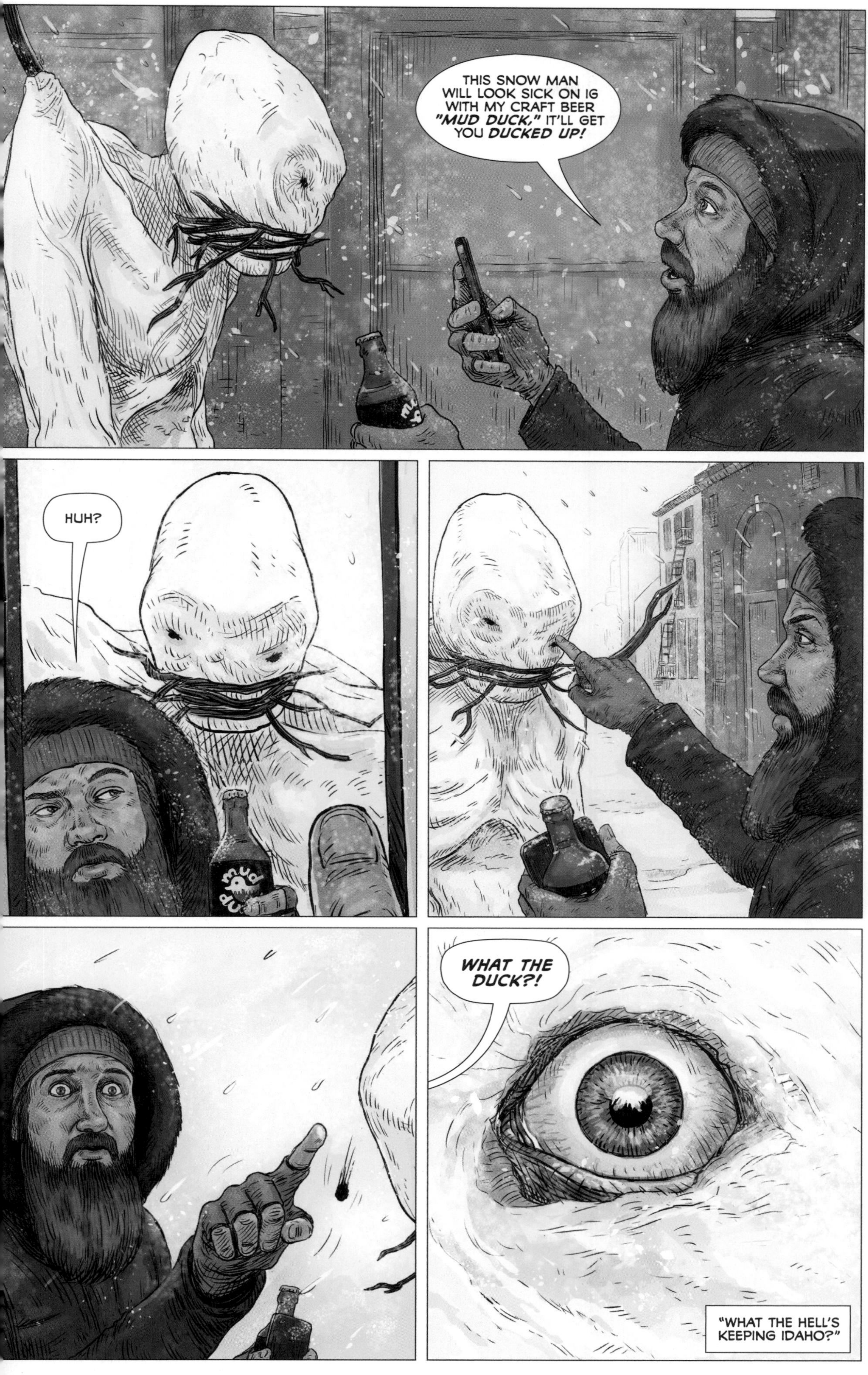
THIS SNOW MAN WILL LOOK SICK ON IG WITH MY CRAFT BEER *"MUD DUCK,"* IT'LL GET YOU *DUCKED UP!*
HUH?
WHAT THE DUCK?!
"WHAT THE HELL'S KEEPING IDAHO?"

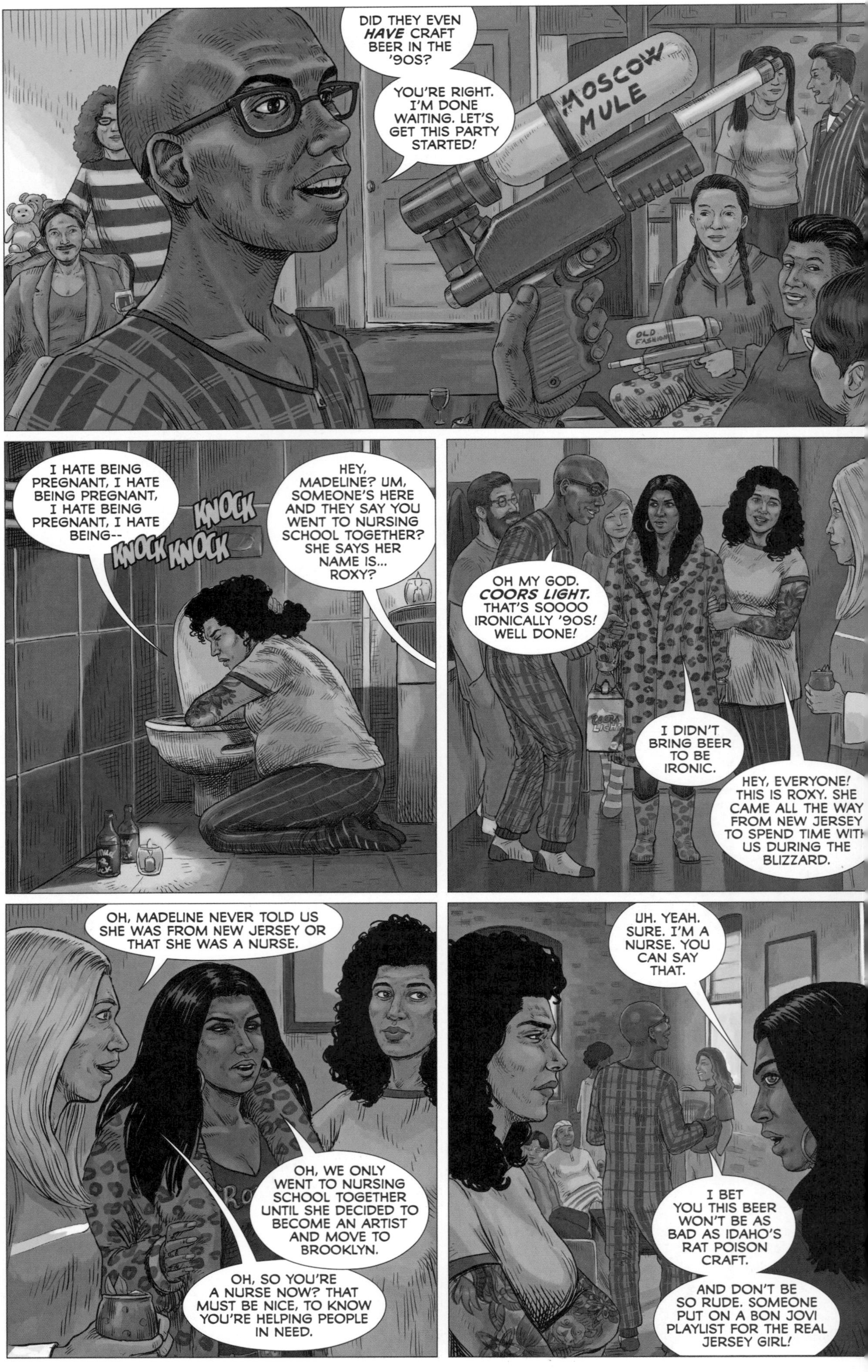

DID THEY EVEN *HAVE* CRAFT BEER IN THE '90S?
YOU'RE RIGHT. I'M DONE WAITING. LET'S GET THIS PARTY STARTED!
MOSCOW MULE
I HATE BEING PREGNANT, I HATE BEING PREGNANT, I HATE BEING PREGNANT, I HATE BEING--
KNOCK
KNOCK KNOCK
HEY, MADELINE? UM, SOMEONE'S HERE AND THEY SAY YOU WENT TO NURSING SCHOOL TOGETHER? SHE SAYS HER NAME IS... ROXY?
OH MY GOD. ***COORS LIGHT.*** THAT'S SOOOO IRONICALLY '90S! WELL DONE!
I DIDN'T BRING BEER TO BE IRONIC.
HEY, EVERYONE! THIS IS ROXY. SHE CAME ALL THE WAY FROM NEW JERSEY TO SPEND TIME WIT US DURING THE BLIZZARD.
OH, MADELINE NEVER TOLD US SHE WAS FROM NEW JERSEY OR THAT SHE WAS A NURSE.
OH, WE ONLY WENT TO NURSING SCHOOL TOGETHER UNTIL SHE DECIDED TO BECOME AN ARTIST AND MOVE TO BROOKLYN.
OH, SO YOU'RE A NURSE NOW? THAT MUST BE NICE, TO KNOW YOU'RE HELPING PEOPLE IN NEED.
UH. YEAH. SURE. I'M A NURSE. YOU CAN SAY THAT.
I BET YOU THIS BEER WON'T BE AS BAD AS IDAHO'S RAT POISON CRAFT.
AND DON'T BE SO RUDE. SOMEONE PUT ON A BON JOVI PLAYLIST FOR THE REAL JERSEY GIRL!

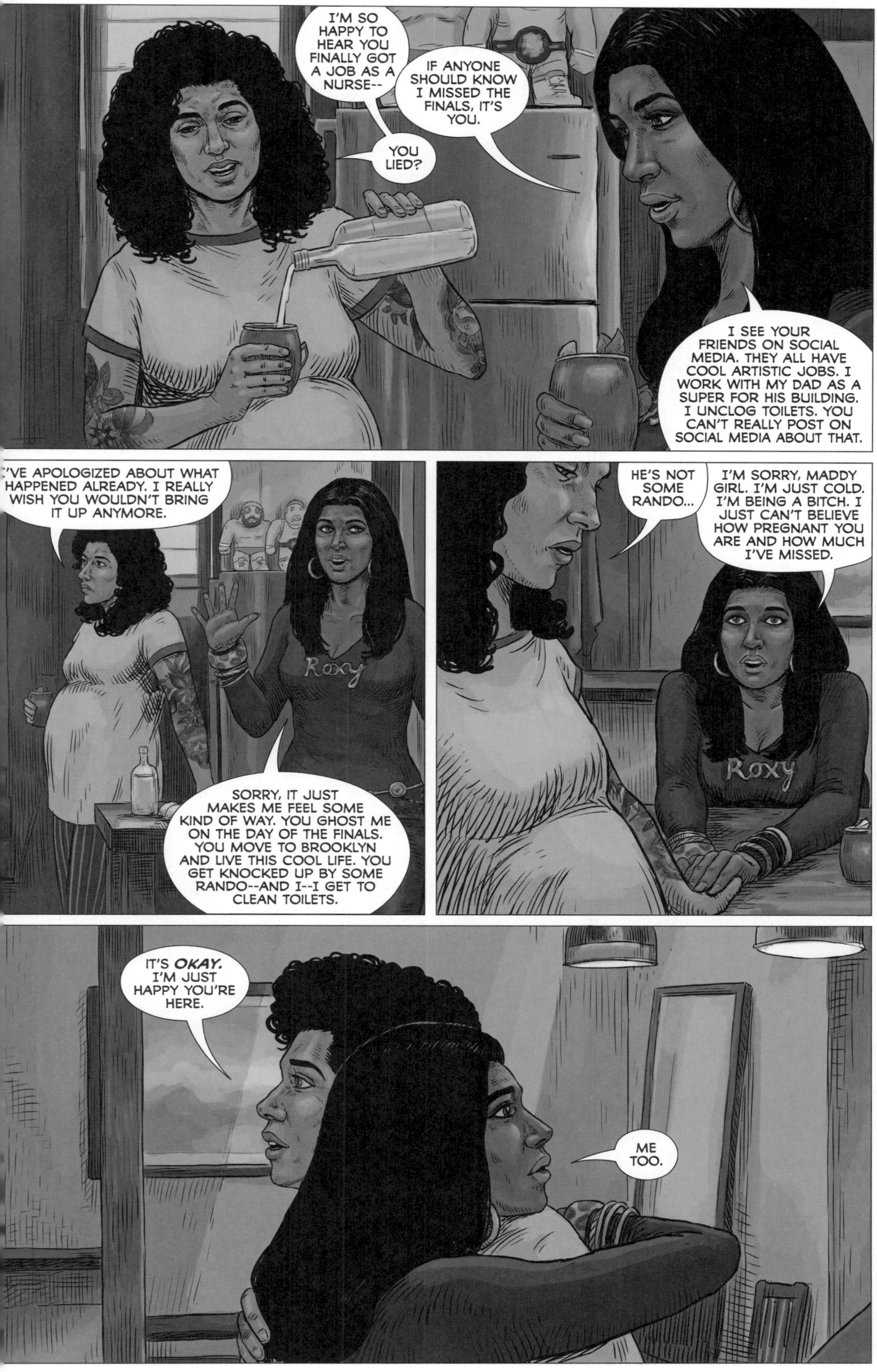
I'M SO HAPPY TO HEAR YOU FINALLY GOT A JOB AS A NURSE--
YOU LIED?
IF ANYONE SHOULD KNOW I MISSED THE FINALS, IT'S YOU.
I SEE YOUR FRIENDS ON SOCIAL MEDIA. THEY ALL HAVE COOL ARTISTIC JOBS. I WORK WITH MY DAD AS A SUPER FOR HIS BUILDING. I UNCLOG TOILETS. YOU CAN'T REALLY POST ON SOCIAL MEDIA ABOUT THAT.
I'VE APOLOGIZED ABOUT WHAT HAPPENED ALREADY. I REALLY WISH YOU WOULDN'T BRING IT UP ANYMORE.
Roxy
SORRY, IT JUST MAKES ME FEEL SOME KIND OF WAY. YOU GHOST ME ON THE DAY OF THE FINALS. YOU MOVE TO BROOKLYN AND LIVE THIS COOL LIFE. YOU GET KNOCKED UP BY SOME RANDO--AND I--I GET TO CLEAN TOILETS.
HE'S NOT SOME RANDO...
I'M SORRY, MADDY GIRL. I'M JUST COLD. I'M BEING A BITCH. I JUST CAN'T BELIEVE HOW PREGNANT YOU ARE AND HOW MUCH I'VE MISSED.
Roxy
IT'S ***OKAY.*** I'M JUST HAPPY YOU'RE HERE.
ME TOO.

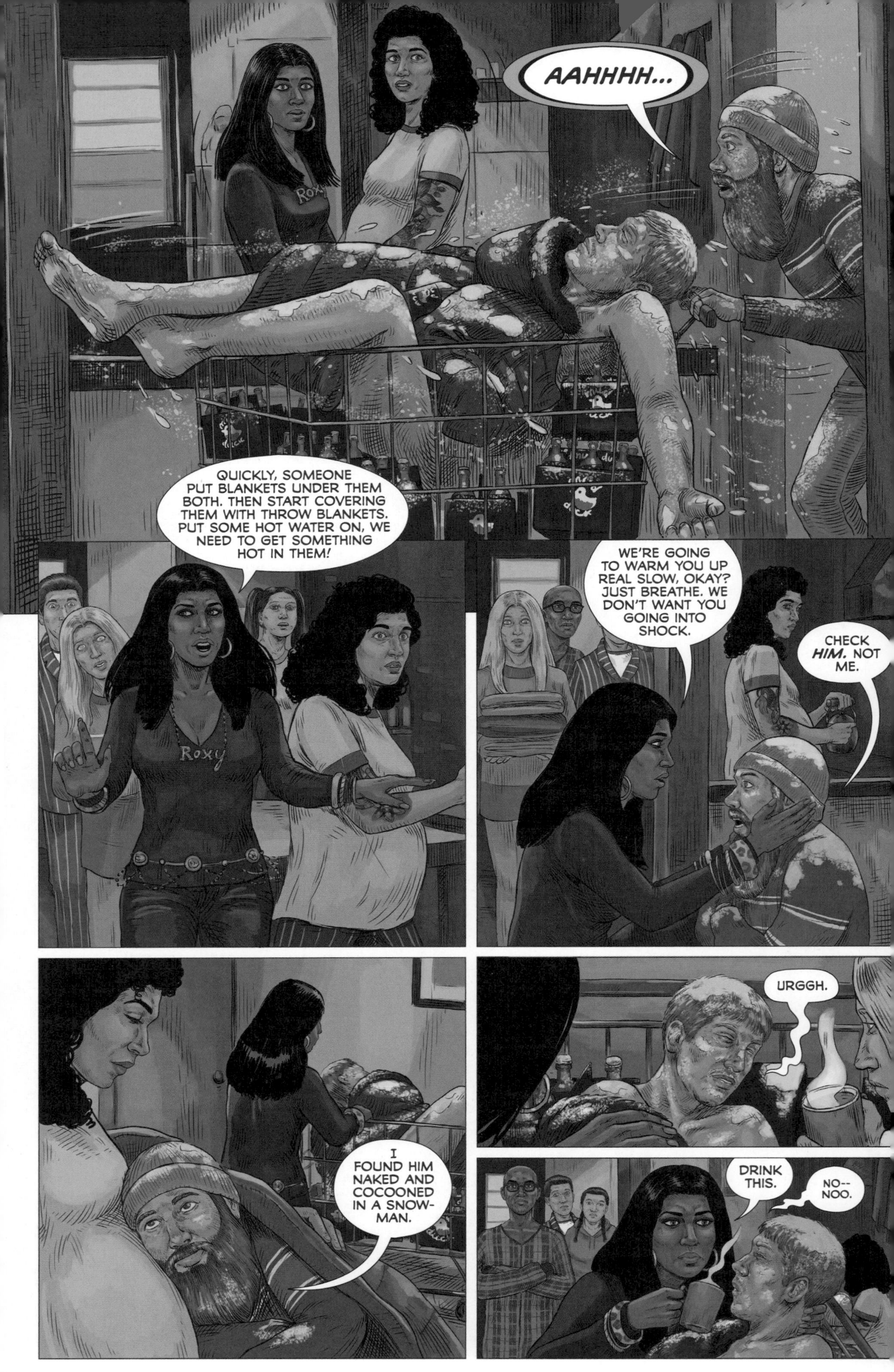
AAHHHH...
QUICKLY, SOMEONE PUT BLANKETS UNDER THEM BOTH. THEN START COVERING THEM WITH THROW BLANKETS. PUT SOME HOT WATER ON, WE NEED TO GET SOMETHING HOT IN THEM!
WE'RE GOING TO WARM YOU UP REAL SLOW, OKAY? JUST BREATHE. WE DON'T WANT YOU GOING INTO SHOCK.
CHECK *HIM*, NOT ME.
I FOUND HIM NAKED AND COCOONED IN A SNOW-MAN.
URGGH.
DRINK THIS.
NO-- NOO.

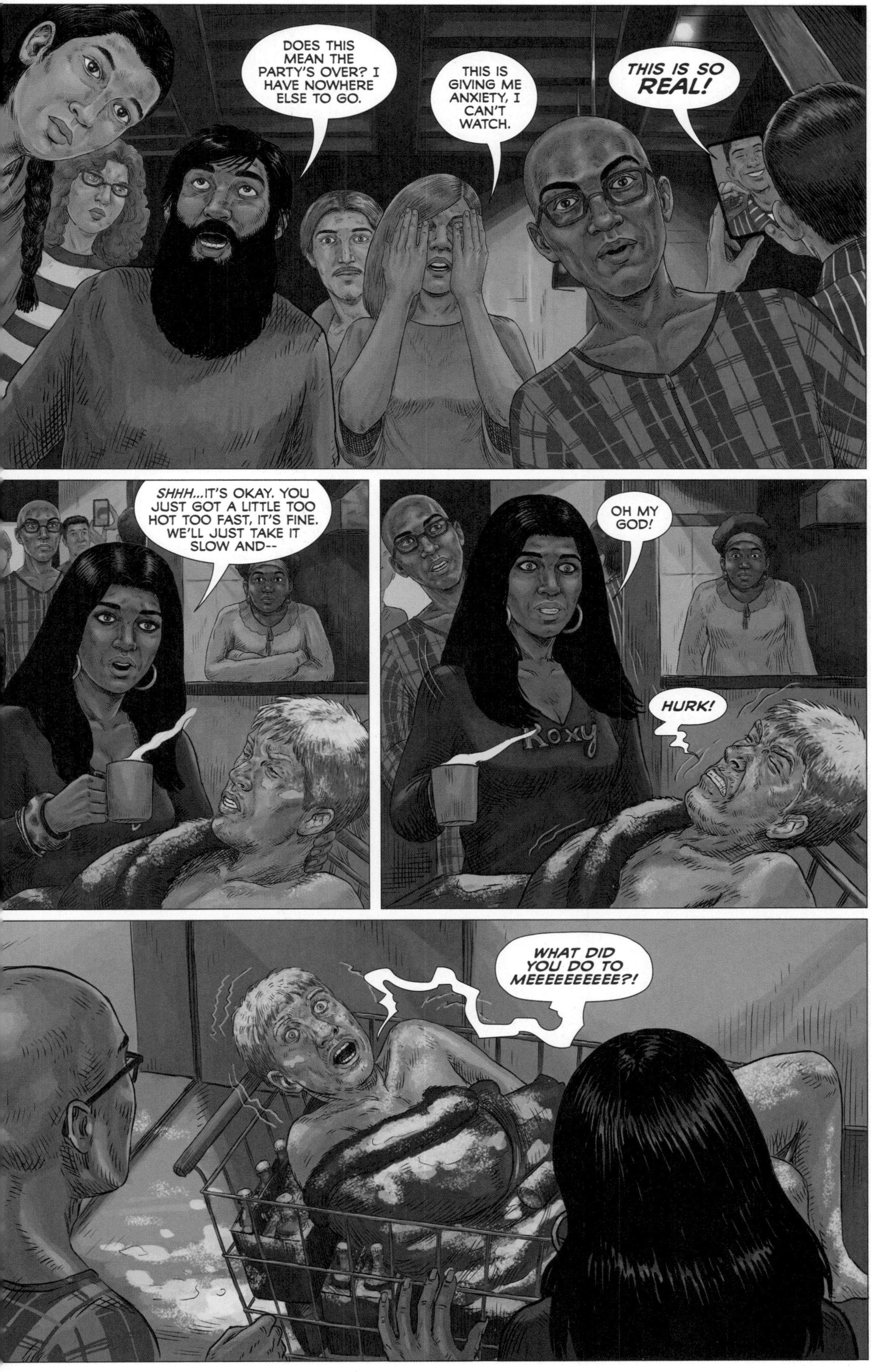
DOES THIS MEAN THE PARTY'S OVER? I HAVE NOWHERE ELSE TO GO.
THIS IS GIVING ME ANXIETY, I CAN'T WATCH.
THIS IS SO REAL!
SHHH...IT'S OKAY. YOU JUST GOT A LITTLE TOO HOT TOO FAST, IT'S FINE. WE'LL JUST TAKE IT SLOW AND--
OH MY GOD!
Roxy
HURK!
WHAT DID YOU DO TO MEEEEEEEEEE?!

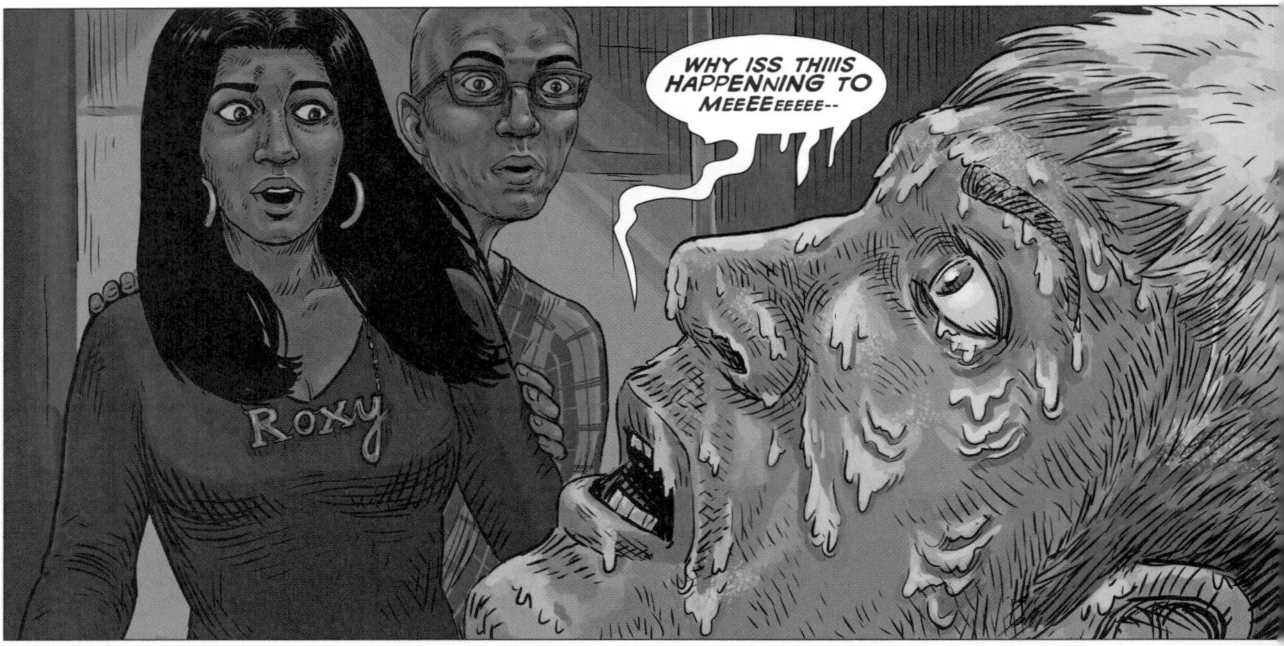
WHY ISS THIIIS HAPPENNING TO MEEEEeeeee--
Roxy

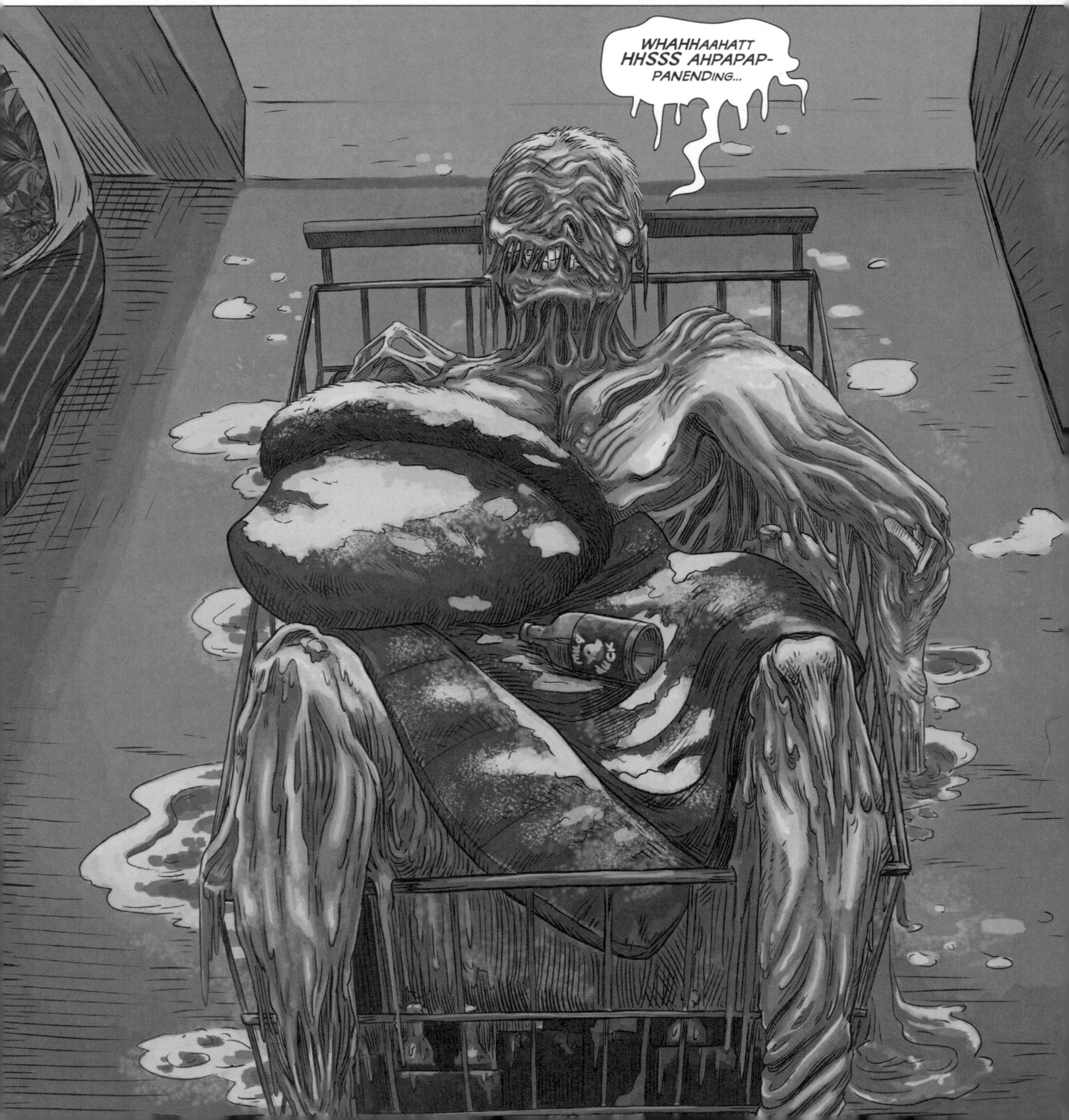
WHAHHAAHATT HHSSS AHPAPAP-PANENDING...

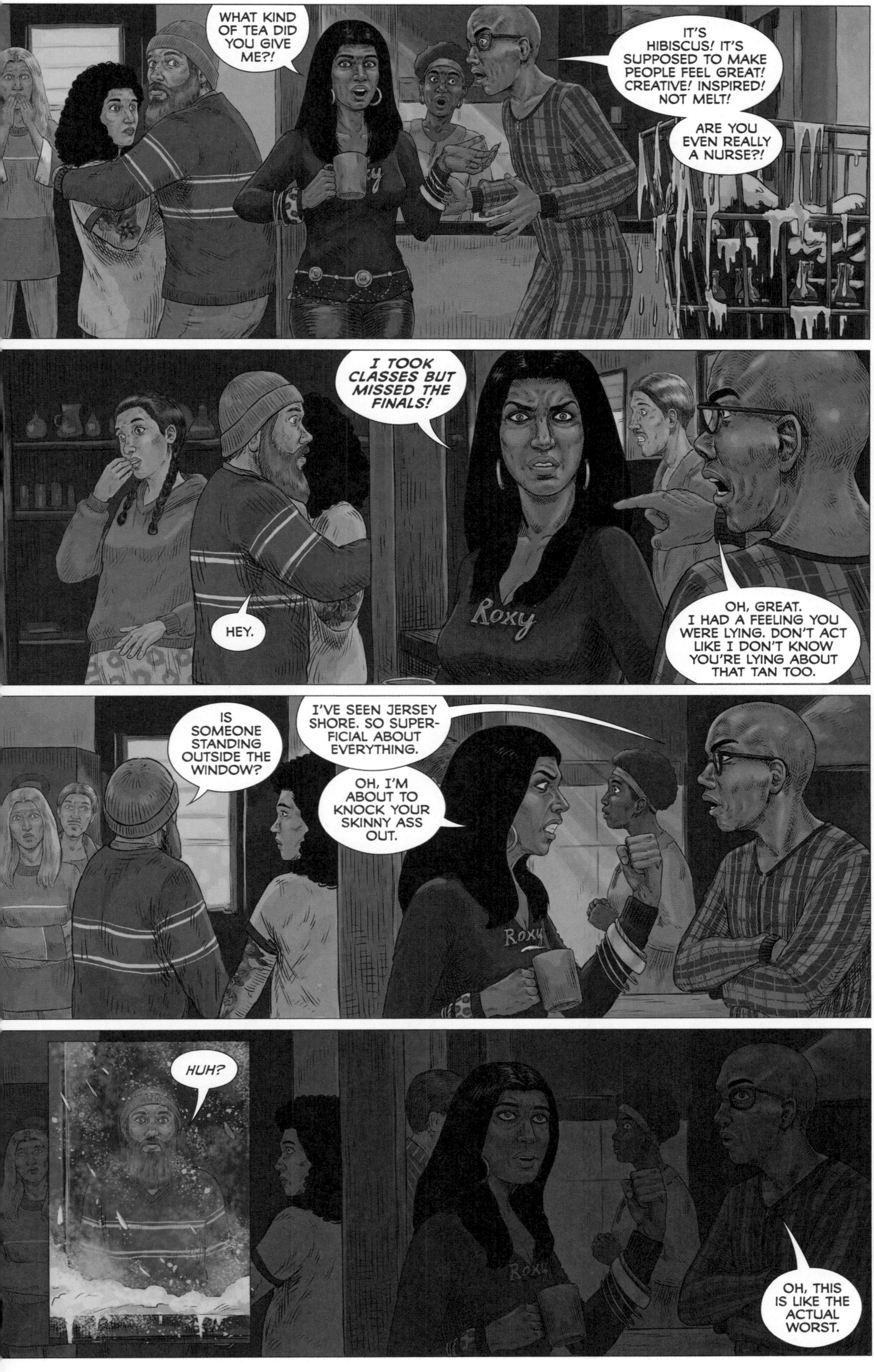
WHAT KIND OF TEA DID YOU GIVE ME?!
IT'S HIBISCUS! IT'S SUPPOSED TO MAKE PEOPLE FEEL GREAT! CREATIVE! INSPIRED! NOT MELT!
ARE YOU EVEN REALLY A NURSE?!
I TOOK CLASSES BUT MISSED THE FINALS!
OH, GREAT. I HAD A FEELING YOU WERE LYING. DON'T ACT LIKE I DON'T KNOW YOU'RE LYING ABOUT THAT TAN TOO.
HEY.
IS SOMEONE STANDING OUTSIDE THE WINDOW?
I'VE SEEN JERSEY SHORE. SO SUPER-FICIAL ABOUT EVERYTHING.
OH, I'M ABOUT TO KNOCK YOUR SKINNY ASS OUT.
HUH?
OH, THIS IS LIKE THE ACTUAL WORST.

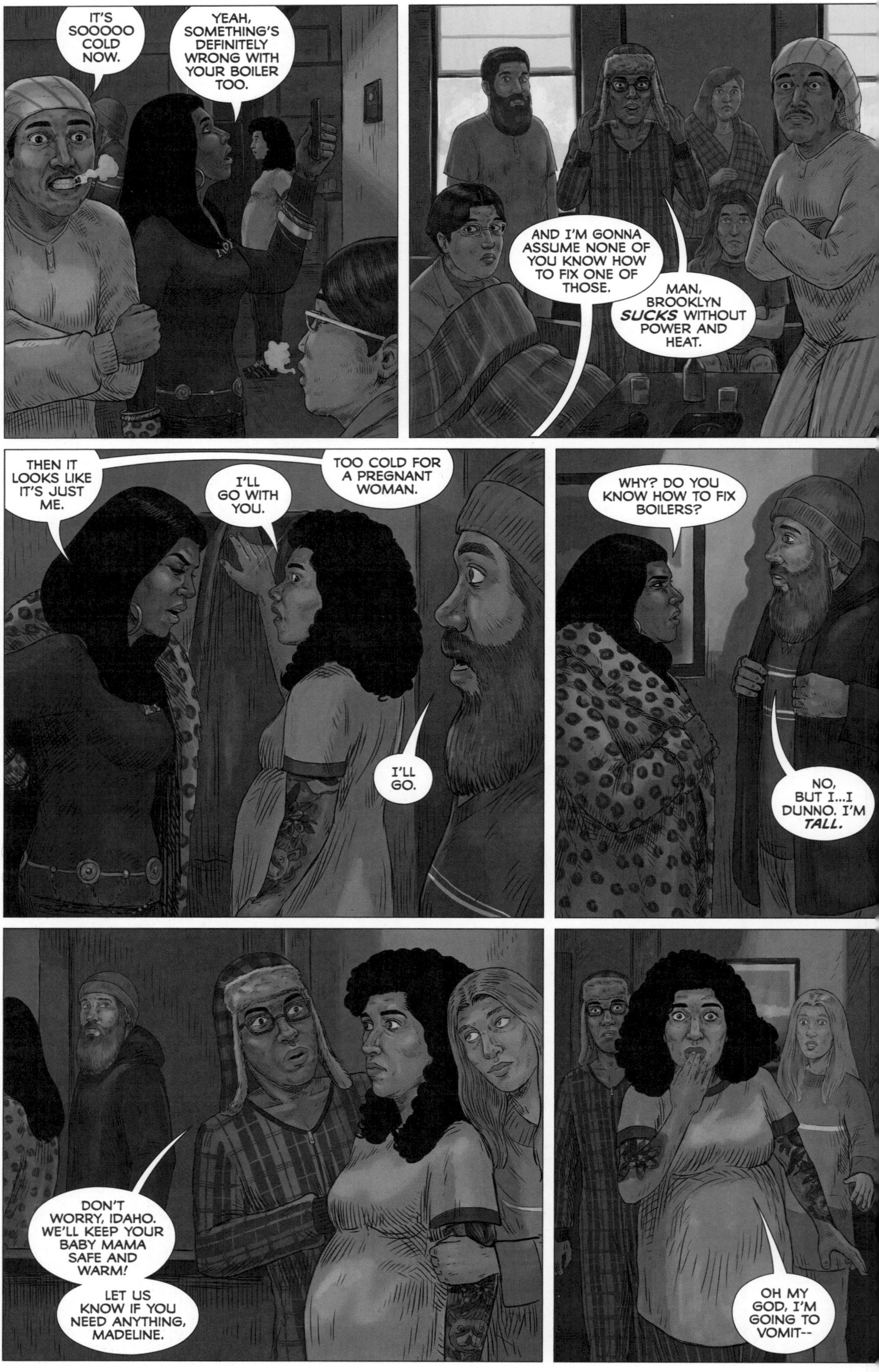
IT'S SOOOOO COLD NOW.
YEAH, SOMETHING'S DEFINITELY WRONG WITH YOUR BOILER TOO.
AND I'M GONNA ASSUME NONE OF YOU KNOW HOW TO FIX ONE OF THOSE.
MAN, BROOKLYN SUCKS WITHOUT POWER AND HEAT.
THEN IT LOOKS LIKE IT'S JUST ME.
TOO COLD FOR A PREGNANT WOMAN.
I'LL GO WITH YOU.
I'LL GO.
WHY? DO YOU KNOW HOW TO FIX BOILERS?
NO, BUT I...I DUNNO. I'M TALL.
DON'T WORRY, IDAHO. WE'LL KEEP YOUR BABY MAMA SAFE AND WARM!
LET US KNOW IF YOU NEED ANYTHING, MADELINE.
OH MY GOD, I'M GOING TO VOMIT--

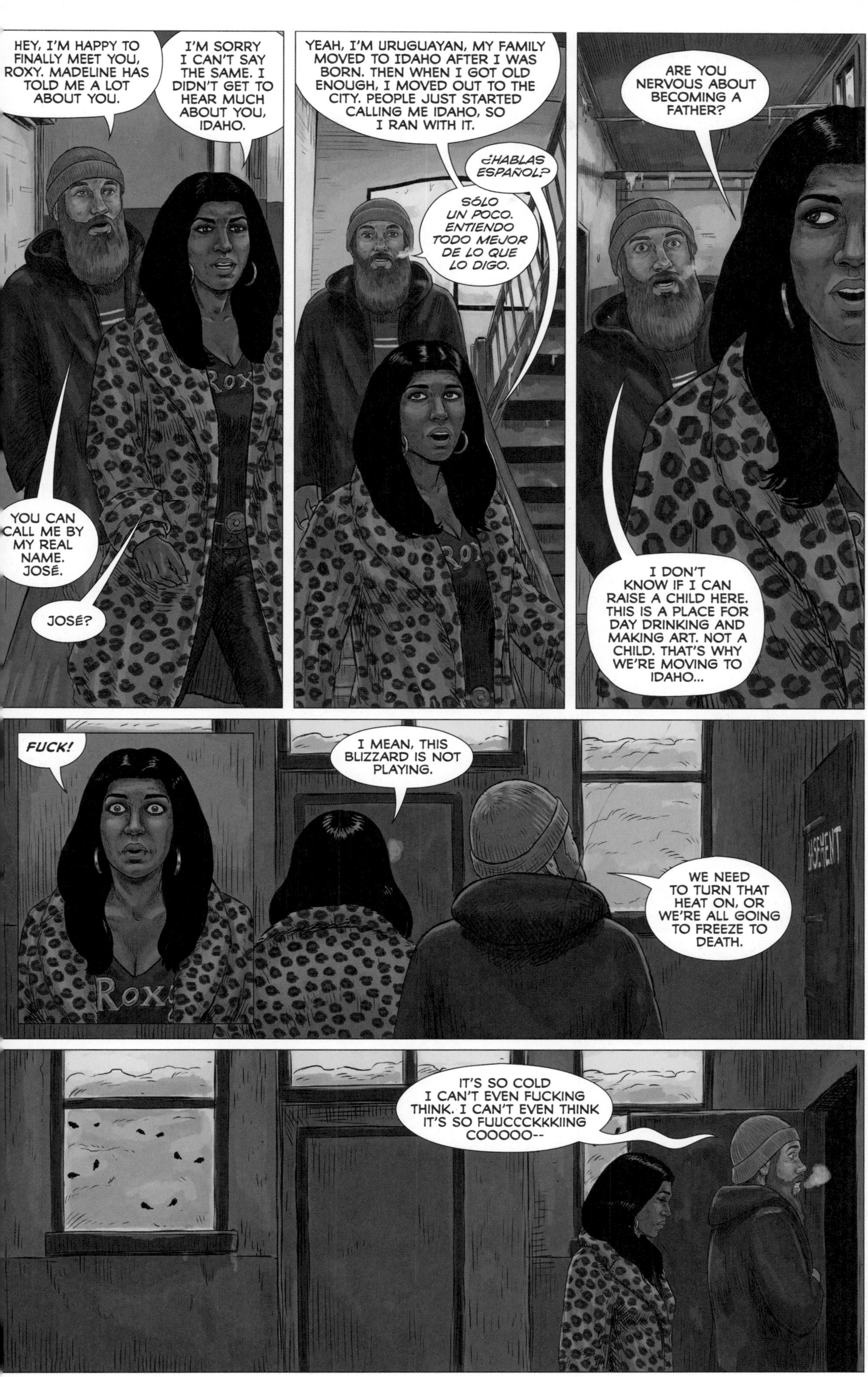
HEY, I'M HAPPY TO FINALLY MEET YOU, ROXY. MADELINE HAS TOLD ME A LOT ABOUT YOU.
I'M SORRY I CAN'T SAY THE SAME. I DIDN'T GET TO HEAR MUCH ABOUT YOU, IDAHO.
YOU CAN CALL ME BY MY REAL NAME. JOSÉ.
JOSÉ?
YEAH, I'M URUGUAYAN, MY FAMILY MOVED TO IDAHO AFTER I WAS BORN. THEN WHEN I GOT OLD ENOUGH, I MOVED OUT TO THE CITY. PEOPLE JUST STARTED CALLING ME IDAHO, SO I RAN WITH IT.
¿HABLAS ESPAÑOL?
SÓLO UN POCO. ENTIENDO TODO MEJOR DE LO QUE LO DIGO.
ARE YOU NERVOUS ABOUT BECOMING A FATHER?
I DON'T KNOW IF I CAN RAISE A CHILD HERE. THIS IS A PLACE FOR DAY DRINKING AND MAKING ART. NOT A CHILD. THAT'S WHY WE'RE MOVING TO IDAHO...
FUCK!
I MEAN, THIS BLIZZARD IS NOT PLAYING.
WE NEED TO TURN THAT HEAT ON, OR WE'RE ALL GOING TO FREEZE TO DEATH.
BASEMENT
IT'S SO COLD I CAN'T EVEN FUCKING THINK. I CAN'T EVEN THINK IT'S SO FUUCCCKKKIING COOOOO--

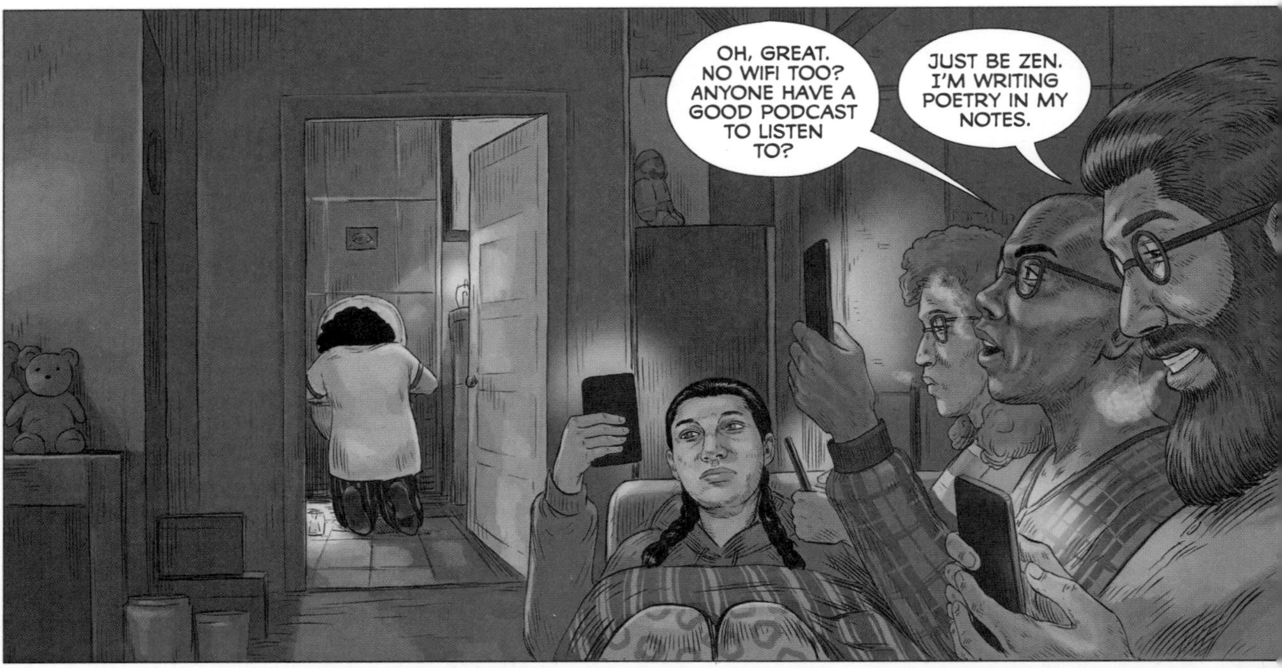
OH, GREAT. NO WIFI TOO? ANYONE HAVE A GOOD PODCAST TO LISTEN TO?
JUST BE ZEN. I'M WRITING POETRY IN MY NOTES.

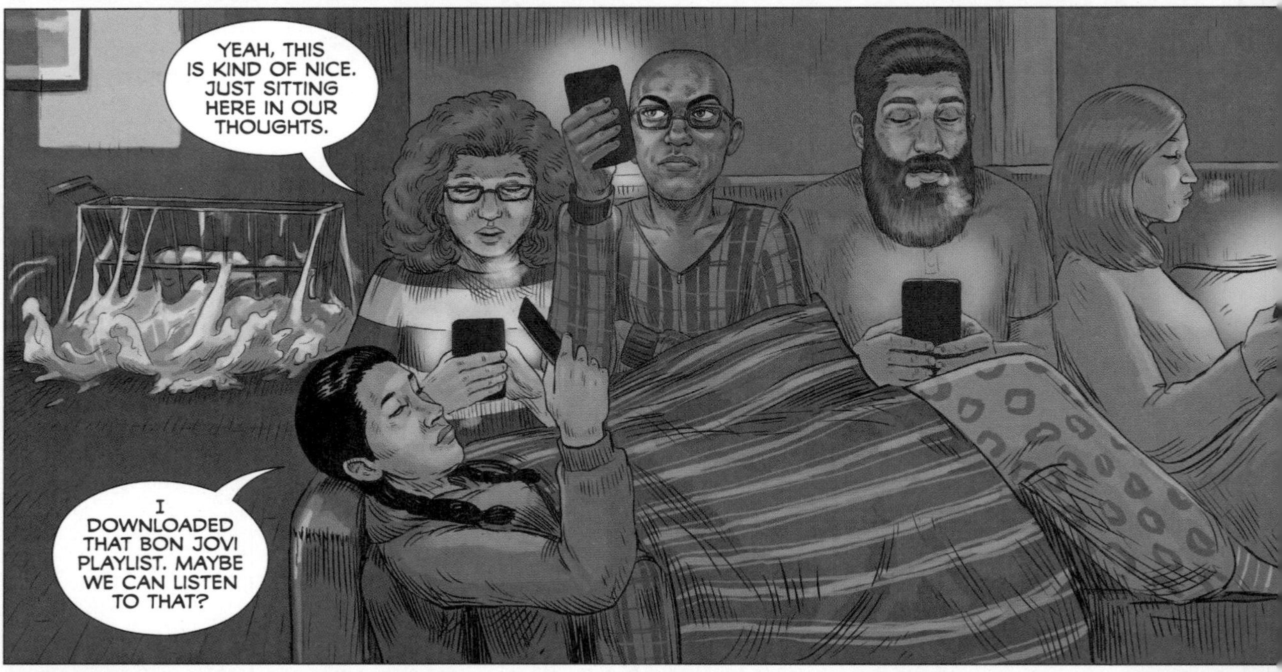
YEAH, THIS IS KIND OF NICE. JUST SITTING HERE IN OUR THOUGHTS.
I DOWNLOADED THAT BON JOVI PLAYLIST. MAYBE WE CAN LISTEN TO THAT?

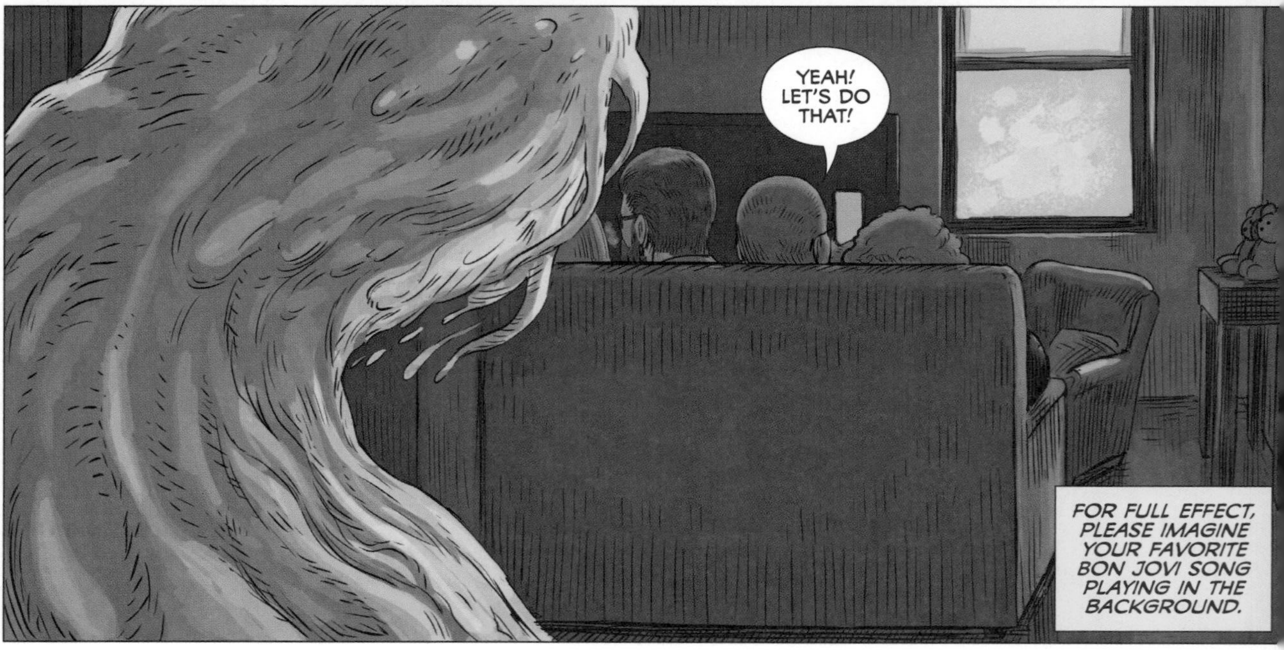
YEAH! LET'S DO THAT!
FOR FULL EFFECT, PLEASE IMAGINE YOUR FAVORITE BON JOVI SONG PLAYING IN THE BACKGROUND.

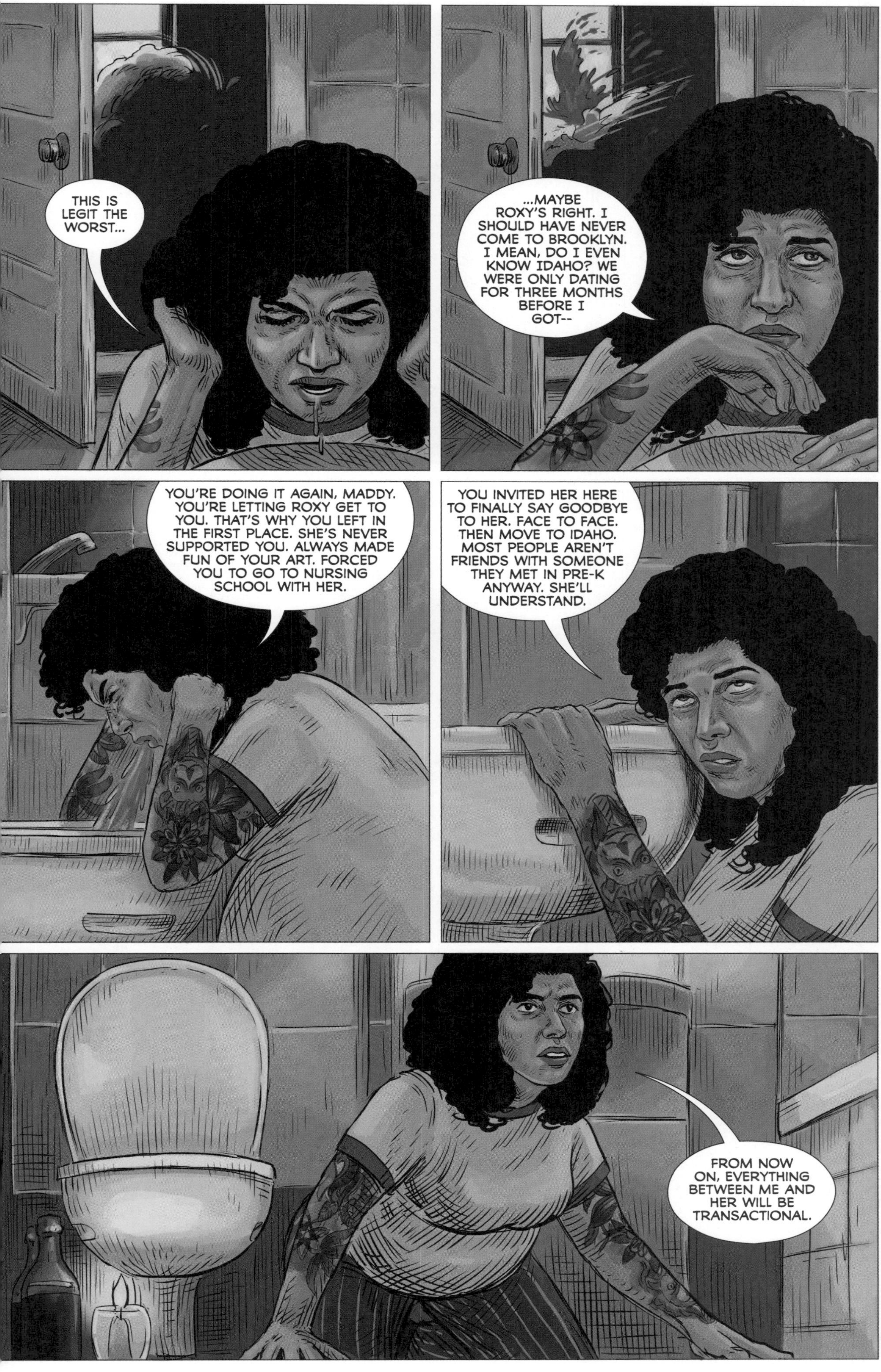
THIS IS LEGIT THE WORST...
...MAYBE ROXY'S RIGHT. I SHOULD HAVE NEVER COME TO BROOKLYN. I MEAN, DO I EVEN KNOW IDAHO? WE WERE ONLY DATING FOR THREE MONTHS BEFORE I GOT--
YOU'RE DOING IT AGAIN, MADDY. YOU'RE LETTING ROXY GET TO YOU. THAT'S WHY YOU LEFT IN THE FIRST PLACE. SHE'S NEVER SUPPORTED YOU. ALWAYS MADE FUN OF YOUR ART. FORCED YOU TO GO TO NURSING SCHOOL WITH HER.
YOU INVITED HER HERE TO FINALLY SAY GOODBYE TO HER. FACE TO FACE. THEN MOVE TO IDAHO. MOST PEOPLE AREN'T FRIENDS WITH SOMEONE THEY MET IN PRE-K ANYWAY. SHE'LL UNDERSTAND.
FROM NOW ON, EVERYTHING BETWEEN ME AND HER WILL BE TRANSACTIONAL.

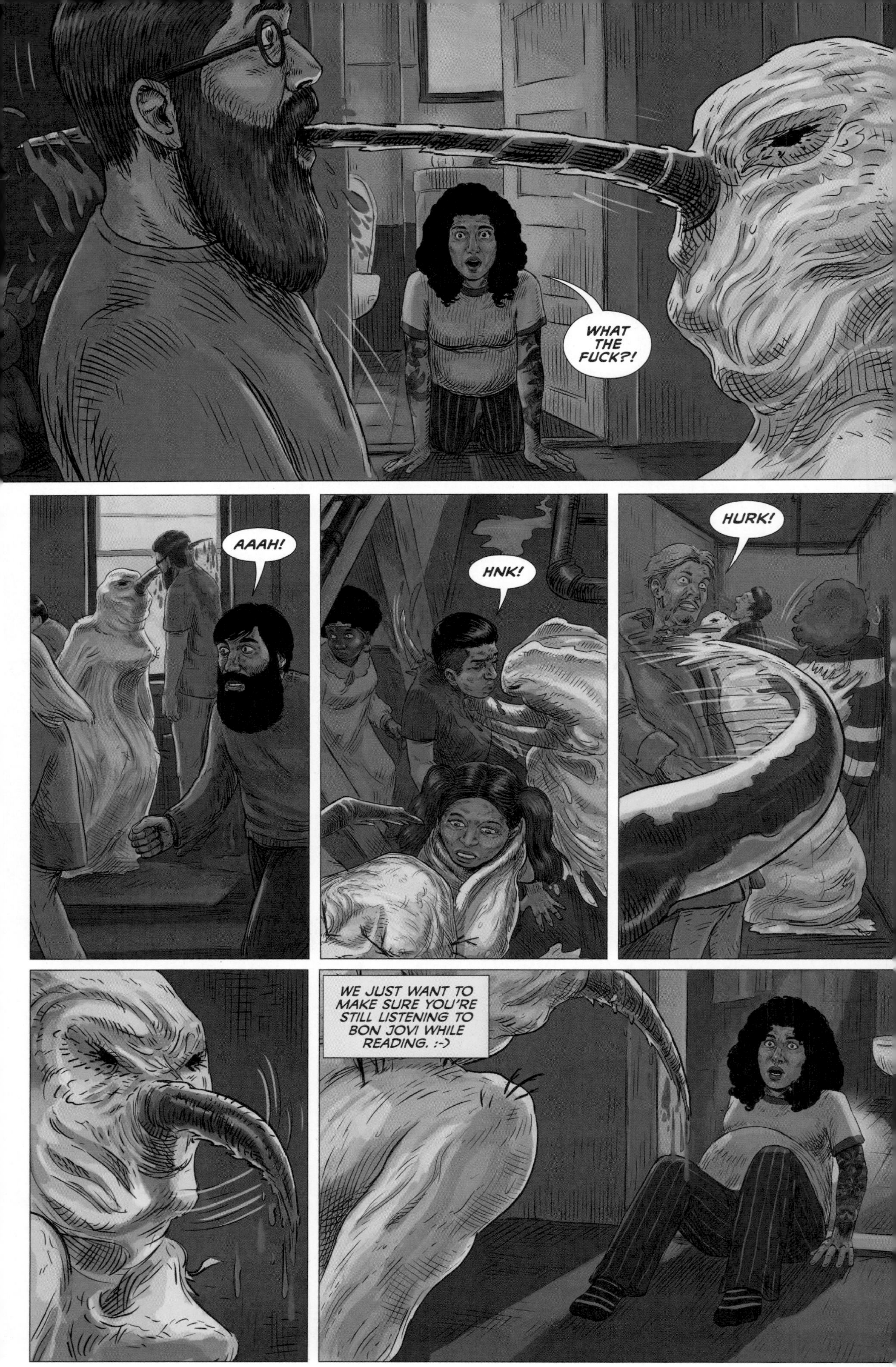
WHAT THE FUCK?!
AAAH!
HNK!
HURK!
WE JUST WANT TO MAKE SURE YOU'RE STILL LISTENING TO BON JOVI WHILE READING. :-)

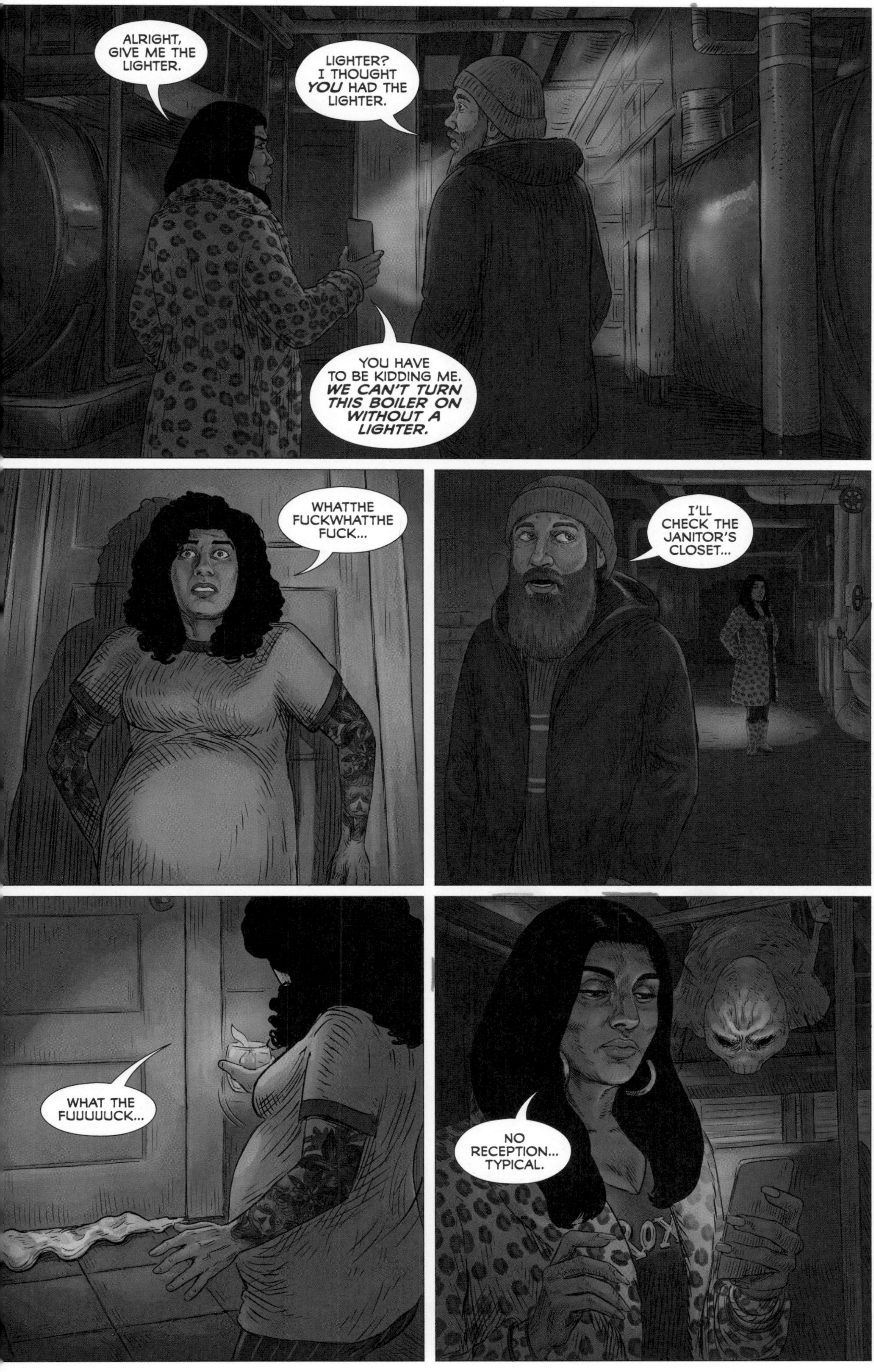
ALRIGHT, GIVE ME THE LIGHTER.
LIGHTER? I THOUGHT *YOU* HAD THE LIGHTER.
YOU HAVE TO BE KIDDING ME. ***WE CAN'T TURN THIS BOILER ON WITHOUT A LIGHTER.***
WHATTHE FUCKWHATTHE FUCK...
I'LL CHECK THE JANITOR'S CLOSET...
WHAT THE FUUUUUCK...
NO RECEPTION... TYPICAL.

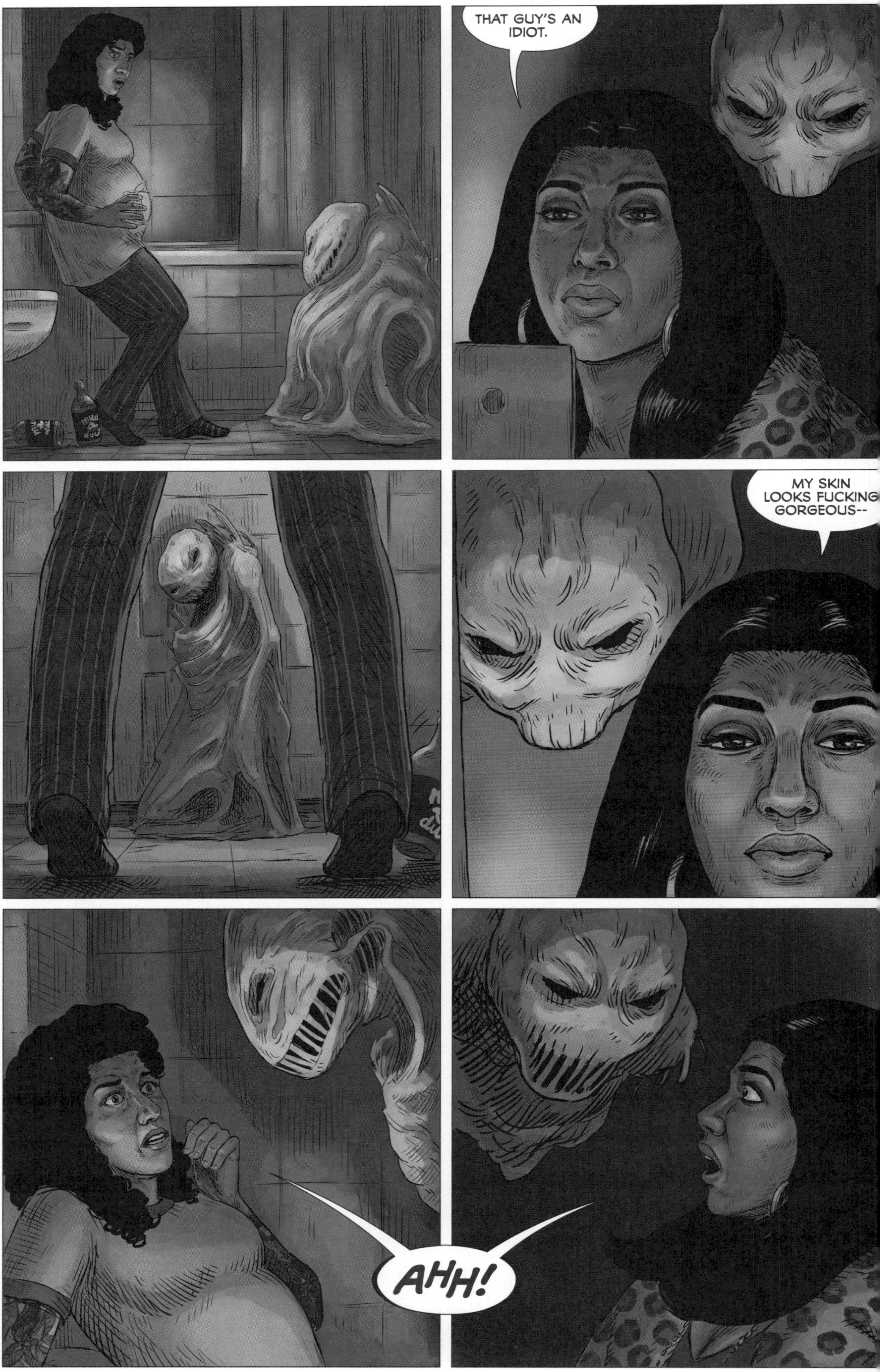
THAT GUY'S AN IDIOT.
MY SKIN LOOKS FUCKING GORGEOUS--
AHH!

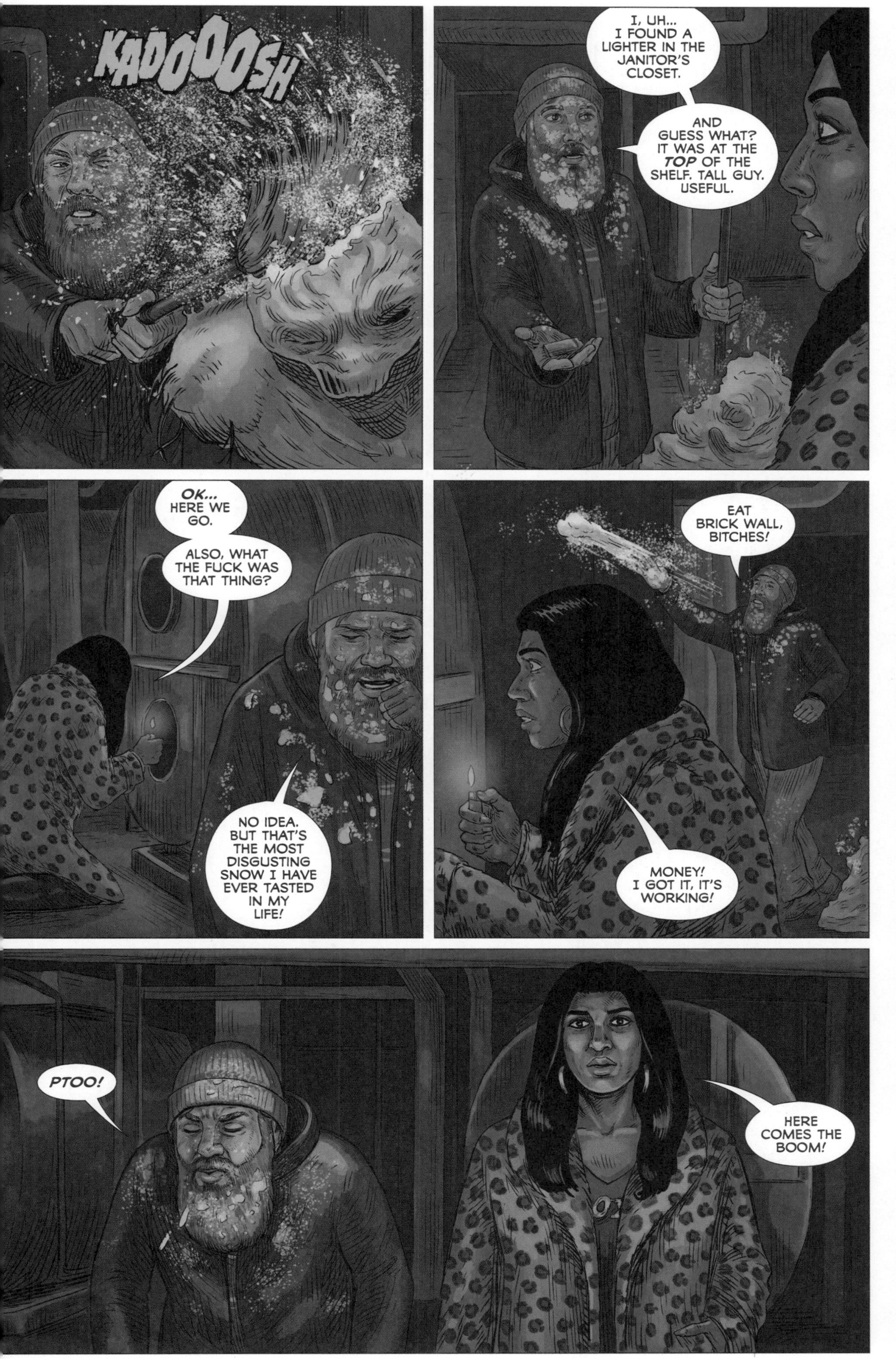
KADOOOOSH
I, UH... I FOUND A LIGHTER IN THE JANITOR'S CLOSET.
AND GUESS WHAT? IT WAS AT THE *TOP* OF THE SHELF. TALL GUY. USEFUL.
OK... HERE WE GO.
ALSO, WHAT THE FUCK WAS THAT THING?
NO IDEA. BUT THAT'S THE MOST DISGUSTING SNOW I HAVE EVER TASTED IN MY LIFE!
EAT BRICK WALL, BITCHES!
MONEY! I GOT IT, IT'S WORKING!
PTOO!
HERE COMES THE BOOM!

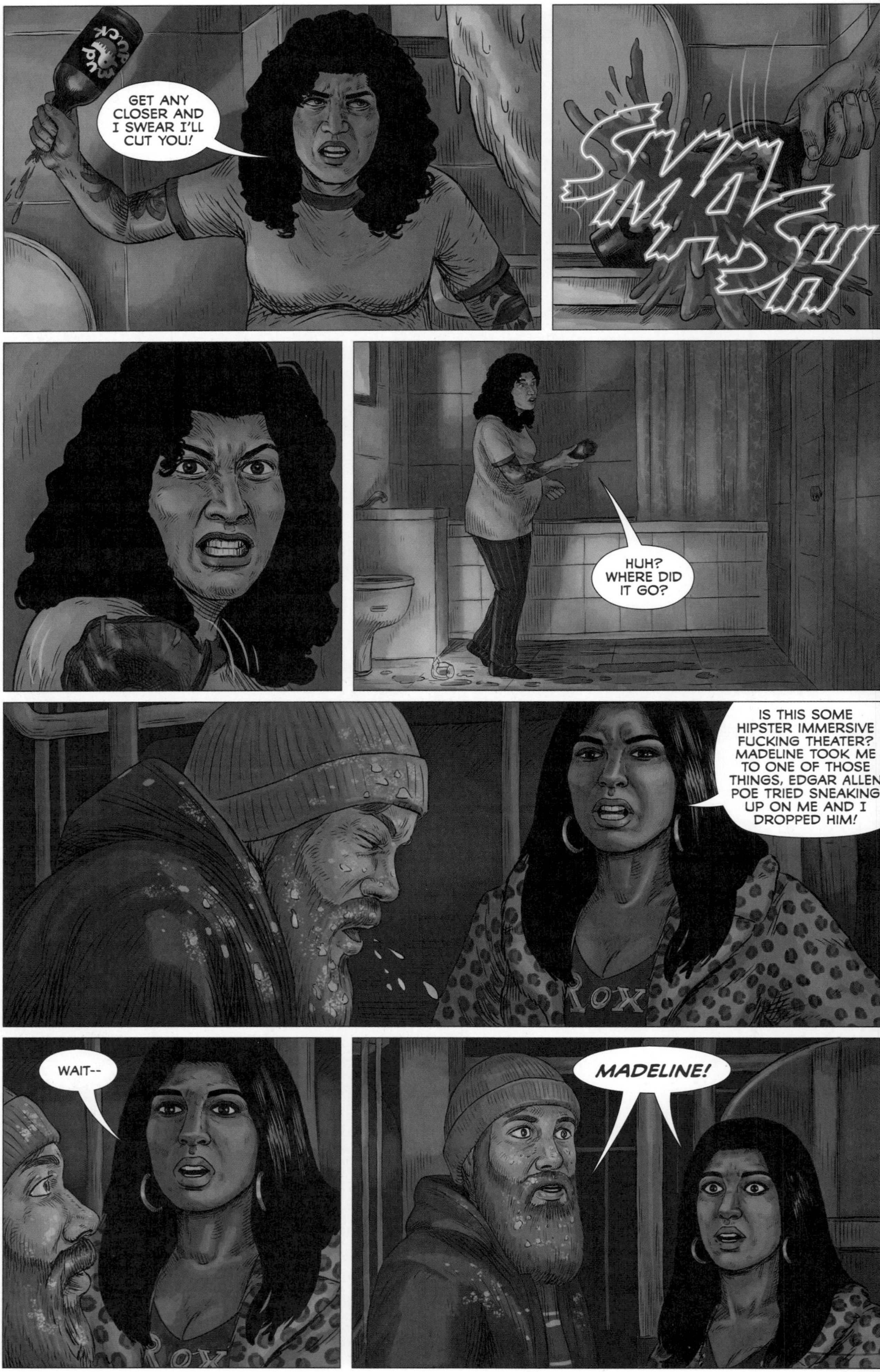
GET ANY CLOSER AND I SWEAR I'LL CUT YOU!
SMASH
HUH? WHERE DID IT GO?
IS THIS SOME HIPSTER IMMERSIVE FUCKING THEATER? MADELINE TOOK ME TO ONE OF THOSE THINGS, EDGAR ALLEN POE TRIED SNEAKING UP ON ME AND I DROPPED HIM!
WAIT--
MADELINE!

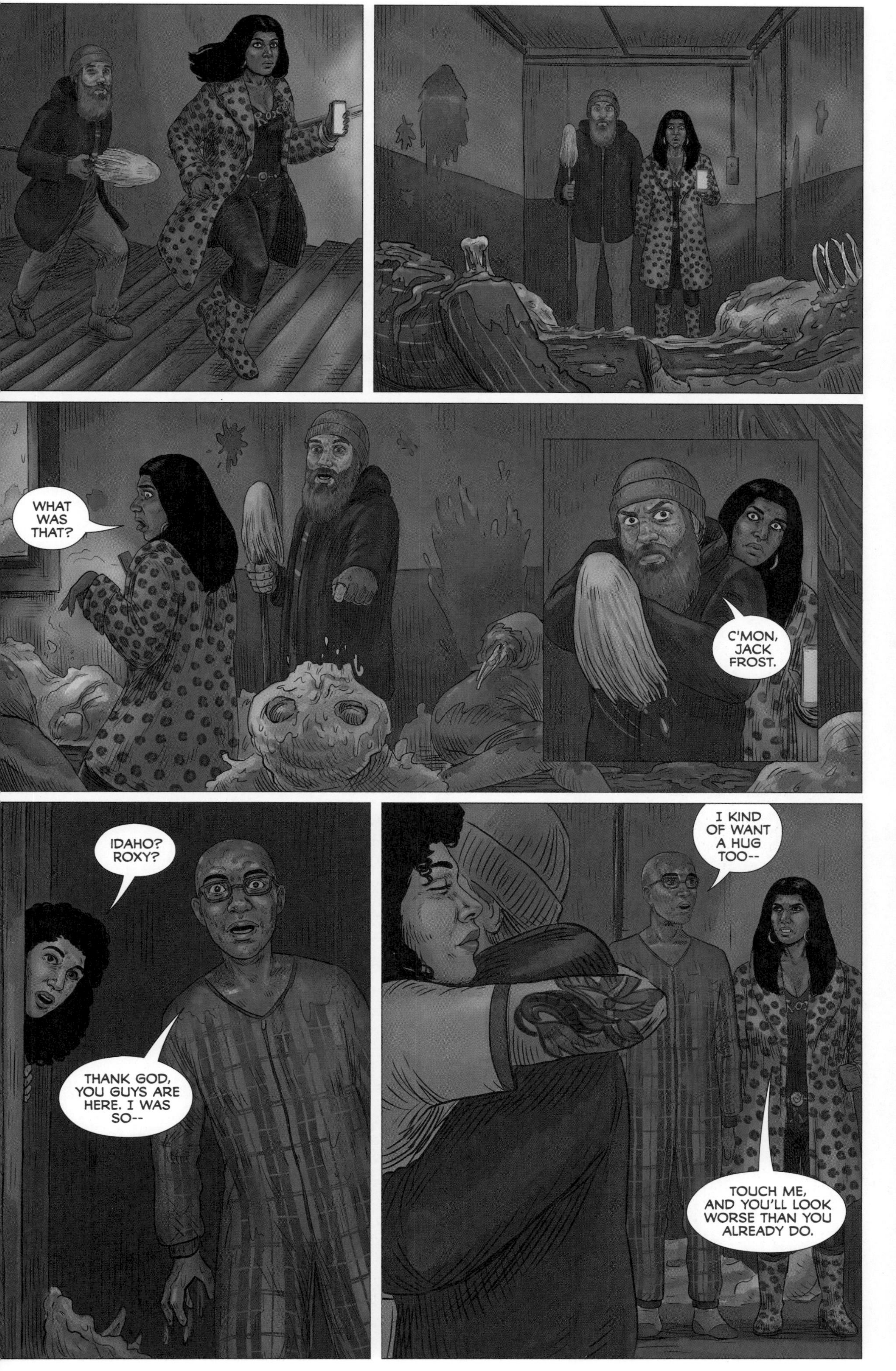
WHAT WAS THAT?
C'MON, JACK FROST.
IDAHO? ROXY?
THANK GOD, YOU GUYS ARE HERE. I WAS SO--
I KIND OF WANT A HUG TOO--
TOUCH ME, AND YOU'LL LOOK WORSE THAN YOU ALREADY DO.

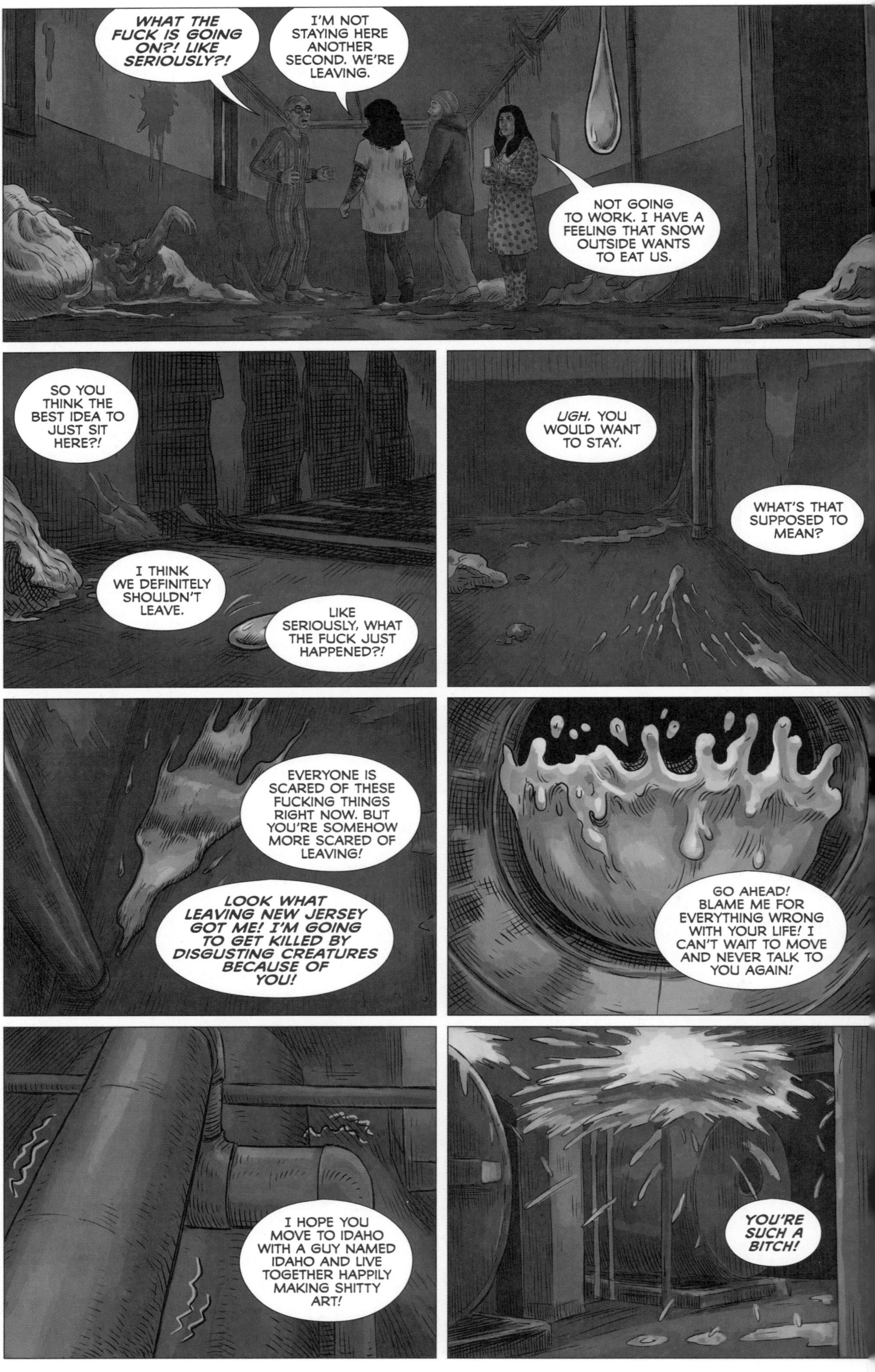
WHAT THE FUCK IS GOING ON?! LIKE SERIOUSLY?!
I'M NOT STAYING HERE ANOTHER SECOND. WE'RE LEAVING.
NOT GOING TO WORK. I HAVE A FEELING THAT SNOW OUTSIDE WANTS TO EAT US.
SO YOU THINK THE BEST IDEA TO JUST SIT HERE?!
I THINK WE DEFINITELY SHOULDN'T LEAVE.
LIKE SERIOUSLY, WHAT THE FUCK JUST HAPPENED?!
UGH. YOU WOULD WANT TO STAY.
WHAT'S THAT SUPPOSED TO MEAN?
EVERYONE IS SCARED OF THESE FUCKING THINGS RIGHT NOW. BUT YOU'RE SOMEHOW MORE SCARED OF LEAVING!
LOOK WHAT LEAVING NEW JERSEY GOT ME! I'M GOING TO GET KILLED BY DISGUSTING CREATURES BECAUSE OF YOU!
GO AHEAD! BLAME ME FOR EVERYTHING WRONG WITH YOUR LIFE! I CAN'T WAIT TO MOVE AND NEVER TALK TO YOU AGAIN!
I HOPE YOU MOVE TO IDAHO WITH A GUY NAMED IDAHO AND LIVE TOGETHER HAPPILY MAKING SHITTY ART!
YOU'RE SUCH A BITCH!

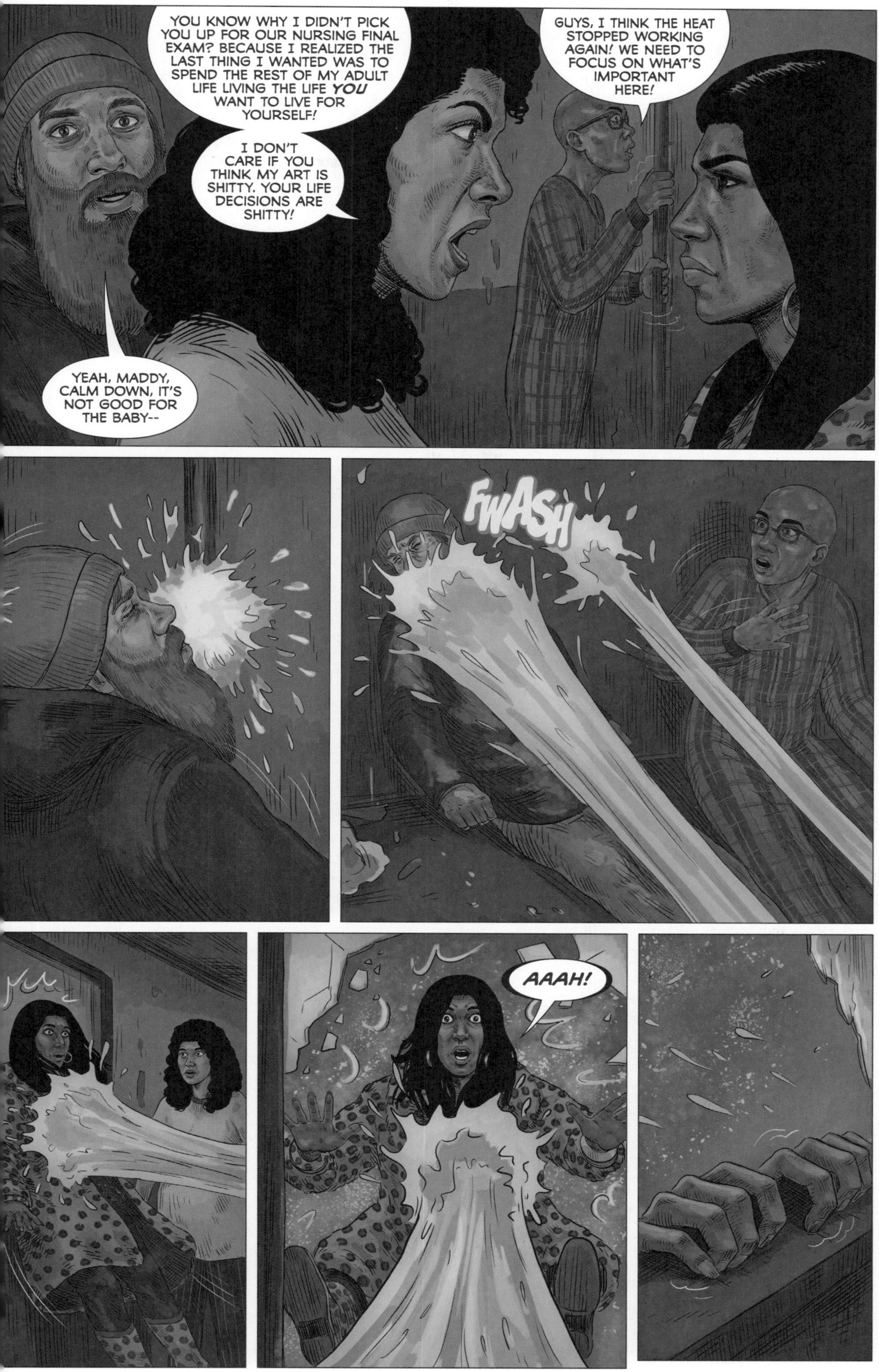
YOU KNOW WHY I DIDN'T PICK YOU UP FOR OUR NURSING FINAL EXAM? BECAUSE I REALIZED THE LAST THING I WANTED WAS TO SPEND THE REST OF MY ADULT LIFE LIVING THE LIFE *YOU* WANT TO LIVE FOR YOURSELF!
I DON'T CARE IF YOU THINK MY ART IS SHITTY. YOUR LIFE DECISIONS ARE SHITTY!
GUYS, I THINK THE HEAT STOPPED WORKING AGAIN! WE NEED TO FOCUS ON WHAT'S IMPORTANT HERE!
YEAH, MADDY, CALM DOWN, IT'S NOT GOOD FOR THE BABY--
FWASH
AAAH!

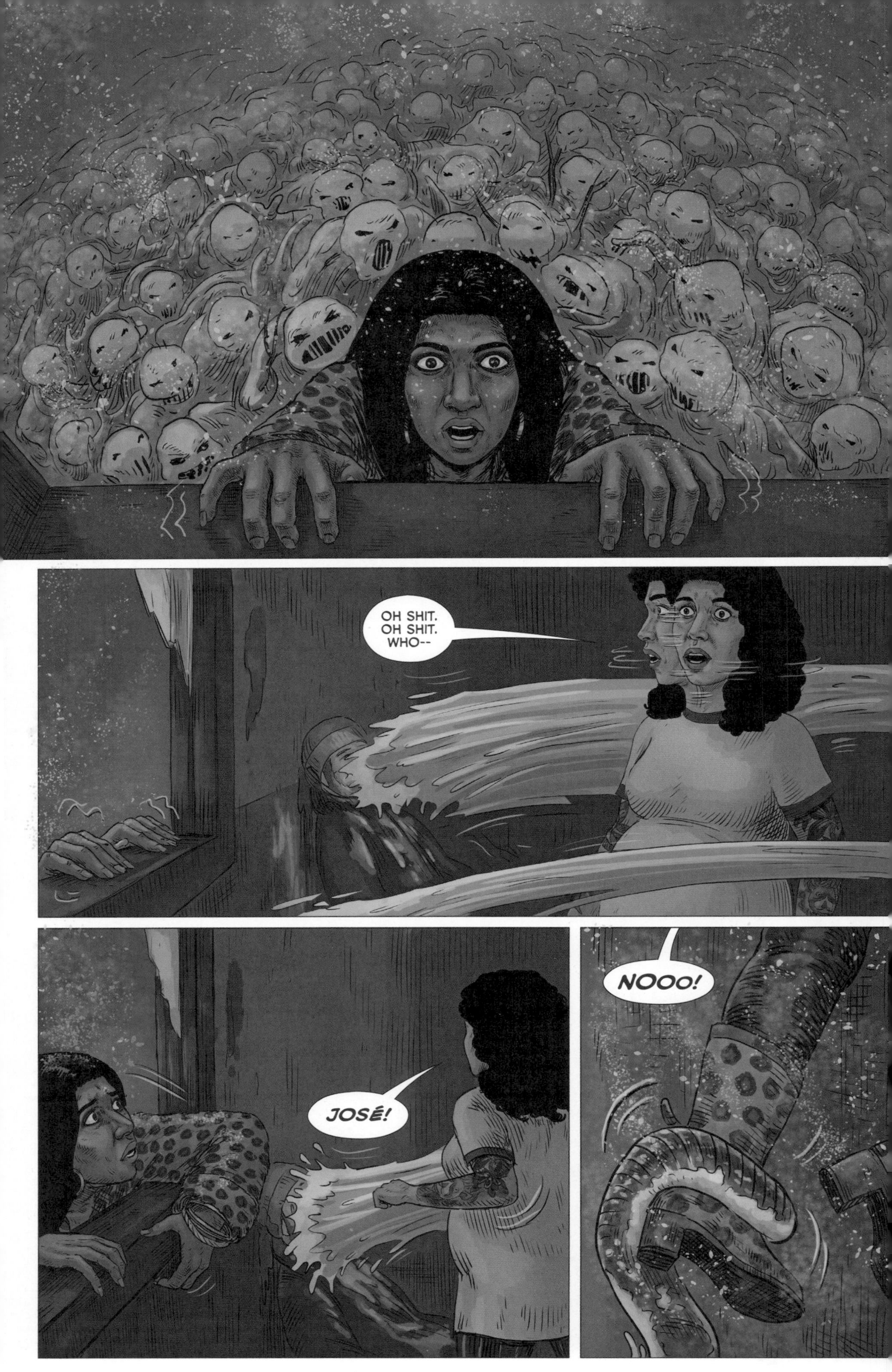
OH SHIT.
OH SHIT.
WHO--
JOSÉ!
NOOO!

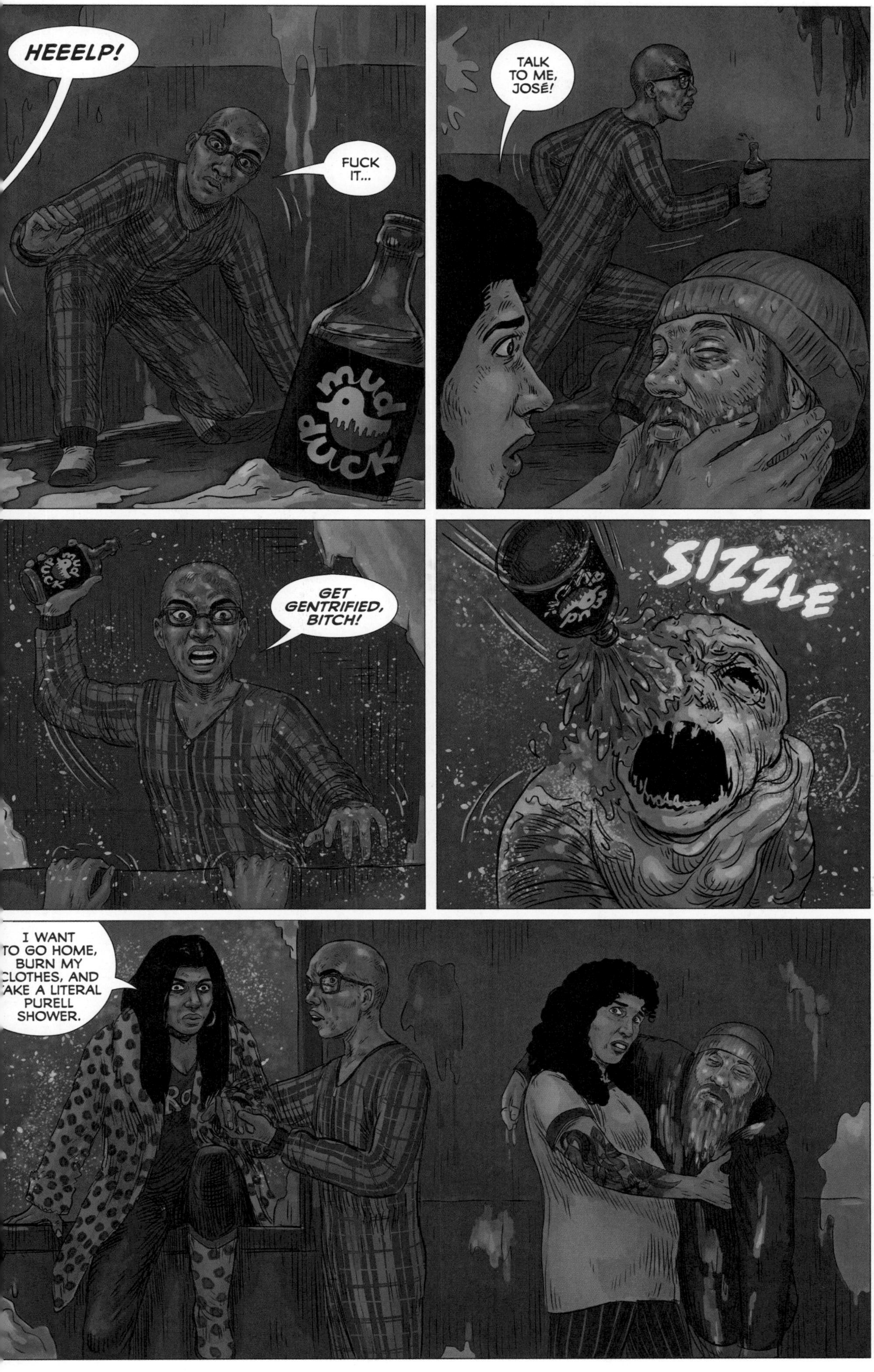
HEEELP!
FUCK IT...
mud duck
TALK TO ME, JOSÉ!
GET GENTRIFIED, BITCH!
SIZZLE
I WANT TO GO HOME, BURN MY CLOTHES, AND TAKE A LITERAL PURELL SHOWER.

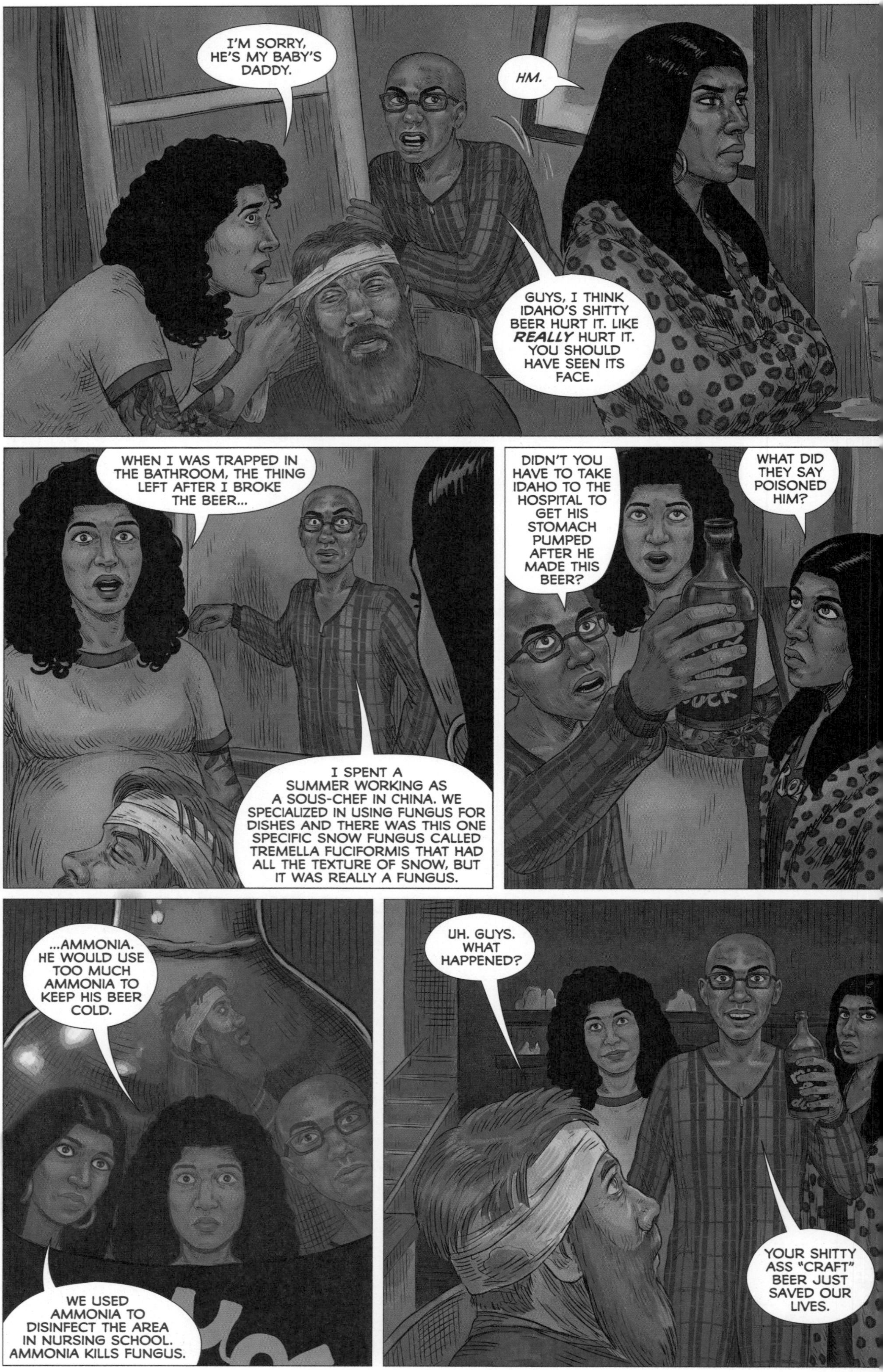
I'M SORRY, HE'S MY BABY'S DADDY.
HM.
GUYS, I THINK IDAHO'S SHITTY BEER HURT IT. LIKE *REALLY* HURT IT. YOU SHOULD HAVE SEEN ITS FACE.
WHEN I WAS TRAPPED IN THE BATHROOM, THE THING LEFT AFTER I BROKE THE BEER...
I SPENT A SUMMER WORKING AS A SOUS-CHEF IN CHINA. WE SPECIALIZED IN USING FUNGUS FOR DISHES AND THERE WAS THIS ONE SPECIFIC SNOW FUNGUS CALLED TREMELLA FUCIFORMIS THAT HAD ALL THE TEXTURE OF SNOW, BUT IT WAS REALLY A FUNGUS.
DIDN'T YOU HAVE TO TAKE IDAHO TO THE HOSPITAL TO GET HIS STOMACH PUMPED AFTER HE MADE THIS BEER?
WHAT DID THEY SAY POISONED HIM?
...AMMONIA. HE WOULD USE TOO MUCH AMMONIA TO KEEP HIS BEER COLD.
WE USED AMMONIA TO DISINFECT THE AREA IN NURSING SCHOOL. AMMONIA KILLS FUNGUS.
UH. GUYS. WHAT HAPPENED?
YOUR SHITTY ASS "CRAFT" BEER JUST SAVED OUR LIVES.

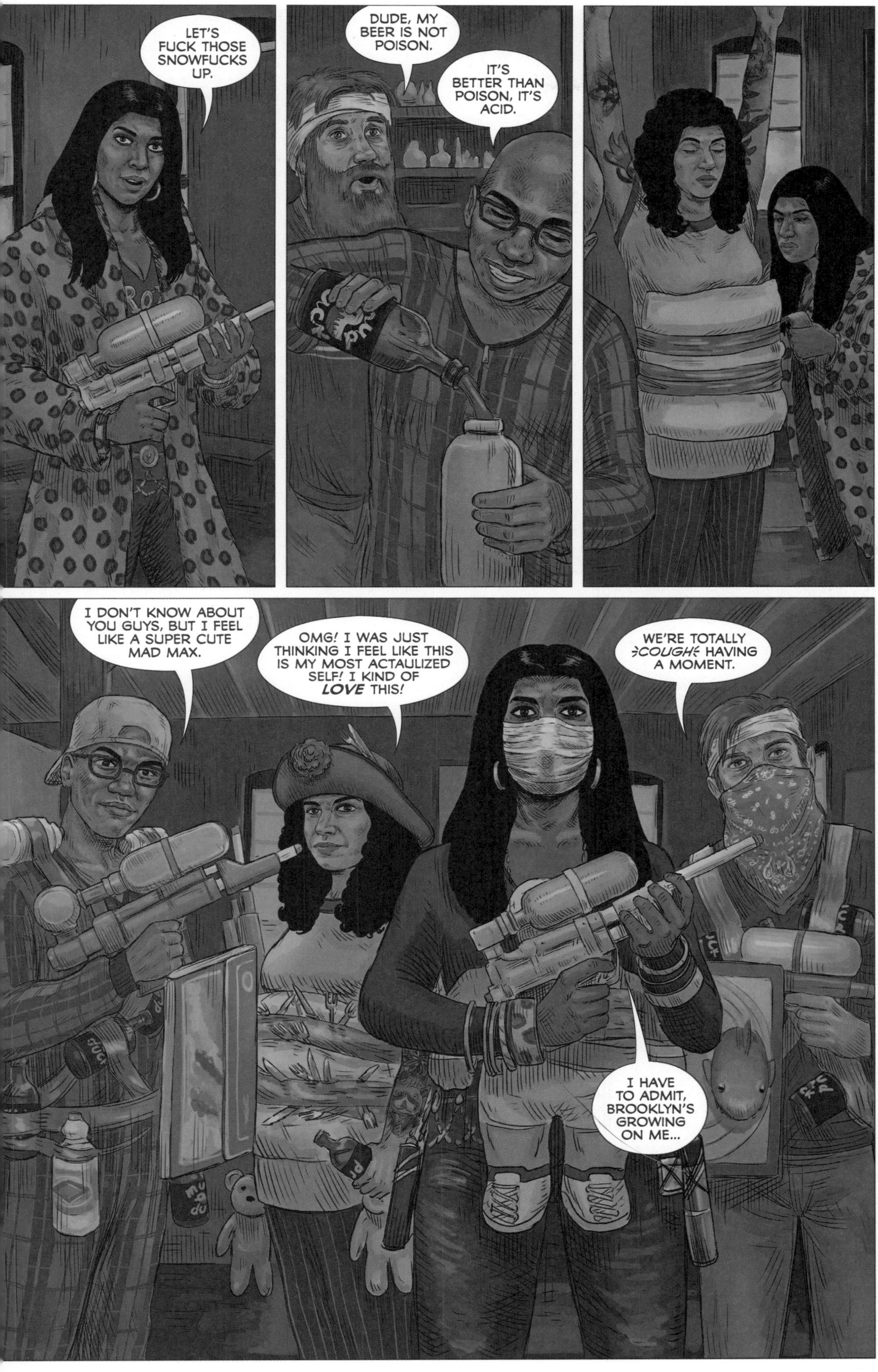
LET'S FUCK THOSE SNOWFUCKS UP.
DUDE, MY BEER IS NOT POISON.
IT'S BETTER THAN POISON, IT'S ACID.
I DON'T KNOW ABOUT YOU GUYS, BUT I FEEL LIKE A SUPER CUTE MAD MAX.
OMG! I WAS JUST THINKING I FEEL LIKE THIS IS MY MOST ACTAULIZED SELF! I KIND OF LOVE THIS!
WE'RE TOTALLY *COUGH* HAVING A MOMENT.
I HAVE TO ADMIT, BROOKLYN'S GROWING ON ME...

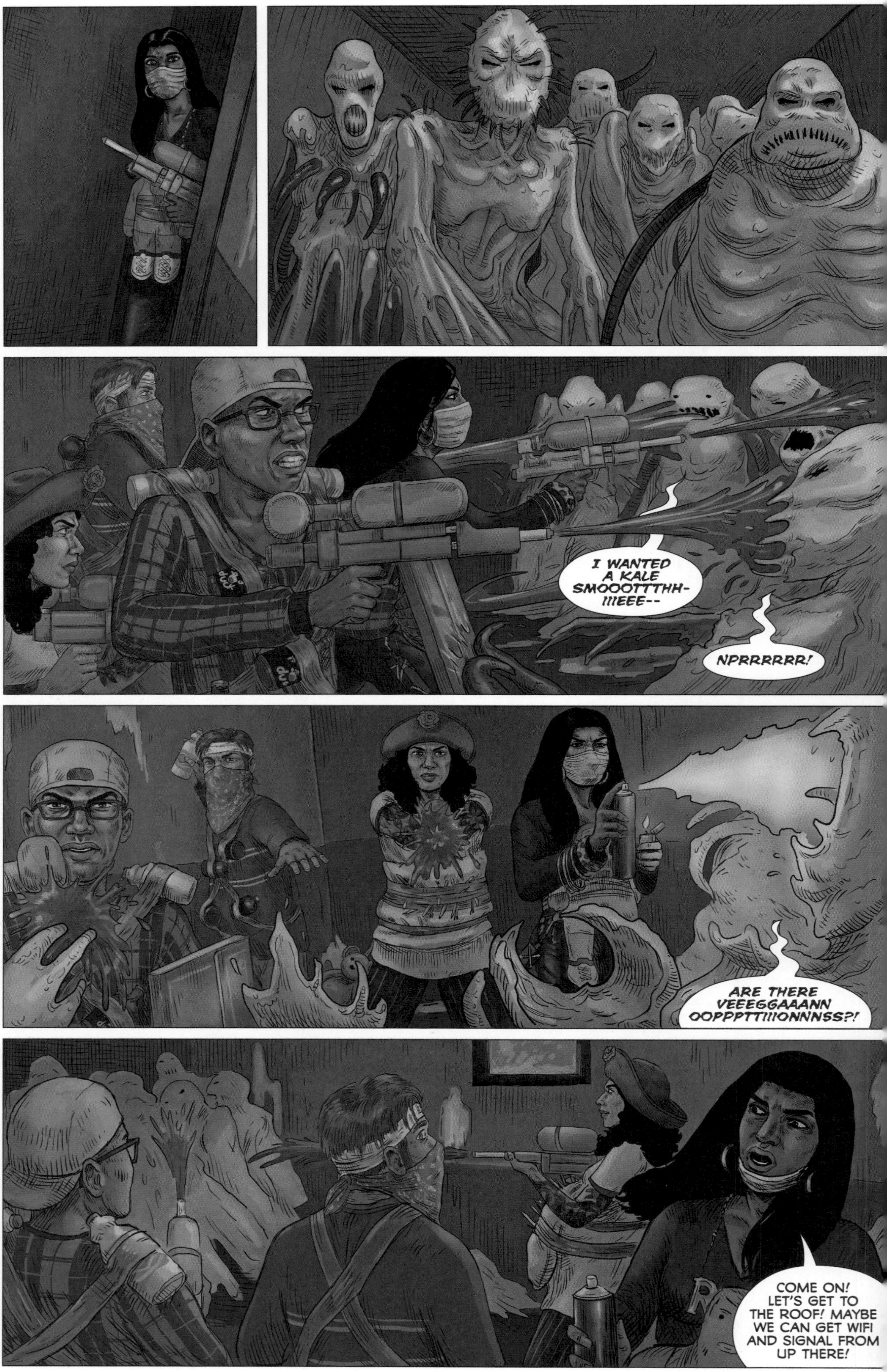
I WANTED A KALE SMOOOTTTHH-IIIEEE--
NPRRRRRR!
ARE THERE VEEEGGAAANN OOPPPTTIIIONNNSS?!
COME ON! LET'S GET TO THE ROOF! MAYBE WE CAN GET WIFI AND SIGNAL FROM UP THERE!

I'M STARTING A POOODDDCCAASSS ttt--

UH...GUYS. IDAHO DOESN'T LOOK GOOD.

OMG-- FRESH AIR, FINALLY.

IDAHO? WHAT THE FUCK IS WRONG WITH YOUR FACE?!

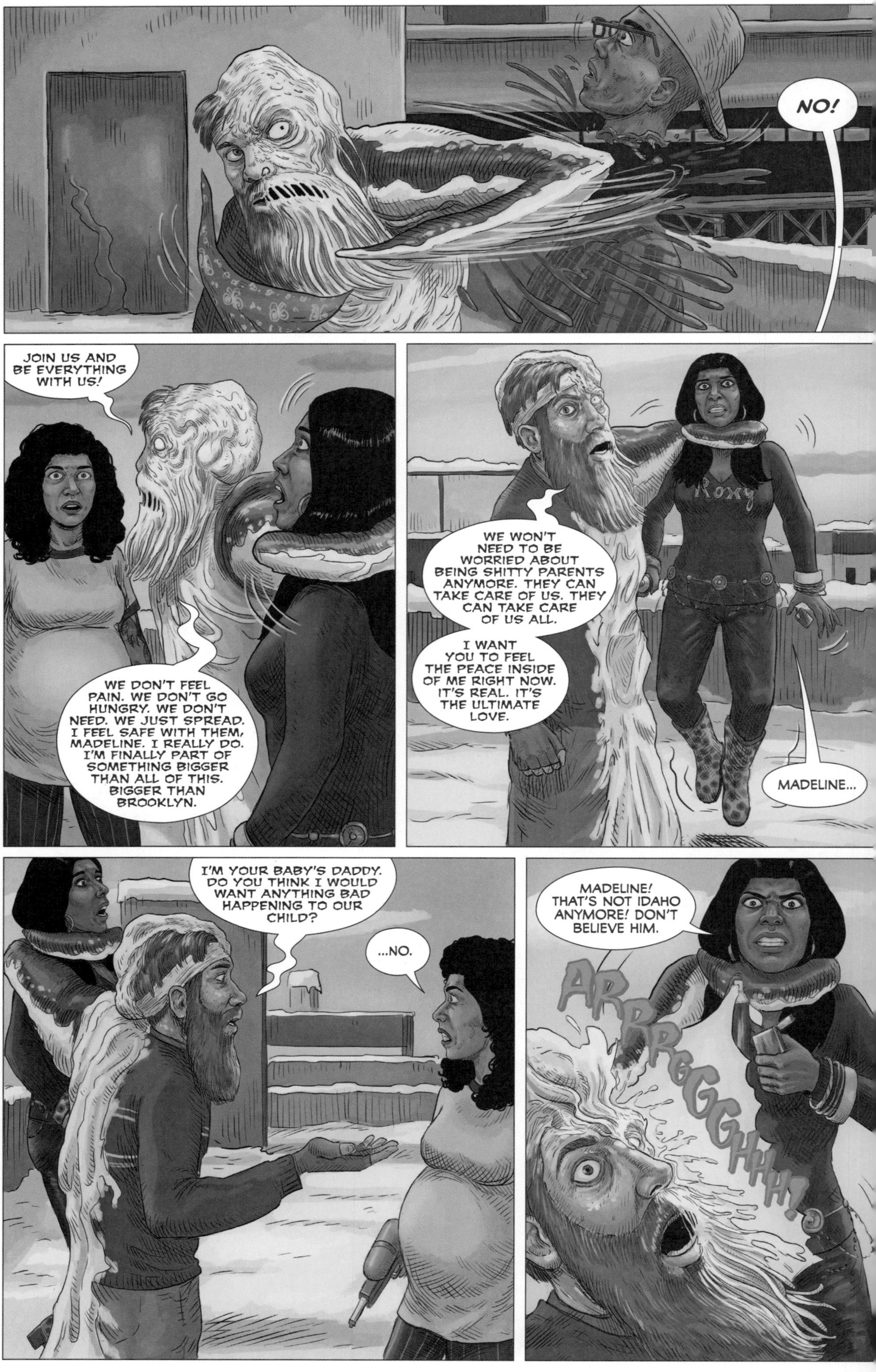
NO!
JOIN US AND BE EVERYTHING WITH US!
WE DON'T FEEL PAIN. WE DON'T GO HUNGRY. WE DON'T NEED. WE JUST SPREAD. I FEEL SAFE WITH THEM, MADELINE. I REALLY DO. I'M FINALLY PART OF SOMETHING BIGGER THAN ALL OF THIS. BIGGER THAN BROOKLYN.
Roxy
WE WON'T NEED TO BE WORRIED ABOUT BEING SHITTY PARENTS ANYMORE. THEY CAN TAKE CARE OF US. THEY CAN TAKE CARE OF US ALL.
I WANT YOU TO FEEL THE PEACE INSIDE OF ME RIGHT NOW. IT'S REAL. IT'S THE ULTIMATE LOVE.
MADELINE...
I'M YOUR BABY'S DADDY. DO YOU THINK I WOULD WANT ANYTHING BAD HAPPENING TO OUR CHILD?
...NO.
MADELINE! THAT'S NOT IDAHO ANYMORE! DON'T BELIEVE HIM.
ARRRGGGHHH!

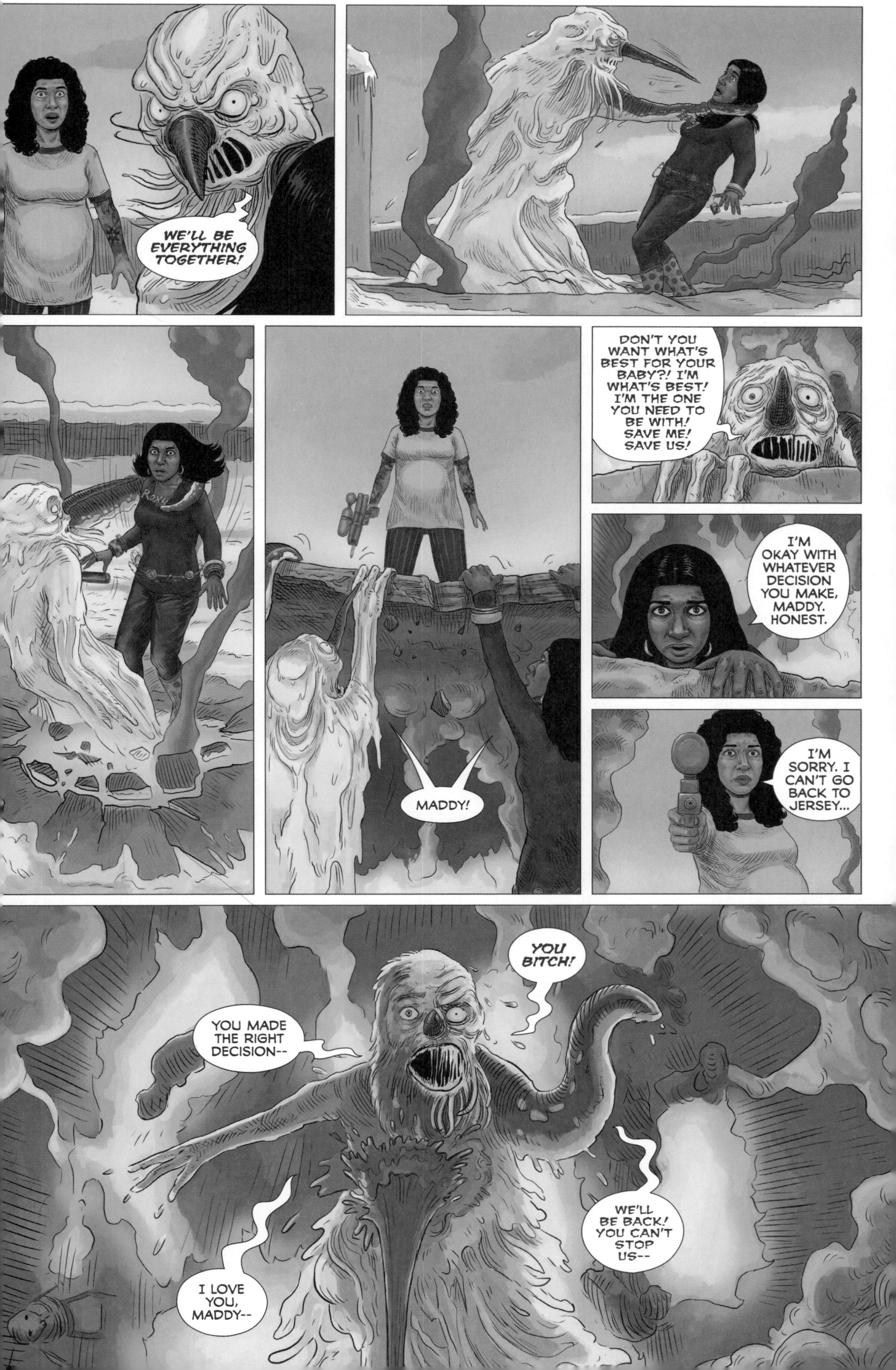
WE'LL BE EVERYTHING TOGETHER!
DON'T YOU WANT WHAT'S BEST FOR YOUR BABY?! I'M WHAT'S BEST! I'M THE ONE YOU NEED TO BE WITH! SAVE ME! SAVE US!
MADDY!
I'M OKAY WITH WHATEVER DECISION YOU MAKE, MADDY. HONEST.
I'M SORRY. I CAN'T GO BACK TO JERSEY...
YOU BITCH!
YOU MADE THE RIGHT DECISION--
WE'LL BE BACK! YOU CAN'T STOP US--
I LOVE YOU, MADDY--

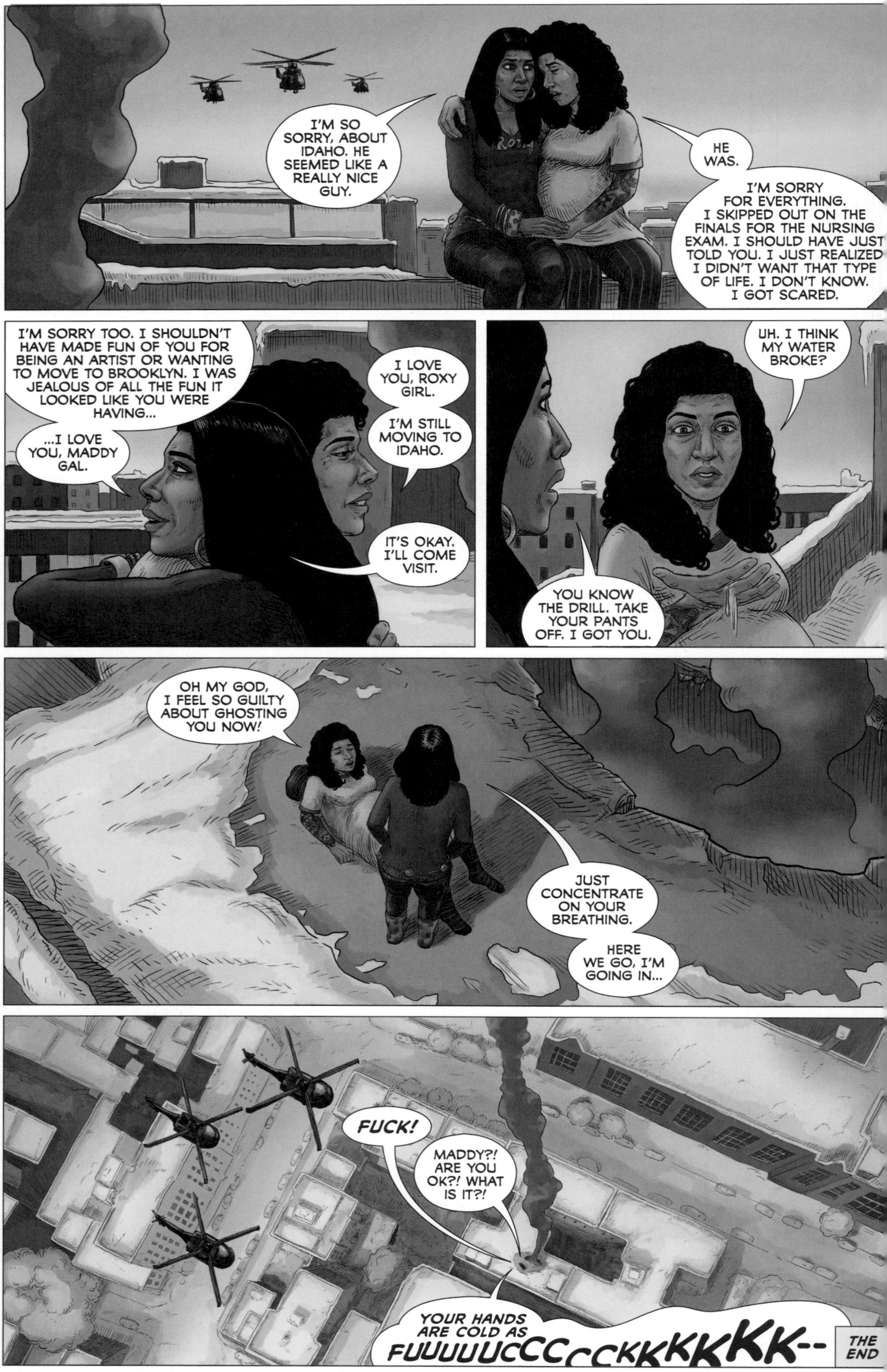
I'M SO SORRY, ABOUT IDAHO. HE SEEMED LIKE A REALLY NICE GUY.
HE WAS.
I'M SORRY FOR EVERYTHING. I SKIPPED OUT ON THE FINALS FOR THE NURSING EXAM. I SHOULD HAVE JUST TOLD YOU. I JUST REALIZED I DIDN'T WANT THAT TYPE OF LIFE. I DON'T KNOW. I GOT SCARED.
I'M SORRY TOO. I SHOULDN'T HAVE MADE FUN OF YOU FOR BEING AN ARTIST OR WANTING TO MOVE TO BROOKLYN. I WAS JEALOUS OF ALL THE FUN IT LOOKED LIKE YOU WERE HAVING...
...I LOVE YOU, MADDY GAL.
I LOVE YOU, ROXY GIRL.
I'M STILL MOVING TO IDAHO.
IT'S OKAY. I'LL COME VISIT.
UH. I THINK MY WATER BROKE?
YOU KNOW THE DRILL. TAKE YOUR PANTS OFF. I GOT YOU.
OH MY GOD, I FEEL SO GUILTY ABOUT GHOSTING YOU NOW!
JUST CONCENTRATE ON YOUR BREATHING.
HERE WE GO, I'M GOING IN...
FUCK!
MADDY?! ARE YOU OK?! WHAT IS IT?!
YOUR HANDS ARE COLD AS FUUUUUCCCCCKKKKKK--
THE END

HAND ME DOWN

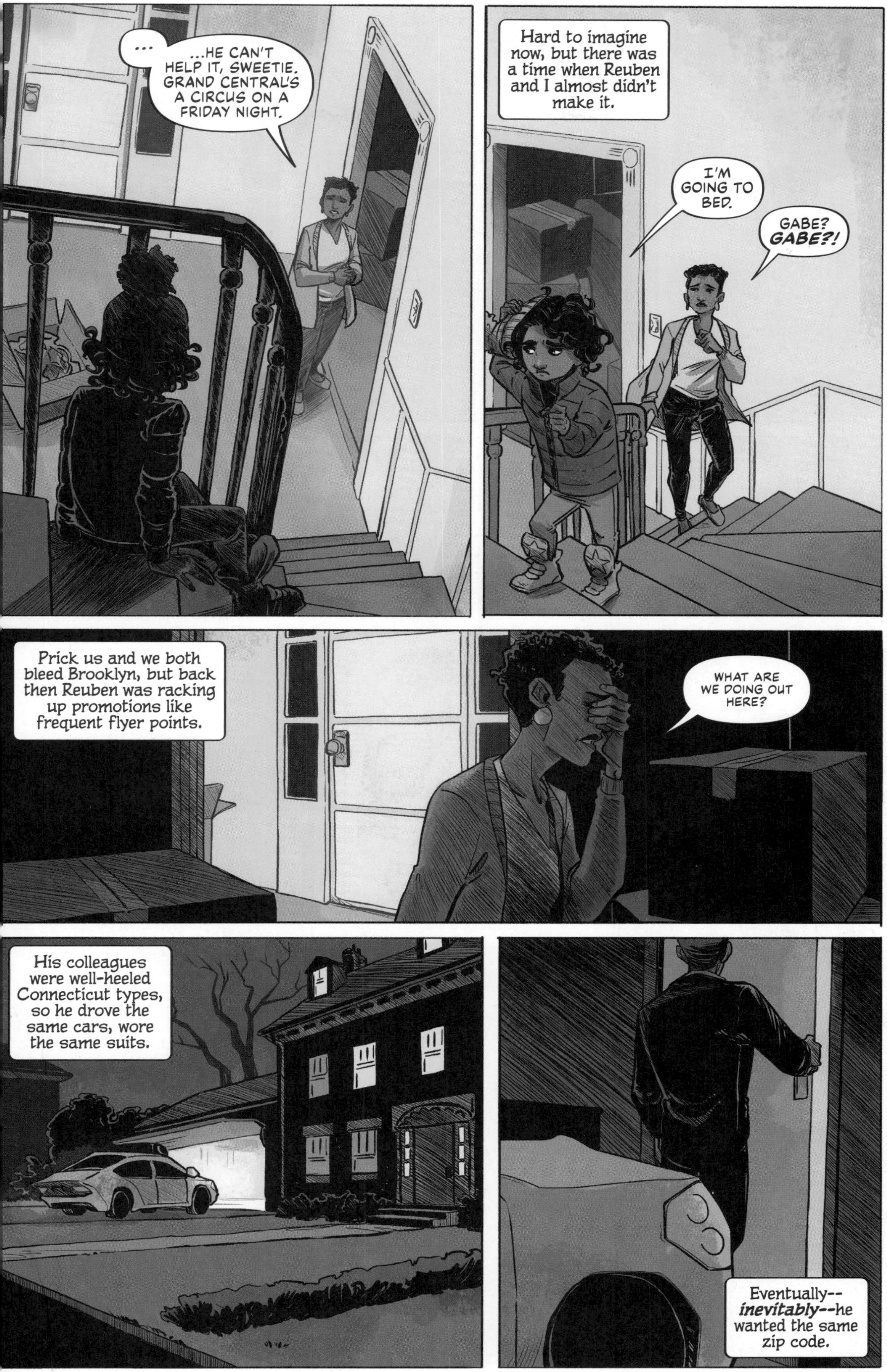
...
...HE CAN'T HELP IT, SWEETIE. GRAND CENTRAL'S A CIRCUS ON A FRIDAY NIGHT.
Hard to imagine now, but there was a time when Reuben and I almost didn't make it.
I'M GOING TO BED.
GABE? GABE?!
Prick us and we both bleed Brooklyn, but back then Reuben was racking up promotions like frequent flyer points.
WHAT ARE WE DOING OUT HERE?
His colleagues were well-heeled Connecticut types, so he drove the same cars, wore the same suits.
Eventually--*inevitably*--he wanted the same zip code.

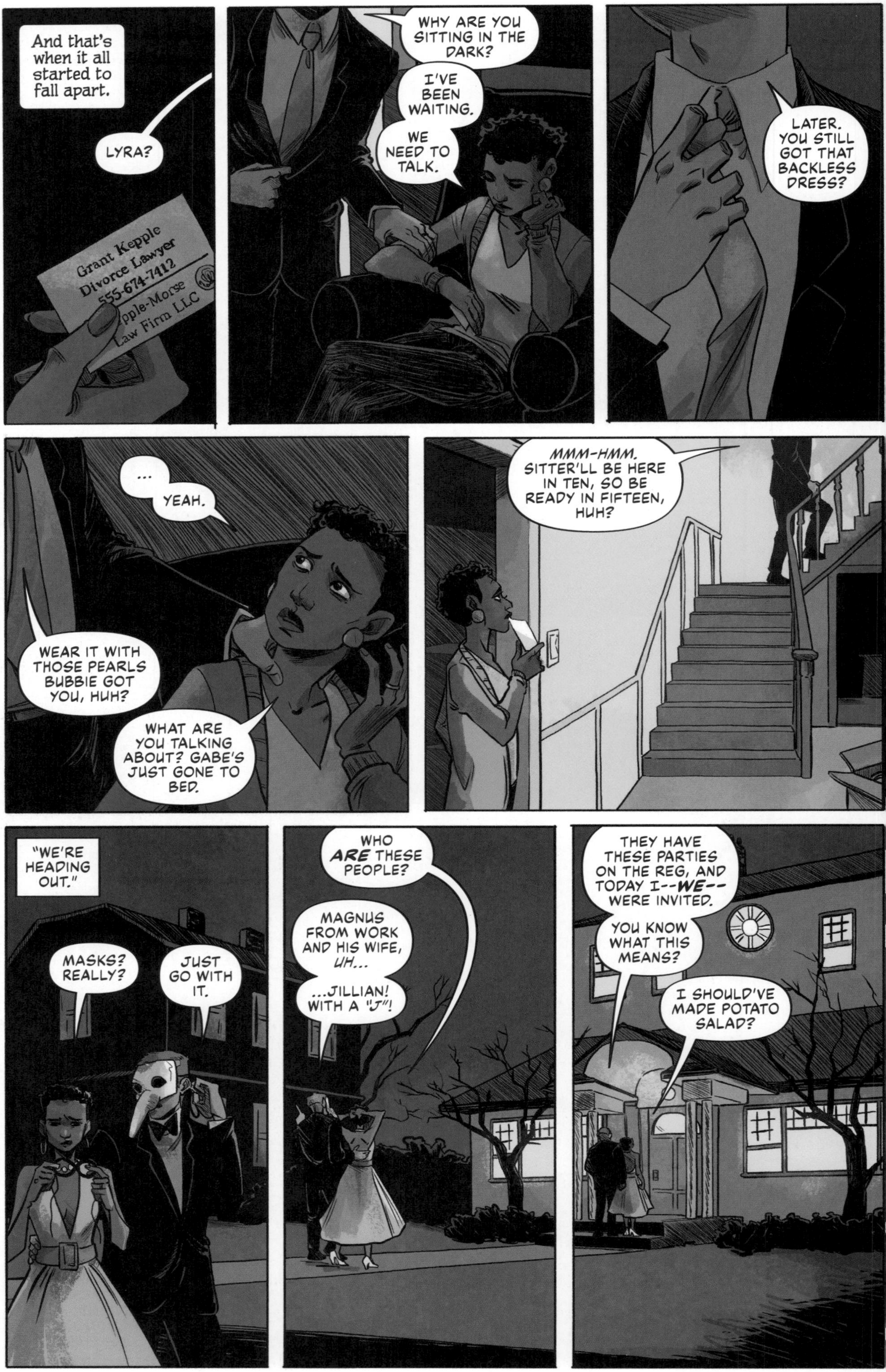
And that's when it all started to fall apart.
LYRA?
Grant Kepple
Divorce Lawyer
555-674-7412
pple-Morse
Law Firm LLC
WHY ARE YOU SITTING IN THE DARK?
I'VE BEEN WAITING.
WE NEED TO TALK.
LATER. YOU STILL GOT THAT BACKLESS DRESS?
... YEAH.
WEAR IT WITH THOSE PEARLS BUBBIE GOT YOU, HUH?
WHAT ARE YOU TALKING ABOUT? GABE'S JUST GONE TO BED.
MMM-HMM. SITTER'LL BE HERE IN TEN, SO BE READY IN FIFTEEN, HUH?
"WE'RE HEADING OUT."
MASKS? REALLY?
JUST GO WITH IT.
WHO ARE THESE PEOPLE?
MAGNUS FROM WORK AND HIS WIFE, UH...
...JILLIAN! WITH A "J"!
THEY HAVE THESE PARTIES ON THE REG, AND TODAY I--WE--WERE INVITED.
YOU KNOW WHAT THIS MEANS?
I SHOULD'VE MADE POTATO SALAD?

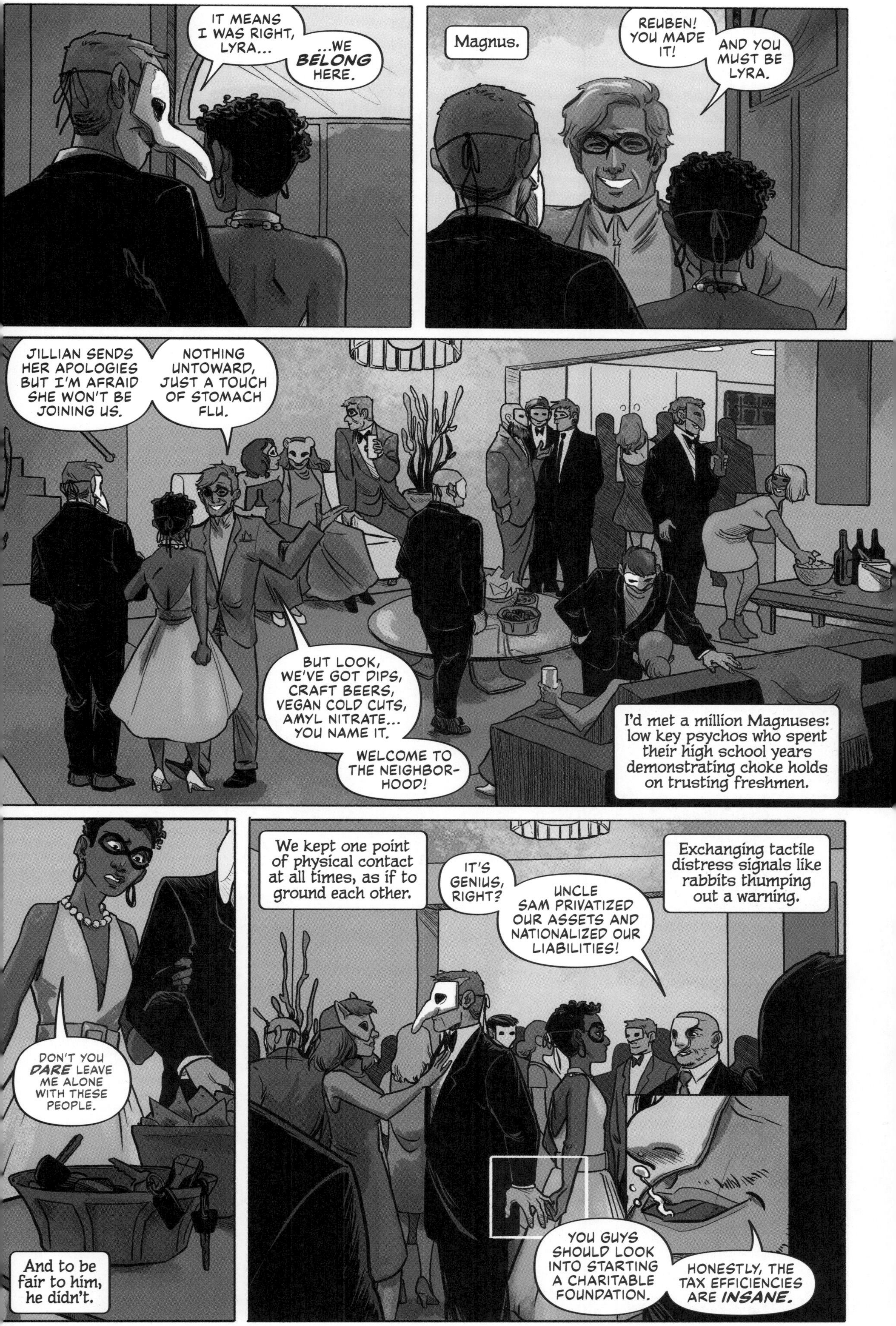
IT MEANS I WAS RIGHT, LYRA...
...WE *BELONG* HERE.
Magnus.
REUBEN! YOU MADE IT!
AND YOU MUST BE LYRA.
JILLIAN SENDS HER APOLOGIES BUT I'M AFRAID SHE WON'T BE JOINING US.
NOTHING UNTOWARD, JUST A TOUCH OF STOMACH FLU.
BUT LOOK, WE'VE GOT DIPS, CRAFT BEERS, VEGAN COLD CUTS, AMYL NITRATE... YOU NAME IT.
WELCOME TO THE NEIGHBOR-HOOD!
I'd met a million Magnuses: low key psychos who spent their high school years demonstrating choke holds on trusting freshmen.
DON'T YOU *DARE* LEAVE ME ALONE WITH THESE PEOPLE.
And to be fair to him, he didn't.
We kept one point of physical contact at all times, as if to ground each other.
IT'S GENIUS, RIGHT?
UNCLE SAM PRIVATIZED OUR ASSETS AND NATIONALIZED OUR LIABILITIES!
Exchanging tactile distress signals like rabbits thumping out a warning.
YOU GUYS SHOULD LOOK INTO STARTING A CHARITABLE FOUNDATION.
HONESTLY, THE TAX EFFICIENCIES ARE *INSANE.*

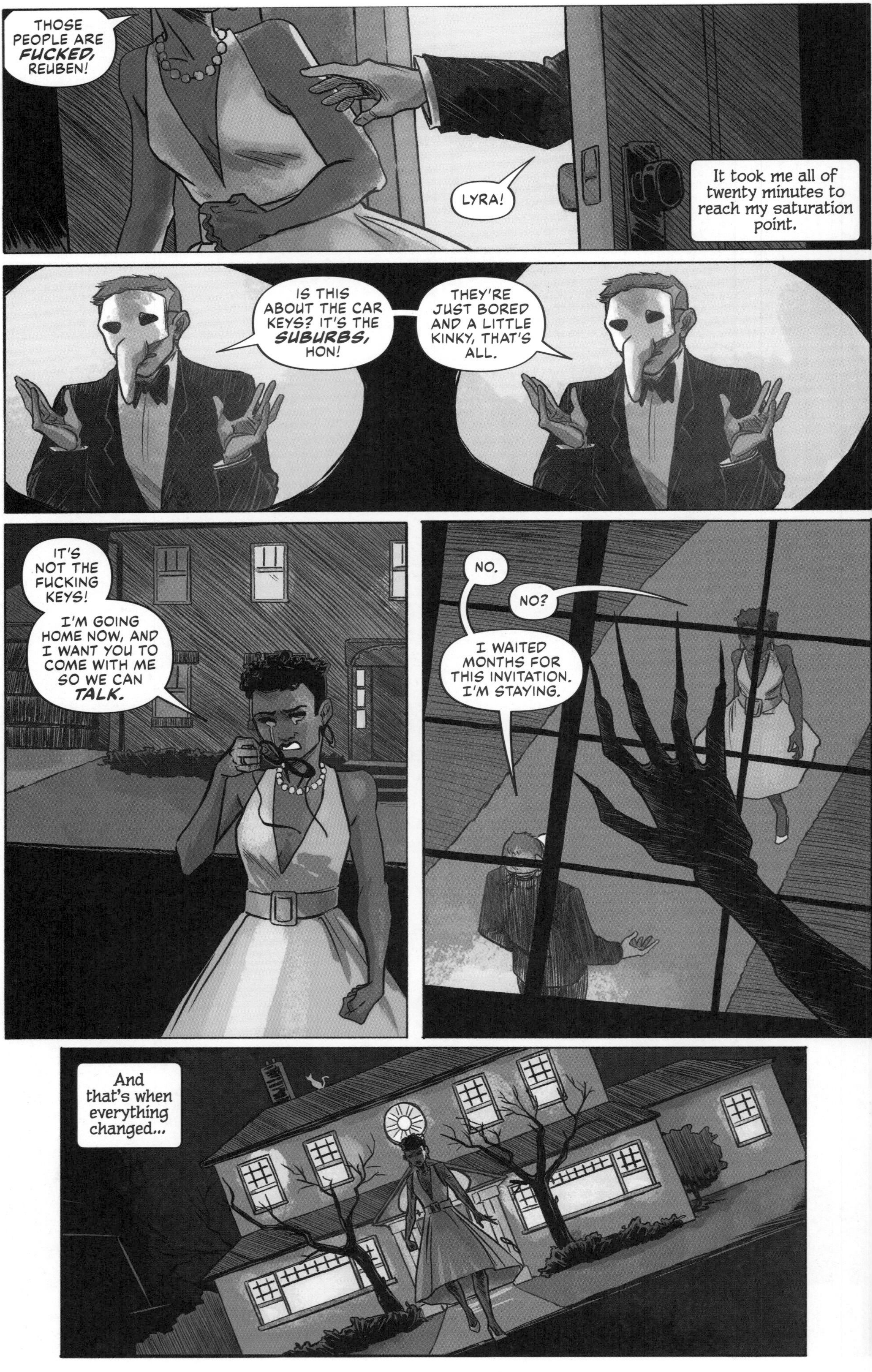
THOSE PEOPLE ARE FUCKED, REUBEN!
LYRA!
It took me all of twenty minutes to reach my saturation point.
IS THIS ABOUT THE CAR KEYS? IT'S THE SUBURBS, HON!
THEY'RE JUST BORED AND A LITTLE KINKY, THAT'S ALL.
IT'S NOT THE FUCKING KEYS!
I'M GOING HOME NOW, AND I WANT YOU TO COME WITH ME SO WE CAN TALK.
NO.
NO?
I WAITED MONTHS FOR THIS INVITATION. I'M STAYING.
And that's when everything changed...

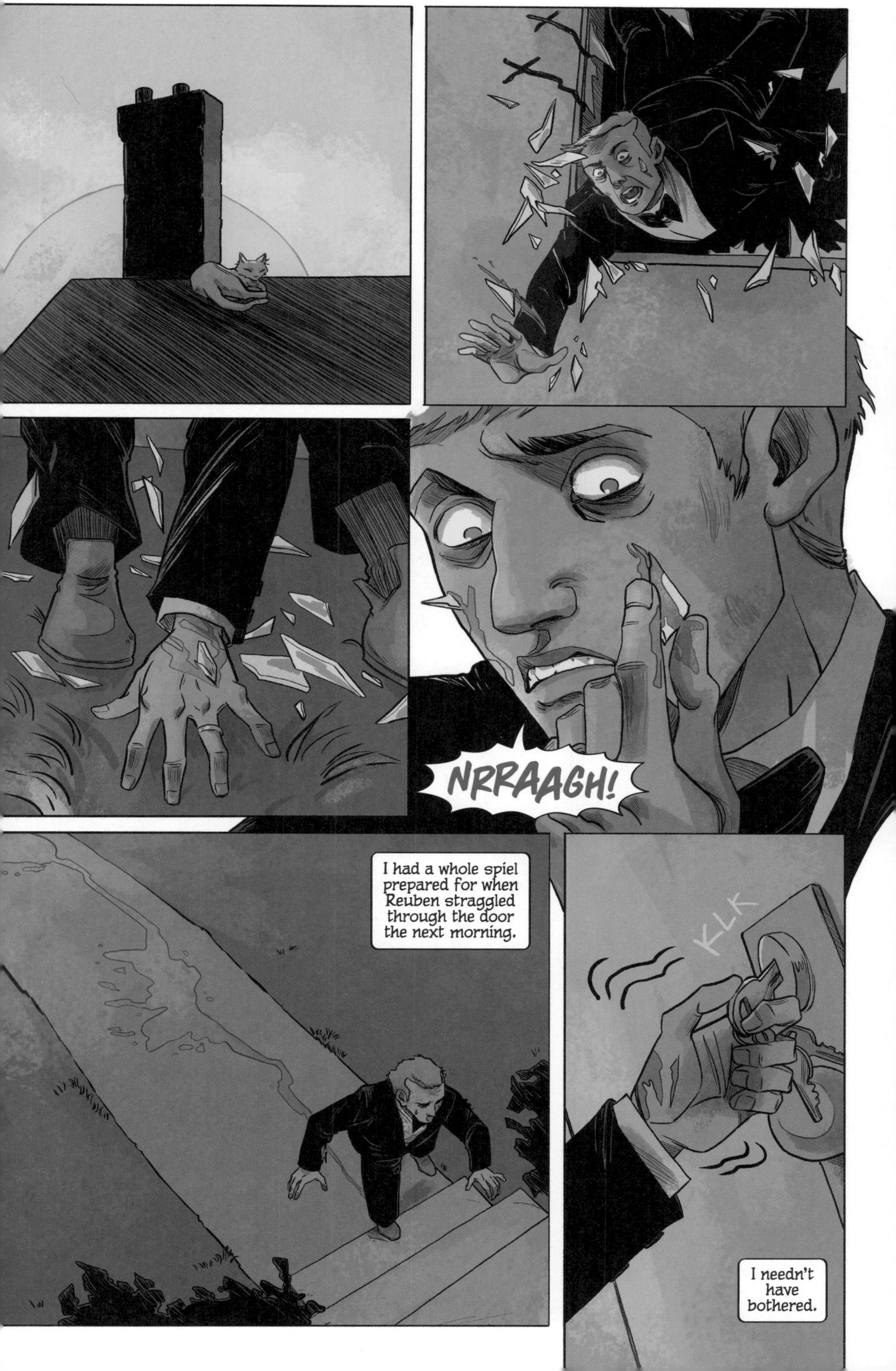
NRRAAGH!
I had a whole spiel prepared for when Reuben straggled through the door the next morning.
KLK
I needn't have bothered.

... JESUS CHRIST.

I DON'T FEEL WELL.

I'M GOING TO BED.

REUBEN!

KRAKK

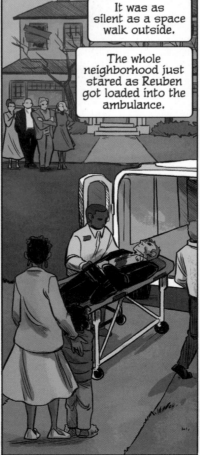
It was as silent as a space walk outside.

The whole neighborhood just stared as Reuben got loaded into the ambulance.

The doctors asked him what happened, but all he'd say was that he had *fallen.*

So they sent him home. With *us.*

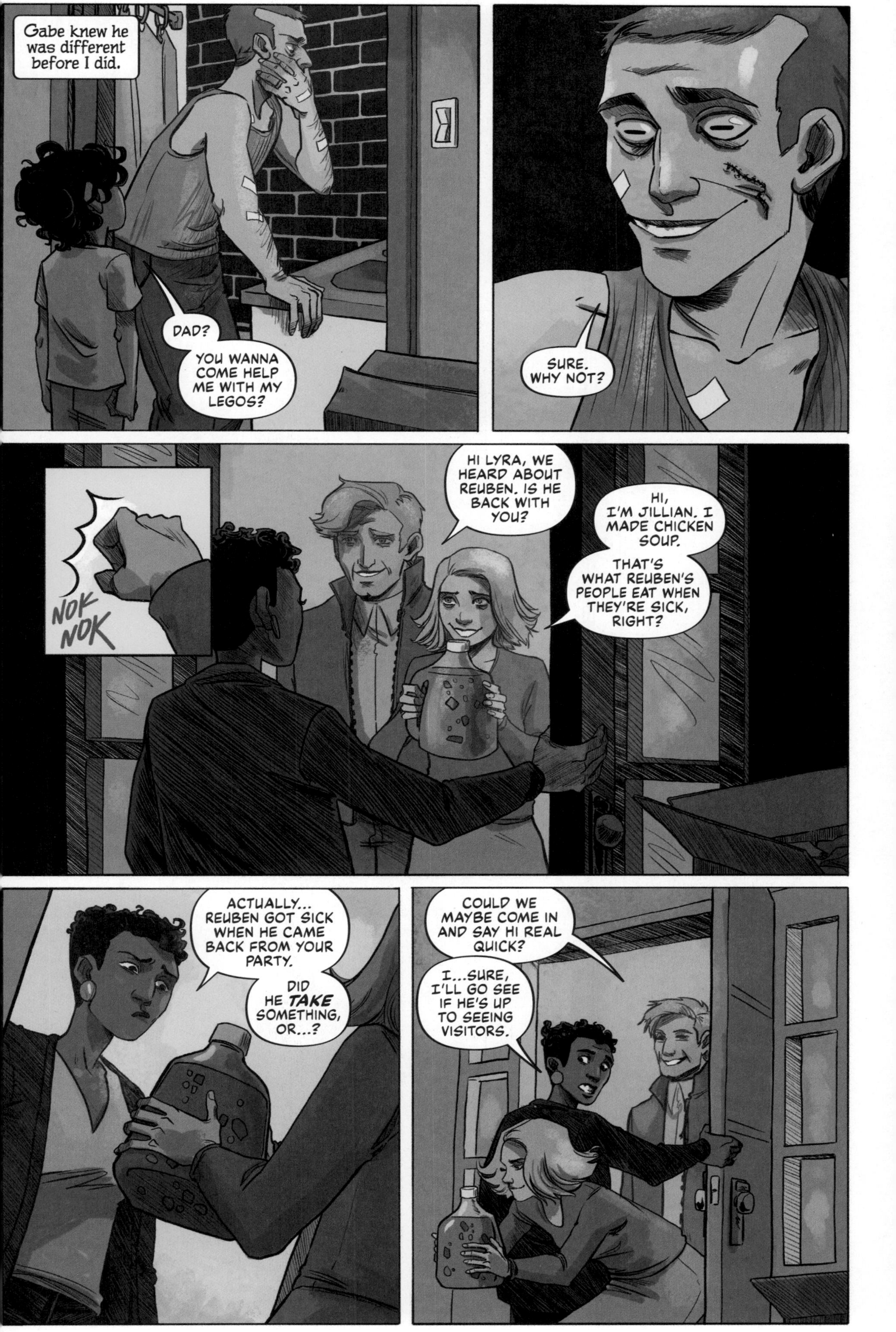
Gabe knew he was different before I did.
DAD?
YOU WANNA COME HELP ME WITH MY LEGOS?
SURE. WHY NOT?
NOK NOK
HI LYRA, WE HEARD ABOUT REUBEN. IS HE BACK WITH YOU?
HI, I'M JILLIAN. I MADE CHICKEN SOUP.
THAT'S WHAT REUBEN'S PEOPLE EAT WHEN THEY'RE SICK, RIGHT?
ACTUALLY... REUBEN GOT SICK WHEN HE CAME BACK FROM YOUR PARTY.
DID HE *TAKE* SOMETHING, OR...?
COULD WE MAYBE COME IN AND SAY HI REAL QUICK?
I...SURE, I'LL GO SEE IF HE'S UP TO SEEING VISITORS.

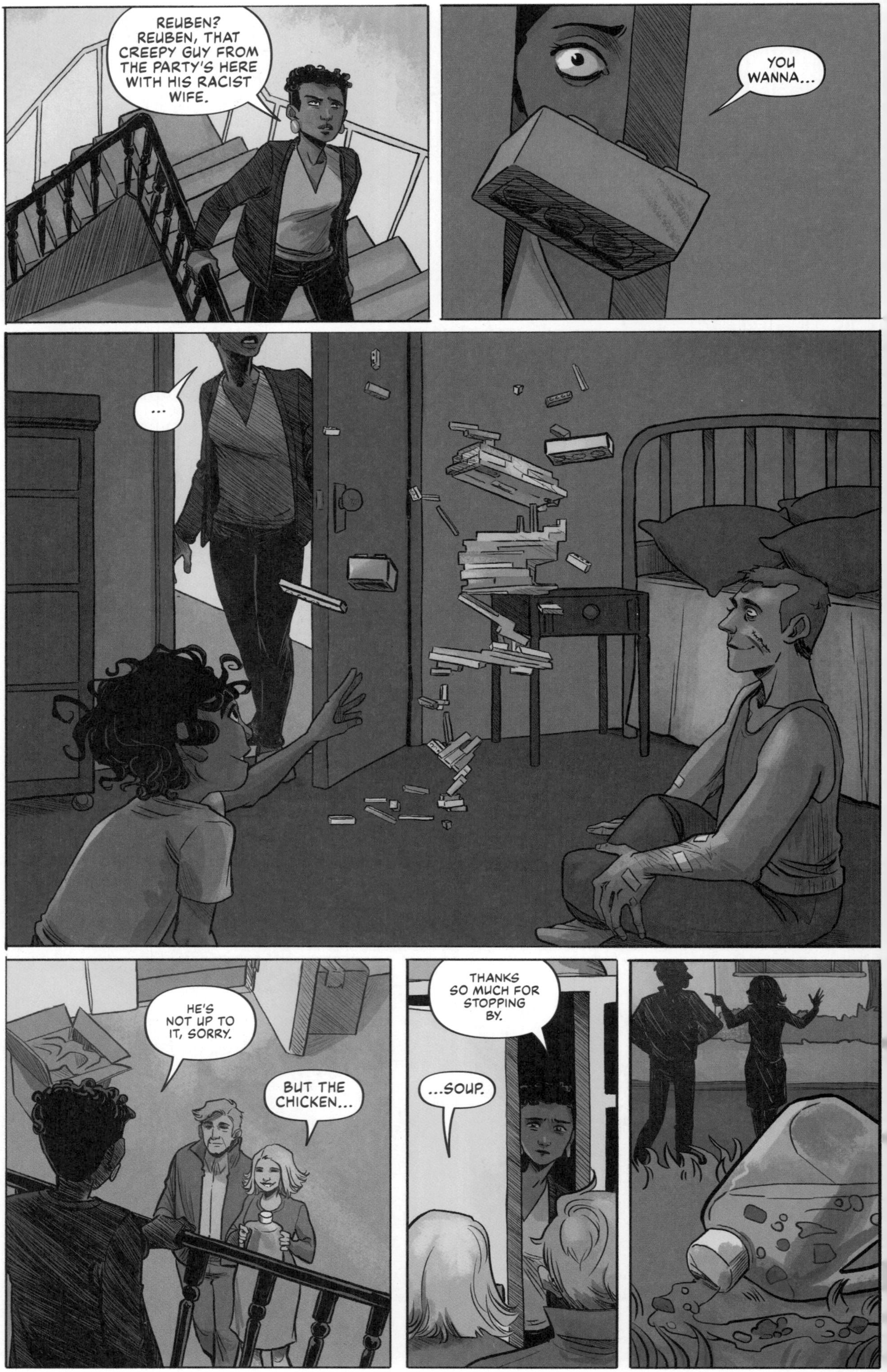
REUBEN? REUBEN, THAT CREEPY GUY FROM THE PARTY'S HERE WITH HIS RACIST WIFE.
YOU WANNA...
...
HE'S NOT UP TO IT, SORRY.
BUT THE CHICKEN...
THANKS SO MUCH FOR STOPPING BY.
...SOUP.

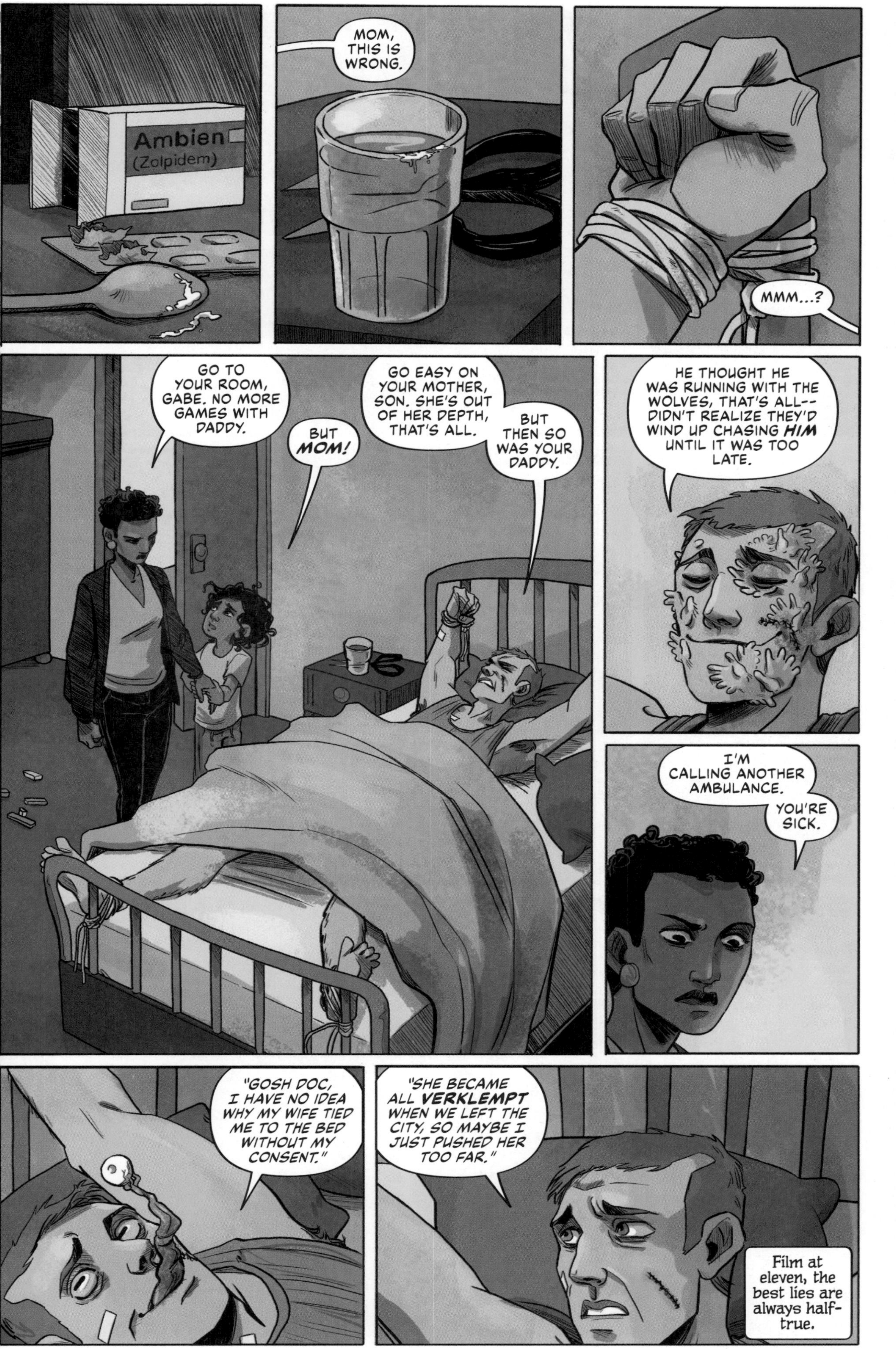
Ambien
(Zolpidem)
MOM, THIS IS WRONG.
MMM...?
GO TO YOUR ROOM, GABE. NO MORE GAMES WITH DADDY.
BUT **MOM!**
GO EASY ON YOUR MOTHER, SON. SHE'S OUT OF HER DEPTH, THAT'S ALL.
BUT THEN SO WAS YOUR DADDY.
HE THOUGHT HE WAS RUNNING WITH THE WOLVES, THAT'S ALL-- DIDN'T REALIZE THEY'D WIND UP CHASING **HIM** UNTIL IT WAS TOO LATE.
I'M CALLING ANOTHER AMBULANCE.
YOU'RE SICK.
"GOSH DOC, I HAVE NO IDEA WHY MY WIFE TIED ME TO THE BED WITHOUT MY CONSENT."
"SHE BECAME ALL **VERKLEMPT** WHEN WE LEFT THE CITY, SO MAYBE I JUST PUSHED HER TOO FAR."
Film at eleven, the best lies are always half-true.

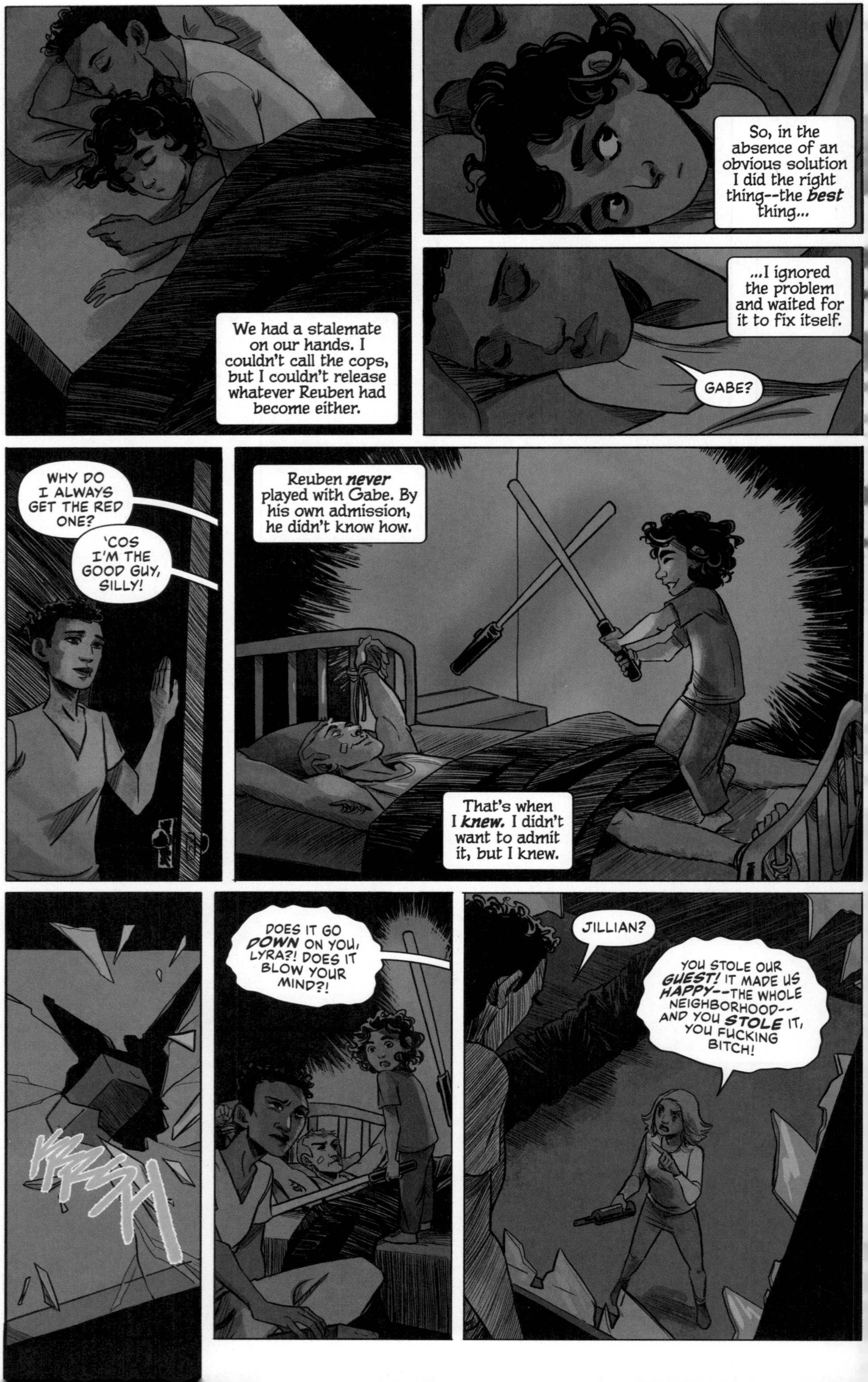
We had a stalemate on our hands. I couldn't call the cops, but I couldn't release whatever Reuben had become either.
So, in the absence of an obvious solution I did the right thing--the *best* thing...
...I ignored the problem and waited for it to fix itself.
GABE?
WHY DO I ALWAYS GET THE RED ONE?
'COS I'M THE GOOD GUY, SILLY!
Reuben *never* played with Gabe. By his own admission, he didn't know how.
That's when I *knew.* I didn't want to admit it, but I knew.
KRRSH
DOES IT GO *DOWN* ON YOU, LYRA?! DOES IT BLOW YOUR MIND?!
JILLIAN?
YOU STOLE OUR *GUEST!* IT MADE US *HAPPY*--THE WHOLE NEIGHBORHOOD--AND YOU *STOLE* IT, YOU FUCKING BITCH!

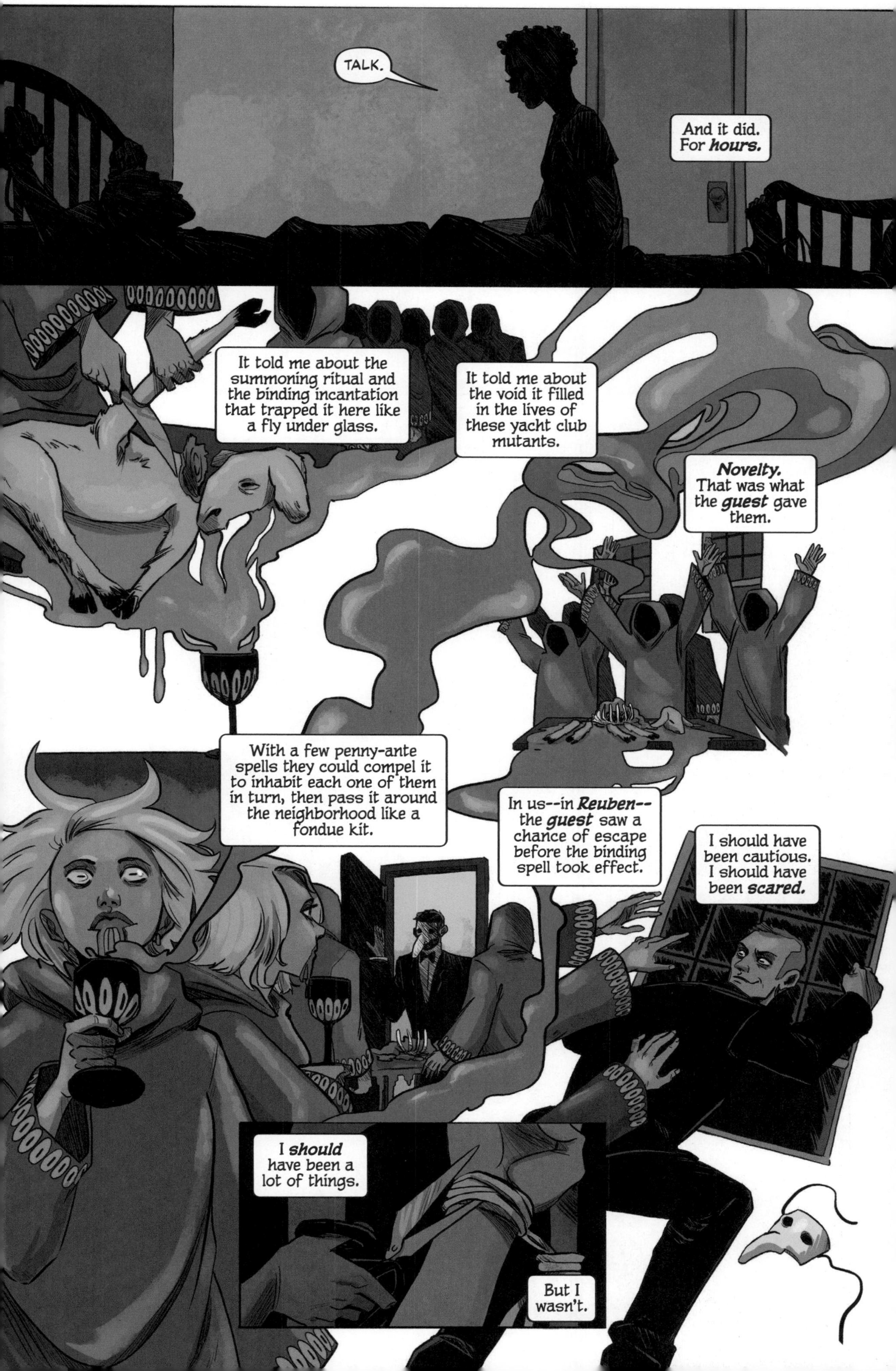

TALK.
And it did. For *hours.*
It told me about the summoning ritual and the binding incantation that trapped it here like a fly under glass.
It told me about the void it filled in the lives of these yacht club mutants.
Novelty. That was what the *guest* gave them.
With a few penny-ante spells they could compel it to inhabit each one of them in turn, then pass it around the neighborhood like a fondue kit.
In us--in *Reuben--* the *guest* saw a chance of escape before the binding spell took effect.
I should have been cautious. I should have been *scared.*
I *should* have been a lot of things.
But I wasn't.

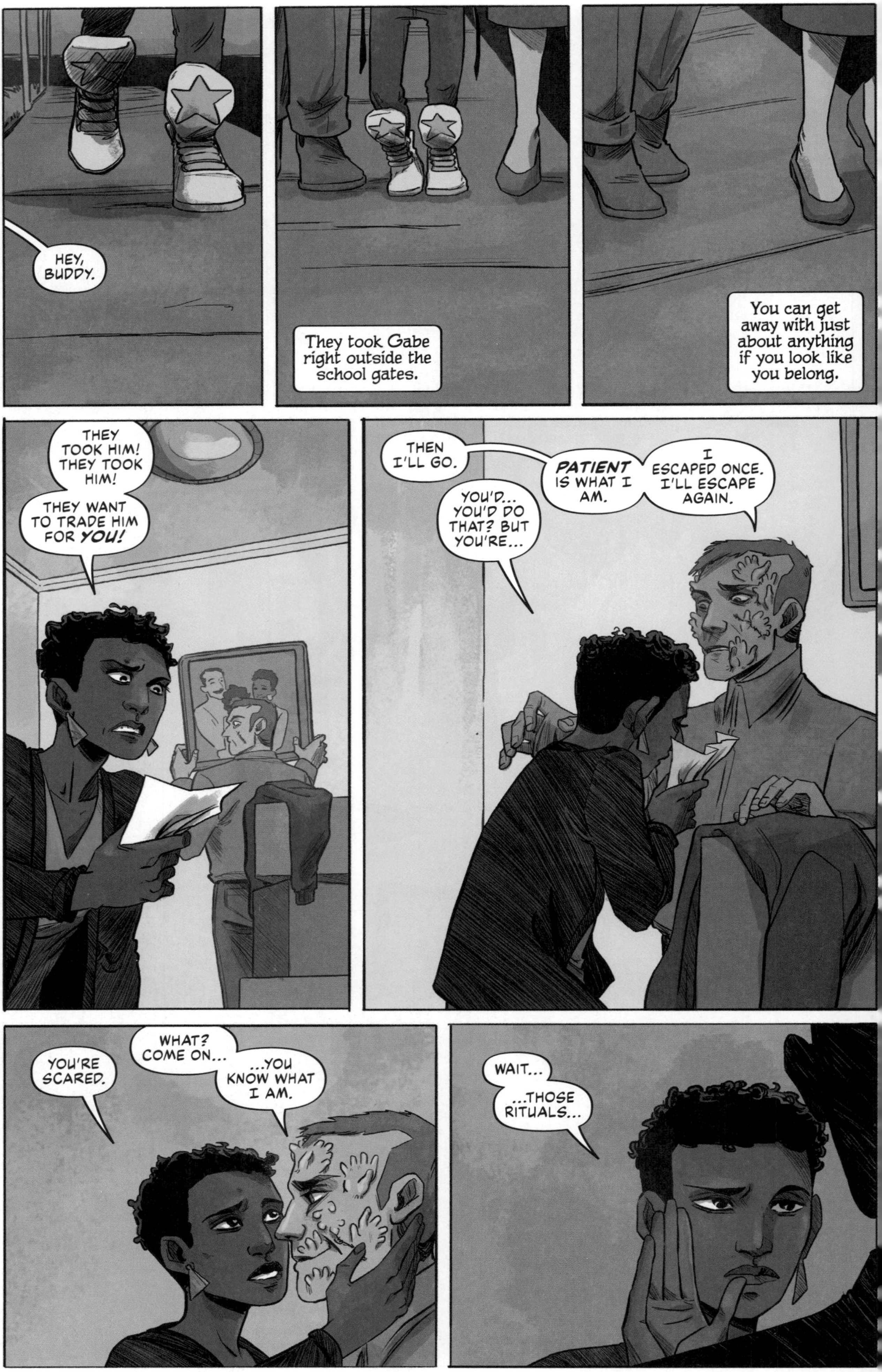
HEY, BUDDY.
They took Gabe right outside the school gates.
You can get away with just about anything if you look like you belong.
THEY TOOK HIM! THEY TOOK HIM!
THEY WANT TO TRADE HIM FOR YOU!
THEN I'LL GO.
YOU'D... YOU'D DO THAT? BUT YOU'RE...
PATIENT IS WHAT I AM.
I ESCAPED ONCE. I'LL ESCAPE AGAIN.
YOU'RE SCARED.
WHAT? COME ON...
...YOU KNOW WHAT I AM.
WAIT...
...THOSE RITUALS...

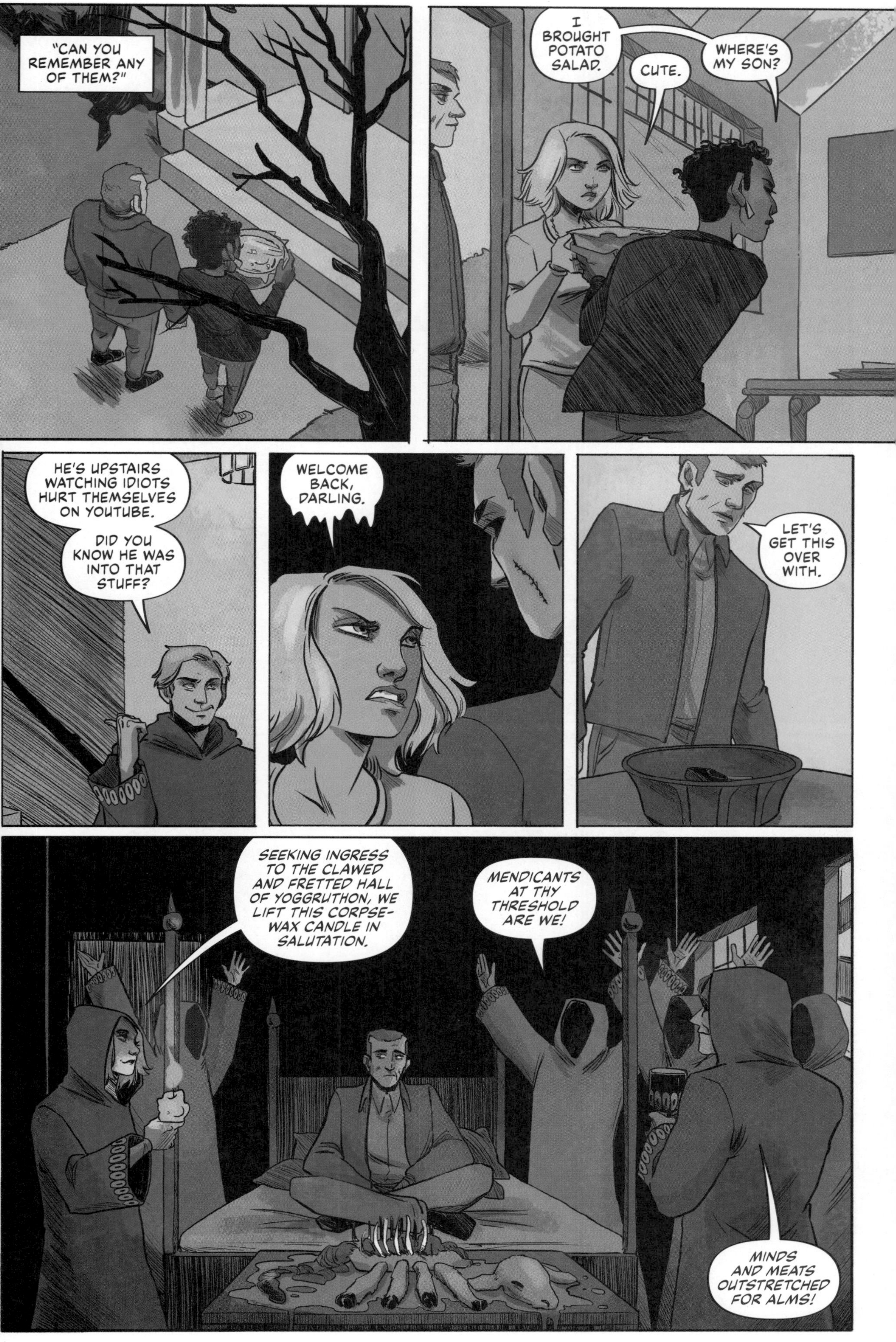
"CAN YOU REMEMBER ANY OF THEM?"
I BROUGHT POTATO SALAD.
CUTE.
WHERE'S MY SON?
HE'S UPSTAIRS WATCHING IDIOTS HURT THEMSELVES ON YOUTUBE.
DID YOU KNOW HE WAS INTO THAT STUFF?
WELCOME BACK, DARLING.
LET'S GET THIS OVER WITH.
SEEKING INGRESS TO THE CLAWED AND FRETTED HALL OF YOGGRUTHON, WE LIFT THIS CORPSE-WAX CANDLE IN SALUTATION.
MENDICANTS AT THY THRESHOLD ARE WE!
MINDS AND MEATS OUTSTRETCHED FOR ALMS!

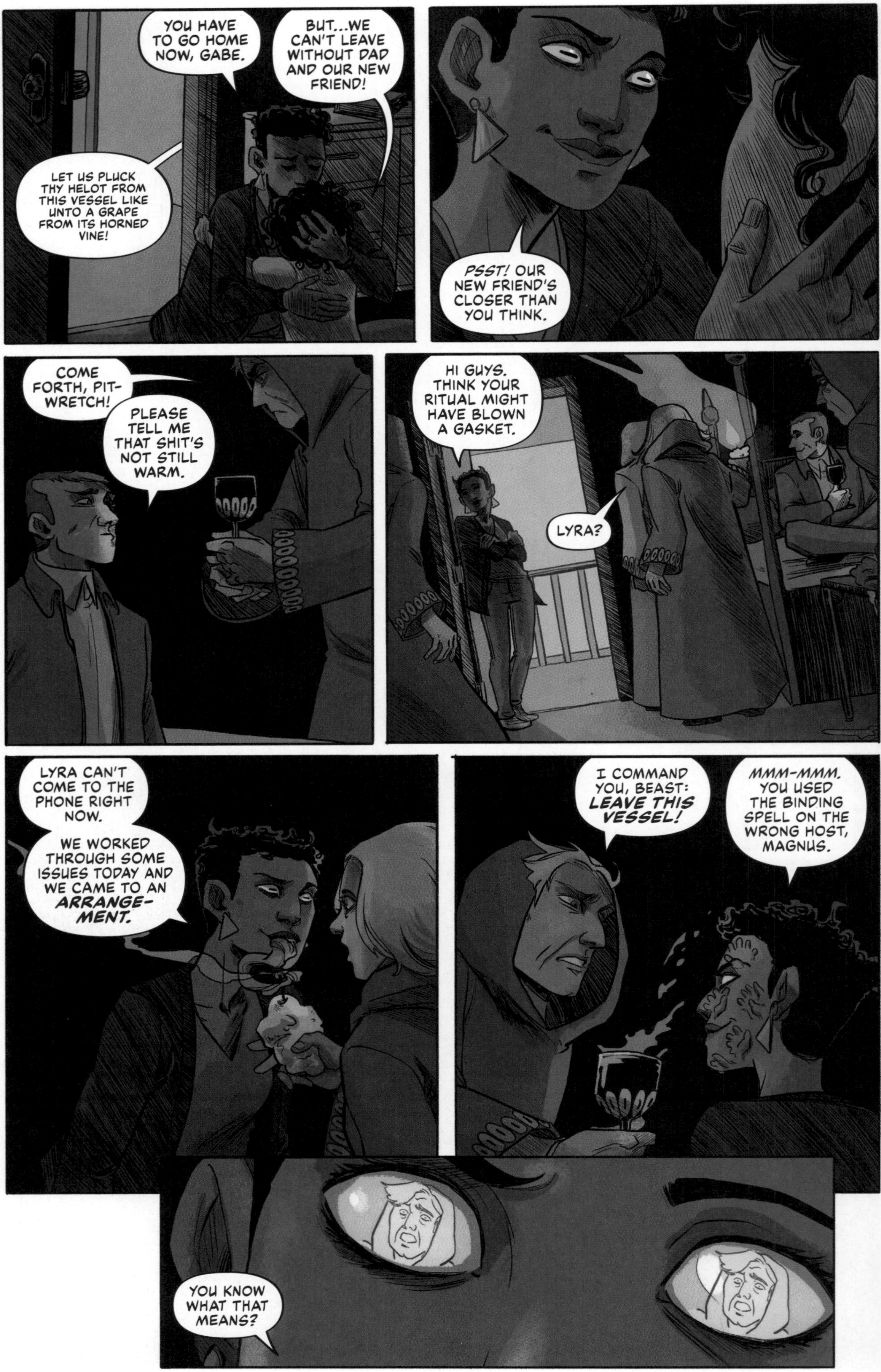
YOU HAVE TO GO HOME NOW, GABE.
BUT...WE CAN'T LEAVE WITHOUT DAD AND OUR NEW FRIEND!
LET US PLUCK THY HELOT FROM THIS VESSEL LIKE UNTO A GRAPE FROM ITS HORNED VINE!
PSST! OUR NEW FRIEND'S CLOSER THAN YOU THINK.
COME FORTH, PIT-WRETCH!
PLEASE TELL ME THAT SHIT'S NOT STILL WARM.
HI GUYS. THINK YOUR RITUAL MIGHT HAVE BLOWN A GASKET.
LYRA?
LYRA CAN'T COME TO THE PHONE RIGHT NOW.
WE WORKED THROUGH SOME ISSUES TODAY AND WE CAME TO AN ***ARRANGE-MENT.***
I COMMAND YOU, BEAST: ***LEAVE THIS VESSEL!***
MMM-MMM. YOU USED THE BINDING SPELL ON THE WRONG HOST, MAGNUS.
YOU KNOW WHAT THAT MEANS?

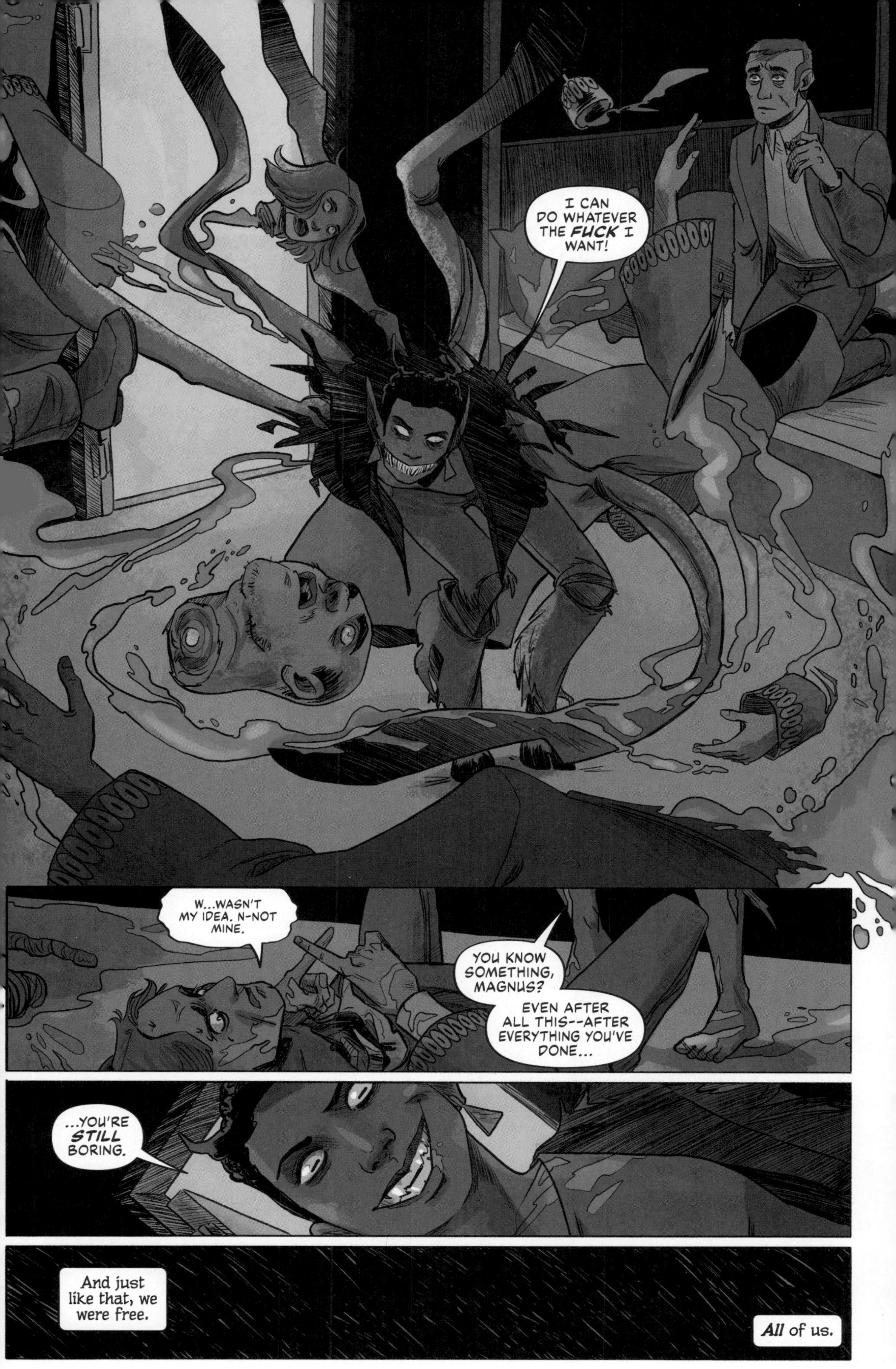
I CAN DO WHATEVER THE *FUCK* I WANT!
W...WASN'T MY IDEA. N-NOT MINE.
YOU KNOW SOMETHING, MAGNUS?
EVEN AFTER ALL THIS--AFTER EVERYTHING YOU'VE DONE...
...YOU'RE *STILL* BORING.
And just like that, we were free.
All of us.

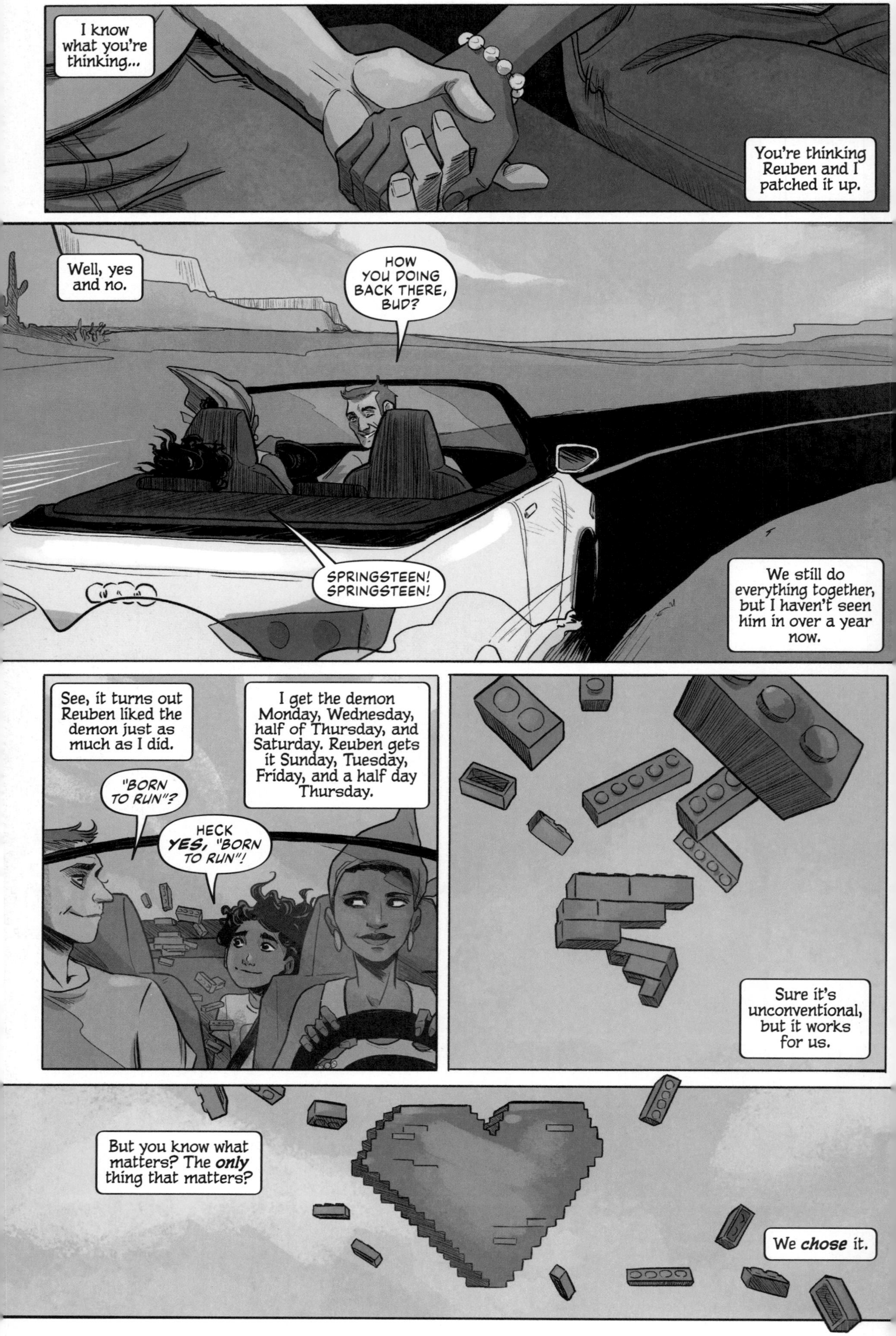

I know what you're thinking...
You're thinking Reuben and I patched it up.
Well, yes and no.
HOW YOU DOING BACK THERE, BUD?
SPRINGSTEEN! SPRINGSTEEN!
We still do everything together, but I haven't seen him in over a year now.
See, it turns out Reuben liked the demon just as much as I did.
I get the demon Monday, Wednesday, half of Thursday, and Saturday. Reuben gets it Sunday, Tuesday, Friday, and a half day Thursday.
"BORN TO RUN"?
HECK *YES*, "BORN TO RUN"!
Sure it's unconventional, but it works for us.
But you know what matters? The *only* thing that matters?
We *chose* it.

CREATORS

LIANA KANGAS | WRITER

Liana Kangas is a comic artist and creator best known for her work on SHE SAID
DESTROY by Vault and other works with 2000AD, Black Mask Studios, and Ringo and
Eisner nominated anthologies. Her clients include Legendary Pictures, King Features,
Z2, Mad Cave, Vices Press, and Scrappy Heart Productions.

JOE CORALLO | WRITER

Joe Corallo is a comics editor whose work includes the Eisner nominated (Best Short
Story) and Ringo Award winning MINE! anthology, the GLAAD nominated KIM & KIM and
the Ringo nominated DEAD BEATS anthology. He also wrote SHE SAID DESTROY which he
co-created with illustrator Liana Kangas at Vault Comics.

PAUL AZACETA | ARTIST

Paul Azaceta is a New Jersey-based artist with a simple but bold style. His past work includes
DAREDEVIL, SPIDER-MAN, PUNISHER NOIR, and B.P.R.D. 1946. He also co-created GRAVEYARD
OF EMPIRES for Image Comics with Mark Sable and OUTCAST with Robert Kirkman.

JEFF POWELL | LETTERER

Jeff Powell has lettered a wide range of titles throughout his lengthy career. His recent
work includes SCALES & SCOUNDRELS, INFIDEL, and THE GOOD ASIAN. In addition, Jeff has
designed books, logos and trade dress for Marvel, Archie, IDW, Image, Valiant, and others.

SEBASTIAN GIRNER | WRITER

Sebastian Girner is a German-born, American-raised comic editor and writer. Since
its launch in 2018 he has served as Editor-in-Chief for TKO STUDIOS. His comic book
writing includes SCALES & SCOUNDRELS, SHIRTLESS BEAR-FIGHTER!, and THE DEVIL'S
RED BRIDE.

BALDEMAR RIVAS | ARTIST

Baldemar Rivas is an artist who specializes in sequential storytelling and is currently
working on the comic book UNEARTH. His style is an amalgamation of eastern and
western comics. He carries a sketchbook everywhere and you can catch him doodling
out in the wild.

STEVE WANDS | LETTERER

Steve Wands is a comic book letterer, artist, and indie author. He works on top titles at DC Comics, Vertigo, Image, and Random House. He's the author of the STAY DEAD series, co-author of TRAIL OF BLOOD, and is a writer of short stories. When not working he spends time with his wife and sons in New Jersey.

STEVE FOXE | WRITER

Steve Foxe is editor and co-creator of RAZORBLADES: THE HORROR MAGAZINE, and the author of more than 50 comics and children's books for properties including Pokémon, Batman, Transformers, Adventure Time, and Steven Universe.

LISANDRO ESTHERREN | ARTIST

Lisandro Estherren (Paraná, 1980) is an Argentine comic artist. His work includes graphic novels, series, and illustration for publishers and magazines in Argentina, Uruguay, Italy, and Spain. In the US, he has produced series for Red5 Comics (SPOK) and BOOM! Studios (THE LAST CONTRACT, STRANGE SKIES OVER EAST BERLIN). He's currently working on REDNECK for Skybound/Image Comics.

PATRICIO DELPECHE | COLOR ARTIST

Patricio Delpeche is a South American comic book artist and graphic designer born and raised in Buenos Aires, Argentina. He works for Vault, Heavy Metal, IDW, Glénat and currently Boom! Studios. His next projects to be published this year are ORIGINS together with Clay McLeod Chapman and Jakub Rebelka and ELLES SE RENDENT PAS COMPTE with JD Morvan.

ALEX PAKNADEL | WRITER

Alex Paknadel is a writer and academic from London, England. His first comics work, the dark sci-fi thriller ARCADIA from Boom! Studios, met with critical acclaim and led to additional projects with a range of publishers including Marvel Entertainment, Vault Comics, Valiant Entertainment, Lion Forge, and Titan Comics. He is also a founding member of White Noise Studio alongside fellow writers Dan Watters, Ram V, and Ryan O'Sullivan

MACEWAN | ARTIST

MacEwan is a cartoonist and illustrator, whose comics work can be seen in SEX, PHET: EARTH WAR, and MCMLXXV with co-creator Joe Casey. He's also known for YANKEE, with writer Jason Leivian, from Floating World Comics. When not drawing cs, he divides his time between illustrating Blu-ray box art, such as Arrow Video le Prisoner Scorpion box set, and obsessing over Harvey Fierstein's dogs.

SAN OTSMANE-ELHAOU | LETTERER

an is the letterer behind comics like UNDONE BY BLOOD, RED SONJA, X-O OWAR, and ENGINEWARD. He's also the editor of the Eisner-winning PANELXPANEL azine, and voice behind the Strip Panel Naked series. You can usually find him aining that comics are definitely a real job.

Y WILLIAMS | WRITER & ARTIST

Williams is a comic creator. He mostly draws, sometimes writes, and always it. He's worked with publishers from Dark Horse to Satan himself and just about yone in between. Not everyone though. That would be lying. He can be summoned rawing comics by playing jazz records backwards and hopping in a circle three s. He is a very serious person.

S! PANGBURN | LETTERER

as a writer, editor, and/or letterer, Chas! Pangburn puts words in balloons. He's fortunate to collaborate with various creators for publishers such as Dark Hors Image, and Scout. In his free time, an angry corgi bosses him around for long s throughout Cincinnati, Ohio.

PILKINGTON | WRITER

as a writer, editor, and/or letterer, Chas! Pangburn puts words in balloons. He's fortunate to collaborate with various creators for publishers such as Dark Hors Image, and Scout. In his free time, an angry corgi bosses him around for long throughout Cincinnati, Ohio

KIT MILLS | ARTIST

Kit Mills is an illustrator, comic artist, and graphic designer who lives in Brooklyn with a ca Kit's work is observational, focusing on the body and the natural world, with a bent toward both humor and horror. More can be found at mitkills.com and on Instagram @kitmills.

ARIANA MAHER | LETTERER

Ariana Maher is a comic book letterer who works with both independent imprints such as LittleFoolery and publishers such as Image Comics, Dynamite Entertainment, and Skybound. Recent projects include NANCY DREW, JAMES BOND 007, RINGSIDE, SFEER THEORY, FLAVOR, and OUTPOST ZERO. She tends to be found wandering around comic book conventions in the Pacific Northwest. Check out her portfolio at arianamaher.com

MICHAEL MORECI | WRITER

Michael Moreci is a bestselling comics author, screenwriter, and novelist. His original work include THE PLOT, CURSE, WASTED SPACE, ROCHE LIMIT, and more. Moreci is currently the lead writer for STAR WARS ADVENTURES, an all-ages Star Wars series published by IDW. He's also written canonical stories for STRANGER THINGS and the DC universe.

JESÚS HERVÁS | ARTIST

Jesús lives in Madrid, and became a cartoonist even though he had studied to be a forest engineer. He started in comics for the French publisher Soleil, where he drew series like DELUGE, ANDROIDS or ORCS & GOBLINS. In the US, he has drawn for series like Clive Barker's HELLRAISER, SONS OF ANARCHY, and THE EMPTY MAN for BOOM!; PENNY DREADFUL for Titan; DARK ARK for Aftershock and TOMORROW for Berger Books

ERICK C. FREITAS | WRITER

Erick Freitas is an Angolan & Portuguese creator living in the NJ/NY area who works in comics & film/TV. He's written three short films and directed one. He's also written for multiple franchise comic books such as JUDGE DREDD, GODZILLA, and TEENAGE MUTANT NINJA TURTLES.

LENA ĐORĐEVIĆ-MAKSIMOVIĆ | ARTIST

mic artist and illustrator from Serbia. A psychologist by education, turned towards
awing comics professionally, mostly for small and independent publishers in Europe
d the USA. Winner of the Grand Prix of the 14th International Comic Festival in
lgrade. Lives between Niš, Serbia and Rome, Italy with her partner Daniele.

N HICKMAN | ARTIST

h Hickman is a visual storyteller from California. Past work includes LONELY
CEIVER, TEST, BEZKAMP, and MOTH & WHISPER. They get really excited about
stopian fiction, good coffee, and drawing hands.

MON BOWLAND | LETTERER

non Bowland has been lettering comics since 2004 and continues to work for publishers
ch as 2000AD, Marvel, DC, Image, Valiant, Dark Horse, and now TKO Studios. He lives in
gland with his colourist wife, Pippa, and their laid-back tabby cat, Jess.